SinSatiable

SinSatiable

Shelia E. Bell

SinSatiable

An insatiable craving for the worldly things in life which feel good, look good, tastes good and brings momentary pleasure, yet in the end yields no lasting satisfaction.

—SinSatiable is a word founded and defined by Author Shelia E. Bell

1

All our dreams can come true, if we have the courage to pursue them. Walt Disney

"How much did you say? Girl, now that's some graduation gift! I wonder how much dough you'll get if you get your Master's degree – a million?"

"Tameria, you're as crazy as they come. My grandparents put this money in a trust for me when I was sixteen years old and the only stipulation to receiving the money was that I had to earn my college degree," Aisha explained.

"I sure wish I had a set of grandparents who left me a little change."

"I just wish they were still alive to see me fulfill my dreams, Tameria."

Aisha Carlisle became teary eyed at the thought of her grandparents' generosity. Growing up as an only child in her household, she was far from spoiled but she was also blessed beyond measure. With the money from her trust fund she planned on fulfilling her dreams of opening a dance studio. Growing up in the Memphis she had a limited opportunity to perfect her gift of dancing like she really wanted. Most of the dance studios in the south catered to country line-dancing, ballet or tap. But she was into more than that. She wanted to incorporate her natural soulful rhythm into her dancing by choreographing her very own dance style. Her dream was to teach young girls how to be both refined and hip in their dancing all at the same time.

She was barely fourteen when she first saw a youth group from a visiting church perform a liturgical dance to the soulful tune *Open Your Heart* by Yolanda Adams. Their grace and perfect rhythm left her breathless. It wasn't long after that she formed a dance group at her own church, Temple Cathedral. Now here she was, seven years later with an undergraduate degree in dance and ready to step out into her future. With God on her side, she knew she could do nothing but soar like an eagle because He had shown favor and blessings upon her life. She still shivered at the thought of how much God loved her. She was a little bushy head preteen when she came to accept him as her personal Lord and Savior. When she first told her mom and dad that she wanted to be saved, they said that she should wait until she was a little older. But Aisha was twelve years old. She refused to wait until her parents thought the time was more appropriate. She had a strong desire to belong to God and no one or anything was going to stop her. So that beautiful Sunday morning in June 1994, she boldly walked to the front of the huge sanctuary of and accepted Jesus as her Lord and Savior. Not once had she ever looked back with regrets, even when she faced tragedy in her small, close-knit family.

Her first meeting with tragedy occurred two days after her sixteenth birthday when her mother's parents who Aisha lovingly called Oma and Opa, had died in a house fire. Aisha recalled the events leading up to their untimely death. Her family and friends had celebrated by surprising her with a lavish sweet sixteen birthday bash. While she was busy opening her gifts, Oma and Opa told her to save their gift and open it last. She did as she was told and after all the other gifts had been *oohed* and *aahhed* over, she nervously unwrapped the pink ribbon from around the pink oblong box, expecting to find a trinket or necklace inside. Her guess was right. There was a white gold locket tucked neatly inside the soft salmon colored tissue paper. The locket had her initials set in tiny diamonds on the back and the words Jeremiah 29:11 engraved on the front. Inside were pictures of her grandparents holding an infant Aisha on the day of her christening.

"Aisha, always remember that God's plan for you is to prosper. He wants you to have a bright future and an eternal hope." Oma beamed with love as she spoke to her granddaughter.

"Aisha, always put God first in your life and whenever life begins to get you down, and the trials and tribulations begin to come, and they will," Opa added, "Cling to that scripture in Jeremiah. It'll remind you of God's will for your life. You hear me?" Her grandfather spoke with such conviction and wisdom. She loved both of them so much.

"Come on, open the other part of your gift," her grandmother urged before Aisha could respond. Aisha pulled out the small envelope tucked neatly inside the box. When she opened it, her eyes grew as big as diamonds. "I can't believe this is for me."

"What is it, Aisha? Tell us what it is," several of her friends and family squealed.

"It's a bank account that's been set aside for me, but it doesn't tell me how much is in it." How much Oma? How much is it for, Opa?"

"We aren't disclosing that to you just yet young lady," her grandfather smiled slyly. "You won't know that until you graduate from college."

"Graduate from college?" But Maaaaa," she whined. "Look how long that'll be."

"Now Aisha, Oma and Opa know exactly what they're doing," her mother said with a look of irritation and impatience. Aisha's mother always thought her daughter was much too whiny and spoiled. Of course, her husband and his parents were to blame and Sandra Carlisle always resented it. They seemed to forget that Benjamin Carlisle had another daughter up North in Michigan. Sandra loved her only child, but another part of her felt as if she was in constant competition with Aisha for Benjamin's affection and his attention. It was Sandra's belief that Aisha managed to be the winner of both every single time. The resentment settled in her heart and whether she chose to admit it or not, Sandra had a difficult time hiding her feelings toward Aisha.

"Aisha, your mother's right," her dad added. "Your grandparents know just like I do, that if they give you a substantial amount of money now, you're just going to either blow it all on clothes or junk. Your current allowance is large enough to provide spending money for your binge buying, so this is a great present for you. You can just let it sit in a Money Market account and draw interest and by the time you graduate from college, you would have accumulated a nice bit of interest on your principal. And besides, by the time you graduate from college you should be more mature and level-headed and be in a better position to make decisions about your money. Honey, you will have had more time to think about what you r-e-a-l-l-y want to do with it. "Oh, okay." As she leaned over to hug her grandparents. Thank you Oma. Thank you Opa for this graduation present. I love you both so much." She planted an affectionate kiss on each of their cheeks.

When Oma and Opa returned to their summer home in Miami tragedy struck while they were asleep. A fire erupted in the modest two-story beach front home. The fire had spread so rapidly that the firemen said that her grandparents didn't stand a chance of escaping. They both died from intense smoke inhalation. .

During this difficult time in her life, Aisha remained focused on God. She spoke at her grandparents' funeral, sharing with everyone her deep love and devotion for them. She spoke like the wonderful young woman she was as she told of her grandparents' love and devotion for God and family. She also performed a touching and emotional dance while fighting back her tears of grief.

2

Before your dreams can come true, you have to have those dreams. Joyce Brothers

Aisha was a college graduate with a little money, an unshakeable faith and trust in God, and a huge world to conquer. She was on her way to the life she had always dreamed about. A life filled with dancing.

Aisha set out to find the perfect place to open her dance studio. It couldn't be just any old place. It had to be centrally located and close to the public transportation line because, the young girls she had identified to be her future students would be mostly from the inner city neighborhoods and transportation for those girls would be practically non-existent if she didn't choose the right area.

"Miss Carlisle, I believe you'll love this piece of property. It's ideal for what you're trying to accomplish." The realtor used his most convincing voice to sell Aisha on the 3,600 square foot space. Aisha's excitement grew by the minute. She felt a mixture of exhaustion and exhilaration at the thought of her dream coming into fruition. *A-Carlisle Studio of Dance and Choreography.* What a nice ring.

"Right this way, Miss Carlisle. I believe you'll agree with me when I say this property simply exudes an upscale style and quality. As you can see the decor of mahogany, marble and bronze sets it apart from the ordinary business space. "

6

"I like it so far. This just might have potential."

"Ma'am, it's ideally located at the focal point of the city." She followed the realtor into the mammoth open space. This was it. She felt it. She had seen over two dozen properties in the past three weeks. This building was the first place that had sparked her interest. The realtor continued to make his sales pitch.

"There's a full service business center adjacent to this property."

"Is the business center accessible at any time?" she asked.

"Yes, you'll have access to the property twenty four hours a day, seven days a week. There are full utility and janitorial services, free parking, a reception and conference area."

"When was it built?"

"This property is only ten years old, Miss Carlisle, which is an added plus."

She immediately fell in love with it.

"Let's walk over to the window," the realtor continued. "This view provides a relaxing atmosphere and helps to remove claustrophobic tendencies. The atrium and courtyard gardens are beautifully landscaped, as you can see. You'll have full access to the courtyards as well. So, what do you think so far?"

"I'd like to know what they're asking. I mean, I like what I have seen so far and it does seem like it could be the ideal place."

"For twenty-six hundred dollars a month you can lease this prestigious business address with an option to buy and without the inconvenience of downtown traffic and parking." When he finally took a moment to rest from his spiel, Aisha was already sold.

"I love it. I absolutely love it!" She couldn't hold back her emotions much longer. She knew within her spirit that this was the place for her studio. In her twenty-four years she had learned how to discern the will of God and what was coming from Satan and his schemes. It wasn't that she was self-righteous, but she was brought up in the church and in some form of Bible study since she was a toddler, so scriptures and the teachings of God were almost second nature to her. She couldn't imagine making any major decision without prayer and sometimes fasting. Now she was at another milestone - owning her on studio. She couldn't begin to thank God enough for all of his blessings.

"I really believe this is the place I'm supposed to have," she explained to the realtor. "It's everything I've been looking for and then some. This is what I'd like to do."

"What is that, Miss Carlisle?"

"By the way, call me Aisha. I'm going to sleep on it and then give you a call tomorrow. If the Holy Spirit is still pushing me toward this direction, then I'll sign the papers and give you one year's rent plus the deposit. How does that sound?"

"No problem at all, Miss Carlisle...Aisha."

"Well, tomorrow it is." Aisha extended her nicely manicured hand out to meet his.

"I'll look forward to hearing from you tomorrow. In the meantime, if you have any questions or concerns, please just give me a call."

◆

"Mom, Dad. I found the perfect place for my dance studio! You have to see it." Aisha couldn't contain her excitement. She paced the room with joy as she told them everything the realtor had told her about the property. .

"Mom, why don't you go with me tomorrow to take a look at it?"

"Aisha, I'd love to, but tomorrow's not a good time. Your half-sister is supposed to be here tomorrow. Maybe you should ask her to go with you." Selena was born to Benjamin Carlisle and his high school sweetheart, Yvette. The two of them rushed to get married when Yvette discovered that she was pregnant. When Selena was three and a half years old, Benjamin met Aisha's mother, Sandra, at Minority Marketplace Expo. She was perusing the aisles with a couple of co-workers when she stopped at Benjamin's company's booth. She eyed the array of African American history books and literature he had set up before she lingered on the tall, handsome, dark haired man with hypnotizing eyes standing behind the booth. Though it was completely out of character for Sandra, she openly flirted with him. Needless to say, he reveled in the much needed attention she showered on him. He certainly wasn't getting any attention at home. She purchased *The Souls of Black Folk* and along with the money for the book, she gave him her business card. Ignoring the gold wedding ring on his long finger, Sandra consciously set out to make him hers. And within two years, she'd gotten what she wanted. Mesmerized by Sandra's beguiling charm, Benjamin filed for divorce from Yvette. Rejected, hurt and destroyed Yvette took Selena and moved to Detroit to be close to her family and far away from Benjamin.

Aisha was disappointed when her mother told her she couldn't go with her to see the building. Though she'd gotten pretty used to her mother's excuses not to be around her, she never stopped trying. "How long is Selena going to be here anyway?" Aisha asked her mother.

"Your sister is coming to visit her cousins on her mother's side and I think your father said she's going to be here for at least three or four days. Maybe the two of you can catch up on what's going on in each of your lives since you never really talk to each other very much."

"Mom, you know Selena and I have never been close. She was raised in Michigan and we've been in Memphis all of our lives. Now Selena and I are both adults and you know she's so much older than I am.

"Honey, she's still your father's child which means she's your sister and the two of you ought to be closer than you are."

"It's not my fault that we live hundreds of miles apart, Mom." Aisha felt herself becoming defensive. Her mother always managed to somehow twist things around when she wanted to avoid talking about something. This time she managed to cleverly switch the conversation from talking about Aisha's dance studio to the distant relationship she had with Selena. "Mom, please I was really hoping you could come and see the building."

"I have a full work load this week, Aisha." Sandra became silent and looked like she was in deep thought. "I tell you what, maybe I can squeeze in a half an hour or so sometime around the lunch hour. But I'm telling you, I can't spend a lot of time from the office tomorrow, I have a huge case file of clients to finish certifying and then I have to have all of them entered into the computer system by the end of the week."

"Okay, lunch time would be great. I had already planned to check out some dance equipment and office furniture first thing in the morning anyway, so I can meet you after that. Oh, mom, I can't believe this is happening. I'm going to have my own dance studio with my very own students. Oh, there is something else that I have to do."

"Slow down child. What do you have to do?" Her daddy asked.

I have to start contacting the people who answered my newspaper ad about dance lessons. I received a lot of positive phone calls about it. I'm going to start calling some of them back and see what kind of interest they really have in dance. Once I secure my building, I'm going to host an open house for potential students, family, friends and everybody!"

"Sounds like you have everything worked out, sweetie," her daddy said smiling at his *baby girl*. "I'm proud of you." He walked over to her and kissed her on the forehead. "I think I'm going to leave you and your mother to yourselves. I have some paperwork to review before I head back to the office.

Benjamin adored Aisha and there was nothing he wouldn't do for his youngest daughter. Unlike Selena, he had seen Aisha grow up from a little girl to a beautiful young woman. He was aware that Sandra had her moments of jealousy, but Aisha was his little girl, the pride and joy of his life and he didn't want her to grow up doubting his love for her, like Selena often did; even though it wasn't Selena's fault. He often blamed himself. As her father, he should have made more of an effort to see her and communicate with her, even though her crazy momma did everything she could do to make it impossible for him to have a relationship with his oldest daughter. She didn't have a problem cashing his child support checks every month, but whenever he tried to see Selena, it had to be on her terms and her terms alone. Those terms turned out to be a week every now and then in the summer. He and Selena had a decent relationship now that she was an adult because she finally understood that her father wasn't entirely to blame for their fragile relationship. But Selena still harbored her share of envy at the exceptionally close relationship he had with Aisha.

3

A friendship can weather most things and thrive in thin soil; but it needs a little mulch of letters and phone calls and small, silly presents every so often - just to save it from drying out completely. Pam Brown

Aisha and Tameria had been best friends since kindergarten and nothing had changed over the years. In kindergarten when they lay down side by side to take an afternoon nap, they often whispered and giggled until they both fell asleep. They have simply been inseparable ever since. They practically spent their entire childhood at each other's homes – eating meals, having sleepovers and even helping to clean each other's bedrooms. The two of them accepted Christ at the same time and were even baptized together at the same church. Since then, Aisha has taken her Christian upbringing seriously by being a hard-working faithful member of Temple Cathedral Church. Her love of dance inspired her to start a youth dance ministry at the church. Her new studio had seen its share of success and some of the girls from the church dance ministry were now her formal students. At times it was hard for her to fathom that she actually owned her own studio. Sometimes she'd walk through the studio's beveled double glass doors and actually pinch herself to make sure she wasn't dreaming.

"Aisha, I can't believe how much the studio has grown in just two years' time. Girl, it's like you've been doing this all of your life. How many children do you have enrolled in your classes now?" Tameria's voice rang with enthusiasm and vigor. She often found herself amazed at the favor of God radiating in her best friend's life.

"I have three classes - Beginners, Intermediate and Advanced with a total of exactly seventy-seven students plus an ever expanding waiting list. I'm growing so fast that I'm going to have to hire another instructor. I can't do it all by myself any longer. Of course that's a good thing so don't think for one minute that I'm complaining."

"I don't see how you do it."

"Why can't you enjoy dance as much as I do, Tameria? We'd make a good team.

"I'm sorry to say, but you know dance just isn't my thing. My passion is in the health-related field. That's my calling. Hey, just think, once I enter into my Residency, I can offer medical assistance to some of your students. God knows you work them hard enough – with all of that bending, twisting, stretching, shaking and jumping, they're going to need a good physician from time to time." The two of them laughed and gave each other a high five.

"You're right about that, girl. But you know for yourself that perfection only comes from commitment, dedication and practice, practice and more practice. These girls know that I will not accept mediocrity. They will need to either give it their all or shut it down. It's all or nothing. Even my younger students have memorized my favorite phrase. *I will dance, I will dance, I will dance unto the Lord.*"

"Yeah I know, but right now can you dance on out of here this evening. It's after six o'clock and we're supposed to be going to that play tonight, remember?

And it starts at exactly eight o'clock. Tameria reminded her.

"Come on, help me straighten up around here and then we can get leave. You know, I have no idea what I'm going to wear.

"Aisha, we've had plans for almost a month to attend this premiere, and you mean to tell me that you haven't decided what you're going to wear? I should have known to check up on you more closely.

"Don't worry. I'll find something in that closet of mine."

It had been a couple of years since the two of them had been to the legendary Orpheum Theatre on Main Street. They had forgotten about the grandeur and elegance it seemed to exude from just walking inside the massive doors. Aisha's teal sleeveless evening dress was perfect for the event. The form fitting dress accentuated her curvaceous body. Her stomach was flat as a pancake and her lean, shapely legs were undoubtedly the legs of a dancer as they made the teal Stuart Weitzman pumps she wore stand out with each sure and certain step she took – she had splurged on the shoes even though she knew they were way out of her price range. She walked like a graceful dancer. She didn't notice the eyes of several gentlemen following her every move. Her auburn colored natural twists hung to her shoulders. She was glad she had finally let go of the permed look. She couldn't imagine relaxing her hair ever again.

"Ladies, please allow me to show you to your seats," the well-groomed usher said extending his white gloved hand.

"Thank you," was Aisha's response. She and Tameria took their lower level seats and began to enjoy the play. At the end of the production, when the little girl in the play was taken from her parents, Aisha found herself crying. Even though it was just a play, she couldn't help but feel the emotions of losing someone. She thought about the tragic death of her grandparents.

"Isn't this touching?" Tameria whispered reaching inside her small beaded purse to pull out a Kleenex. "This play is *soooo* good. Look at the two of us crying like babies." They both let out a soft snicker being careful not to disturb anyone with their chatter.

"Girl, you know we have to do better. I didn't go through all of that trouble putting on make-up just to have it smeared all over my face. We look like raccoons. " Tameria said as they prepared to exit the theatre.

"I know that's right. But I just couldn't help it. It was so moving and so surreal. Now what are we going to do to lift out spirits after this tear jerker?" Aisha asked.

"How about having a drink with me?" The gentleman standing next to them spoke. Aisha turned swiftly in his direction.

"Excuse me?" She said trying not to show her annoyance at the gentleman for listening in on their conversation.

"I didn't mean to eavesdrop," he said. "But I couldn't help but over hear you. I saw the two of you during the intermission but I couldn't get through the crowd to say anything. Let me introduce myself. I'm Chandler, Chandler Larson. And may I ask your names?" He said, extending his hand and focusing his baby browns on Aisha.

"No, I don't think so," Aisha responded. "I'm not in the habit of just giving my name out to strange men." Her voice resonated her anger and cautiousness. She had no idea where this man had come from. *What does he mean, he couldn't get to us during intermission? How long has this fool been watching us?* She felt quite uncomfortable.

Grabbing hold of Tameria's elbow, she said, "Excuse us. Come on Tameria. Let's get out of here."

Tameria followed her best friend with a tad bit of reservation. This Chandler Larson was quite a looker. His black tuxedoed suit clung to his tall frame flawlessly. His coal black dreads rested neatly against his scalp and tapered off at the nape of his neck. His eyebrows were thick and when he spoke they seemed to carry on a conversation of their own. Every word he spoke revealed glistening white teeth which had to have been bleached His muscular physique could easily make a girl feel secure and protected.

"Tameria, come on," Aisha moved her hand to Tameria's wrist pulling her toward the door. "Let's get out of here before another crazed maniac walks up. I can't believe the nerve of that guy."

"Aisha, get over it. He was only flirting with you. Stop getting so uptight. Just because a man approaches you like that doesn't mean he's some serial killer or rapist. That was just his pick-up line to get a conversation going with us."

"Well, he obviously needs to get a new one because that one surely won't work with me. You might fall for some okie dokie line like that but as for me, I think he must be nuts. You just don't walk up to somebody you don't know and eavesdrop on their conversation."

"Aisha, ease up. Come on, before you go berserk."

"Now you're talking," was Aisha's response.

Tameria steered her champagne colored Mazda onto MLK Boulevard. "Aisha you need to ease up some. Don't be on the defensive so much. You can't possibly expect to find Mr. Right if you keep brushing off every man that tries to get next to you?"

"For one thing, you know me, right?"

"Uh huh."

"Then you ought to know that I am not out searching for Mr. Right. I'm leaving that all up to God. He's going to handle that. "

"How do you know that God didn't send what's his name? Chandler. And look what you did. You all but told the poor guy to get out of your face. You're a trip." Tameria smiled pulling up into the crowded parking lot of Logan's Steakhouse.

"Enough of that, Tameria. I see we're eating steak tonight. I'm glad. I've only eaten a blueberry muffin today and I'm absolutely famished. They went into the restaurant and within seconds were escorted to a booth.

It didn't take long for the two of them to decide on what they were having. Tameria enjoyed the thickly sliced T-bone, prepared medium well with a Caesar salad and steamed vegetables. Aisha ordered a tender sirloin tip, well done with a green salad and a loaded baked potato. They laughed and talked, enjoying each other's company like they always did.

"Tell me, how's it going with your new beau?" Aisha asked.

"Chase is quite a guy," Tameria answered. "I really like him. He's attentive, he loves the outdoors like I do and he adores his mother. That's a huge plus right there. I've heard that if a man treats his momma right then he surely will treat his lady with some real respect and admiration. And the fact that we're both in the medical field is great because he understands that my schedule is hectic and our time together is quite limited. He's already doing his Residency in Neurosurgery. To tell you the truth, I can't find a single thing wrong with him."

"A neurosurgeon? Wow, that's fantastic. But uh, what about his beliefs, Tameria? Is he a Christian? You know you shouldn't date someone who doesn't share the same Christian beliefs as you."

"Didn't I tell you that I can't find anything wrong with the man? He is a Christian and has been since he was thirteen years old. He's active in his church and works with the youth ministry when he isn't on call at the hospital. I really believe that God has his hand in this relationship Aisha."

"I'm so glad for you. That one time I met him, even though it wasn't for long, he appeared to be a nice guy. He was all over you and quite affectionate too."

"Yeah, he's like that. I have to admit that I'm crazy about him. I think I'm actually falling in love with him."

" Really? Oh, Tameria, that's good. Do you think he feels the same about you?"

"Yep, he even told me as much the other night."

"He told you that he loved you and you didn't tell me?"

"I've been busy, Aisha. You know how medical school is and you know how busy you always are. By the time we make it home, it's too late to talk on the phone and we're both wiped out."

"You're right about that. Our schedules are hectic as all get out. This is the first time we've had a chance to chill out and talk in quite a while. Just be prayerful and take it slow. And please don't give up the booty. Make him wait, girl."

Tameria stopped eating. A look of guilt spread across her face.

Aisha knew her friend too well. She was holding something back. She hoped it wasn't what she was thinking. Surely Tameria hadn't given up her virginity to Chase. She didn't care how great he was. She wanted her friend to honor the commitment they first made when they both started dating, not only to each other but to God - to remain virgins until their wedding day.

"Tameria, please tell me you haven't? Please."

"No, we haven't done anything. But things are really getting hot and heavy. I've never felt like this before. Even Kevin Dixon didn't arouse the kind of feelings in me that I have when I'm with Chase. And you know how crazy I was about him in high school."

Aisha remembered all too well. Kevin Dixon had been Tameria's first and only boyfriend in high school. The three of them attended Christ the King Academy. Kevin was the star quarterback of the varsity football team and he was crazy about Tameria Matthews the prettiest girl on the varsity cheerleading squad. During their junior year of high school, they were inseparable. Tameria believed he was going to be the man she would marry one day-until his daddy's job transferred him up North. Tameria was devastated. She didn't eat for almost two weeks and lost about ten pounds. In the beginning they emailed each other every day and talked on the phone just about every weekend, but after a couple of months the phone calls and emails tapered off and by the end of their senior year, Kevin and Tameria hadn't spoken to each other in almost three months. The distance proved to be too much for the young high school sweethearts. Since that time she hadn't been seriously involved with anyone, until she met Chase at University of Tennessee Medical school. They hit if off like they had known each other all of their lives.

Aisha was delighted to see Tameria happy once again. And Chase did seem like quite a catch. He had that special charisma that drew people to him like a magnet. Yet Aisha was still cautious and she wanted her friend to be even more cautious. She didn't want to see Tameria's heart broken.

"Tameria, you have to be careful. I told you not to put yourself in a position where you would be tempted. What ever happened to hanging out with other friends instead of just the two of you being alone? You don't need to be alone with him especially in private."

"I know and you're right. But it's hard."

Aisha didn't let up. "Everything will go much better for you in a group setting. Anytime you find yourself alone with him, you know your hormones and HIS are going to start raging girl. You have to be more careful. If he really is the one, remember that everything will work out. He'll respect the fact that you are celibate and a virgin and he won't try to push you to do anything rash."

"I know that Aisha. And like I said, you're right. Our last few dates have been just the two of us in his apartment. And I have to put a stop to it. I don't plan on giving it up until I'm standing before a minister and saying those two little words, *I do*."

"I know that's right," Aisha grinned. "Now that's what I'm talking about. She took a bite of her steak. "Girl, this is the best sirloin I've tasted in a long time. How is your T-bone?"

"Great, but the food here is always good. Now, I want you to admit something."

"Admit what?"

"That the man at the theatre tonight was really fine." Tameria laughed. "Come on, admit it."

"Girl, when I turned around and looked up at him, I could feel my face turning ten shades of red," Aisha grinned. "He was so good looking I could barely stand to look at him."

"I knew it. Boy am I glad to hear that."

"Glad about what."

"Glad that you still got some feelings inside of you, some yearnings for a man. You stay too uptight."

"You're so silly. You know dancing is what matters to me. It's the only relationship I have time for right now and of course putting my all into being the woman God wants me to be."

"Aisha, just give somebody a chance. At least go on a date from time to time."

"I do. Remember when I went to dinner and a gospel concert with Gaston from church."

"Aisha, that was almost six months ago."

"Gnaw, it wasn't that long ago. Was it?"

Tameria eyed Aisha, raising one eyebrow and then nodded her head in an up and down motion.

"I can't help it, Tameria. I just can't see myself allowing a man to get too close to me. I believe when that time comes along, God will awaken those special feelings inside of me and that's when I'll know it's time. But He hasn't done that yet, which is absolutely fine with me."

"Well, I'm going to start praying a little bit harder for you. You haven't had a real boyfriend– not ever. You're waaay overdue for one. We're both twenty-four years old. And you, my dear, have never even been kissed."

"Yes, I have." Aisha laughed loudly. "I can't believe you said that."

"When then? Tell me. And I'm not talking about the time Gaston kissed you on your hand either," both ladies laughed so loud that heads turned in their direction.

The ladies finished their dinner then went to Tameria's apartment. Like they did when they were teenagers, they undressed down to their undies and put on flannel pajama pants and white t-shirts. Curling up in Tameria's queen size bed with a bowl of buttered popcorn, they talked some more while flipping the remote between BET, MTV and Discovery Health. Aisha soon nodded off. Tameria's light snore woke her up and she got up and went into the other bedroom.

"I'm out of here," she mumbled to Tameria.

"Um, huh," Tameria sleepily responded while she turned to her side and pulled the quilt over her head.

23

4

Choosing goals that are important to you is one of the most essential things you can do in order to live your dreams. Les Brown

"Girls, how many times do I have to tell you? We have to get this routine right? We have a recital in three and a half weeks and we're still making the same mistakes. Now let's start again. One..two…three….turn. One…two…three…bend…One…two three… left….One…two three… right. Great. Now, let's do it again. This time we're going to dance to the music. Remember, count in your mind. Don't look at the person next to you. Concentrate, relax and allow the steps to flow naturally. Remember, you're angels, graceful, light on your feet. Now let's take it from the top."

♦

"Aisha, you have a call on line two," the receptionist's pleasant voice rang over the intercom.

"Keep it up girls. I'll be right back." She turned and walked hurriedly to her office to answer the call.

"Hello, this is Aisha."

"Aisha. Good afternoon. Thaddeus Phelps here."

"Oh, hi Thaddeus. What's up?"

"I'm calling about the lease on your building. As you know, it expires in three months.

"Yes, I'm aware of that. But like I told you last month, I am planning to renew my lease before it expires.

I can't find another location as perfect as this one and I'm totally pleased with it."

"That's great to hear Miss Carlisle."

"Miss Carlisle?" Aisha began to feel somewhat uneasy. She and Thaddeus had been on a first name since she had begun leasing the building three years ago. Now he wanted to come at her all formal. She couldn't understand why he was taking such a professional tone with her now.

"Thaddeus, is something wrong? You're sounding different. Tell me. What is it?"

"Well, I have some good news and some bad news."

"Just tell me."

"The good news is that the owner wants you to remain in the building. He believes your dance studio is a great outlet for these young girls you're teaching. You've been a great tenant and we couldn't ask for anyone better."

"Okay, Thaddeus what's going on? You're scaring me."

"Look Aisha. The bottom line is that the owner of the building has decided to sell it. He's run into some financial hardships and has to liquidate several of his properties and your location happens to be one of them."

"What? Are you telling me that he's selling this property? But he can't do that Thaddeus. I've put too much into this building. There's no way I can find a place like this with the space, the perks and all at a price I can afford. Doesn't he have some other property he can sell?"

"I'm sorry, Aisha. He's made up his mind. He's going to get rid of it. The good news is that we're giving you a heads up on this so if you want to, you can purchase the building. All you need is a down payment of thirty-five thousand dollars."

"Thirty-five thousand dollars! I don't have that kind of money. I've already invested every bit of my inheritance into remodeling this studio, Thaddeus. And you know that. Over half of my students are inner city youths which mean they're paying according to their income levels. I barely have enough to cover the rent every month, now you expect me to come up with thirty-five thousand dollars?" Aisha couldn't believe what she was hearing. All she could see was her dream going down the drain. Maybe she could relocate. Maybe she could find somewhere else. But with what? She had no funds and she was already using her small savings account to pay the rent on her apartment and her car note. What could she do?

"Look, Thaddeus, just give me six months or so and maybe I can find a way to come up with the money. Or maybe, with a little prayer and fasting I can get the owner to change his mind about selling this building."

"Unfortunately, you don't have six months, Aisha. The most I can give you is ninety days. After that, if you don't have the money, you've got to move. This is a prime location and they're lots of people who would pay top dollar for this building. I'm sorry. There's nothing I can do."

Aisha hung up the phone and a feeling of hopelessness began to consume her. She turned to God. "Lord, what can I do? I can't give up this place. I just can't. You know that my credit isn't the best since opening the studio. I'm up to my head in debt already trying to keep the studio going. I can't afford to start over somewhere else. I need you to intervene in this situation Lord and I need you to do it in a hurry." she cried out.

◆

Tameria couldn't believe it when Aisha told her about her conversation with Thaddeus. "What are you going to do Aisha? That's money we can only dream about having. I wish I could do something to help you. Shoots, I only have about $1,500 I can loan you. You already know that I'm up to my neck in student loans just to stay in med school."

"Thanks, Tameria. But I can't accept your money anyway. Shoots, you're trying to make it just like I am. God will make a way. He has to."

"Have you talked to your parents?" Tameria asked. A frown etched across her forehead.

"No, I didn't ask mom and dad. I mean they're still trying to manage living off their pensions. I can't do that to them. And even if they did have it to loan to me, I have no idea when or if I could pay it back anytime soon. You know the studio is barely turning a profit Tameria." Aisha looked shakened.

"What are you going to do?"

"I have an appointment at the bank tomorrow morning. I'm going to see if I can possibly get a small business loan again. Something will work out. It just has too." Aisha tried hard to make herself believe the very words she was saying to Tameria. She couldn't fathom the idea of giving up the studio. It was her life. Surely God wouldn't allow her to lose it.

5

"Miss Carlisle, we've reviewed your loan history with us, the loan officer spoke in a cold detached voice. Though your payment history has been fair, I have noticed that there have been quite a few times you've been delinquent with your payments."

"Yes, that's correct. But that's only like you said, a few times. Most of my students are from the inner city and pay on a sliding income scale. At times, I have to wait until I secure these payments and I might run a few days late in paying you. But I always call and let you know and I've never missed a payment. So please, I really need this loan. If I don't get it, I can lose my studio all together and I just can't let that happen."

The loan officer paused, not once did she look at Aisha. She continued to peruse the file before her, shaking her head from side to side every so often.

Aisha's hands were sweating. She prayed underneath her breath. "Please help me, Lord."

Finally, after what seemed like an eternity, the woman looked up. "To be truthful Miss Carlisle I don't see much that we can do to help you. With what you already owe us, and the thirty-five thousand you're asking for, I just don't see how we can approve any more loans for you."

"Ma'am, please. I need this loan. You have to do something." Aisha pleaded.

"Let me look over some figures here for just a minute." The woman entered number after number into her desk top computer. When she finished this time she looked up at Aisha. "Miss Carlisle."

"Yes," Aisha beamed. She felt like a breakthrough had just occurred. God had come through for her once again.

"I believe we could pay off your existing loan and refinance it as one new loan. If we do that, the most we could loan you will be fourteen thousand-five hundred. And of course your payment will increase substantially, by about thirty-five percent."

Aisha's face turned sour. What was she going to do? She knew one thing was for sure. She couldn't turn this down. She would just have to accept it and then figure out some other way to get the remainder of the money. But what? "I'd like to do that."

"Okay, but let me remind you again Miss Carlisle that your monthly payments will increase considerably. Right now your debt ratio is hovering on the edge. You can't afford to get another loan anytime soon and you won't be able to get anything from us until you have at least paid this loan down by more than half of your recomputed balance."

"Thank you, ma'am. Just write up the papers. God and I will have to deal with the rest. Thank you," she answered again.

After spending an hour and a half at the bank, she left with a somewhat sigh of relief about the loan. But she would have to get very creative in a heartbeat in order to find a way to come up with the remaining $20,500. She had a little less than three months to get the money to Thaddeus. She buttoned her black leather bomber jacket, pulled her matching leather cap down over her head and raced to the coffee shop a couple of blocks from her studio. She'd soothe herself with a tall cappuccino with loads of whipped cream on top. Usually she stayed away from the caffeine but today she felt like she could use an extra boost of energy. She would go to the studio and work it off later. She sat down at the small round table, sipping on her cappuccino and reading over her loan papers. She then decided to make a list of possible things she could do to get the rest of the money. She was in deep thought, in her own world when she heard the captivating, distinct voice hovering above her head.

"Hi there. Looks like we have something in common."

Aisha quickly raised her head toward the voice. It was him. The guy from the theatre. She couldn't believe she recognized him after all this time. What was he doing here? Had he been following her? Surely not, it had been over two months since they were at the theatre. She gathered her thoughts quickly, trying not to show her displeasure of being interrupted.

"And what exactly do we have in common?" she responded tersely while stuffing her loan papers in her purse.

"Cappuccino, of course." He flashed a boyish smile at her.

"Is that right? So what does this warrant?" Aisha asked him. "Since we have soooo much in common, do I owe you a gold ribbon or something?"

"My, my aren't we the feisty one. Look , let's start over again. I'm Chandler Larson. He extended his manicured hand out toward Aisha while he kept on talking. "I'm not trying to come on to you. But I do find you attractive. I'd just like to sit here and share a cappuccino with you. That's all."

Aisha ignored his outstretched hand. She didn't know what to think. She began to really look at him. He seemed harmless and she was in a public place. She didn't have to tell him anything about her so maybe it was okay to let him sit down and drink his cappuccino.

"Okay, sure. Have a seat. But I'm very busy and I don't have a lot of time."

"That's fine. I promise not to wear out my welcome.

"So, Chandler, what type of work do you do?" Aisha's curiosity had the best of her. "Are you a private eye or something?" She asked sarcastically. "I mean, you appear at the most unlikely times."

Chandler flashed a broad grin. Aisha couldn't help but think to herself how handsome he was. She quickly dispelled the thought and concentrated on his answer.

"You're quite the humorous one aren't you? By the way, funny lady do you have a name? I've told you mine so at least you can tell me yours. Can't you?" His eyes pleaded innocently.

"Aisha. I believe that's all you need to know.

"Ahhh, Aisha. What a pretty name. But of course it goes with such a pretty face." His infectious smile captivated her and she knew that a blush must surely have spread across her face.

She quickly changed the subject. "Now, like I asked, are you a private investigator?"

"No, of course not. I'm a land developer. Far from a private eye, huh?"

"You're right about that." Aisha muttered underneath her breath. She took another sip of cappuccino.

"Come again?" he asked.

"Oh nothing. I was just thinking out loud."

"What about you?" Chandler asked.

"What about me what?" Aisha replied looking confused.

"What do you do for a living?"

"I own a dance studio."

"Oh, a dance studio. Why am I not surprised?" His voice was sure and she didn't know why this man captivated her so.

"Why are you not surprised?"

"Because you look so graceful and poised. And that teal evening dress you had on at the theatre revealed that you do some serious working out," he flirted.

That uneasy feeling began to rise up in Aisha. She just wasn't used to having some guy come on so strong. She was used to being in control of situations and making the other person feel uneasy. Now the tables were turned.

"Look, it's been nice talking to you. But I have to leave now. I have some business to take care of."

"Sure, I understand. I certainly didn't mean to detain you, Aisha. But look, will you give me a call sometime?" Chandler reached inside his jacket and pulled out his business card.

"Why on earth would I want to do that?" she asked. "Now, if you'll excuse me. Good day, Mr. Larson."

Before he could respond to her cold remark, she grabbed her Nine West purse and dashed for the door. When Chandler moved from the table he spotted the thin leather wallet lying on the floor next to the chair where she had been sitting. Chandler assumed that when she stood up abruptly she must have forced the wallet out of her purse. He bent over and picked it up and immediately raced through the door after her. He looked up and down the street but she was nowhere in sight. How could she have vanished so quickly? Leafing through the wallet he saw the beautiful face of this strange woman on her driver's license. He read the address on the license. *Looks like I'm going to have the chance to see you again after all Aisha Carlisle*. Tucking the wallet safely away in his inside jacket pocket, he smiled as he walked casually to his car.

6

A dream doesn't become reality through magic; it takes sweat, determination and hard work. Unknown

"Look, girls. We only have three weeks before your dance presentation. Everything has to be flawless. I will accept nothing less. From the beat and rhythm, to the musical forms, everything must be perfect. Performing at the Mayor's charity ball is a once in a lifetime opportunity for us and I won't blow it. So take a fiver and then back to the dance floor you go.

Aisha couldn't hold back the fact that she was on edge about the future of the studio. It wasn't just having to come up with the rest of the money to buy the building that was stressing her out, she was also behind on practically all of her bills. She had to do something, but what. Her attitude toward her students was changing and her receptionist noticed it along with some of the parents.

"Aisha, look I'm not trying to but into your business, but I know something is wrong," the receptionist Angie said. "Do you want to talk about it?"

"No, not right now, Angie. I've got too many things to do. Anyway, it's nothing. I'm just trying to get things in order for the charity ball. This is going to be a fantastic opportunity for the girls as well as for the studio.. I just don't want to blow it."

Angie knew better. Ever since her boss had received the phone call from Thaddeus last week, she had been a totally different person. She was usually quite even tempered and patient with her students, but now she often heard Aisha raising her voice at them and making them do their routines repeatedly without resting. Something was wrong, but Angie didn't know what.

"Thanks for being concerned. Look I need to get back to work. Oh and Angie," Aisha said turning around in a spin.

"Yes?"

"Have you seen my wallet? I can't find it. You know how bad I am about misplacing stuff."

"No, I haven't seen it. I'll keep my eyes open though."

"Okay," Aisha turned and went back into the studio. She would look for her wallet a little later. She was glad that she had deposited the loan check into her business account. Thank God for small miracles. If it hadn't been for her distraction by that Chandler guy, maybe she wouldn't have been thrown off track. She quickly dismissed any thought of him.

"Break's over girls…let's get back to work!" She yelled while clapping her hands loudly.

◆

"Aisha, have you decided what you're going to do about the rest of the money for the building?" Tameria inquired.

"Nope. And I don't have much time left so I've got to do something. I'm going to have to meet with my students' parents. I can't put it off much longer. I'm going to increase my fees. I know that might mean losing a few students, actually I might lose more than a few but I have to increase the tuition. Then I'm going to call some of the kids on the waiting list and hold an audition for more students.

"More students!" Tameria was upset at hearing this. She knew that Aisha couldn't take on any more students right now. She was already pushing herself over the top. "How in the world are you going to pull that off? I know you can't be talking about enrolling any more kids. Girl, you must be crazy."

"No, I'm not crazy, Tameria. I have to do what I have to do. Don't you know how important this is to me? It was obvious that Aisha was about to break. Tameria hated to see her dearest friend come apart like this.

"Oh, I'm sorry," I didn't mean to interrupt. Tameria and Aisha both looked up at the same time. The tall, dark haired lady stood in the doorway. Elisa Santana was the mother of one of her more talented students, Gabby.

"Oh, no, you're not interrupting. We were just talking," Aisha tried to wipe the tear away from her eye that was about to find its way down her red cheeks. "Please come on in."

"Look, I'm going to go in the studio, Aisha and watch the kids practice their routine. I know they're going to do great at the ball," Tameria replied.

"Alright. We'll talk later. Now, what can I do for you Miss Santana?"

"Gabby told me that you are going to meet with the parents tomorrow afternoon. I won't be able to attend. I have to go in to work early tomorrow. So do you think you could let me know why you want to meet with us?" Elisa Santana was a pencil thin, tall and quite attractive woman with olive skin. Her daughter, Gabby, looked a lot like her mother. She had the same features and was just as pretty. Elisa used to be an exotic dancer. Her stealth legs were supported by three inch violet heels. The sleek fitting mini dress she wore hugged every curve on her body and the hem of the dress almost met up with her thick auburn tresses flowing down her back.

"Miss Santana, I'm sorry to have to do this to my parents. But I'm going to have to go up on the tuition. My expenses are increasing and unfortunately I have to pass some of that cost on to my students. If I don't raise my rates then I'm afraid that I'll have to make some serious cuts in other areas in order to keep the studio going. I know you're a single mother trying to raise a teenage daughter and take care of your own, but I hope you understand." Aisha tried to break it to Miss Santana as easily as she could. She wouldn't be surprised if she withdrew Gabby from the dance classes.

"I understand. And really, it's no problem. Just tell me when the new rate goes into effect and I'll take care of it."

Aisha was amazed. Elisa Santana hadn't bothered to even ask her how much of an increase. She didn't seem the least bit upset or bothered by the notice of an increase.

"Don't you want to know how much the increase is going to be?" Aisha asked trying not to sound too astonished.

"Why, of course," Elisa said, while slinging her tresses over her shoulder. "But it really won't make any difference because Gabby isn't going anywhere else. She loves you and I love the way you teach and that's that. The money is no problem."

"Wow," Aisha mumbled. *Does she have a rich boyfriend somewhere lurking in the background or what?* Aisha slightly grinned.

Sure enough, when Aisha told Elisa that the tuition was going up by twenty five percent, Elisa answered with an "okay," and nothing else was said.

"If only the other parents would be so easy," Aisha told Tameria after Elisa Santana and Gabby left.

"Girl, what is she doing? She always looks just like she just stepped out of a fashion magazine. She drives a BMW and you said she has a house to die for. Maybe I'm in the wrong field of study," Tameria laughed.

"I know that's right," Aisha responded. When Aisha offered to take Gabby home after practice one day, she was surprised at the multi-level structure and the perfectly landscaped lawn. It wasn't that she was surprised that some of her students were not from the inner city. However it was somewhat surprising that Elisa lived in an upscale neighborhood as a single parent on a dancer's income. On the other hand, Aisha remembered somebody telling her that some exotic dancers made a pretty hefty salary. Obviously what she had heard was right, at least in Elisa's case.

"Come on, I've got to get out of here. I have to run some errands before I go to Bible study tonight. Since I can't find my wallet, I guess I'll have to go ahead and replace my driver's license and social security card. I'm glad I had my small purse. If I had been carrying my other purse I would have had the wallet with all my credit cards and pictures and other stuff inside. Girl, God is good. He knows he looks out for me." Aisha let out a long sigh. "Come on, let's get out of here."

Aisha told Angie goodnight and she and Tameria left for the afternoon.

"Tameria, I can't believe I forgot to tell you." Aisha whirled around as soon as they walked through the glass double doors leading from the building.

"What? What is it?" Tameria asked.

"You remember that guy we saw at the Orpheum a couple of months ago? You know the one that walked up on us while we were talking, and you said he was only trying to throw us a line?"

"Yeah, I remember that fine hunk of flesh, but I said he was trying to throw you a line, not me. Anyway, what about him?" she countered, her curiosity piqued to the fullest.

"I ran into him when I was leaving the bank today. I was at the coffee shop having a cappuccino when I heard this heavy charming voice say hello. And when I looked up, it was none other than Chandler Larson."

"Chandler Larson? What happened? I want to know everything," Tameria said while they raced down the busy Memphis expressway.

7

If you have built castles in the air, your work need not be lost; that is where they should be. Now put the foundations under them. Henry Thoreau

"We're going to continue our study on peace. The Hebrew meaning of peace is shalom, which means complete, whole, nothing missing." Pastor Shipley was an excellent Bible scholar. He had a way of making the word of God plain enough for everyone to understand. Since becoming Pastor of *(put the name of the church here)* eight years ago, the membership had more than tripled in size and was continuing to grow by leaps and bounds. It definitely was getting closer to fitting the description of a mega church. He drew in a great deal of young people as well as older adults. "Now if you want some of this peace, you have to stay focused on God," he said. "God wants his children whole. How can you be whole if you're consumed with worry, if you're troubled by financial woes and sickness and heartache? God doesn't want that for his children. He stands ready to deliver you and make you complete. But you have to be willing to obey His word. You have to be willing to praise Him even in the midst of troubled times. The word of God says that many are the afflictions of the righteous, but the Lord delivereth them out of them all! God's word is true and his promises are real," Pastor Shipley emphasized to the members.

Aisha understood that everything Pastor Shipley said was true. And if she just remained faithful and obedient then things would work out just fine. After leaving church an hour and a half later, she stopped off at the corner store before heading to her two-bedroom townhouse. When she drove her midnight blue Acura into the circular drive, she mouthed a prayer of thanksgiving to God. She pulled out her keys, grabbed the bag of groceries, and raced up the marble walkway leading to her humble abode. She placed the key in the lock and the lights inside the living room automatically came on. She walked into the silence of the apartment, stepping out of each shoe as she walked along the Oriental rug covering her dark stained hardwood floors. She sat the groceries on the kitchen island and began carefully pulling out the head of lettuce, shaved turkey breast and sourdough bread. Standing in front of the fridge, she yanked it open and checked to see if she had mustard and a piece of red onion for the sandwich she planned to make for her dinner. "Oh, yes," she said breathing a sigh of relief when she found the items. She went into her bedroom, pulled off her capris and blouse. She couldn't wait to climb into a hot steamy shower, and then prepare her sandwich in time for the new episode of American Idol.

The water pounding against her body felt like tiny electric currents that energized her yet made her feel relaxed at the same time. She held her head back with her eyes closed and allowed the warm water to bathe her ebony skin. She carefully took the bath sponge and moved it up and down the length of her perfectly sculptured body and muscular legs. After twenty minutes, she felt the water cooling down and stepped carefully out of the shower stall on to the soft white bath rug. When the cool air kissed her body a shiver raced up and down her spine. She quickly grabbed her towel and wrapped it around her upper body. After drying off, she took the fuchsia cotton robe off of her bed and placed it over her body in place of the towel, stepped into her cloth slippers and walked into the kitchen to prepare her turkey sandwich.

While preparing her dinner she checked her voice mail messages. *You have six new messages. To listen to your messages press one now,"* the automated voice said.

"Aisha, it's your daddy. I'm just checking on you." *Press two to save, press three to erase or press four to go to the next message,* the voice instructed. Aisha continued to listen to all six of her messages. Surprisingly there was a message from her sister, Selena and another call was from a church member about the upcoming new members' banquet. Aisha was part of the New Members' Committee and had volunteered to help make the arrangements for the quarterly banquet. Her last message was from one of the parents from the studio.

"Hi, Aisha, I'm sorry to bother you, but I'm calling about Cherise. She won't be at rehearsal tomorrow. She has strep throat. I sure hope none of the other girls come down with it. Call me if you have any questions. We'll see you next week. Bye."

Shucks, that's all I need is for my girls to come down with strep. Oh well, I'm not going to worry about anything tonight. She erased the message and continued to fix her sandwich before settling down in her bed to watch *American Idol*.

◆

The blare of the alarm clock jarred her from her sleep. Aisha turned over sleepily, rubbing her eyes and glancing over at the clock. She turned the alarm off, eased out of the bed and walked into the bathroom. She washed her face and brushed her teeth and then cleaned up the mess she'd left on her nightstand the night before. She must have really been tired. She couldn't remember what happened after American Idol went off. She had even fallen asleep without saying her prayers. "Lord, forgive me," she mouthed out loud. Dragging her feet along, she went into the kitchen, poured herself a glass of V8 and released another slow yawn as she retrieved her morning paper from her doorstep. The sound of the phone interrupted her routine.

"Good morning, sweetheart. How are you?" Her daddy asked.

"Hi, Daddy, I'm fine. I'm sorry I didn't call you back last night. I fell asleep."

"Oh, that's okay. I just wanted to check on you and make sure everything was going all right. You doing okay, sweetie?"

"Sure, Dad. I told you. I'm fine. I've been working on the recital for the Mayor's charity ball so I'm pretty wiped out. I want everything to be sensational. This is a once in a lifetime opportunity for my dance studio."

"I know that honey. But you still have to take care of yourself. Okay? Your mom and I are proud of you Aisha, you know that. Let us know if we can help you in any way for the ball. Now, have a good day. Call me later on if you get a chance."

"I will. Bye, Daddy," Aisha said and then blew a kiss into the receiver.

"Bye, baby."

Aisha began dialing Tameria's phone number but then stopped abruptly when she realized that Tameria was doing a thirty six hour med rotation at the hospital. She was going to miss talking to her. But she knew she might as well get used to not talking to Tameria all of the time. Becoming a doctor was quite the challenge and revamping her social and personal life would be the sacrifice Tameria would have to make in order to succeed. If anyone understood, it was Aisha. She had to do the same thing to make her dance studio successful too. Now she faced a whole new dilemma, holding on to it. With the morning came the fresh onslaught of her problem. Perhaps today would be the day things would turn around for her. She remembered that she still hadn't located her wallet. She leafed through her purse and her dance duffel bag but the wallet was nowhere to be found. She ran outside and searched her car and still it wasn't there.

Oh, well, forget it. If it turns up fine and if it doesn't then so be it, she said out loud. *It certainly won't be the first time I've misplaced my wallet.*

She took another quick shower before putting on a thigh length jean skirt over her dance leotards and body suit, then packed her duffel bag with a change of clothes, a couple of energy bars and a can of V8 Splash before heading out the door.

8

Having aspirations is nice; fulfilling them is exhilarating.
Unknown

Lead Detective Chandler Larson's job in the Memphis Police Department's Undercover Division was one he'd dreamed about all of his life. Ever since he was a little boy he often day dreamed of being a cop and an undercover agent. He lived for the excitement and danger that he encountered on an almost daily basis. Imagine, scrawny Chandler Larson, had grown up to be a big bad police detective, saving the world from the evil guy. Chandler snickered at the thought of how far he'd come from a skinny, pimple faced little country boy in Montgomery.

His thoughts quickly zeroed in on the mysterious Aisha Carlisle. Never in a million years did he think he would ever see her again. For weeks after he first laid eyes on her at the Orpheum, he thought about how it would be to come up with her. He needed a nice sophisticated lady by his side. He was tired of going home to an empty apartment. But unfortunately his job didn't allow him the time he needed to really find that special someone. The hit and run kind of relationships were beginning to be a bore to him. He realized that at thirty-one years of age the playa in him had played out and he was ready to settle down and get serious with a lady.

44

He glanced over at one of his partners. "Hey, Jay, did I tell you about this dime piece I ran into earlier today?" Chandler's face was beet red as he thought about the mysterious bombshell.

"You're always meeting some so called dime piece," his co-worker teased. "Tell me just how hot this one is. I'll believe anything just as long as it gives me a minute to take a break from this computer. Man my eyes are beginning to cross. I've been staring at this screen so long. I can't run a trace on this suspected carjacker yet. I've run addresses, aliases and tats and still I'm coming up empty. So tell me. What's she like?" Jay leaned back in his chair, crossed his legs and put both hands behind his neck. His beer belly peaked through his celery green polo.

"This one might just be it Jay. This isn't the first time I've seen her either. I spotted her at the Orpheum a couple of months ago but she got away from me before I could make my move. I thought I'd never see her again and so I told myself that it just wasn't meant to be and left it at that. Then today, here I am at the coffee shop, right?"

"Yeah, and."

"And I look over and see this fine young thing sitting at the table all by her lonesome. Man, this girl has got it going on. Her hair was laid back man, flowing down her back, natural and all. Just the way I like it. I'm talking about silky black thick twists. Oooh, wee. Mercy!" Chandler squealed.

Sounds like she might just be hot if she has you going off like that, man." Jay laughed. "Come on, tell me more."

"Well, like I said, her hair was pretty as silk, man. She had on a salmon colored pant set and those high pumps I love to see the ladies wearing. Her fingernails were manicured and I can tell that the lady was all about the business."

"So what'd you do? Did you say anything to her?"

"What? Are you crazy? You know I wasn't about to let her walk out of my life a second time. So, tell you what I did."

"What?" A look of utter enjoyment was plastered across Jay's round plump face.

I took my smooth, charming self over to her table man." Chandler made an oomph sound, and continued with his story.

Jay stopped fumbling with the pile of papers on his desk, looked up and gave Chandler his full attention.

"Man, I was determined to use my best line on this one. You know, the one I reserve for the special little honeys," Chandler spoke with total confidence as he flashed a wide toothy grin at Jay.

"Let's hear what you said, man."

"First, I walked up to her and introduced myself. I reminded her that I'd seen her at the Orpheum."

"And what'd she say?"

"What do you mean what'd she say. She let me sit down beside her. I said to myself, yea, yea, yea."

"She let you sit down? Man, how do you do it?"

"Man, I just do it because I got it like that." Chandler spoke with a bit of cockiness. "Anyway, we talked a few minutes. I could tell she liked me even though she was playing hard to get. Girl got it all going on. She has great conversation and a mean streak to boot. Yea, I'd like to really get to know her."

"The thing is does she want to get to know you?" Jay laughed hard almost causing the chair to tilt over from the weight of his chunky body

"Not to worry about that. I know how to handle that situation. Anyway, when she left, I spotted a wallet lying on the floor beside where she was sitting. I opened it up and it was hers. I ran outside and tried to catch her but I couldn't. Lucky me."

"Lucky you? You said she got away didn't you?"

"Yeah, but now I know where she lives."

"Are you going over to her house?"

"Naw, I'm not going to be that bold. I'm going to run a check on her and see if I can find a phone number. Once I do that, I'll give her a ring, let her know I found her wallet and offer to bring it over. Boing…then I make my move."

"Your move? What kind of move, man?"

"Nope, can't tell. I can't let you in on all my playa secrets, not just yet, Jay." Chandler let out a laugh. "Now, let me run this check and get some work done around here for a minute." Chandler said.

"Yeah, me too. I've got to get some leads on this fool before I leave here today. I'm sick of this punk going around carjacking innocent folks like he's somebody or something." Jay's face showed the obvious anger he had over the suspected carjacker that had continued to elude capture.

◆

Chandler listened as the phone rang once, twice, three, four times. "Does she have an answering machine," he thought to himself.

"Hi, you've reached 555.8976. I can't take your call at the moment, but please leave a message or stay on the line and your call will be forwarded to me." Chandler decided to hang on and see if the call would reach her. Within a few seconds he heard the soft, sexy voice on the other end.

"Hello."

"Uh, hello, he stammered. "May I speak to Aisha Carlisle please?" Chandler didn't know why he was nervous. He just knew that he was.

"This is Aisha, who's calling please?" Aisha didn't recognize the voice on the other end. But whoever it was sure did sound good. The voice resonated sexiness and confidence. His deep baritone voice sent a tiny shiver up and down her spine.

"Hi, Aisha, this is Chandler. Chandler Larson, you know from the coffee shop."

Aisha couldn't believe this guy. How did he get her number? Was he some kind of fatal attraction or what? She was disturbed by this invasion of privacy. "Look Chandler, I don't appreciate you stalking me. I told you at the coffee shop that I had no reason to call you. What's up with you?" she asked angrily.

"Look, Miss Carlisle, it's not at all like you think. I'm not a stalker so don't worry about anything like that." He wasn't about to tell her that he had run an NCI on her at the station by using her driver's license.

"Well, how can I help you, Mr. Larson?"

"I think it's how I can help you. You see after you ran away from me at the coffee shop you happened to drop your wallet. I saw it and picked it up. I tried to catch up to you but you disappeared without a trace. I was calling now to see how we might arrange for you to get it. I didn't want to just show up on your doorstep unexpectedly, you see."

Aisha felt stupid for being so short with Chandler. She didn't know why this man made her stay in a defensive mode. "Oh, thanks Mr. Larson. I can come and pick it up if you'll just tell me where. I've been trying to figure out where I could possibly have lost it. And when I went back to the coffee shop, no one had turned it in at the counter. I even looked around the table but I didn't see it there either."

"Look, I don't want you to have to come to my place. I mean, I live all the way across town. I tell you what I can do. Do you work in the area of the coffee shop? If so, we could meet up there or I could drop it off by your place of work. Whatever you say, I'm at your beck and call," he laughed.

Aisha couldn't help but smile. Her defenses began to drop and she started to hear the kindness in Chandler's voice. She felt like he was truly being sincere and just trying to help her out. But she was used to keeping up her guard when it came to men. She'd dated a few guys here and there but none seriously. Her dance studio took up so much of her time and when she wasn't at the studio she was at church or trying to get in a little R&R between down times. A serious relationship was the farthest thing from her mind.

"I tell you what we can do. My dance studio is about two blocks from that coffee shop. You can bring it there if you don't mind."

"That sounds great. How about tomorrow around eleven?" he asked.

"Eleven will be fine. The address is four fifty-seven East Bellevue. If things change you can call me and we can make some other arrangements. The number to the studio is 555.9877.

"Okay, I've got it. And you do still have my card don't you or did you throw it away?"

Aisha was glad he couldn't see her face as it turned a flushed color. She stammered. "Yea, yes I believe I still have it." Aisha knew that she still had the card. She had looked at it a couple of times and for some reason she had decided to keep it. "If something comes up then I'll give you a call too," she answered. "Goodnight and thank you, Mr. Larson."

"Goodnight, Miss Carlisle. And look before I hang up can we cut the formalities. Just call me Chandler, okay?"

"Okay, and you may call me Aisha. Goodnight, Chandler."

"Goodnight, Aisha."

9

Sometimes what you're looking for comes when you're not looking. Goodquotes

Chandler expertly guided the black Infiniti into the parking space. His black trousers swayed with the wind as he maneuvered his long muscular legs down the parking lot corridor. The melon silk shirt wrapped around his chest outlined his massive chest. The black leather jacket hit his hips as the soft material protected him against the brisk wintry day. Snow was forecasted over the next couple of days and Chandler thought to himself that a leather jacket wasn't going to cut it much longer. He pushed the elevator button for the second floor. When he stepped off he immediately saw the sign facing him. *A-Carlisle Studio of Dance and Choreography.* He turned the doorknob and walked inside, feeling a bit of nervousness at the thought of seeing her again.

"Good morning, how may I help you?" The polite receptionist asked.

"Chandler Larson, I'm here to see Aisha Carlisle." Angie thought to herself how fine this Chandler Larson truly was. When Aisha told her that he would be coming by to bring her wallet, Angie had no idea he would be the knockout that he was. That was the one thing Aisha failed to tell her. "Humph," Angie moaned under her breath. *If fineness was against the law, this brother would be locked up for life.* "Let me get her for you Mr. Larson. Have a seat please."

"Thanks. And please call me Chandler."

"Oh, all right, Chandler. Aisha will be right with you."

Angie went into Aisha's office and immediately saw how upset she was. She was on the phone and it was obvious she was pleading with someone. About what, Angie had no idea? She hated to see her boss in apparent distress.

"Excuse me, just a minute please," Aisha told whoever was on the other end. "What is it Angie? she asked rather curtly.

"A Mr. Chandler Larson is in the lobby."

"Oh, dog, is it eleven already? Just get my wallet from him. No, on second thought, I'll be out in a minute."

Aisha turned and resumed her conversation. "Look just give me a little more time. I'm doing all I can to come up with the money. I can't lose this place. I just can't. Talk to the owner and see if I can get any kind of extension. Please Thaddeus. "

"Look, I told you. There's no extension. This guy has to sell and he wants his money now. I know you said you had part of it and I'll come by later this evening and get that but you don't have much time to come up with the rest. I'm sorry, Aisha. I hate that it has to be this way. I'll see you later." Thaddeus hung up the phone and Aisha fell back into the cloth covered swivel office chair. She had to get herself together. No time for tears. She mouthed a quick prayer. "Lord, I need you to come through for me on this. I can't do this without your help. You know how important this studio is to me." She stood up, pressed her hands against her red leotards, smoothed out her matching red knit top and proceeded to welcome the stranger on the other side of the door.

"Mr. Larson, thank you so much for coming by to bring my wallet. I really appreciate it." She extended her hand to meet his and flashed a fake smile his way. He looked more handsome than she had remembered from the coffee shop and the Orpheum. It was as if she was seeing him for the first time. He stood towering over her, appearing to be almost six feet. She knew that he worked out from the way his clothes hung so perfectly over his chiseled body. His broad shoulders oozed manliness. His goatee and well-trimmed mustache accentuated his smile and his pearly whites. Be still my heart.

"You're quite welcome, Aisha. It's all my pleasure. I believe this has to be fate, don't you?"

"I don't know if I agree with that statement or not. And what makes you say that anyway."

"Because three times I've had the pleasure of running into you. Now here's your wallet, and if you should ever lose it again, may I be so lucky again as to find it." His smile spread even further.

Aisha couldn't help but blush. Again she felt a tingle run up and down the course of her spine. "How can I repay you?"

"I have the perfect answer to that question, Miss Carlisle."

"And what is the perfect answer?"

"May I have the pleasure of your company at dinner this evening?" he asked boldly. He thought he might as well go for it. After all, she asked how he could be repaid.

"Well," she hesitated.

"Uh, uh, let's not even go there. You asked what you could do to repay me. I promise not to bite you, Aisha. I just want to enjoy getting to know you a little better, that's all. Nothing more, nothing less."

"Okay. Dinner will be fine. How does six thirty sound?"

"Six thirty sounds great. Where do you want me to pick you up?"

"Since you already know where I live why not come by my place. As a matter of fact, I have a great idea," Aisha said.

"What's that?"

"Why don't I prepare dinner for you? I mean it's the least I can do after all the trouble you've gone through to get my wallet back to me. And I have to admit that I'm an awfully good cook."

"That sounds even better. I'll be over around six thirty. Before I leave, do you have time to give me a quick tour of your studio? From what I've seen already it's truly state of the art. I'm quite impressed."

"Why, thank you, Mr. Larson."

"Why do you insist on being so formal? Call me Chandler, remember."

"Yes, of course I remember. Since I have a few minutes before my next class, I'd love to show you around – Chandler. Follow me." Aisha was excited that he wanted to tour the studio. She loved it when others appreciated her work. She pushed back the memories of the problems she faced and instead concentrated her efforts on giving Chandler a full-scale tour.

"Right around this corner and down the corridor is another practice room. I use it for my advanced class. "

"I see." He clasped his hands behind his back and leaned forward to view inside the classroom.

"This room holds about five to six students."

The next room is the dressing room. There's a wardrobe area right across the hall."

"Wow, you have a fantastic setup here. I had no idea this place was as large as it is. You can't tell when you first walk in."

"Yeah, I know. It's deceiving isn't it?"

"Girl, you have it going on."

Aisha smiled. "Do you dance?"

"Me, I don't think you could call doing the electric slide dancing."

She released a giggle. "Come on, I know you have to know how to step don't you? And what about slow dancing?"

"Sure, in that case, the answer to your question is yes." Before they both realized it forty-five minutes had gone by. He glanced at the clock on the mint green painted wall. "My, the time is slipping by. I'd better go and let you get back to doing your thing. Thanks for the grand tour."

"You're most welcome."

"I'll see you later this evening."

"Okay. And you did say lasagna would be fine, didn't you?"

"Yes, lasagna is fine. If you'll give me a chance you'll find out just how easy I am to please Aisha. Bye." He strolled out of the door feeling exhilarated.

Aisha blushed again and Angie smiled. *Something's starting to brew between those two.* Maybe this Chandler guy will be the one to penetrate her boss's shell. Just maybe.

10

One day someone will walk into your life and make you see why it never worked out with anyone else. Unknown

"The lasagna tastes superb," Chandler complimented as he finished off a second helping.

"I'm glad you liked it. It's made from an old recipe my grandmother gave me when I was a teenager."

"Tell me a little about yourself, Aisha." He stared directly into her eyes, making her feel somewhat captivated by his magnetism. She had to admit to herself that she was really enjoying his company. It had been such a long time since she'd entertained a man and it felt good, especially with him.

They continued sipping on a glass of red wine. Do you want dessert now? I made a raspberry cheesecake.

"Lady, you've really outdone yourself. Maybe you should lose something else and let me be so fortunate as to find it," he chuckled.

Aisha returned the laugh with one of her own. "I love it when people like my cooking so I just might have to entertain that idea Chandler," she joked. "Now, how about that cheesecake."

"Bring it on, girl. Bring it on." The two of them laughed and talked for several hours. Aisha found herself telling Chandler how she started the studio, about the death of her grandparents, and all about her students. The one thing she didn't mention was the financial trouble she was facing with the studio. In return, he told her about his so called job as a land developer, purposely failing to divulge that he was actually a detective in the Memphis Undercover Special Units division. There was no way he would tell her that.

"Tell me, do you like doing what you do? You know building things."

"Yeah, I do. I've never thought of being anything else. My father was a land developer and for as long as I can remember, he taught me everything about it." Chandler didn't really consider himself as lying, not totally anyway. His father might be considered as a land developer to some. It didn't matter that anyone else would have merely stated that his dad was a carpenter.

"Wow, that's interesting, but I know how you feel. I've dreamed of being a dancer since I was a little girl. My momma said I used to dance around the house as soon as I took my first step," Aisha giggled.

"It's good to be able to live your dream, don't you think."

"Yes, I do. I thank God every day that I'm living mine." Aisha paused before asking him, "Do you mind if I get a little more personal."

"No, what is it."

"Do you have a special someone in your life?" She didn't want to come off too brash, but she had to know. A man as fine as Chandler had to be involved with someone.

"No, I don't. I was serious about a girl back home at one time."

"Where is back home?" she asked him.

"Montgomery, Alabama."

"I have a couple of cousins who live in Alabama."

"Is that right?"

"Yeah.

"See, we have quite a few things in common, Aisha."
He flashed his hypnotizing smile.

"Come on. Finish telling me about this girl."

"We met in college and became serious. I thought
she was the one I would spend my life with."

"What happened?"

"It's a long story, but to sum it up, I caught her, and I
mean literally caught her and a good buddy of mine in the
act."

"Oh, that's terrible, Chandler."

"Tell me about it. After that I decided to move to
Memphis, get a fresh start on things, you know."

"I'm really sorry that happened to you."

"I lost a lot of trust when that happened," Chandler
admitted to Aisha. A tinge of sadness began to overcome
him as he reminisced about the break up.

"It happens sometimes," Aisha told him. "I don't
know what your religious beliefs are, but I know that
whenever I'm facing a difficulty or trial in life, I turn to
God. Without my faith, I know I wouldn't have made it
through a lot of situations that arose in my life."

"Yea, I know what you mean and I feel you on that. I
don't attend church as often as I should with my work
schedule and all, but I do believe in the man upstairs, no
doubt, no doubt." Chandler emphasized.

"That's great to hear. Tell me, how's the
cheesecake?"

"Heavenly, simply heavenly," they both laughed.

Aisha felt at ease and comfortable with him. She
breathed in his manly aroma as they sat on the chocolate
sectional. Finally, Chandler decided to call things to an
end. He didn't want to wear out his welcome. He wanted
the chance to come back again. "Hey, it's getting late and
I have an early day tomorrow, so I'm going to get out of

your hair. I can't thank you enough for the wonderful dinner and the lovely conversation."

"The pleasure was all mine. You saved me from going through a lot of changes when you found my wallet and returned it. So the thanks goes to you. Plus I really enjoyed your company this evening, Chandler." She admitted.

"You see?"

"See what?" she responded.

"If you had been receptive to me from the get go then we would be good friends by now, little lady. But no, at the Orpheum and at the coffee shop you had to diss a brother like he had the plague or something." Again a grin stretched across Chandler's chiseled face.

"Okay, you're right. I'm a big enough girl to admit when I'm wrong. But you also know that in this day and age, a girl has to be careful, real careful. And men do too for that matter."

"Okay I'll let you off the hook with that. But I do want to see you again. Can I see you again?" He asked as he moved in closer to her space. She felt her breath becoming somewhat heavy and her heart began to race as he moved within a hair of her body.

"What do you say, Aisha? Can I see you again?"

"I, I'd like that. But I want to warn you. I'm not interested in a relationship. Friendship, yes but if you have anything else on your mind, look elsewhere.

"Ooh, aren't we the testy little one. But I only had friendship in mind myself. I don't believe in moving too fast either. But I also want to be honest. I am attracted to you. You're a beautiful, sexy woman." Chandler didn't want to come on too strong. And part of what he said was actually true. He was definitely attracted to her. But he was looking for more than friendship. He wanted to take things a step further. But only in time. Only in time.

She couldn't allow herself to get romantically involved with anyone right now, no matter how attracted she was to Chandler. She had to concentrate all of her efforts on getting the money for the dance studio. Maybe after she crossed that hurdle and if she and Chandler were still friends, then perhaps she could entertain the notion.

Will you call me?

Sure, I'll call you. And Chandler.

"Yes?"

"Thanks for returning my wallet." She stood on tiptoe and planted a soft kiss on his left cheek. He was taken aback but tried not to show it. He felt that the best way for him to respond was not to respond at all. Instead he wrapped his long thick fingers around the pewter doorknob and carefully opened it.

"Goodnight. We'll talk soon."

11

In the waves of change we find out direction.
Motivational quotes

"Daddy, are you and Mom getting ready?"

"Not yet, sweetheart. We have plenty of time. I know what you're thinking. I may be a little slow but don't worry, I won't make us late for the gala. I know how important tonight is to you. It's not every day you get to show off in front of the Mayor and his guests."

"You're right about that, Daddy. Just make sure you and Mom make it on time. As for me, I'm going to hang up now. I need to get a shower and start getting ready. I told the girls to meet me two hours before the gala starts. We've already practiced a couple of times at the Cannon Center but I want to do a last minute run through."

"Girl, you know you work those girls hard. But anyway, okay, Aisha. We'll see you later on tonight."

"Bye, Daddy." Aisha hung up the phone and dashed into the oversize all white bathroom. She reached through the shower stall and grabbed the brass knob and turned on the shower while at the same time coming out of her clothes. The warm steaming water kissed every inch of her body. Aisha began to relax and let go of all of her pinned up anxiety over tonight's gala. Without giving her any warning, her mind quickly turned to Chandler Larson. *It's been well over a week since he returned my wallet. I can't believe he hasn't bothered to call. But then again, I haven't put forth an effort to call him either. I can't help it if I'm not an aggressive girl. I like to be pursued. Well, what's the big deal anyway?* Suddenly, the script was flipped and Aisha's thoughts of Chandler were replaced by her present dilemma with the building. How was she ever going to get the rest of the money to keep her studio? She'd looked at other perspective sites but none suited her. Plus, there wasn't a bank or mortgage company out there that would give her the time of day with the kind of debt ratio she had. Her only hope of keeping the studio alive was to hold on to the building she was already in.

"Lord," she cried out loud while the beads of water continued to pound her milk ebony flesh. "You say that if I believe in you and your word that I can ask what I may and it will be done. Well, Lord, I'm asking you to open a window and pour me out a huge blessing. I can't lose this studio. I just can't." The water began to turn cool and Aisha jumped out of the shower, grabbed her plush tangerine bath towel and dashed off into her room, drying off with every step she made. She slipped on a midnight blue jacquard corset-back dress. Her blue satin heels bore a crossover front strap and knotted gold metal ornament encrusted in crystals. She sprayed on a splash of Adore before she styled her hair into a single curl twist traveling down the course of her back. She reached along the side of the oak sleigh bed and retrieved her duffel bag, checking inside to make sure her dance clothes were all in place. She took one last glance in front of the full length mirror and said out loud, "Aisha Carlisle you don't look too bad there girl. Knock 'em dead tonight!"

♦

Crystal chandeliers extended from the high beam ceilings of the Cannon Center ballroom. A separate cocktail area was host to a bevy of drinks from hard liquor to high teas to diet sodas. The balcony offered a serene panoramic view for people watching. The pedestal stage offered an abundance of room for Aisha and her dance troupe as the crowd gathered around to watch the dynamic dance team. The upbeat music Aisha chose showed off the skillful maneuvers of the young girls before they ended some ten minutes later with a high-twist and boogie step. The girls were perfect. Aisha felt a ball rising up from the pit of her stomach to her throat as she surveyed the crowd. The applause sounded heavenly to her ears. She signaled for the girls to take another bow before they pranced off the stage. Aisha remained for a final bow and one last look at all the faces. *Thank you Lord,* she said to herself.

Aisha changed back into her evening clothes and set out to locate her parents. She didn't have to look far as the strikingly beautiful couple headed her way.

"Honey, you were great. I know you must be very proud of the girls," her father spoke with obvious pride. He hugged his youngest daughter before continuing. "I don't think they made one awkward step during the entire routine."

Her mom responded before Aisha could say anything. "If they did, we couldn't tell anyway. Just like your father said, we're proud of you."

'Thanks, Momma. Thanks, Daddy. I'm just glad the two of you are here. When I looked out in the crowd and I didn't see you, I thought you got held up or something."

"Excuse me." The voice behind her sounded somewhat familiar to her. She hesitated slightly before turning around. There stood the towering Chandler Larson. His black on black Sean John tuxedo suit was tailored perfectly, fitting him to a tee. The handsome features of this man mesmerized her. She breathed in the heavenly aroma of his cologne while peering into his mysteriously dark, sexy eyes.

"Chandler," she mumbled. "How are you?"

"I'm great."

That's an understatement if I ever heard one.

"Look, I'm sorry to interrupt but I wanted to tell you how much I enjoyed the performance. I had no idea you'd be attending this evening's event."

"Why, yes. I must say, I'm equally as surprised to see you here. By the way, these are my parents, Mr. and Mrs. Benjamin Carlisle. Mom, Dad this is the man I told you about. You know, the one who found my wallet . Chandler Larson."

"Nice to meet you both." He extended his manicured hand out to each of them. He quickly saw features of Aisha in both parents. She had her father's high cheekbones and her mother's thick mane and tantalizingly sexy almond shaped eyes.

"It's good to know there are still some honest people around," Mr. Carlisle said staring Chandler straight in the eyes.

"Thank you sir. I think honesty is always the best policy. My momma used to say it's better to suffer the consequences from telling the truth than to suffer the consequences from telling a lie. I try to remember that in everything I do. It's carried me a long way, sir."

"Your mother is a wise woman, Chandler. A wise woman indeed."

Mrs. Carlisle nodded in agreement with her husband of forty two years.

"Daddy, Mother, if you don't mind I'm going to do a little socializing."

"Go on baby, do your thing." Her father urged proudly.

Aisha felt Chandler's hand cuff the small of her back. A warm sensation came over her at the gentleness of his massive hand. She turned and glanced up at him. His smile fascinated her as he extended his free hand in front of him, directing her step. Like a partner leading her to the dance floor, she allowed him to maneuver her through the bevy of guests that filled the Cannon Center.

"You're quite a gentleman, Chandler. But really, there's no need for you to chaperone me. I'm quite comfortable mingling on my own."

"So, you're trying to get rid of me, huh."

"No. Of course not. I'm only saying that I'm used to these types of functions but I'm not used to having someone following my every move, if you know what I mean."

"Yes, I know what you mean and I understand. I'll leave you to do your thing." He tried to hide his obvious disappointment. He hadn't meant to come on too strong, but this woman was hypnotic.

"Maybe I'll catch up to you before the evening is over."

"Sure," he responded. "I see a couple of familiar faces myself. See you later Aisha."

"Thanks for understanding."

"No problem, no problem at all." He reluctantly walked off in the opposite direction.

12

"Aisha, the girls were fantastic this evening."

"Thank you, Miss Santana. That means a lot coming from you." Elisa Santana's daughter, Gabby, was one of Aisha's star students. The compliment from Miss Santana elevated Aisha to another level of excitement.

"Their routine was so original. Did you choreograph the entire dance routine?"

"Yes, ma'am."

"Please, I've told you, don't say ma'am to me. And call me Elisa. I insist."

"Okay, Elisa. How did you like Gabby's solo? I think she's a natural."

"Well, of course you might think I'm partial to her because she's my daughter, but actually I'm not. She was exceptionally good tonight. Sometimes I tend to be a little tough on her I know, but it's really paying off. She loves your class too."

"That's great to hear. But to be honest, I don't know how much longer I'm going to have the dance studio."

"You can't be serious. You run one of the best studios in the city. Where are you going?"

"I wish I wasn't going anywhere. I guess I should have waited to tell all of my parents at once, and I am going to have a meeting in a couple of days, but needless to say, things are falling apart."

"You're not making any sense Aisha. Come on. Let's go out on the terrace where we can talk privately. I want all the details."

Aisha proceeded to pour out her dilemma to Elisa Santana. Once she started talking she couldn't stop. A half hour later, they were still out on the terrace.

"Aisha, you can't give up the studio. That's that."

"Elisa, didn't you hear anything I just said? I don't have the money. I don't have a choice."

"Aisha, I have an idea. Let me check on something first and I'll give you a call tomorrow afternoon."

"Are you sure? What do you have in mind?"

"Just wait, let me look into some things first. I don't want to give you false hope. But I'm almost sure something can be done to save your dance studio. Tomorrow, okay?"

"Tomorrow it is. Thank you Miss Santana, I mean Elisa." Aisha reached over and hugged the alluring woman. "Don't thank me yet. I'm going to find Gabby and then I'm out of here. I have to work tonight."

"Tonight? It's almost ten o'clock."

"I know, but try telling that to my boss. Gotta go, we'll talk tomorrow." Elisa Santana whirled around. Her rhinestone t-strapped black stilettos clicked in perfect rhythm with the sashay of the draping ruffles on her black three-tiered halter dress as she proceeded to locate her daughter.

"Gabby, come on. We have to leave. I don't want to be late."

"But, mom," the fourteen-year old pleaded. "I wanted to stay a little longer. There's no one else leaving this early."

"Not tonight, Gabby. I have to work and you know it."

"Can't I go home with Cherise and her mom? She has already said it was okay."

"What have I told you about going behind my back and making plans and then telling me at the last minute."

"I didn't go behind your back. Cherise asked her momma if I could spend the night and I said I would have to check with you first. Please mom, tomorrow's Saturday and I don't want to be at home by myself."

"Don't start Gabby. I don't have time for this." Elisa was quickly becoming frustrated with her only child. Actually it would save her a considerable amount of time if Gabby could spend the night with Cherise. She was glad Gabby made friends so easily. When she first met Cherise at the dance studio, Gabby and her hit if off immediately. Cherise's mom, Stacey, didn't work and she often volunteered to chauffeur the girls to their dance recitals and rehearsal. "Let me check with Stacey. Where are they?"

"Right over there by the refreshment table," Gabby pointed a few feet away.

Elisa Santana's long sculpted legs strolled across the room and walked up to Stacey just as she was about to put an hors d'oeuvre in her mouth. "Hi, Stacey."

"Hi Elisa. And yes, I said Gabby could spend the night. You don't even have to ask and you know it. I love having her over."

"I just don't want her to wear out her welcome Stacey. You know that."

"Girl, please, you should know better by now. Gabby's an angel."

"No you're the angel, I don't know what I'd do without you."

"Elisa, really, it's nothing."

"Well I've gotta go. I don't want to be late for work." She kissed Gabby on the forehead, said her goodbyes to Cherise and Stacey and rushed down the escalators of the Cannon Center. Within minutes she had maneuvered the baby blue Z4 Roadster on to the open stretch of Highway 205. She turned up the volume on the surround sound system and listened to Destiny's Child. She moved to the beat of, *I need a soldier someone who can take care of me. One who carries big things if you know what I mean."*

13

Elisa Santana keyed in her secret code and the massive wrought iron gates of the private parking garage swung open. She sped inside and pulled the BMW into the space that read *Diamond's Spot*, her professional name.

When she swung open the door to The Lynx Association, she stepped on to the thick plush carpet in the main entryway. The forty-foot limestone fireplace revealed the obvious, that the members of the Lynx were no ordinary people. The grandeur of the lobby with its granite countertops, marble floors and solid gold hardware gave off an aura of warmth and wealth.

"Good evening Miss Santana," the tuxedo-clad bellman spoke.

"Evenin' Thomas." Elisa never stopped walking. She continued down the winding mahogany paneled corridor until she reached the private elevator for employees. Smiling at her reflection through the mirrored elevator doors, she leaned in closer and pouted her lips before reaching in her bag and pulling out the oversized silver and black key. She placed it inside the matching keyhole and turned. The elevator doors closed and she breathed a sigh of relief.

God, it's been a long day already and I still have four hours to go. Wake up girl, she said out loud while continuing to glare at her flawless reflection. She fumbled through her purse again and pulled out the thumb sized glass vial, opened it and snorted a portion up her nose, and placed a dab of it on her tongue. *Now, that should do it...who ever said diamonds are a girl's best friend was definitely wrong.*

The elevator doors swung open to deafening music but she had grown accustomed to it. She swayed her hips to the beat of rapper, 50 Cents song, *Candy Shop.*

"What's up, Diamond." One of the bartenders yelled out over the music.

"If you have to ask, you don't need to know," she smiled. "Gotta go." She rushed past him and the staring eyes of the well-dressed men sitting at the tables. Several young ladies danced erotically up on the elevated platform keeping up with every beat booming from the sexually explicit lyrics.

"Diamond, where have you been? I thought you were off tonight." A young scantily clad Puerto Rican girl said walking up to her.

"No, Gabby had to perform tonight at the Mayor's charity ball. Don't you remember me telling you that?"

"Oh yeah, I just forgot that's all. It's been wild around here. How'd she do?"

"Great as usual."

They continued talking until they reached Elisa's dressing room. She stepped out of her stilettos and eased her dress down over her firm round hips. "So things have been jumping tonight, huh?"

"Yes indeed. But you know I'm not complaining. It's a gold mine in here tonight and I got the cheddar to prove it." The girl pulled out a thick wad of one hundred dollar bills from between her size triple D breasts.

"Sookie, sookie now." Elisa responded. "Let me take a shower and get ready so I can get my fair share. I'll check you later. Oh, is Jason here tonight? I need to talk to him about something."

"Yeah, the boss man is somewhere around here."

"Thanks. I'll catch him after my spot ends."

14

The only journey is the journey within. Rainer Rilke

Tameria sat in Aisha's office with her legs propped up on the chair next to her. Munching on a bag of hot Cheetos that she had gotten out of the vending machine, she told Aisha about a woman who was brought into the emergency room with a knife embedded in her shoulder. Aisha enjoyed hearing about Tameria's hospital experiences. The fact that Tameria had the ability to help the sick and injured was a tremendous thrill to Aisha.

"Tameria, sounds like you never have a dull moment at that hospital. It must work on you though, seeing the worse of the worse injuries and even death coming through those emergency room doors." Aisha suggested.

"That's true, but I have to learn how to leave it behind when I walk out those hospital doors. Sometimes it's easier said than done."

"I can only imagine." Changing the subject Aisha asked, "Where's that man of yours, the great Resident Neurosurgeon Dr. Chase Gray?"

"He has four days off so he went home to St. Louis to visit his family. That's a rarity for him. He hasn't seen them in about six or seven months." Tameria answered her friend.

"No wonder you're here keeping me company. Maybe Chase needs to leave town more often. That way I can get to have my best friend to myself."

73

"Yeah, yeah," Tameria waved her hand toward Aisha and laughed. "Tell me the latest on your dilemma. Have you figured out what you're going to do?"

"Not really. I'm still seeking God's direction. But one of the parents did offer to help me."

"Offered to help you? Offered to help you how and with what?"

She looked around to see if she saw anyone in earshot of her office then continued talking. "You know. With the studio."

"And like I said, how is she supposed to do that?"

"Look, Tameria, I don't know just yet. She's supposed to call me. She has to check on some things first."

"Just who is this person, Aisha?"

"Her name is Elisa Santana. I think I've mentioned her to you before. Her daughter's name is Gabby, one of my lead dancers. Her mother is a dancer too."

"Oh yeah, I vaguely remember seeing her. But how did she know about your problem?"

"We were talking at the ball the other night."

"Aisha, I thought you said you were going to wait to see what you could come up with before you told anyone."

"It wasn't like I meant to tell her. It just came out. Anyway, who knows what's going to happen. She may not be able to help me after all and then she just might. I know that wherever she works, she's doing pretty well for herself financially."

Tameria stared at her best friend with obvious concern. "And how do you know that?"

Aisha moved around anxiously in her chair. "Cause she has a nice ride and the woman is always dressed to the nines. The girl's got style and plenty of it too."

"Just be careful about telling folks your business. You know how that can backfire."

"Sure, I know. I'm thinking that she may know the owner of this builder. The sucker won't reveal himself to me. He always has Thaddeus to call me. What do you think about that?"

"I guess I'm not surprised. The man probably has a lot of properties. Why would he want to meet his tenants anyway? That's what property managers like Thaddeus are paid to do. What's the owner's name? "

"I have no idea. And I'm not going to worry about it right now. Come on. Let's get out of here and go get something to eat."

"That's right on time because I'm on call tonight and that means no food for at least the next twenty something hours."

Aisha and Tameria went to the Hard Rock Cafe on Beale Street for lunch. Afterwards the two friends walked up and down the famous street and did a little window shopping. Aisha confided in Tameria about her spark of interest in Chandler. He didn't call often but when he did, she enjoyed their conversation. Chandler was an easy going kind of man, something Aisha liked. She didn't want to feel pressured into anything with anyone. Admitting to Tameria, that she was attracted to him was a big step for her. Tameria reminded Aisha that she was young and beautiful with feelings and emotions and that there was nothing wrong with liking Chandler. Aisha swung her arms back and forth while they peeped inside some of the quaint shops lining the busy street. At the end of their stroll, they stopped off at A *Schwab*, the store that has simply everything imaginatible, and purchased a bag of old fashioned soft peppermint candy sticks. Two hours after leaving, Tameria drove Aisha back to the studio in time for her afternoon dance class.

◆

Elisa made her entrance into the dance studio and as usual, all eyes fell on her sleek cat-like moves. Dressed in fashionable flared black athletic pants, a bright yellow sports bra, and crisp white running shoes, she walked to the receptionist desk and, as if in slow motion, she approached the receptionist counter.

Angie immediately greeted her. "Good afternoon Miss Santana."

"Hello Angie. Is Aisha here or has she already left for the afternoon?"

"No, she's still here. She's in her office on the phone. As soon as I see her phone light go off, I'll let her know you're here. You can have a seat if you'd like."

"No, thanks. Just tell her I'll be in the back in one of the classrooms. I might as well do a few stretches while I wait. That is all right isn't it?"

"Sure, I know she won't mind. I'll send her back there when she hangs up. Check Classroom 4. It should be empty."

◆

Aisha relaxed in her chair and listened to Chandler trying to convince her to spend some time with him. "Chandler, I don't know if I can make it tonight. I'm beat and I still have errands to run after I leave the studio."

Chandler held on to the other end of the phone and exhaled. He hadn't seen Aisha since their first and only dinner date three and a half weeks ago. But he was not going to give up on trying to persuade her to see him again. Her reserved demeanor only made him want her more. Whatever it took to get Aisha Carlisle he had resolved to do. He wasn't used to women turning him down. Aisha was different too. She piqued the playa in him. On purpose he didn't respond to her answer of no. Instead he remained silent and waited for her to say something.

"Are you still there?" she asked.

"Yes, of course. I was just thinking." He used his special voice that was a mixture of sadness and sexiness.

"Thinking about what?"

"About how I can get you to share just a small fraction of your time with me. I'll tell you what. Why don't I come by the studio in say, an hour?"

"I..."

He cut her off before she could continue. "Stop right there. I won't take no for an answer. I want to see you Aisha. Won't you at least have dinner with me, nothing else? And I promise not to keep you out pass your bedtime. I'll even run your errands for you while you rest," he agreed.

She found him particularly amusing. Whenever she talked to him, he always managed to make her laugh about something before they hung up. But she still reminded herself to tread lightly with Chandler. She didn't want to get too involved too quickly. "Oh, okay. You've twisted my arm. I'll see you in an hour."

"An hour it is."

Aisha barely had time to hang up the phone when Angie buzzed in. "Yes Angie?"

"Gabby's mother is here. She's in classroom four doing stretches."

"Thanks. I'll go find her." Aisha glanced at the clock sitting on the window ledge. "Remember to lock up before you leave Angie. And have a good evening."

"Thanks. I'll holler at you when I'm walking out."

Aisha proceeded down the hallway, anxious to find out what the mysterious Elisa Santana had to say. As she approached classroom four where Elisa was, Aisha stopped and watched her. Elisa moved with the delicate grace of a gazelle.

Elisa signaled for Aisha to join her as she entered the room. Aisha moved in behind her, grabbed the rail and began to sway to the sound of the music being pumped in through the surround sound speakers. The two of them moved simultaneously away from the rail and started their individual dance moves. Elisa gyrated her hips in a circular rhythm, taking steps back, forward and to the side. Her arms took on moves of their own as she glided across the floor. Aisha was oblivious to Elisa as she became lost in the music herself. Aisha's body moved along the dance floor and her fingers snapped to the beat of the song. The two of them continued their free style dancing until the song ended.

"You're good, Elisa."

"Thank you. That means a lot coming from a professional like yourself."

"When the truth is the truth tell it, is what I always say." She proceeded to walk over to the towel cabinet and grabbed a couple of towels, tossing one to Elisa.

"Thanks," Elisa wiped the beads of sweat from her brow. "Do you want to talk in here?"

"Angie will be leaving in a few minutes so I'd prefer to go up front. I'm expecting a friend to drop by in about an hour and that way I can hear him when he sounds the buzzer."

"No problem." They proceeded to the front of the dance studio and Aisha led her into the break room."

"Would you like some coffee, soda, water?"

"Water will do just fine unless you have a PowerAde or something."

"Sure, PowerAde it is." Aisha opened the door to the refrigerator and pulled out two ice cold PowerAde's. "Hope you like strawberry."

"Love it. Thanks." Elisa responded and reached for the beverage. After taking a couple of gulps, Elisa started talking. "First of all, let me start by telling you that I think I have a solution to your problem. That is if you'll listen with an open mind."

Red flags went off in Aisha's head when Elisa advised her to listen with an open mind. *Must be something illegal or too far-fetched.* "Sure, let's hear it."

"You know that I'm a dancer. I just haven't told you all there is to know because until now it hasn't been necessary."

Aisha nodded her head up and down in slow motion, unsure as to what this had to do with her financial woes.

"I work for a privately run association.

"What kind of privately run association," Aisha's eyebrows furrowed together. She was curious as to what Elisa meant.

"I'm employed at The Lynx Association. You have heard of it, haven't you?"

Another red flag.

"Yes, I've heard of it, but I don't know what it entails. I only know it's supposed to be some sort of upscale country club."

"Basically you're right."

"You don't have another job?"

"Nope, The Lynx is it. I have clients there who pay me a hefty salary to do private dancing. Plus the Lynx pays me a base salary of $1,000 a week."

"The Lynx?" Aisha looked puzzled.

"Yes, The Lynx."

"And did you say one thousand dollars a week?"

Aisha spoke in an exasperated voice saying, "That's simply unbelievable."

"Believe me, it's true. Some weeks I bring in as much as $3,500 to $5,000. That's chump change considering the money these men have and they're not stingy with it either. Especially when they're getting what they want out of the deal."

"And exactly what are they getting for their money, Elisa? This sounds like something that calls for more than shaking your booty."

"If you want it to be more than that, then I'm sure these gentlemen won't turn you down, but as for me, I'm strictly a private dancer. Whatever they want me to do during the time they're paying me, then I do it."

"I see. What does that include Elisa?" Aisha was hesitant about asking her, afraid of what her answer would be.

"I know what you're hinting at. And the answer is I draw the line when it comes to certain things and other things I don't divulge to anyone. But I will say this much, if they want me to take off my clothes, I do it. If they want me to drop it like it's hot, I do it. If they want me to put it in their face, then I put it in their face. I'm making a living and a doggone good living for me and Gabby, don't you think?"

"I can't deny that. But why are you telling me this? How can what you do help my situation? Do you think one of these gentlemen will invest in the studio or do they own a bank or what?"

"Honey, they own banks, car dealerships, sports teams, radio stations, you name it and I betcha there's someone there who owns it. They're doctors, lawyers, executives too."

"I hear you. But I still don't understand what all this has to do with me."

"Here's how you play into the deal. A couple of weeks ago one of the girls had to leave town because of illness in her family. One of her parents is really sick. She won't be coming back for a few months, if she comes back at all."

"No, Elisa, I know where you're going with this. I could never do such a thing as strip. That's what this adds up to. I'm a Christian and you know it. I can't do it. I appreciate the fact that you're concerned about me and the dance studio, but."

Elisa stood up and cut her off by showing the palm of her hand. "Aisha, I'm not going to sit here and beg you or try to convince you to do something that goes against your beliefs. So suit yourself. But I'm telling you. The Lynx Association is a classy, discreet and well respected organization. It's exclusive and it's not some sleazy strip joint. You've got it all wrong. I tell you what. Before you make up your mind, why don't you be my guest tomorrow night?"

"I, I, don't know about that Elisa. I don't think it's a good idea."

"I'm not asking you to do anything but come and have a glass of wine or a diet soda if you prefer," she said jokingly. "You can check out the atmosphere and meet a couple of the other ladies who work there. Come on, I promise no one will get out of line or make you uncomfortable. And if you find out that it's something you wouldn't feel right about doing, then so be it. You just up and leave. No harm done." Elisa raised her eyebrows and placed one hand on her waist.

Aisha thought about it a few seconds and then answered, "Let me think about it but I already know that my answer is still going to be no." The buzzer on the front door sounded. "That must be my friend and I'm not even close to being ready."

"Go, scoot. We can talk later. I'll go out the back entrance."

"That's not necessary, really."

"No, it's all right. My car is parked out back anyway. I'll call you tomorrow and let you know what time I'm picking you up." Elisa smiled and rushed toward the back door, leaving Aisha with a dumbfounded look plastered across her face. She waved both hands in the air in frustration then turned to go and unlock the door. She spotted Chandler on the other side with a sexy grin on his handsome face.

Chandler marveled in the fact that he'd convinced Aisha to have dinner with him. She appeared to be intelligent but naïve at the same time, something he considered a challenge and a win-win for him.

Over the years, especially since his heart had been crushed, he'd become cold, hard and callous when it came to women. There was no way he was going to let another woman get as close to him as he had allowed his ex-fiancée Tracye to get. At times, he could swear that he felt the remnants of heartbreak that she'd left stamped indelibly on his heart. After the initial shock of seeing her naked body underneath one of his friends, he turned and walked out of the apartment they had shared for over two years. Each time she called and pleaded for his forgiveness, he attacked her with the most derogatory words he could think of. He just couldn't forgive her infidelity. He did a 360 after that and changed from being kind, thoughtful, loving Chandler to a misogynistic brute full of unleashed anger. Despite his angry actions towards her, Tracye had refused to back off and continued to beg him to take her back. Several weeks after their breakup, Chandler gave in to her persistence and agreed to meet her at the apartment. Using his key, he walked in and saw her standing near the living room door. Chandler didn't bother to say one word. He briskly walked over to her, yanked her shoulder length hair so hard that it snapped her neck back. He gritted his teeth and forced his hands between her thighs. Tracye tried to break free from his grasp but the hold he had on her was too powerful. He smothered her screams with brutal kisses while pushing her down hard on the cold tile floor. Using his knees to pin her legs down, he violated her over and over again. Chandler was surprised at how much rage he had but at this point he couldn't stop, refused to stop. He wanted to hurt her like she had hurt him. After he finished his assault, he stood up over her, straightened his clothes then spit in her face before walking out the door.

Shortly after his retaliation against Tracye, Chandler packed up his bags, left Montgomery and moved to Memphis. Not once had he regretted his attack on Tracye, someone he once loved. When he applied for the position as a police officer with the Memphis Police Department, he found that he enjoyed his job more than he had anticipated. There were times when he thought of how he got his revenge on Tracye and in a weird way, he believed his ability to rape and assault her without feeling remorse was actually a good trait because on the streets of Memphis there was no time to feel anything for anyone who was breaking the law. As for Aisha, he was drawn to her shyness and naiveté. He planned on using her attributes to reel her in just where he wanted her to be. And getting her to have dinner with him was his first conquest in breaking her down.

Chandler took her to a quaint little Italian bistro in South Memphis. They dined on shrimp primavera and sipped on white Zinfandel. Though Aisha was not a drinker per se, she would indulge in a glass of wine on special occasions. Dining with Chandler was on that list. Chandler used his playa expertise to make her feel at ease by talking about things that interested her, such as her love of dancing. The sparkle in her eyes told him that she liked him. His self-esteem was slowly returning. Maybe Aisha Carlisle could help him regain a small bit of trust in women again - just maybe.

Aisha listened to Chandler talk about his love of dancing. It was good to hear someone who shared her passion of dance. Tameria was right. It felt good to be out with someone of the opposite sex. The conversation, the ambiance of the romantic setting of the restaurant, wine, good food, all of it made her feel exceptionally special. The last time she found herself sitting across the table from a man was when she attended the Mayor's Charity Ball. For a moment, she was able to forget her troubles and enjoy the moment. The glass of wine helped to ease her tension along with Chandler's soothing personality.

On the way home, the two of them continued chatting. In between conversation, they listened to the radio. Arriving at her apartment, Aisha invited Chandler to come in for a cup of coffee and a slice of mother's homemade butter pound cake.

Aisha took the time to express her gratitude. "Thanks for dinner Chandler and for running my errands too," she laughed.

"No problem. I told you, I'd do anything to see you and spend some time with you." Chandler took a bite of the cake and leaned back.

She rested her head against the plush thickness of the sofa and sighed.

"What is it?" he asked.

"Oh, I'm just tired and I have a lot on my mind, that's all."

"Anything you want to talk about?

She wished it was that easy. *Talk about your problems and they'll go away. Ha, what a laugh.* She thought to herself. "No, I'll be fine. And I hate to end the evening so early, but I really am ready to call it a night. I have another long day tomorrow.""

"So this is how you treat the fellas, huh. Get them to feed you, run your errands, hold conversation with you then you throw them out." He teased her.

"I thought that's what men liked," she teased back.

"I guess some of us do. But before I leave, may I use your bathroom?"

"Of course, it's down the hall and to the left."

"Thanks, I'll be right back."

◆

What's he doing in there? He's been in there an awfully long time. Just when she decided to call his name, he came down the hall. She smelled the aroma of the incense sticks she had in the bathroom for those not so pleasant bathroom stops. She giggled slightly as she thought about what he must have done in the bathroom.

"You okay?" she asked him.

"Sure, I'm fine. But I think I made a mess in your bathroom."

"What do you mean?" she looked confused.

"I better show you. Come here for a minute." She hesitated before getting up.

"I'm sure it's nothing that can't be fixed."

"I hope you're right. But you still better take a look." She ambled down the hallway to the bathroom. She stopped at the doorway and gasped.

"Oh my God," she said and placed both hands over her mouth in total surprise.

"Chandler I don't believe this." The tub was filled with bubbles and the scent of jasmine incense wafted through her nostrils. "Thank you *soooo* much."

"No problem. I'd do anything to see that look you have on your face again and again. He grabbed her hand. "Come on so you can lock the door behind me. Then I expect you to go and relax in your bubble bath."

She walked him to the door. He looked down on her radiant beauty and wanted her.

"Chandler, thanks for everything," she responded.

"I'll call you tomorrow, if that's all right with you."

"I'd like that."

He kissed her on the forehead and left. She watched as he walked down the stairway and a smiled covered her face and his.

15

*Manipulation, fueled with good intent, can be a blessing.
But when used wickedly, it is the beginning of a
magician's karmic calamity.* T.F. Hodge

Aisha couldn't believe she'd succumbed to Elisa's offer to visit The Lynx. All of her instincts had told her not to go, but yet, here she was standing in what she'd classified as none other than a high class strip joint. If her pastor could see her now he would probably stroke out. Not to mention her daddy and her mother. And Tameria? What would she think of her Holy Roller best friend now? Stepping inside The Lynx, her previous thoughts were put on hold as she walked into the magnificently luxurious foyer.

"Elisa, this place is like wow. It reeks of money."

"Honey, this place is money. Come on, let me show you around. The Lynx is designed like a five star hotel with private suites. An individual suite runs anywhere from five to ten thousand dollars."

"Whaaat? That's unbelievable. Why so much?"

"Because these guys mean business. Some of them live in the city and own their suites and come and go at their leisure. Others live out of town and fly here for a few days or a weekend and they want to guarantee their exclusivity."

"Okay, I understand that much. But what's there to hide?"

Elisa stopped walking and glared at Aisha. "Most of these men have families. They're owners of corporations and a few are even movie stars.. The Lynx provides them with a means to freely do whatever it is they want to do within the confines of these walls. Remember when I told you that some of the girls are private entertainers?"

"Yeah."

"Well, take me for instance. I have two gentlemen here that I entertain exclusively in the privacy of their suites. One comes the fourth weekend of every month and the other gentleman is here a few times a month. Then on my free nights, I might dance for some of the regulars and make several hundred or even a thousand or more a night. I mostly do that on the dance platform, not in the suites. Come on. I'll show you where the open area is."

"What's the open area?"

"It's where the bar and the dance stage are located. Follow me."

They got back on the elevator and Aisha noticed the number pad next to the fourth floor button. "Hey, what's on the fourth floor that requires a keypad?"

"It's the owner's private space. No one's ever been up there except a select few and I mean a few."

"Are you?"

"Am I what?" Elisa asked.

"Are you one of those select few?"

"Nope, and I don't think any of the other ladies who work here have been there either. And plus, I don't even know the owner. None of the girls here do."

"That's unbelievable. Why is everything so secretive? I don't understand."

Elisa sniffed and wiped her nose. "Aisha, like I already said, this is no run of the mill kind of place. Most of these men live totally different lives outside of these walls. They pay for their privacy and they pay handsomely. I don't know who owns this place and I really don't care. "Now, come on, let's go see what you can do."

"What are you talking about?"

"I'm talking about dancing."

"No, no, I can't."

"Yes, you can." They walked through the open area. Some of the men were dressed in fine Italian suits and others in more leisurely attire. Aisha's eyes grew big as she watched two ladies dancing seductively on a raised stage. They caressed the pole like it was a man. Their breasts bobbled up and down slowly, and Aisha saw that they had the full attention of the gentlemen seated around the tables.

"Here's my dressing room." Elisa ushered her into a well-designed, expensively furnished room that reminded her of a hotel suite. She went over to the mini - bar and fixed herself a martini. "What can I get you?"

"Nothing, I don't drink. Not really."

"There's a first time for everything. Let me fix you an apple martini. I promise to go light on the alcohol. You'll love it. It'll help ease some of your jitters."

Aisha paused before she nodded her head. "Okay." Tonight she was definitely not the Aisha people were used to seeing. Everything was evolving so quickly for her. She'd gone from a do right, uptight Christian woman to sitting among a room full of sinners in nothing more than an upscale strip joint. It wasn't that she looked down on Elisa or any of the other ladies she'd seen at The Lynx, but no one could ever have told her that she would be in the midst of them contemplating if she was going to be one of them. She sipped on the apple martini. It was slightly bitter but tasty and though Elisa told her she only put less than a shot of liquor in the drink, Aisha's head felt lighter by the time she finished the drink. Strike two, she thought and glued her eyes on the empty glass. Not only am I sitting among these people, I'm drinking with them. Maybe she was looking down on them. Her mind reflected on the words she'd read in the Bible though she couldn't recall what passage. There was a man that said he found himself standing around some sinners looking at and listening to what they were saying and doing. Before long he was sitting among them and soon he found himself not only sitting among the sinners, but he was actually doing what they were doing. Aisha felt somehow that she was on her way to doing the same thing that she once criticized people like Elisa for doing. How had she arrived at this point in her life? Now was the time for her to get up and get as far away as she could from The Lynx and all that it represented. But she didn't budge from her chair. Instead she watched as Elisa changed into a skimpy one piece outfit that reminded Aisha of Frederick's of Hollywood lingerie. Aisha couldn't move. It wasn't until she felt Elisa touching her on her shoulder when she focused in on her surroundings again and came out of her daydream.

"Aisha, you look like you're in a trance or something. Don't tell me that one itty bitty apple martini has you drunk?" Elisa laughed.

"No, no, it's nothing like that. Look Elisa. Thanks for trying to help me save the studio. But really, I don't think this is the way. I just don't. I've got to get out of here," Aisha declared and proceeded to stand up.

"Okay, okay. Tell you what. Can you just hold on for about an hour or two? I have to at least do a few dances before I can leave. Remember, this is my job. You can stay here in my dressing room or you can come along with me and sit in the open area. I'll tell one of the other girls to keep you company. How's that?" Elisa offered with sincerity.

"I guess that'll be all right. And Elisa?"

"What is it Aisha?"

"I'm sorry I had you to bring me all the way out here for nothing. I really am."

"Hey, don't worry about it. Now come on. Let me introduce you to Kim. She's been working here for about three years. She'll be glad to sit with you while I do my thing. And you'll see for yourself, how easy this job is."

Aisha watched as Elisa confidently strolled out on the stage. With each step she took, she captivated her audience. The beat of the music along with the martinis she'd had, drew Elisa into a world that was void of anything going on around her except the music. Elisa's seductive moves across the dance stage oozed sexuality. Aisha realized how talented Elisa really was. If only she'd chosen to use her skills in another environment she would be the envy of many in the art of dance, including Aisha. Sneaking looks at the men scattered around in the open area, Aisha could tell they were mesmerized by Elisa's performance. Elisa swayed her hips with each beat of the song playing. Several poles were on the stage as well. Elisa danced her way over to them. Her long dance legs caressed the pole while she moved her hands and butt in a manner that Elisa had only seen girls do on the movie channel. Yet, Elisa didn't look vulgar at all. Aisha studied her expert moves and choreography and felt herself drawn into Elisa and her talent. She was actually an excellent performer. Taking another sneak peek at the men, Aisha noticed there were note pads of some sort in front of each man. From time to time, Aisha would see them write something on the pads. She leaned over and asked Kim what they were doing. Kim explained to her that at The Lynx if a man wanted to show his pleasure for the dancer, he would keep something like a running tab. The note pads had each dancer's name on it and whatever amount he wanted to give her was placed on the pad and turned in to Jason. Jason was a wealthy banker who was also on the board of directors at The Lynx and the overseer of the girls. In turn, Jason collected the money at the end of the night and after taking The Lynx' fifteen percent the rest would go to the dancer. When she and Elisa finally left The Lynx, Elisa had made a cool $2,300. And that was for less than two hours of dancing. Aisha was astonished. Could this possibly be my way out? Could it? *Maybe God could use a den of ill repute to bless me. He did say that the wealth of the wicked would be laid up for the righteous, Aisha told herself. Maybe this is the way. Why else would it come so easy for me?* Remaining quiet on the way home, Aisha contemplated her next move. By the time Elisa pulled up in front of her apartment, Aisha had made up her mind. "Elisa, how soon can I start?"

16

Our true self is being who we are. Lailah Akita

The two of them laughed in unison with the rest of the movie goers when Big Mama waddled across the screen in a bright yellow bathing suit.

Holding her hand as they exited the movie theatre, Chandler asked her, "You having a good time?"

"I haven't enjoyed myself like this in a long time Chandler. That Martin Lawrence knows he's a fool," Aisha laughed and moved in closer to Chandler. "You know, usually if I'm not at some church function, I'm at my dance studio."

"Well, I say it's time you start taking some time to relax and enjoy life. Don't get me wrong, I know you're driven to succeed and that's great. But you need to cool out every now and then. You know what I'm saying?"

"Yea, I know. My best friend Tameria, you know the one you saw at the Orpheum?"

"Yea, I remember her."

"Well, she's in medical school. Her boyfriend is a third or fourth year Neurosurgeon Resident. So even though they're always working, most of the times their rotations are the same so they still get a chance to spend time with each other. So you see they share a lot in common. But as for me, there aren't many guys who understand my passion for dance. I live and breathe dancing."

"I beg to differ," was Chandler's response. He brought her in closer to him as they walked along Tom Lee Park. "I like to watch you dance. I like to see how you work with your students. You're good at what you do, Aisha. That was evident when I saw the performance at the Mayor's Ball. And earlier today, when I came by the studio, I could tell you were born to dance."

"That's nice of you to say, Chandler. My father is the only other man who understands what I feel about my dancing. He always pushes me to follow my dreams and never stop even when I reach that pot of gold at the end of the rainbow. I love him for that." Aisha's eyes gleamed when she spoke about her father.

"You a daddy's girl?" Chandler teased.

"Sure am. Always have been too."

"Do you have sisters and brothers?"

"I have a half-sister who lives in Detroit. I don't see or talk to her that often. Her name is Selena."

"Selena," he said the name slowly. "That's a pretty name too. But I'm partial to Aisha." He laughed, stopped and pointed her in the direction of a bench and the two of them sat down. Wrapping his arm around her shoulders, she snuggled in against his chest.

"Aisha?"

"Yes?"

"I really do like you. You know that?"

"I know it now because you just told me," she giggled like a school girl.

"Hey," he pulled her face around to meet his. When his lips caressed hers, her heart raced and her pulse beat wildly. The chemistry they felt for one another was intense. Aisha returned his kiss and wrapped both of her arms around his neck.

Chandler thought of how Aisha's lips tasted like sweet honey nectar. She was not only pretty, smart, intelligent but she made him feel what he had kept under wraps for so long. He liked this girl a lot and his intention was to make her feel the same way about him.

They sat underneath the twinkling stars at Tom Lee Park until the breeze picked up. "Come on. I'll take you home."

Aisha agreed. "I'd like that. It's gotten a little chilly out here."

On the way to her apartment they laughed and talked some more about some of everything. Aisha felt relaxed around him. It had been a long time since she'd been out on a date and the attention felt especially nice. She made each of them a cup of spiced tea after they arrived at her apartment.

Chandler complimented her. "This tastes good." He sipped on the warm tea again before setting it down on the table.

"I'm glad you like it. I'm a lover of tea. Hot, cold, regular, green, spiced. It makes no difference. Just as long as it's tea," she grinned.

"Ahhh, now I know the way to your heart," he teased.

She threw her head back and laughed. "You think so?"

"Yeah, I do." He gently moved back the twist of hair that had fallen in her face. Leaning in, he lightly kissed her on the neck.

◆

"Hi, come on in." Chase kissed Tameria on the cheek as he entered her midsize two bedroom flat. Reaching for his rain soaked jacket and umbrella she said, "Let me get that."

"Thanks, baby. It's really coming down out there. No sign of it letting up either."

"It's a good thing we don't have to report to the hospital tonight."

"I know that's right." Chase walked up behind Tameria and surprised her by grabbing her around the waist and twirling her around to face him. Chase was a jokester. His cheerful, love of life personality was one of the things that had attracted Tameria to him in the first place. He could always bring a smile to her face. Plus the fact that they both were medical students helped too. He understood the stress and commitment of being in med school. The two of them often pulled thirty-six hour shifts, sometimes not seeing each other but a few minutes in passing. But after dating for almost seven months, Tameria knew he was the man of her dreams. Chase teased, "Umm, you smell good. Just like fried chicken with red beans and rice."

She thumped him lightly on the head and said, "Boy please, you're so silly. Just for that I'm not feeding you."

"You mean you cooked for me? You must really love me." Moving her back and forth in his arms, he squeezed her tightly.

"Ummm, you think?" She rubbed the right side of her face across the smoothness of his right cheek. They laughed at each other before exchanging another kiss. She loved the way she fit perfectly inside his arms. She nestled in closer and returned his fervor with that of her own, skillfully manipulating her tongue with flickering motions in between his moist lips. In turn he lightly sucked on hers. She didn't flinch when his hands moved over the familiar areas of her mounds and on to her large proportioned butt. Her sounds of satisfaction echoed off the thin walls of the apartment.

"Hey, what about dinner?" she whispered and pulled away. "I fixed your favorite."

In a husky voice he answered, "You're my favorite." He didn't stop kissing her as he moved in closer to his destination. He eased her back on the sofa with one hand and used his fingers to gently massage her private places like a skilled surgeon. As if on cue, she opened her gate to allow him easy access to her most intimate spots.

What would Aisha think if she saw me now? She hated when thoughts of Aisha invaded such moments as this. But just as quickly as she thought of Aisha, those same thoughts vanished and she arched her back to meet his every stroke. The thunderous roar of the storm raging outside deafened their sounds of passion. She gave in to his every desire and he fueled her burning flame with his torch of love.

Tameria and Chase had been sexually intimate for almost two months. The flames of guilt over committing fornication had basically died out. Her concentration was centered around the relationship she shared with Chase. She'd sought forgiveness over and over in the beginning when she gave her virginity to him. But now, Tameria felt no shame. The only reason she hadn't confided in Aisha was because she didn't want to get into a confrontation with her. She cared about her friendship with Aisha and respected her beliefs because Aisha's beliefs used to be her beliefs as well. But love had changed all of that. Chase was the man she planned to spend the rest of her life with and that was enough justification for her. There was a time she thought she would be shy about being intimate with Chase or any man for that matter. Her petite full figured body made her uncomfortable at times. But thanks to Chase loving her just the way she was and of course her mentor, the infamous thespian, "M'onique, Tameria had learned to love every inch of her 198 pounds voluptuous frame.

As for Aisha…well there was no time to think about her right now. The pleasure she was experiencing with Chase captured her mind, body and soul and for now, there was no room for anything or anyone else.

17

Best be yourself, imperial, plain and true!
Robert Browning

Chandler turned over in his bed, raised his head and looked lazily at the clock up on his chest of drawers. He yawned and stretched while thinking about his undercover assignment in Nashville, Tennessee. Normally, he would have a three hour drive to Nashville. But it had been snowing most of the day and it was still coming down hard so he was in for an even longer drive. But he had a job to do, rain, sleet or snow. Being an undercover cop kept his adrenaline pumping. He couldn't see himself being anything else in law enforcement. Granted, it was a dangerous job and he basically had to act much like some of the lowlifes he helped to put away. Not knowing when or if someone would shout five-o. Hiding his true identity, always having to look over his shoulder during an assignment was part of it too. His mother's brother had worked undercover in Toledo, Ohio for almost twenty years before he succumbed to lung cancer. Smoking three packs of menthol cigarettes a day until the day he died, his uncle had been a true man of the law. He lived and breathed law enforcement, forsaking his family for long, dangerous assignments. The one thing that was different for Chandler was that he didn't have anyone to report to but himself. After his break up with Tracye, he didn't think twice about relocating when he found out the MPD was recruiting for new officers. And after she'd provoked him into losing his temper the way he had, he knew the best thing for him to do would be to leave Montgomery and start a new life for himself before he found himself in deep trouble. He completed the MPD online application and within weeks he'd been contacted and scheduled for his first round interview. His Associates Degree in Criminal Justice helped him tremendously. Working the city streets of Memphis made him feel invigorated. It was a dream come true when he was accepted into the Memphis Police Academy. The training had been rigorous but he had persevered. When graduation day arrived, he stood proudly to receive his badge and uniform.

He stretched his arms out and released one last yawn before raising his towering frame from underneath the quilt that his great grandmother had made many years ago. He didn't bother grabbing his robe. He was already fully dressed in the same outfit he'd worn when he made his entrance into the world thirty-one years ago. He loved being naked. It made him feel free, unbound by any and everything. Strolling slowly into the bathroom, he turned on the shower, walked over to the linen closet, grabbed a couple of towels and then stepped underneath the water, allowing the beads of warm water to massage his skin.

Ring. Ring. He stopped soaping himself and listened. *Every time I get in the freaking shower, the phone rings. Well, whoever it is this time will just have to wait.* He moved his head swiftly from side to side to shake the water off of his face before starting his ritual. He made a frothy lather by rubbing the soap briskly between his massive hands. He reached down and grabbed his best friend and gently massaged it, being thorough in cleaning it. He followed the same method for his taut buttocks and chiseled calves. As soon as he felt the water cooling down, he finished rinsing himself off and stepped out of the shower to welcome the coolness that embraced him.

♦

"Hey, Smooth, let's roll man. We got five kilos coming in about half an hour. Get up and let's move it," he ordered followed by a couple of four letter words. "If I miss out on this deal, you can put on your concrete suit, cause you're headed for your new home – the river.

"Look, Nash, don't talk that trash to me. You think I'm about to blow this. Hell naw, we got millions riding on this one and I plan to get my fair share. Come on, let's roll."

Chandler and his unsuspecting partner, Smooth, climbed in the black on black H3. Chandler's job gave him a high that no drug could ever do. He had worked this undercover assignment for almost a year under the alias, Nash, a member of a notorious drug cartel. Finally it was all about to come to an end. He'd gained the total trust of his associates, and they thought of him as one of their 'to the death' brothers. But in a few hours he would put away several members of the cartel for a long time to come including the fall guy, Smooth, who he'd worked closely with since he started this assignment. He concentrated his efforts on the job at hand and he and Smooth headed for their destination.

When the shipment of cocaine arrived as scheduled, Chandler's back-up was already strategically planted in inconspicuous places along the drop off area. He strolled along the boardwalk, confident that he was about to bust a major gang and take several million dollars' worth of drugs off the street along with its top suppliers.

Everything had gone as planned. He could still see the piercing set of blue eyes as they changed colors when he made the exchange and Chandler flashed his badge.

"You're five-o." the gang banger yelled. If looks could have killed him, Chandler would have been dead on the spot. Several of the gang members reached for their weapons, but the back-up police officers were too quick for them and the bust ended nonviolently with eleven arrests.

◆

The next evening, Chandler slowly opened the door to his apartment. He had left Nashville the moment he finished writing his report. Hanging around the city after such a major bust was not a good idea. He was glad to get home. He had a few days to relax before starting a new assignment. Before he plopped down on the cushiony sofa he ambled over to his bar and poured himself a shot of vodka with a spot of cranberry juice Then he laid down on the sofa, pushed the button on his answering machine and prepared to listen to his messages.

When he woke up, it was the next morning. "I must have been more tired than I realized," he said out loud. He eased up from the couch and looked around in a state of confusion. Whenever he had a long term assignment, it took him a while to adjust to being at home in his own bed, in familiar surroundings. He focused on the view in front of him displayed through the large picture window. He thought of Aisha and their last time together. *Man, I'd like to see her. I will make her my priority for today.*

18

Knowing yourself is the beginning of all wisdom.
Aristotle

On her way to The Lynx Aisha felt a jittery feeling in her stomach. Telling herself that God had a hand in her decision to accept Elisa's job offer at The Lynx, Aisha tried to justify what she was about to do by praying. *Lord, I don't always understand your way of working things out. I only hope that I can do this and get through it so that I can keep the studio.*

Elisa assured her that she could make the money she needed and then some. And Aisha didn't have a problem accepting what Elisa said as the truth. She'd seen for herself the money Elisa made in a short period of time the night she went with her to The Lynx.

Walking nervously inside, Aisha asked the doorman to page Elisa.

Elisa saw the nervous look on Aisha's face as she approached her. Elisa reached out and gave her new friend a hug of support and reassurance.

"I'm scared. I shouldn't be doing this. Suppose I make a fool of myself."

"That's hardly possible. You're a great dancer, choreographer and you're beautiful too. Now let's go get you dressed."

Aisha paused before putting on the skimpy front buttoned micro mini dress with a wide vinyl belt that rested on her narrow but shapely hips. The matching thong and spiked bracelet accessories caused her to shiver. How could she have resulted to doing something like this? she asked herself. But when she thought of the financial dilemma she was in she knew something had to be done. *It's only for a few weeks then I'll have enough cash to make the down payment on the building*, she managed to convince herself.

"You are going to make a bank load tonight with that outfit. When I first saw it, I knew it was you. Here, take a sniff of this." Elisa passed her a vial with a white powdery substance inside. There was a tiny spoon attached to the side of the vial.

"What is this?" Aisha stared questionably at the vial.

"Just a little something to make you more relaxed, that's all. Don't worry. It's not habit forming. It's just crushed valium. My doctor prescribes it for me. I crush it up so it'll get into my system faster. Believe me. It's safe. Plus I know you've heard of valium.

"Yes I've heard of it, but I'm not into doing drugs." Aisha had never done any kind of drug. She'd never been drawn into that world. The only thing she'd ever taken close to strong drugs was when her orthopedist prescribed Tylenol with codeine after she sprang her ankle dancing a couple of years ago.

"Look, take a hit. Don't be such a prude, girl." She pushed the vial toward Aisha and then placed it in her hand.

Without thinking any further, Aisha took a snort in each nostril of the yellowish-white substance. Within minutes, she began to feel relaxed and her anxiety had passed. She allowed Elisa to lead her to the open area.

The blaring rap music pumped into The Lynx. Unsure at first, Aisha almost stumbled on to the stage. Seeing the men from the stage view frightened her beyond measure. Just as she turned to walk off the stage,

Aisha spotted Elisa standing on the side of the stage behind the curtain. Elisa waved her hands back and forth and mouthed words of encouragement to Aisha. Slowly, Aisha turned back to the stage and began to move to the beat of the music. She closed her eyes and allowed herself to imagine she was on stage at the Orpheum dancing for dignitaries and high society people who'd come just to watch her perform. Her rhythm picked up and the wild beat of another artist rapping carried her into the world she loved best. The world of dance. Before long, Aisha was working the stage like she'd been performing at The Lynx for years. Wrapping her slender legs around the pole, she held on with one hand and threw her head back while moving seductively keeping up with each beat of the song. She swayed her hips, closed her eyes and allowed the drugs and music to take her into another world. She slowly slid to the floor in a Chinese split oblivious to the approval of the gentlemen gathered in the lounge. When she stepped off the stage some ten minutes later to thunderous applause, her shyness and apprehension had disappeared. She had become one with the music. She jumped up and down in front of Elisa. The exhilaration she felt was overpowering.

"Hey, you really knocked them off their feet tonight," Elisa commented. "I didn't see a shy bone in your body, girl."

"Thanks. I took your advice. I closed my eyes, listened to the music and pretended I was a famous dancer on Broadway. It worked. It really worked."

"See, I told you it wasn't going to be so bad, didn't I? Before you know it, you're going to be able to buy that building, and you're going to have enough cash left over to buy anything else you might want." Elisa hooked her arm inside of Aisha's and both women laughed as Aisha went to change into a different outfit for her next dance.

It was three thirty in the morning when Aisha returned to her apartment. She thought she would be exhausted. But much to her surprise, she wasn't sleepy at all. Walking over to her sofa, she threw her duffel bag on the floor and her cell phone on the table and sat down. Tonight had been better than she could ever have imagined and her feelings of guilt at what she was doing quickly dissipated. Her first night at her new part-time job had netted her over sixteen hundred dollars. Throwing the money up in the air, she looked up and said thank you, thank you, thank you God then prepared herself for bed.

The next morning Aisha was awakened by the sound of thunder and lightning. Rain pounded against her bedroom window. Yawning and stretching she sat up in the bed, reliving the previous night's events. Several minutes passed before she climbed out of her bed and took a hot shower. Afterwards, she called Angie and told her to cancel today's classes after listening to the news saying that severe thunderstorms and tornado warnings were expected throughout the day. When she made a cup of spiced tea, she remembered what Elisa had told her before she left for home. "I left you a little something inside your purse. After tonight, you're going to need a little something to pick you up." Aisha hadn't bothered to look in her purse to see what Elisa meant and had soon forgotten that she'd even told her that. But her memory was beginning to take focus and she searched inside her purse until she saw a vial like the one Elisa had told her to take a sniff from the night before. Aisha's first instinct told her to throw the vial away but the loud ringing of the phone stopped her and she placed it in her nightstand drawer.

"Hello," Aisha answered. Elisa was on the other end.

"Good morning. You up yet?"

"Yeah, this storm woke me up. So I called in and cancelled lessons for today."

"Yeah, I know Angie just called and told me. By the way, did you find the little present I left you?"

"Yes, I did. But Elisa, please don't do that again. I told you. I am not into drugs. I know I did it last night but I'm not going to do that again."

"Like I said, it's up to you. But if you change your mind, you'll have it. I know you're beat and sometimes you need something to get you started, that's all. If you do decide you want to try a hit every now and then, there's a doctor who's a member at The Lynx who'll be glad to write you your own script."

"I don't think so."

"Well, look, I was just checking on you. I'm going to fix Gabby some breakfast and then I'm going back to bed. I'll talk to you later on."

"Okay. Bye." Aisha hung up the phone and walked over to the nightstand. She opened the drawer and reached inside for the vial. Kneading it around in her hand, she stared at its contents. Turning the black top with the tiniest spoon she'd ever seen connected to it, Aisha put it underneath her nose and sniffed.

19

I think that somehow we learn who we really are and then live with that decision. Eleanor Roosevelt

Aisha had been dancing at The Lynx for almost three and a half weeks. She'd managed to accumulate quite a little nest egg. Each time she danced, she began to feel more energized. Tonight she was going to perform her first private dance. Elisa had managed to set it up despite Jason's protests. Jason wanted the girls to have at least three to four months of experience working at The Lynx before he promoted them to private dancer status. Somehow, Elisa convinced him to do otherwise. Aisha had her suspicions of what Elisa did to make Jason change his mind, but she pushed her suspicions aside and repeated what Elisa often said, "A girl's gotta do what a girl's gotta do."

Ring, ring, ring. It was Tameria.

"Hey, Tameria."

"Girl, what have you been up too? It's been God knows how long since I've heard from you. Every time I call you that answering machine of yours pops on. And you don't need a cell phone 'cuz you never have it turned on either."

"You know I've been trying to raise the money I need to keep the studio. I've been out hustling girl, trying to get investors and working a part time job too. Plus, I know your schedule is so screwed up with school that I haven't bothered to call you. I knew you would get in touch with me when you had a chance. So there." Aisha declared.

"Did you say you have a part time job? Tameria interjected, disregarding the part Aisha said about med school. "A part time job? Doing what?"

Aisha had to think fast. What lie could she tell her best friend? "Uh, I've been teaching dance lessons at a private dance studio way on the other side of town."

"Oh, that's great. How are things going?" Tameria was truly concerned about the studio. She knew how much it meant to Aisha.

"Actually, I think everything is going to work out. I'm saving the money I make from this night job. And I've lined up some potential investors who've shown an interest in the studio." With each sentence, Aisha found it easier to lie. She was relaxed and no longer bothered by anything Tameria said. She was glad she had agreed to let Elisa introduce her to the doctor with the hook up. He hadn't mind writing her a prescription for her own supply of valium.

"That's a blessing. Well, do you have to work tonight? Or are you going to be able to come to Bible study?"

"Yeah, I'll be there. I don't have to work tonight. So I'll meet you there around six forty five."

Before leaving the apartment for Bible study, Aisha took a hit of what she had come to call *baby girl*. In the past, she would never have thought to do such a thing, but that was in the past. Today was another day, and Aisha had to do what Aisha had to do. God surely would understand. Life for her had quickly changed in such a short span of time.

When she arrived at church, it was still early enough for her and Tameria to have a chance to talk. Tameria wasted no time asking Aisha to tell her what was going on in her life.

"Have you heard from what's his name?"

"Who are you talking about? Chandler?"

"Yeah."

"I talked to him earlier this afternoon. Since I have tonight off, I'm going to meet him for coffee after Bible study."

"That's good to hear. At least you haven't shut everyone out of your life."

Ignoring Tameria's remark, Aisha asked her, "And what about you and Chase?"

"Things couldn't be better. I think I'm in love with him."

"Oh, Tameria, I'm so happy for you. Do you think he loves you too?"

"Yeah, I really do. He tells me all the time." Aisha embraced Tameria in a firm bear hug. She was ecstatic at hearing the news. Tameria nudged her friend. "Look come on, we'd better go inside. Bible study will be starting in a few minutes."

♦

"How was Bible study?" Chandler asked.

"Good as usual. Pastor Shipley is the greatest. The man makes things so clear and easy to follow. I love his method of teaching."

"I'll have to come along and hear him some time."

"Okay, I'd like that. So tell me, what's been up with you these past couple of weeks."

"I've been busy trying to close a couple of deals. You know my job believe it or not can be quite exhausting, not to mention time consuming and stressful.

But seeing you tonight eases all of my tension." He flirted.

Aisha smiled broadly before answering. "It's good to see you too. I've been rather busy myself." She sipped on her cup of hot tea and looked out the restaurant window. Frost had formed on the window, making it almost impossible to see the trail of people moving quickly up and down the busy sidewalk.

After they finished their coffee and tea, Chandler invited her to his apartment and she freely accepted his invitation. She yearned for some genuine affection and attention. Night after night men at The Lynx stared lustfully and sometimes propositioned her. But that was only for her body. She wanted to be wanted for who she was on the inside. Not as a sex toy. Soon she would be doing more private dances. Elisa had told her that two members at The Lynx had already discussed it with the illusive owner of the association. In turn, the offer had made its way down to Elisa, who was more like a communications representative as well as a dancer. Aisha had thought about it the past couple of days and the idea was extremely appealing. She'd made almost $12,000 over the past few weeks. Now she had a chance of making that and much more on a regular basis, dancing for a few nights a month exclusively for her clients. She would be able to make the down payment to buy the studio in another week but she hadn't planned on quitting The Lynx. At least not yet. Her plan was to get as much as she could while she could.

She excused herself and went into the bathroom and took a hit of her feel good medicine before she returned to the living room of Chandler's simple apartment. Only this time, the vial contained something other than valium. When she first took a hit of the substance inside her little vial a couple of weeks prior, she didn't suspect that it could be something other than valium. But the numbness she felt when she placed it on her tongue and the exhilarating feeling was quite different from that of valium. Elisa saw Aisha's positive reaction when she snorted the unknown substance. She freely admitted to Aisha that she had given her something a little stronger and better because Aisha had been using more and more of the valium trying to feel the same effects she had when she first tried it. Aisha was angry at first when she found out Elisa had put cocaine in her vial while she was dancing one evening. Soon her anger left when the drug made her feel better than she had ever felt before.

"How do you like my place? I know it's not as nicely decorated as yours, but it's home."

"I like it, Chandler. It's soothing and comfortable. I love your art." Aisha walked around admiring his apartment. "And your antique pieces are lovely."

"They belonged to my great, great paternal grandmother."

"I see. Well, they're beautiful pieces."

Chandler strolled over to the entertainment center and put on KEM's latest CD before he went to the bar and poured each of them a glass of white wine.

"Here, pretty lady." He sat down close beside her on the plush high back sofa. They sipped on the wine and Aisha relaxed back in his colossal arms. They snuggled for several minutes. Chandler inhaled the fruity scent of her hair and then kissed her on the forehead before turning her face to meet his. He kissed her intensely and a flame of passion was ignited between them.

A moan escaped her lips and she pulled back in surprise from his embrace. "Don't you think we're moving too fast?"

"No, I think we're moving according to how we feel about each other," he whispered while planting butterfly kisses along the side of her neck. He pulled her back in closer to him, tilting her head toward his. His tongue sought desperately to find hers.

"But, Chandler," she spoke between his kisses. "I don't think we should." She couldn't hold back any longer. His kisses were too demanding and the touch of his hands moving expertly over the contours of her body set a fire ablaze inside of her. She had to make him stop before there was no turning back. Her mind suddenly thought about the very advice she'd given Tameria. *Don't put yourself in a situation where you're along with Chase. If you do, you're setting yourself up for things to get way out of hand.* Now, who was she to talk? She was in Chandler's luxurious bachelor pad, with KEM crooning in the background and a fine man doing things to her she'd often dreamed of.

"Chandler, wait," she pleaded softly. "There's something I have to tell you."

He leaned back and looked longingly into her hazel eyes. "What is it, baby? Talk to me." Before she could respond, he kissed her again lightly on her lips. His rough but gentle hands moved slowly up and down the length of her thighs.

Why did I have to wear a skirt of all nights? I should have put on my fuchsia pantsuit like I originally planned.

"I'm listening, tell me what's wrong, Aisha. Tell me, baby." The warmth penetrating through her body made it difficult for her to speak.

"I've. I've never been. Oooh, Chandler. Please, don't."

"You've never been what?" He stopped caressing her and waited to hear what she had to say. He didn't want to run her off. He liked her too much, way too much.

"I've never, you know, been with a man."

"Did you say never?" He couldn't believe what he just heard. *A twenty five year old virgin. No way. Not in this day and age.*

"Never."

"I see." He didn't know what to say. He was stunned. Here he was sitting next to the most beautiful woman he'd ever seen, a woman who brought out feelings in him that he thought he'd never experience again and she's telling him that she's a virgin. "Aisha, this is, man this is something I'm not used to hearing every day. You know?"

"Yeah, I know. But it's true. So you see, that's why we can't let this get out of control. I can't put myself in this position. I think it's time that you took me home."

"Look, I don't want to take you home. I like you Aisha. I really, really like you. And I can tell that you like me too. Don't you?" He waited to hear what he knew was in her heart.

"Yes, I do, but."

"No buts. Let's just take things one day at a time. I promise I won't pressure you to do anything you don't want to do." He had no idea how he was going to keep his hands off of her. But he was a man of his word and he wanted to earn her trust and respect. He stood up, walked over to the stereo and turned it off. Then he grabbed the remote and turned on the big screen.

With her eyes, she quietly followed his every move. *Ooh, I want him so bad. Lord, help me. I can't give in to this temptation. I can't.* Chandler sat back down on the sofa, pulled her in his arms, allowing her to snuggle against him. He flipped the remote until they decided to watch Crash on the Showtime Channel. Engrossed in the movie, Aisha was relaxed and no longer felt like she was losing control of her emotions.

The ringing of her cell phone disrupted their moment. She looked at the caller ID. It was Elisa. "Sorry, but I have to take this call." He nodded his head up and down and gingerly removed his arm from underneath her head. She answered the call while simultaneously standing up and going out to stand on the apartment balcony. "Hey. What's going on?"

"What are you doing?"

"I'm with my friend."

"Oh, sorry. But look, how would you like to make a couple of grand later on tonight?" Aisha leaned her slender dance body against the cold concrete wall. She spoke low so Chandler wouldn't hear her.

"A couple of grand? How can I say no to that? But tell me first. What's the catch? What do I have to do?"

"What you do best." Elisa laughed over the phone. "Dance, of course. Except this time it's for one of the clients who I told you is looking for a private dancer. There's nothing but good things being said about you around The Lynx, and you know it. So, here's your big chance. You wanna go for it?"

"I'll be there in less than an hour." Aisha walked back into the warmth of the living room, looking flustered with cheeks as red as an apple.

"Everything all right?" Chandler asked, his wrinkled brow revealed his concern.

"Sure, it's just that I have to leave. A friend of mine is in trouble."

"I'll come with you," he offered.

"No, please. That won't be necessary. I need to handle this by myself. Plus, I don't think she'd appreciate me bringing a stranger along with me. It's a sensitive situation."

"I see."

"I'm really sorry, Chandler. But I can't let this person down. She's done too much for me." She grabbed her lavender cashmere jacket from the teak wood coat rack. Without giving him a chance to show his obvious disappointment, she gave him a peck on the cheek, grabbed her purse and rushed out the door. "I'll call you tomorrow. Bye now."

Hurrying to get to The Lynx, Aisha put the pedal to the medal on E-way 240. She fussed at herself for almost blowing her cover with Chandler. There was no way he believed that she was going to some friend's rescue at ten thirty at night. But she was thankful that Elisa had called. It got her out of a situation that could have turned into something she didn't want with Chandler. Well, she did want to be intimate with him, but she knew that no matter how much she shook her tail at The Lynx, she wasn't about to show it to Chandler. That was still taboo on her list of no no's.

Pulling up to The Lynx, her tires squealed as she put on brakes and parked her car. She hurried inside, said hello to the bellman and headed for her dressing room. Her client, she was told, was a cowboy at heart. So Aisha wore her blue tight fitting rubber cowgirl mini with blue stilettos. She pulled her twists up in a poof up on her head, along with a pair of blue oversized earrings, surveyed herself in the mirror and smiled. Before leaving to meet him, she said hello to *baby girl* and proceeded to walk to the private suite elevator.

The morning after her private dance session, Aisha made a phone call. An hour later Thaddeus arrived at the studio.

"Come on in, Thaddeus." Aisha welcomed him into her studio office. Her private dance session the night before provided her with the rest of the money she needed to make the payment on the building. "Could I offer you a cup of coffee, tea or soda?"

"No, I'm fine. Thanks. I'd really like to get down to business. I have another appointment that I must get to and it's all the way on the other side of town." Thaddeus hoped that Aisha hadn't called him over to beg for more time. The owner of the building wanted out and he made it clear to Thaddeus that he wouldn't take any more extensions. Thaddeus had heard the owner was already in debt up to the ying yang and worst of all that he faced big trouble with the IRS. It was necessary for him to liquidate some of his assets as quickly as he could to pay them off or they would take everything he'd worked hard for.

Aisha sat on the edge of her oblong walnut desk and reached over to the side drawer. Unlocking it, she reached inside and pulled out a green envelope and passed it over to Thaddeus.

"What do you have for me here?" He eyed the envelope with curiosity, turning it over in his hands before opening it. His eyes grew large as saucers when he spied the cashier's check for the exact amount of the building. "You do mean business don't you?"

"Yes, I most certainly do."

"I'm impressed. You definitely go after what you want don't you?"

"Yes, and you make sure the owner of this building knows that."

"Did you say the owner of this building?"

"Yes, I sure did."

"Well let's take care of that by finalizing this deal and filling out these other papers. And the owner of this building will be YOU."

She breathed a huge sigh of relief. Though she hated the fact that she had to become an exotic dancer to get the money, she was glad to be blessed with the talent to make the kind of money she'd always dreamed of making by doing what she always loved.

20

"Every time I come to church, I get a free workout."
Tameria burst into laughter. "This church is way too
huge. I see why people are starting to call it a mega
church."

"That just lets us know that we're reaching people,
Tameria," was Aisha's reply. "If a church isn't growing,
then something's drastically wrong. That's the purpose of
the pastor and the different ministries. To reach the lost."

"Yea, I know that. But I still miss that small, cozy
family type atmosphere that you find in small churches."

"Me too, but we can't have it all. Is Chase coming
tonight? He's tagged along with you the last few times
you came to church."

"He's on call tonight. And I have to report to the
hospital at midnight myself. How's everything coming
along with raising the money for the down payment?"

Aisha couldn't tell Tameria the truth. She would
have too many questions and there was no way she would
be able to explain why she was dancing at The Lynx. So
she remained quiet and told her that things were coming
along fine and that she had secured a few investors that
pledged to help her. Sitting in church on the padded
pews, she felt a bit of guilt at the lie and the undercover

life she was leading. But God would forgive her. That she believed for sure so she opened her Bible and listened to Pastor Shipley.

"God desires for His children to have a personal relationship with Him. He wants us to be holy and pure. We all have sinned and fallen short of the glory of God. That much is true. But we don't have a right to freely sin and go against God's commandments," he taught. "People, God has a plan for our lives. Let's begin to listen to His voice. Take heed to His message and live a life of holiness dedicated to loving and living for Him."

Aisha squirmed in her chair as she listened to Pastor Shipley's every word. She felt uneasy about her secret life but she had no choice. She had to do what she had to do in order to keep the studio. Anyway, she had convinced herself that God had opened the door for her to receive her blessing. And so what if it was at the Lynx. It was no strip joint. It was a private upscale club, just another job. And as for the cocaine, she only did it every now and then. She needed a boost of energy after leaving her studio every evening. She wasn't hooked on it or anything. Because when she searched for information about cocaine on the internet she found out it was not addictive anyway. She just liked the way it made her feel. Aisha refocused on Pastor Shipley's closing remarks.

"Remember, if sin didn't feel good, look good, and taste good, there would be nothing for you to worry about. You see sin is a great disguiser. Merriam Webster's defines it as an offense against God, a weakened state of human nature in which the self is estranged from God. Then there's the word insatiable. Insatiable is when you have a craving for something but you can never get satisfied or full of it. No matter what you do, you can never get enough of it. Sin is like that. It feels so good and looks so good sometimes that you find yourself craving it more and more. You want more money. More sex. More cars. More houses. More men. More women. More things of this world. All the time, you're being deceived, trapped by the devil. I call it, Sinsatiable. But there's something false about these Sinsatiable desires and feelings. They're fleeting, and only for a moment does it feel good. So be wise my brothas and sistas. Resist the schemes of the devil as if your very life depended on it. Because it does."

After speaking to several of the church members after Bible study, Aisha said goodbye to Tameria, rushed out of the sanctuary, and dashed to her car. She was infuriated when the screeching set of tires against the wet blacktop pulled in front of her. The oncoming car barely missed her steel gray Acura as she pulled out of the church parking lot. Thoughts of Pastor Shipley's remarks were easily replaced with a string of expletives flowing from her mouth. She sped off down the winding street until she reached I-240. Glancing at the console, the digital clock read 8:45. She had less than an hour to get to The Lynx, shower and change. She had a client who thrived on promptness so being late wasn't an option. She reached over in her purse, fumbled for the rectangular pill box instead of her brown vial. When she found it, she popped open its latch and pulled out a tiny round blue pill with a cut out V design. "*Ahhh,* nothing like a little valium to relax one's nerves," she said and sped off.

Aisha made it to the Lynx in seventeen minutes flat. She rushed inside and ran past the armed doorman. "Good evening, Miss C."

"Hello, Thomas," she responded in an exasperated voice. She walked briskly to the elevator, pressed the button and without waiting on it, raced to the stairwell and walked up to the second floor. The first person she ran into was Elisa. She looked radiant as usual. Every time Aisha saw her, Elisa was perfectly dressed from head to toe. Tonight she had on a revealing black flared mini. The front of the dress had a plunging V like neck line that stopped at her belly button. The sleeveless dress sparkled from tiny sequins. The black king toed stilettos she wore and sheer black hose added an extra dose of sex appeal to Elisa's already perfect body. Elisa greeted her friend as she walked into the lounge.

"Slow down, girl. You aren't late you know."

"I know but if I don't hurry up and get changed I will be."

"Who's the lucky man tonight?" the well-dressed man asked as he walked up to her and Elisa."

"Jason, you know we can't divulge who our private clients are," Elisa responded before Aisha could answer herself.

Of course Jason knew all of the members already. He was fully aware that the name of their high paying, exclusive clientele list was never to be mentioned unless it was behind closed doors. He continued to tease the two of them, especially flirting with Aisha. He found her exceptionally beautiful and her innocent persona made him desire her that much more. She'd danced privately for him once and as bad as he wanted her to be his private dancer, he wasn't allowed that privilege on a permanent basis. None of the board of directors were entitled to have their own private dancer but they could have a private dancer of their choice once every three months. Other than that, their pleasure was derived from the bevy of young beauties that gyrated sensuously in the open area of the gentleman's lounge.

"Aisha, whoever the lucky man is, I sure envy him."

"Jason, you have a wife and four kids at home. Don't you think you need to lay low? I think you're getting more than enough action already," Aisha teased. Elisa laughed and Jason turned beet red before walking off.

"Girl, why you dog that man like that? You know he just wants to get a little something on the side."

"Please. Jason needs to be at home spending time with his family instead of leading a double life. From what I've heard, he has a gorgeous wife. I don't understand men like him."

"You still have a lot to learn. Take a look around. Most of these men have families at home, gorgeous wives, mistresses and lots of money. Some of them are even preachers, elders and deacons at church so wake up and smell the roses my friend. This is life and no matter how you think it ought to be, it is what it is."

"I know, but I'm just saying. I don't understand that's all."

"Look, we'll talk later. You better go and get ready. You don't want to disappoint your new client."

"Yeah, you're right. I'll see you later on."

Aisha soon learned that The Lynx was not all it portrayed itself to be. She could sense it. She didn't know what the real deal was or who the owner was but the last few weeks she'd worked there, she began to notice how some of the girls were treated rather roughly. Whenever she asked Elisa about it, Elisa found some excuse to dismiss her suspicions. Some of the girls looked a little young. But Elisa managed to brush off Aisha's curiosity by telling her that every girl at The Lynx had to be at least eighteen years old. Aisha dismissed the suspicious feelings she had about the Association time and time again. She told herself that if there was any illegal business going on then it wasn't any of her business. She was there to make money and whatever else may have been going on, she wasn't interested in it.

After she finished her shower, Aisha stood in front of the full length mirror and surveyed herself. All of her life she had been raised to be a 'good girl.' She was taught to carry herself like a lady at all times. Her father often emphasized to her while she was growing up the importance of respecting her own body. He told her that she should demand that any man who called themselves interested in her should respect her as well. To Aisha, her father represented all that she wanted to have in a man. Being raised by Christian parents, she spent more than half her life in and out of church. Every morning before she went off to school her father prayed with her. And every single Wednesday night and Sunday evening they attended Bible study. She basically knew the Bible like the back of her hand.

As she studied herself in the mirror, she felt ashamed of where she had allowed herself to be in life. She was going around lecturing Tameria about not going too far with Chase but look at her. Here she was leading a double life of her own, stripping for money. No matter how she tried to justify her actions, she felt at this moment that she was no better than the girls who danced around a pole in the strip clubs lining Brooks Road and Lamar Avenue. Maybe she hadn't slept with anyone but she was still no better than a common whore, at least that's what the face in the mirror called her. She shifted her eyes over her dressing room and they rested on the brown vial on the round table. Walking slowly from the mirror, she moved toward the nightstand and picked up the vial. Again, doing what she never thought she would do, she opened the top and inhaled the white substance up each of her nostrils before she proceeded to get dressed.

When she stood in front of the mirror this time, the shame she'd felt a few minutes earlier had disappeared. She felt relaxed, without a care in the world. She inhaled another hit of the powdery substance and smiled at the image in the mirror. She wore a strapless white halter top along with a sheer sarong that revealed her white thong underneath. Her twists were gathered up and held together by a white and silver band. The large silver diamond cut hoops glistened as they dangled from her ears. She lightly squirted Gucci Rush on each wrist and added a squirt at the base of her throat. Lastly, she placed her freshly pedicured feet into her white leather stilettos then placed her top coat over her outfit and proceeded down the back hall way that lead to the private elevator. Pulling out her elevator key and placing it in the key hole, she then pushed the button next to the word Private Suites.

By the time she made it to the Private Suites floor she was relaxed and confident in her talents. She wasn't going to allow the devil to make her feel inadequate. Not tonight. As she walked along the corridor, she convinced herself that what she was doing wasn't wrong. She wasn't fornicating. She wasn't stealing or robbing or hurting anybody. She was merely doing a job, using her talents to satisfy other people. And making money. She proudly strode to room 1066 and lightly tapped on the door. The voice on the other end invited her inside. Removing her top coat, Aisha responded to the gentleman on the other side by stepping inside. *Another day and many more dollars..*

21

*The difference between who you are and who you want to
be is what you do.* Anonymous

Chandler was glad when the Chief informed him that
he wouldn't have to go out of town for his next
undercover assignment. This would give him more time
to get closer to Aisha. It was hard trying to establish a
relationship when he had to keep his unexplained
whereabouts a secret and when he had to lie about the
type of work he did. When he told Aisha he was a land
developer, he understood that he was deceiving her. In
the past, it hadn't really mattered with the girls he had
dated, but Aisha was different. For some reason, he didn't
want to lie to her. But right now, he had no choice. He
had a job, a dangerous job at that. And if he wanted to
maintain a sense of safety he had to keep everything
confidential.

The assignment, the chief explained, called for him
to play the part of an older gentleman with lots of money.
He laughed at the description when the Chief told him he
would be posing as a high powered company executive.

To aid his transformation to a wealthy gentleman,
Chandler's first stop was at an exclusive men's store in
Cordova, a small city on the outskirts of Memphis. He
looked at some of the most expensive, top of the line
clothing. He settled on two pair of Sean John slacks with
coordinating shirts and blazers, three Armani suits and

126

one Gucci linen slack set with shoes to match each of the outfits. Before leaving out of the store, he picked out a pair of three hundred and fifty dollar Versace sunglasses. He went back to the station and waited on one of his fellow officers to take him to his next destination-Hertz Car Rental where a black onyx Lexus LS 430 had been reserved for him in the name of Kyle Taylor, his latest undercover alias.

"Man, I wish I could get some of the assignments you get," the young officer told him as he pulled into the rental car establishment.

"I've been at this for a couple of years. And I had to work hard to get where I am. You have to gain the trust of your superiors and show them that you can do the job. It'll happen for you, if you really want to be an undercover cop. But it's not all peaches and cream out here in these streets. And doing this can be more dangerous than patrolling the streets in your cruiser. So you think about it long and hard before you jump off into this area of law enforcement."

"Thanks man," the officer responded in an appreciative sounding voice, "I'll be sure to take what you said to heart."

Flashing his newly fabricated identification to the reservation clerk, Kyle walked out of the rental office with the keys to the luxury vehicle. After he picked up the SUV he looked at the next destination written on his list—3289 Riverside Drive. He pushed the navigation button in the middle of the vehicle console and entered the destination address into the system, listening as the mechanical voice gave him step by step directions to his destination. When he pulled up in front of the gated house, he exhaled loudly. "Wow, this Kyle Taylor definitely has it going on. I could get used to this kind of living for real," he said to the mechanical voice. The house was a tri-level mansion resembling a medieval castle. The steps leading up to the house were marble and the porch stretched the length of the house. He pulled out the pouch inside his briefcase and saw the key marked with the address. Walking up the brick steps, Chandler turned the key and entered the 13,000 square foot dwelling. The foyer with its 20-feet ceiling was elegant and lead to a rounding double staircase with intricate wrought iron railings. On the main level to the left were the living room, dining room, gourmet kitchen and family room. To the right of the foyer he entered the huge master bedroom suite with vaulted ceilings and windows that extended from the floor to the ceiling. The master bath included a gigantic walk in closet, standalone steam shower, sauna and a Jacuzzi. A separate whirlpool tub sat in the middle of the slate floor. Chandler checked out the other two levels of the house before he went outside and brought in his recent purchases. The home was furnished like an HGTV dream house and the landscaped grounds added even more class to the already dramatic home. For the next several weeks at least, this would be his residence. After searching through the fully stocked black and chrome sub-zero refrigerator, he pulled out all the fixings for a fresh deli style turkey and ham sandwich.

He toured the remaining floors of the house while he munched on his sandwich and gulped his soda. After looking over the entire house, he finally settled into the library and pulled out his briefcase to read about the details of his assignment.

The paper read, "The Lynx, a privately owned gentleman's association is located on the outskirts of Memphis in the secluded Southwind area. Owner suspected of human trafficking of young girls, mostly whom are under age. , Girls suspected of being used as sexual slaves by clientele made up of some of the wealthiest men in the city and throughout the country." Chandler continued to read while he lightly tapped the tip of his pen up and down on the cherry wood desk. "You are to portray one Kyle Taylor. Kyle is supposed to be a man in his early fifties who lives a secluded life on the downtown banks of the Mississippi. He runs a multimillion dollar technology company. Kyle is a quiet but charming gentleman with an insatiable desire for beautiful women. We'll have one of our inside guys set you up with the right person at The Lynx so you can become one of their VIP members. Kyle has mingled gray hair at the temples, a mustache and a neatly trimmed beard. He wears a Presidential Rolex, a gold diamond ring on his left index finger and a gold cluster on his right pinkie finger. You will find all of the necessary items needed to transform yourself into Kyle Taylor in the master suite."

Chandler smiled as he finished reading the description of Kyle Taylor. He loved getting into character. Before deciding on law enforcement, he'd thought about becoming an actor but decided differently after being told repeatedly by his parents that becoming a successful actor was like searching for a needle in a haystack. When he became an undercover policeman, he immediately fell in love with his job. It gave him the chance to take on different characters and he took each assignment like he was the star of a blockbuster movie. He could fool the best of the best. That's one of the reasons he was so good at his job. Crime surely didn't pay when Chandler Larson was on the job. And soon, whoever the owner of The Lynx was would be added to his list of conquests along with anyone else that had a hand in this illegal operation.

22

Real integrity is doing the right thing, knowing that nobody's going to know whether you did it or not.
Oprah Winfrey

"How did your new client look?" Elisa asked. "Did he try to get freaky with you?"

"Nope. You know I'm not going to stand for anything other than entertaining him and getting out of there. He looked okay but there was something about him. He looked familiar, like somebody I've seen before.

"You may very well run into somebody you know every blue moon, but that's highly unlikely, girl. These men pay too much for their privacy and we don't see men like them walking the Average Joe streets of Memphis, you know."

"Yeah, I know, but he still looked familiar, that's all. Anyway, he was nice enough though. He was an older guy, salt and pepper hair, tall, dark and rugged looking. The brother was dressed to the nines and smelled even better. He wanted me to slow dance with him. At first I was like, no way, but after I took a snort of *baby girl*, I was ready," Aisha laughed.

She would never admit how much she depended on cocaine and valium to get her through the day. Whether she was at her dance studio or at The Lynx or sometimes even at church, it was nothing for her to go into a

130

bathroom stall whenever the urge hit her and take a couple of snorts.

"You slow danced with him? You are getting bold aren't you? I thought a Christian girl like you wouldn't want a man rubbing up against her. Especially since you say that you're a virgin. Unless the virgin tale is just that, a tale." Elisa boldly confronted her. "Do I detect a change here, girlfriend," Elisa questioned, raising her arched eyebrows.

Aisha stared at her, and her ebony complexion appeared to change to a tinted red hue. She was totally embarrassed and defensive. "I AM a Christian and don't you forget it Elisa. I know I'm doing some things totally out of character but I'm going to stop. You'll see. As a matter of fact, I'm going to stop at the end of the month," she screamed.

"What? That's only three weeks away. You can't be serious. Can't you take a joke? I wasn't trying to make you feel bad. I swear. You take life way too serious sometimes."

"Look, it's not you. You just reminded me that I shouldn't be doing this anyway. I've got what I wanted out of this. I saved my studio and I have a rather fat bank account now. But, still. I mean look at me. I actually snort cocaine and valium Elisa. Me, of all people."

"What do you mean by *you of all people?* You're human just like the rest of us. You think that just because you call yourself all into God and stuff that you're supposed to be little miss perfect, better than the rest of us or something? Well, you're not. You're no better than me or the rest of these girls. Look around honey. What separates us from you? Aisha's face turned crimson and Elisa continued reading her. "That's why I can't get into the God thing. 'Cause there are a lot of so-called Christians right here at The Lynx, including you. These rich men parade in here night after night lusting after me then go home to their wives and their children like they're so perfect and all. Sitting up in church pretending to be so holy, righteous and all of that. None of them are for real if you ask me. Just a bunch of hypocrites. And I don't mean any harm, but no one can tell by looking at you or listening to you that you're a so-called Christian. But still, I ain't mad at you." Elisa sat down and took a couple of snorts from her own personal vial, followed by a swig of her favorite apple martini.

"I didn't say I was better than anybody," Aisha shot back. "And you're right. I'm on the wrong road right now. I know that things in my life have gotten out of control and I shouldn't be doing what I'm doing. I should have trusted God in the beginning. But *noooo* I had to take matters into my own hands. Now here I am dancing for men, letting them ease up on me, and snorting drugs. Lord, forgive me!"

"Well, you better hope God really is the forgiving kind sweetheart because you have a lot of forgiveness to ask for. But don't worry. You're still a good girl Aisha. I'm not trying to put you down. I just wanted you to see that we're all the same and nobody, I mean nobody is perfect. Right?"

"You're right."

"Now, come on. Let's get out of here. I'm beat and I promised Gabby that I would be home early tonight."

During the thirty minute drive home, Aisha became more consumed with guilt. What happened and how had she turned into the person she was now? Where had her faith failed her? Everything Elisa said to her was on target. She was no more than the unsaved people she encountered every day. As a matter of fact, she was even worse. Because they weren't pretending to be something other than what they were like she was. Tears crested in the corners of her eyes and she took one hand to wipe them away. She had to make a change before things got any worse. Her cell phone rang, pulling her away from the condemning thoughts that invaded her mind.

"Hello," she spoke softly into the razor thin phone.

"Hi, Aisha. Where are you? I called you at home but you didn't answer."

"Mom, remember I told you that I work part-time. I'm on my way home."

"I know you work part-time. But it seems more like a full-time job to me. You're never home anymore and I can barely reach you on your cell."

"I know, Mother, and I'm sorry. But I have some things I'm trying to do and in order to do them, I need this job." Aisha was trying to hide the irritation she felt at her mother's inquisition.

"Well, still, you shouldn't be working so much. Remember Beverly? Well she told me that she hasn't seen you at church or Bible study lately. Beverly was one of her mother's friends who resided in a retirement community owned and operated by the church. "Nothing should come before God and church Aisha. You know I tell you that all the time. Always, and I mean always put God first," her mother scolded.

Her mother's words stung her and added to the guilt she already felt. "Mom, I know I haven't been to church lately, but you and Daddy also taught me that it's not the number of times a person does or doesn't attend church. It's what's in your heart. And Jesus is in my heart," Aisha declared.

"Don't try to use my words against me, Aisha Denise Carlisle. When you get through justifying putting God, not to mention me and your daddy, on the back burner, you're still wrong. If I didn't call you, then I don't know when I would hear from you. And you know that your daddy hasn't been feeling the best lately."

"What's wrong with Daddy? I thought he just had a nasty cold."

"If you would come to see us more often, then you'd know that it's more than a cold. Your daddy went to the doctor a couple of days ago and they ran some tests and took some x-rays."

"What kind of tests?" Aisha stomped on the brakes when she saw that she was about to run the traffic light. "Mom, look, I'll be home in about ten minutes. Let me call you as soon as I make it to the house. I want to know what's going on."

"Okay, call me as soon as you get home." She would never forgive herself if something major was wrong with her daddy and she hadn't been around to see about him. She rushed inside the empty apartment, kicked off her shoes at the same time the auto lights popped on in the foyer. She dropped her duffel bag full of her costumes, threw her purse on the table and headed straight to the den to call her mom.

"Hi, Mom. I'm home."

"You better stop driving so fast, Aisha. I know it hasn't been ten minutes since we hung up."

"Mom, please. Tell me what's going on with Daddy," she asked ignoring her mother's sharp criticism. Sometimes she felt there was nothing she could do well enough in her mother's eyes. Sandra Carlisle had been the disciplinarian in the family. Growing up Aisha felt her mother's wrath more than a few times. She wasn't abusive but she could cut Aisha with her words. And the look in her eyes when she was angry could stop a train in its tracks. There were times when Aisha was young that she preferred an outright whipping rather than listen to her mother's verbal slashing.

"The doctors think he has some kind of respiratory problem. We won't know for sure until the tests come back."

"Where is Daddy now?"

"He's asleep. He complains of muscle aches and he has a really bad cough too. He's been awfully tired lately and having migraine headaches. He's been laying around the house a lot for the past couple of weeks. It's just not like him."

Aisha was livid. Why hadn't her mother called and told her any of this? Sandra Carlisle could be quite vindictive but Aisha hated to think that this was her mother's way of punishing her for not being around or calling them as much. Ever since she started working at The Lynx, Aisha had found it more difficult to find time to visit as much as she used to. She mostly relied on phone communication to keep her abreast of what was going on, but of course her mother didn't see things the same way. The two women were stubborn and often butted heads.

"Mother, I can't believe you haven't said anything about this to me. I know I've been working non-stop and I haven't been over there lately. But I'm still entitled to know what's going on with you and Daddy." Aisha ranted on the cordless phone while she walked through the house.

"If you really wanted to see us, you'd make the time to do it. Maybe if you slowed down a little and took a look around at the things that are or *should* be," she emphasized, "important to you other than making money and more money, then you would know what's going on."

Aisha knew by her mother's last remarks that she was definitely punishing her. She began to cry, but managed to keep her mother from hearing it in her voice.

"I'll head over there first thing tomorrow morning. I'll talk to you then," Aisha remarked without responding to her mother's cutting words. She said goodbye and went into her bedroom and plopped down on the bed where she allowed the heavy flow of tears to have their way. She was too tired and way too upset to hold them back. She buried her face in her pillow to muffle the sound. Without flinching, she reached over on the nightstand next to her king-sized bed and pulled out *baby girl*. After taking a few hits, she fell into a deep, restless sleep.

23

With lies you may go ahead in the world, but you can never go back. Proverb

"Welcome to The Lynx, Mr. Taylor." Jason extended his hand out to the newest member of their circle.

"Thank you, Jason. And now that we're comrades, call me Kyle.

"Of course, Kyle," Jason responded.

"From the looks of this establishment, I believe I've made the right decision to become a member. But as you know, I can't be totally sure until I see what this place has to offer other than elegance of structure. If you know what I mean?" Kyle Taylor was smooth talking and much like his true self, he had the charisma that drew people to him.

"Now that you've toured your new home away from home, let me show you the perks that come along with being a V.I.P. member of *The Lynx*. After that, I'll show you to your suite. You must be tired after such a long flight.

Kyle nodded, "Yes I am. I had the driver to bring me here without stopping at my Memphis home. But I'm about business, so let's see what you have to show me."

"Of course." Jason led him into the lounge area. It was close to midnight, and the ambiance of the lounge was impressive. Kyle's eyes lingered on the host of stunning scantily clad women sitting and standing around in the lounge. From the cocktail waitresses to the voluptuous blonde and brunette dancers that moved back and forth over the raised floor, they were hot. Their assets moved invitingly along with them as they kept up with the beat of the hip hop song playing. Their attire left little to the imagination.

"What do you think, Kyle? Do you like what you see so far?"

"I do, I do. But I've seen even better where I've just come from."

"Is that right? Where might that be?" If I might ask."

"St. Thomas."

"I've made several trips to St. Thomas myself. They have some fine women there but they can't compete with the ladies you'll find here at The Lynx. I believe you're well aware of that. Successful brothers like us don't pay for services that we aren't one hundred percent sure about," Jason laughed.

"Well said, Jason. And, oh so true. Show me more," Kyle prodded. I want to make sure I did the right thing when I purchased a home in Memphis.

"Come, I'll take you to your suite." Kyle allowed Jason to lead him down the same corridor Aisha had taken earlier that led to the private elevator.

"I believe you'll find that the key to the elevator is already in your possession."

"Is that so?" Kyle asked rather curious.

"Just push the black square on the elevator and hold it there for ten seconds."

Kyle did as he was instructed and the elevator door opened. "Ah, another plus. You've already programmed my fingerprints, huh. How clever."

"The men at The Lynx are not your typical run of the mill men. We have the best of the best in every field. That includes the best of work technology that you could ever imagine." They stepped on to the elevator and Jason guided Kyle again. This time he told him to push the blue square button that read 11. Kyle did as he was told and when the elevator reached the eleventh floor they stepped out, turned right and walked down the wide hallway until the two of them stood in front of Suite 1177. The two bedroom Presidential suite occupied the entire eleventh floor. When Kyle walked inside, he stepped on to black marble floors. The first bathroom had mahogany ceilings. To his right, was the sitting room which featured unique glazed faux finish walls, an entertainment center and Victorian antiques. Through another entrance leading from the sitting area was a study that had a mahogany and leather desk with matching leather both from the *Ernest Hemingway* collection. Another area of the study was equipped with a state of the art computer. Each room of the suite was lavishly decorated and furnished. Chandler thought to himself, I can easily get used to being Kyle Taylor. He turned and looked at Jason when they walked out on to the private balcony. Before he could say anything, Jason spoke.

"Your clothes have already been brought up to your room. Someone will be up shortly, or whenever you say the word to unpack them for you."

"Okay. But give me a few minutes to relax and make some business calls, then you can send the person up."

"Sure, and we'll talk tomorrow. You'll get a chance to meet some of the other members at that time. Goodnight."

"Goodnight." Kyle went back into the master suite and looked around. Next to the walnut California king size bed was an antique side table. A key rested on top of it in a solid gold tray. Kyle tried to see if it was the key to the locked drawer on the table, and it was. He pulled out the drawer and saw a black octagon shaped box. He opened it and couldn't believe what he was seeing. The white powder stung his tongue when he tasted it. Pure cocaine. Well, I'll be…." he swore. He placed the box back inside the drawer and locked it back, placing the key on his key ring. He talked to himself out loud. "I'm going to take a bath and then I'll call Aisha. I haven't seen or talked to her in a few days." Just as he started into the bathroom, he heard a light knock on the door.

"Who's there?"

"I'm here to unpack your things sir," the demure voice said from the other side of the door.

Chandler opened the door and was in awe at the beauty of the young girl who stood before him. Her hair was the color of onyx and her eyes sparkled like diamonds. Her sweet fragrance wafted through his nostrils. Yet he wasn't the least bit moved or aroused by her presence. She looked far too young and reminded him of his fourteen year old niece in Birmingham. He resisted the urge to pull the terrified looking girl inside his suite and tell her that everything would be all right. The frightened look on her face pushed him to his limit. But he had to play his part well if he was to be successful in nabbing these oversexed, drug dealing, perverted men he was about to encounter at The Lynx.

"Come in, young lady," Chandler spoke as politely as possible without sounding too mushy or suspicious.

"Sir, are you ready for me to unpack your things?" He could barely hear her, as she spoke just above a whisper. She shied away from looking directly at him as she moved deeper inside the suite.

"Yes, I'd like that. What's your name?"

"Hallie," she said quickly.

"Hallie. That's a lovely name. I'm Kyle"

He wanted to make her feel somewhat at ease. He hoped to be able to gain her trust over the next few days and then get her to confide in him. He was sure she was at The Lynx against her will and from what he'd discovered in his room, there was a lot of other illegal activity to be uncovered and he was just the cop to do the job. He focused his attention back on Hallie. He watched as she carefully removed each piece of clothing from his suitcase and hung them on the wooden hangars in the closet or placed them in the drawers. When she finally finished, she slowly turned toward him and began to peel each layer of her own clothing. She slid the delicate sleeves of the lavender dress down off her shoulders and was about to push the one piece dress down over her hips when Chandler ordered her to stop. He didn't mean to frighten her with his fatherly tone, but at that moment he saw a child standing before him, not a woman.

"Hallie, what are you doing?"

"I'm here to please you, sir."

He rushed over to her side and pulled her dress back up over her shoulders. The girl cowered in fear. "Please me? What are you talking about, please me?"

"I'm here for you, to serve your needs, Mr. Kyle. What would you like me to do? How can I show you how much I want to satisfy you?"

"You're just a child. Tell me something, Hallie?"

"Yes, what is it sir?" she asked, eager to respond to his request.

"How old are you?"

Hallie's face turned ashen. She didn't know what to say. Why would he ask her such a thing? She had been brought to The Lynx three months ago and she was still new to what was expected of her. She longed to be back home in St. Thomas with her three younger brothers and two little sisters. When her father woke her up that terrible night, she didn't know that her life was about to change. Some of her friends on the island had suddenly disappeared over the past two years without a trace and she'd heard frightening stories about what happened to them. But she didn't want to believe the horrid things she heard about them being kidnapped, raped, sold as sex slaves and child laborers. "Hallie, wake up," her father had demanded that horrible night. He shook her hard and yanked her out of the bed. "Hallie," he screamed again. "Hurry, they're waiting on you."

"Who, Father?" she asked. "Who's waiting on me? Is everything okay?"

"You have to go. It's time for you to do something to help the family. I can't do it alone anymore. You're thirteen years old now. You must fulfill your responsibilities as a woman." He pushed her toward the front door. She saw her mother and siblings hovering inside the dingy hut they called home. A look of helplessness and despair lay openly over her mother's face. Her brothers and sisters watched as her father continued to pull her toward the bamboo door. When he opened it, she saw three men she'd seen from time to time on the island. She'd heard terrible rumors about the reason the men scaled the island. Tonight it seemed as if the rumors weren't rumors at all. They really were who people said they were – men looking to buy young girls and sometimes boys from the poorest inhabitants on the island.

"Daddy, please. Please don't do this." She felt fear rise up inside and envelop her newly developing body.

"Come on, Hallie. Everything will be all right." She kicked and screamed against the darkness.

The three men laughed. One of them remarked, "She's a feisty little thing isn't she." Another one of the men passed a wad of money to Hallie's father. She met the empty gaze of her father as he turned and walked back in the house. He push the door closed behind him.

"Hallie, I asked you a question," Chandler repeated. "How old are you?"

"Almost fourteen, Mr. Taylor," she responded, sounding even more like a little girl to Chandler than she had just moments before.

"Get out of here, Hallie."

"What did I do wrong, Mr. Kyle? Please, I'll do whatever you want. Just tell me. I don't want any trouble," she begged.

"Trouble? What kind of trouble?" Chandler asked the terrified child.

"I, I don't want them to hurt me anymore. I'll do whatever you want."

"Then what I want is for you to go. I'm tired and I don't want to be bothered," he insisted. He couldn't trust her with his true identity and real reason for being at The Lynx just yet. The young girl hurried toward the door. A look of relief washed over her innocent face.

"Goodnight sir.. I'll be here early tomorrow with your breakfast."

"Fine. Now go. I told you, I'm tired." When she closed the door, he formed his hand into a fist and slammed it against the wall. He couldn't suppress the thoughts of the vile, filthy, disgusting acts that were probably being done to Hallie and the other girls who were there against their will. He hurried to bathroom, ran some more hot water to warm up his now cold bath water. He soaked for almost forty five minutes before climbing out and checking the time.

"Dang, it's almost two in the morning. Too late to call Aisha. I'll call her first thing tomorrow morning. I want to see her and talk to her so bad. I'm craving her." He turned back the thick covers on the bed and climbed between the pure white 1000 thread count Egyptian sheets. He fell asleep immediately.

24

One father is more than a hundred schoolmasters.
George Herbert

"Aisha, pick up the phone," Tameria screamed into the answering machine. "Aisha, if you're there, please pick up the phone. It's an emergency!" Aisha shifted her body in the bed as she slowly awakened to the screaming woman who interrupted dreams of her and Chandler walking hand in hand along the river walk.

Still half asleep, she clumsily felt around on the bed for her cordless phone. "Hello, whuzzup, Tameria? What time is it?" Aisha asked, too sleepy to be angry.

"Wake up. You need to get to the hospital right away."

As if someone had suddenly prodded her with a hot poker, Aisha jumped upright in the bed. "What's wrong? Tell me Tameria, what's wrong?" She screamed frantically.

"It's Mr. Carlisle. He came through the emergency room about an hour ago. You need to get here as soon as you can." Tameria hated to be the one to have to call her best friend with such horrific news, but better her than some other doctor or nurse who didn't know anything about Aisha or the Carlisle family.

"My daddy. Oh my God. Tameria, is he all right?" She moved across the cold hardwood floor with the

144

swiftness of a jaguar, grabbing a pair of sweats off the back of the door.

"Just try to take it easy and get here as soon as you can. Come to the first floor Critical Care Unit."

"Oh, Jesus, have mercy," Aisha cried. Her hands shook and big tears rolled down her round face. . She dropped the phone and slammed the door behind her.

"Oh, Lord, I need you to hear me. I need you to answer me. Please make my daddy be okay." She pleaded as she sped to St. Francis Hospital on Park Avenue. Her tears almost blinded her and thoughts of her father possibly dying flooded her mind. He was always in her corner. She was Daddy's little girl. Whenever her mother criticized, ridiculed or punished her, she would run to the safety of her daddy's arms. Though short in stature, his love for Aisha was mammoth. No one ever meant more to him than his daughter. Sometimes Aisha believed that her mother was jealous of her relationship with her father. Maybe that's why she acted like Aisha could never do anything right. Aisha used one hand to steer the car and the other to ramble in her purse for her cell phone. After several seconds of holding down the speed dial button, the phone dialed her mother's cell number. The phone immediately went to voice mail. "Dang, Momma, why haven't you called me? Fifteen minutes later, she turned off the Poplar-Germantown exit toward Ridgeway Boulevard. Her heart pounded as she saw the lights of the hospital. She talked to herself. *Daddy, you're all right. You've just got a virus, nothing serious.* She turned swiftly into the full emergency room parking lot, barely missing the bumper of a parked car. She frantically drove around the parking lot in search of a parking space. *Lord, come on. Don't allow this to happen. I've got to find a place to park. I've got to get to my daddy.* After circling the lot a few more times, she decided to park in a handicapped space. She couldn't worry about a ticket or being towed. All her thoughts were on her father. She jumped out of the car and raced to the information desk and asked for directions to Critical Care.

"I need to know about my father, Benjamin Carlisle," she told the clerk at the window. Exceptionally nice, the middle aged redhead pointed in the direction of the far right corner of the comfortably furnished waiting area. Aisha saw her mother with her head in her hands, looking like she'd aged overnight.

She rushed over to her and sat in the pearl gray leather chair next to her. "Mother, tell me what's happened to Daddy?"

"Aisha, I tried to call you earlier but you wouldn't answer your cell phone. Your father has a brain aneurysm that burst. He's unconscious. They don't know if he's going to make it," she cried.

"I've got to see him." She immediately ran back to the window clerk. "Please, tell me where I can go to see my father?"

"Sweetie, the doctors are working on Mr. Carlisle right now. I'll let the floor nurse know you're here. Are you his daughter?"

"Yes, yes I am and I need to talk to the doctor about seeing my father." Aisha couldn't contain her fear. Her mother walked up beside her and wrapped her arms around her shoulders.

"Aisha, they're doing all they can. We have to pray and believe God for healing. Let the doctors do what needs to be done."

"Aisha, your mother is right. We'll let you know when you can see him. The nurse or doctor will call as soon as they can and let you know what's going on. I'll call you up here when they do and you're to go right around that corner," the clerk pointed to a corridor next to her reception area. "There're several phones lined up on the walls with a number over each one. I'll tell you which phone to answer. I promise, as soon as I hear something, you'll be the first to know," Aisha's face was pallid and she began to feel sick to her stomach. Sweat formed on her brow.

"Are you okay?" The clerk stood quickly and came out of her enclosed glass booth. "Come on. Why don't you sit down?" She led Aisha over to a chair close by the reception area. "Sit here. I'll get you some water. I'll be right back."

"Aisha, get yourself together," her mother said in a scolding voice. "You look like hell. This is no time for your dramatics. Your father needs us and he needs us to be strong. This is not about you. What you need to be doing is praying not weeping. And my God, when was the last time you ate? You look anorexic."

Aisha looked at her mother with a coldness in her eyes. All the years her mother had professed to be such a saint. But if only the people at church knew how she treated her own daughter. Aisha felt like she was always in competition with her mother, always trying to prove to her mother that she was a good girl. But Sandra Carlisle shielded her emotions like Fort Knox protected its gold. She wouldn't let anyone get too close to her. Her mother had been the same way. She often told Sandra that showing affection was a sign of weakness. True Christians should be strong, not weak is what Sandra had been taught. Sandra looked at Aisha again. The compassion she wanted to feel toward her only child just wasn't there. Instead she reached into the pocket of her jacket and pulled out her purse sized Bible. She turned to the twenty third Psalms and began to read the Bible verses she already knew so well.

"Tameria, thank God." Aisha rushed to the arms of her best friend.

"I would have come down earlier, but things are hectic in CCU and I couldn't get a break. I only have a few minutes now." Tameria could barely contain the sick feeling that formed in the base of her throat when she saw Aisha. It had been several weeks since the last time they'd actually been in each other's presence. Between Tameria's medical rotation shifts and Aisha's full and part time jobs, they rarely had the chance to spend time with each other. Something was terribly wrong with Aisha but Tameria didn't know what it was. She slowly approached the pencil thin frame of her friend and Mrs. Carlisle.

"How's my father, Tameria?"

Tameria could barely look at Aisha. Mr. Carlisle was hanging on by a thread. After emergency surgery he'd lapsed into a coma and his prognosis wasn't good. Tameria was not about to share this heartbreaking news with them. She would leave that up to Chase.

"Tameria, I want to see Benjamin. I want to see my husband."

"Mrs. Carlisle, I'm going to take you up to CCU now. Come with me." Tameria stopped at the window clerk's desk to inform her that she was taking the family to see Benjamin Carlisle.

On the way to CCU, the elevator ride seemed to move in slow motion. "Tameria, you never told us. How is my daddy?"

"Aisha, I'm sorry to say, but he's not doing so well. The surgery was performed in an effort to clip the ruptured aneurysm and reduce the risk of rebleeding. Chase is up there too. He can tell you more since he's a Neurosurgery Resident.

"Thanks, Tameria. We thank God for you," Sandra Carlisle said in a humble voice.

When she walked into CCU and saw her father lying on the cold white pristine sheets, with tubes in his arms and down his throat, Aisha almost collapsed. The same feeling of weakness and nausea she felt earlier revisited her again. Her mother ignored Aisha and walked over to the side of her husband's bed and grabbed his hand. The gentleness she displayed toward him was seldom shown toward Aisha.

"Bennie, Bennie I'm here darling," she whispered. "You're going to be all right. I know you are. Just hang on and have faith baby. God is with you." The only sound that pushed from his lips was the sound of the breathing tube. His eyes were swollen and his head was wrapped in white gauze.

Aisha couldn't hold back her tears any longer. She moved in on the other side of her father's hospital bed. "Daddy. Daddy I'm so sorry I haven't been around like I should. But I love you Daddy. I love you so much," she whispered softly to him. Tameria moved closer to Aisha and placed her arm around Aisha's bony shoulder to uphold her. When her arm rested on her skinny frame, she thought Aisha would break. Tameria began to mentally diagnose Aisha while she stood next to her for support. *Maybe she's working too hard and not eating enough. I know she's not anorexic or bulimic, at least I hope that's not the case. What could it be*, she continued her thoughts as she did a side glance at Aisha.

"Daddy, can you hear me? Please say something, Daddy." Aisha stared at her father intensely and guilt consumed her. If only she had been around more for her father instead of doing obscene dancing for perverted men. She felt the sudden urge to find relief in her vial of *baby girl* that was tucked safely inside the zip pouch of her handbag. Before she could leave his side to find a bathroom, a mild mannered voice clashed her thoughts. She looked up and saw the hefty built doctor standing next to her mother.

"Mrs. Carlisle, I'm Dr. Johnston." The Neurosurgeon said to Sandra Carlisle. "Why don't you come to the consultation area with me and I'll tell you what's going on with your husband."

She followed the doctor to the consultation room and Aisha scurried behind the two of them.

"I'm going to go and check on my patients and I'll be back soon," Tameria reassured them.

"Okay, I'll see you later," Aisha said.

"Mrs. Carlisle and Miss…" he paused looking at Aisha.

"Aisha Carlisle. Benjamin Carlisle is my father. Doctor is my father going to be all right?" Before the doctor could respond, Chase walked in and joined him. His look revealed what Aisha denied in her heart. "Aisha, hello. Mrs. Carlisle," Chase nodded.

Aisha couldn't find the words to respond. Her mind was saturated with thoughts about her father's condition.

"Your father had an aneurysm that ruptured and caused bleeding in the brain. We've managed to clamp off the aneurysm and stop the bleeding but there's always the possibility that the bleeding will start again and cause additional aneurysms." He turned to Mrs. Carlisle. The two ladies were obviously distraught. This was one part of his job he hated. It never became easier, no matter how many times he'd experienced less than favorable prognosis of patients. This was such a time but it was still not a time to mince words and give them false hope either.

"I'm sorry to say," Chase added. But Mr. Carlisle's condition is out of our hands now. We've done all we can do."

"Nooo," Sandra Carlisle screamed. "God, I do not accept what this doctor has said. Satan I rebuke you now in the name of Jesus. Doctor Johnston and you to too Chase. Both of you listen to me," her voice commanded. Aisha's sobs were ignored. "God is the one true doctor and I cannot and will not accept this sentence you've placed over my husband's life. I will not."

"I understand what you're saying, Mrs. Carlisle and I respect your religion, but I'm a specialist, a neurosurgeon and I'm telling you what the prognosis is for your husband. I don't want to deceive you, ma'am. The chances for his survival are quite slim." Chase explained while Dr. Johnston stood with his hands folded over his chest in total silence.

"Chase, please, there has to be something else you can do. There just has to be," Aisha intercepted.

"I wish there was."

"We really do," Dr. Johnston emphasized.

The pain that consumed Aisha was far too much for her to bear. The doctor's words ripped at her heart over and over again. She ran out of the room and didn't stop until she saw the sign on the door that said 'Exit - Stairs.' She pushed open the heavy steel door and sat down on the first step. Without hesitation she reached inside her handbag and pulled out *baby girl*. She uttered a prayer between each snort, pleading and begging God to save her father, promising him that she would change her life if only he would save him.

◆

"Chase. Something's not right with Aisha."

"Something like what? The woman is distraught about her father's critical state. What's not right about that?"

"You know I haven't seen her for several weeks because of our schedules. She looks bad, Chase. I mean Aisha has always been one to keep herself in perfect shape. Now she looks like a weekend crack head or something. That's the best way I can describe her."

"You don't think she's doing drugs do you?"

"No. Of course not. Aisha's too smart to get caught up in something like that. She's too into God to get hung up on drugs."

"Well what do you think the problem is?" Chase was concerned about anything that bothered Tameria. He loved her and hoped to make her his wife when he finished his residency and secured a more permanent position. Anything that he could do to alleviate any pressure or anxiety she felt, he was willing to do that. The fact that Aisha was in trouble, concerned Tameria and Chase wanted to help her get to the bottom of Aisha's problems.

"Look, why don't you go back to CCU and see if you can get her to meet you later on when you go on break. Then you two can talk a little and maybe you can find out what's got her looking so stressed. But being worried about her father probably has a lot to do with it. Then you told me that she's working two jobs too. That's enough to stress anybody out."

"Everything you've said is true. But, Chase, the girl looks like she's lost almost twenty pounds in a matter of weeks." Tameria lowered her head and wrung her hands together. Chase reached over and tilted her face toward his and kissed her lightly on the lips.

"Hey, I don't want my favorite girl to get all worked up about this. Everything will be all right. You'll see. Now go and find Aisha and make those plans to meet her later, okay?" His smile always warmed Tameria's heart. The touch of his lips against hers relaxed her and for a moment, thoughts about Aisha disappeared.

25

Love is composed of a single soul inhabiting two bodies.
Unknown

Aisha looked down at her cell phone. A grin enveloped her weary face when she saw the call was from Chandler.

"Hi, you. Long time no hear from," she said gingerly.

"Hi, yourself. You know that works both ways. You have my number and I don't recall seeing your digits flash across my screen," he responded. "Tell me, what's a man got to do to get some attention from you?"

"Let me see," she made a humming sound over the phone pretending like she was in deep thought.

"I'm waiting," he said flirtatiously.

"I'd really like to see you, Chandler," she confessed. Then taking a more serious tone she explained to him about her father's illness. "I've been spending as much time as I can at the hospital."

"I'm sorry to hear that about your dad, Aisha. Why don't I come over later and take you to dinner. Or if you're going to be at the hospital, I can bring you something to eat. Just tell me what you want me to do."

Each time he heard Aisha's voice a tiny piece of him surrendered to his feelings for her. He hoped his undercover assignment would be ending soon. At least in the next few weeks or so. So far he'd found out how the girls were being brought in to The Lynx. Most of them were being lured from shopping malls all over the United States with promises of modeling careers. Others were runaways or homeless teens. Most of the time two well-dressed decoys, usually a man and a woman, approached vulnerable looking girls, and sometimes boys, who were alone in the mall. The decoys would strike up a conversation, often telling the girl how pretty she was and how she would make a perfect model. It really didn't take much to talk most of them into listening to their scripted diversion before they lured them outside to a waiting car. From that point on, they were shuffled around like cattle to a predesignated city. Some ended up at The Lynx and others ended up in cities far from their original pick up location. Still others were sent overseas and sold as sex slaves to drug cartels. The end result wasn't pretty because there were girls like Hallie whose very childhood had been stolen and the right to live a life of safety was long gone.

"Chandler, I don't know about seeing you tonight. I don't think it's such a good idea for you to come to the hospital. It's depressing here and I don't want my mood to rub off on you."

"I want to come, Aisha. Are you at the hospital now?"

"I'm actually on my way back to the hospital. I had to go and pick up a few things from my apartment and run a couple of errands for my mom."

"How long will it be before you get there and what hospital is your father in?"

"He's at St. Francis and I should be pulling into their parking lot in about ten or fifteen minutes. He's in CCU so I can meet you in the downstairs CCU waiting area, in say about forty or fifty minutes. That'll give me time to check on my father and see about my mom. Is that all right with you?"

"Yeah, sure. I'll see you then."

Chandler washed the grey rinse out of his hair, removed the fake moustache and goatee and changed into his normal attire. He was Chandler Larson again and it felt good. Like a person with a split personality, he sent Kyle Taylor away. The night belonged to Chandler and Aisha and he was going to take advantage of every bit of it. Before leaving the house on the river, he checked in with the Police Chief and filled him in on what he'd found out so far about The Lynx.

◆

Aisha's pale face lit up when Chandler walked into the CCU waiting area. His charcoal shuttle jeans and printed shirt made him stand out like a fashion model.

"Hi, Chandler," she blushed.

It took several seconds for him to respond. He was taken aback by her ghostly appearance. She'd lost quite a bit of weight since the last time he'd seen her and her face looked sunken and almost hollow. He imagined that she'd been through a tremendous amount of pressure with her father being so ill, along with her trying to operate the studio and work a second job. He felt sorry for her. He wanted to whisk her away from all of the problems she faced at this time, but his own career kept him from doing a lot of the things he desired to do in life. It was because of his job that he had shied away from long term relationships. But Aisha was different. He wanted something more than a fly by night fling with her. She stood for everything he wanted in a woman. She was ambitious, smart, intelligent, family oriented and beautiful. When she smiled, her whole body smiled and he loved that about her. When he touched her, she was soft like cotton candy and she smelled like the sweetest of fragrances.

Why is he staring at me like that? Aisha asked herself. I know Tameria said I'd lost a lot of weight and maybe I have but dang, he doesn't have to look like he's in another time zone or something.

"Hey, don't I get a hello, whuzzup or something," Aisha spoke up.

"No, you get more than that." He pulled her into his massive arms and held her against his chest. The sweet scent of her hair aroused his desire for her.

She relaxed in the safety of his arms and allowed herself to enjoy being held and comforted. When they pulled away from each other, he caressed her face with the back of his hand and then led her to the sofa in the back area of the waiting room. When they sat down, he placed the bag he brought in on the table next to them.

"You didn't tell me what to bring, so I stopped and picked up a couple of subs. I hope you like turkey and ham."

"That's fine, thanks for doing this, Chandler."

"No thanks is necessary. I brought enough for your mom too. I didn't know if she'd eaten or not, but I know how it can be when you're in a situation like this. It drains you and you find very little time to do the things you normally do every day."

"You're right about that? But how do you know?"

"I've been through this same sort of situation before. I had a brother who had muscular dystrophy. We stayed in and out of the hospital with him. He passed away when I was fifteen."

"Oh, I didn't know. I'm sorry to hear that, Chandler."

"Anyway, that's how I know. Now, come on, I want you to eat a little something."

"I will, but not right now. I want to spend some time with you for now. I promise, I'll eat something later."

"Okay. Tell me, how is your father?" A real sound of concern was in his voice.

"He's still in a coma and on a respirator. The doctors don't give him much hope but I know that God is in the healing business. I believe that with all of my heart."

"I know you do, Aisha. And I hope he makes it through this. You know what?"

"Yes, Chandler," she spoke in a soft voice.

"I admire your faith. You're the kind of person who isn't ashamed of her beliefs and that says a lot about you."

Suddenly Aisha felt ashamed. How could she talk about God and faith when her life was so screwed up? Here she was sitting across from a man that had penetrated her shell and she was living a lie. She dropped her head and turned away from Chandler's stare.

"What is it, Aisha? Did I say something wrong?"

"No, of course not. It's just that I don't want you putting me up on this high pedestal and all. Like I'm little Miss Perfect. I'm far from perfect you know and my faith gets shaky sometimes too."

"I know you're not perfect. I never said that you were. I just said that I admire you and that's what I meant. Anyway, I think you're perfect for me," he confessed. She turned her head quickly to meet his gaze. They stared at each other before he pulled her next to him. She rested her head against his shoulder. Within minutes he heard her labored breathing. He allowed her to sleep in the crest of his arms. Gently rubbing her hair away from her closed eyes, he kissed her forehead, leaned back into the soft leather of the sofa and watched CNN on the waiting room TV.

Chandler soon followed suit and drifted off into a light sleep. He was awakened by the feel of someone moving or shaking next to him. When he opened his eyes, he saw a strikingly beautiful older version of Aisha hovered over her, jabbing Aisha on the arm.

"Aisha, wake up. Wake up," the woman ordered. Chandler rubbed his eyes and sat upright on the sofa.

"Oh, hi, Mrs. Carlisle."

"And you are?" Mrs. Carlisle inquired gruffly.

"Chandler Larson. I met you several months ago at the Mayor's Gala. I'm a friend of Aisha's."

"Oh, yes, I think I remember meeting you."

"Mom, what's wrong? Is Daddy okay?"

"He's the same, Aisha. I came down here to see if you were still here. I think I'm going to go home and change and check on the house. Can you stay here until I get back? I shouldn't be gone for more than a couple of hours."

"Of course...I'll stay."

Before abruptly turning to leave Mrs. Carlisle looked over at Chandler. "Nice to see you again, Chandler."

"Mrs. Carlisle, would you like to take something to eat with you? I brought a couple of subs for you and Aisha."

"No, but thanks for thinking of us. I don't have an appetite right now."

"I want to tell you that I hate that we had to meet again under these circumstances, Mrs. Carlisle. I hope everything turns out fine for your husband. And if there's anything I can do, please by all means tell Aisha and I'll be glad to do it."

"Thank you, young man," she responded without feeling.

"That was nice of you, Chandler."

"I just said what I meant. I told you, I'm here for you Aisha."

Aisha's cell phone began to ring the familiar tone that let her know it was Elisa calling.

"Excuse me, Chandler, I have to get this."

"Sure, go right ahead. I'm going to stretch my legs for a minute. I'll be back." He stood up and headed into the outer hospital area.

"How's your father, Aisha?" Elisa asked.

"Not so good I'm afraid."

"I'm sorry to hear that."

"What's up with you?"

"I was just calling to check on you. You haven't been here in a couple of days and I haven't heard from you. Jason said he hadn't either. I wanted to make sure you were all right."

"Yeah, I'll be okay. My friend is here. You know the one I've been seeing."

"Uh, Chandler isn't it?"

"That's right. What's going on? Anything I should know about."

"Well, we have a couple of new members. Both of them are quite handsome too girl. That's another reason I was calling."

Aisha hoped Elisa wasn't about to ask her to come to work. She had no time to think about dancing. She hadn't even been to her own dance studio in two days. Her mind was on her father and nothing else.

"If you're thinking about asking me to come in, you must be crazy. I'm not leaving this hospital." The irritation in Aisha's voice was evident but Elisa didn't back down.

"Hey, I know you're going through some tough things right now. But listen, we all are. That's life. You have to learn how to roll with the punches."

"Roll with the punches," Aisha shouted. Eyes from some of the others in the waiting room zeroed in on her when she shouted. She placed her hand over her mouth and the miniature cell phone and continued talking. "Look, this is more than rolling with the punches as you put it. My father is in Critical Care. I don't know if he's going to get better and you want me to come in and shake my tail because of some new clients. Girl, puhleeze. You must be snorting more than coke."

"Jason insists that you come. All you have to do is entertain one of the new clients for an hour or two and then you're out of here. There's a huge bonus in it for you too. Plus, you don't have to be here until around eleven tonight. That gives you a few more hours to spend at the hospital. You can come here, do your thing, and go right back to the hospital."

Aisha spotted Chandler walking back into the CCU Waiting Area. "Look, I'll call you back. Let me think about it."

"Don't call me. Just come. Like I said, it's going to be well worth your time. Bye now."

"Don't hang up on my account," Chandler told her.

"No, it's nothing like that. The conversation was over anyway." He sat down beside her again and held her hand.

"What time can you go see your father?"

Aisha glanced at her watch before answering. "Visiting hours are for fifteen minutes every two hours. " I can go up in about thirty minutes."

"Well, that gives you time to taste some of this food you promised me you'd eat. I won't leave here until you do," he smiled.

"If you insist, Chandler." She took several small bites of the sub sandwich before folding the remainder inside the crinkled wrapping. "Now are you satisfied?"

"Not really. I was hoping you would have eaten a little more, but I won't nag this time around," he teased.

"Good. For that you get a kiss." She laughed and kissed him lightly on his full lips.

"Ummm. I like that," he crooned sexily in her ear.

"Now you go on and get out of here. Didn't you say you had a client to meet later?"

"Yeah, I do. But I'll sit here with you until you get ready to visit your dad, then I'll be on my way. I'll still have plenty of time to get to my appointment."

"If you don't mind my asking, what kind of land deal is it?"

Chandler didn't stutter at all when the lie dripped from his lips. He was used to fudging the truth with family, friends and the criminals he found himself working around. "It's a deal for an apartment unit. I've been working with this guy for a couple of weeks now and I think we're going to seal the deal tonight."

"That'll be great. We'll have to celebrate soon, I hope."

"Yes soon. But right now it's time for you to head upstairs. I'm going to get out of here. I'll try to call you later, okay?" They both stood and exited the CCU waiting area. Chandler walked her to the elevator. "See you," he looked in her eyes, missing her already.

"See you," she responded with the same reply. He leaned down, drew her into his arms and kissed her passionately oblivious to any one standing around them. The ding sound of the elevator startled them. Chandler pulled away from Aisha and speaking in their own silent language they went their separate ways.

26

In time of test, family is best. Burmese Proverb

Aisha called the dance studio and left a voice mail message for Angie. She gave her an update about her father's condition and told her she would be by the studio the next day. Because of her ever growing bank account, she was able to hire two additional dance instructors. That way she was able to keep the studio open while she spent time at the hospital. Working at The Lynx had its perks and whenever her spirit nudged her to give it up, she somehow managed to find a reason not to. This time she convinced herself that all of the extra money she was making helped provide so much more for her students. What she said was true, but she still felt dirty and hypocritical for doing what she did at The Lynx. Yet, it wasn't enough to make her quit like she had told Elisa she was going to do.

She turned into her personal parking space and stepped out of the car into the warm muggy night. It was almost Easter and normally she would be fasting for Lent but no such thoughts had entered her mind this time. This year she wasn't willing to give up anything for 40 days. *Lord, I promise you that I'm going to stop this,* she mumbled under her breath as she took long strides toward the entrance.

"Elisa, what did Aisha say? Is she going to show up or not?" Jason didn't want to aggravate their newest member, Kyle Taylor.

"I haven't talked back to her. But if I know Aisha like I think I know Aisha, she'll be walking through that door any second now. She's hooked on making this money."

"I hope you know what you're talking about. We have a lot at stake. I told you in the beginning that I didn't like to recruit girls like her. We should stick to the ones we traffic in instead of women like Aisha. This establishment has managed to maintain its status and stay out of the Fed limelight. Girls like her can bring trouble."

"Jason, stop bugging won't you?" Elisa threw her hand up in the air. "You're being way too paranoid. Aisha is one of the best dancers we have and she's naïve as hell. That's why she's one of our most requested private dancers. And now that she's hooked on coke, we don't have anything to worry about."

Jason cast a strange look at Elisa.

"What's up with that look you're giving me?" she asked, placing a hand on her hip. The tangerine dress she wore barely covered her luscious thighs and her butt reminded him of Jennifer Lopez's luscious booty.

"I remember when you first came to The Lynx. You were a scared, frightened fifteen-year old runaway. When I saw you standing alone at the entrance of the mall in Maryland, you looked like you were starving to death. When I walked up to you, your eyes grew big as Bo dollars," Jason grinned.

"Jason, that was a long time ago. I've learned a lot since then. I've learned how to survive. I've learned that this world won't give you anything. You have to go out and get it for yourself any way you can."

"And you did just that Elisa. Look at you now. You're basically running this whole operation. You're doing a fantastic job of it too. That's why you get paid the top dollars. And Gabby will never have to worry about a thing."

Suddenly Elisa's face turned ghostly at the mention of her daughter. "Jason, don't even go there," she lashed out.

"Woe, hold up. What did I say? Gabby's a beautiful girl but you don't have to worry about her being brought into this business," he paused. "Unless of course, you decide differently," he remarked in a threatening voice that Elisa knew all too well. It was true, she did make plenty of money. But if she ever thought about leaving the business, she had been subtlety warned about what would happen to Gabby. She helped bring in young girls all the time, sometimes traveling around the United States to snatch homeless, starry-eyed teens and runaways. She'd even gone to some of the islands as well and organized the transport of girls, not to mention a few boys to satisfy the perverted taste of some of The Lynx clientele.

"Do I know what I'm talking about or not? Look who's coming through the door." Elisa spoke to Jason under her breath. "Well, I'll be…" Jason said and shook his head back and forth. "You are good, Elisa." He walked over to meet Aisha. "Aisha, sweetheart, how's your father?" he asked her pretending to be truly concerned.

"If you really gave a crap, you wouldn't have insisted that I be here tonight," she huffed at him.

"Darling, you're stressed. Take it easy. I promise, tonight will be a breeze. A couple of hours will be gone before you know it. Now, go on and get dressed up real nice for me. We're going to meet him at his place." Jason instructed her.

Aisha shot back, "Why are we going to his place? I thought we only did that for a very small number of our members. What makes this one so special?"

"Don't you worry yourself about such minor details. Just go and get dolled up." Aisha swiftly jerked her body around without responding to Jason. The last thing she wanted to do was go to some client's house, but she also thought, the sooner she did this, the sooner she could get back to the hospital.

Aisha showered and changed into a violet slip style mini dress in stretch lace. with a v neck that rested closer to her thighs than her knees. Her extra drug thin frame was supported by a pair of matching strappy Giuseppe sandals with a five inch heel. She resembled one of America's Next Top Models.

The drive to the client's house led along a stretch of dark roads with twists and curves. She was amazed that there were still parts of Memphis she was unfamiliar with and this was one such time. The long drive led them to a gated community on the bluffs. Aisha's eyes widened as they approached the large estate. They followed the circular drive and pulled up in front of the massive stained glass doors leading to the front entrance.

Going up the stairs, Aisha reminded Jason one final time about the night's event. "Jason, I'm telling you, I'm not going to be here all night. Two hours tops and I'm outta here, even if I have to leave here walking. "

"I hear you. Just come on."

Jason rang the doorbell and an older full figured Asian woman dressed in a traditional maid's uniform answered the door.

"We're here to see Mr. Taylor. He's expecting us," Jason remarked. Without responding the woman directed them inside the foyer with the wave of her hand. She glared at Aisha with a look of distaste.

As they followed her lead, the maid spoke for the first time. With a thick accent she said, "Have a seat in here please. Mr. Taylor will be with you momentarily." They walked into the living room that was richly painted in textured butter cream and accented with oversized printed furniture lined with traces of butter cream and splashes of red. The massive stone fireplace curved along the soaring ceilings radiating an aura of peace and tranquility. After waiting several minutes, the maid re-entered the living room with a tray of h'ordeuvres. "May I get you something to drink?"

"I'd like a shot of grey goose with cranberry juice," Jason quickly answered. He turned and looked at Aisha.

"A martini for me, please."

"I'll be back shortly with your drinks."

Aisha reached inside her handbag and pulled out her *baby girl*. After taking a snort in each nose she offered the vial to Jason.

"None for me tonight." He motioned the vial away with his hand. Aisha took another hit and immediately felt a sense of relaxation. She didn't notice the gentleman who had quietly entered the room. Kyle Taylor watched the mysterious woman put what he thought to be coke in each nostril. Her back was to him, but he could make out the side profile of her despite her flowing black twists.

"Umm," he said pretending to clear his throat. "I'm sorry to have kept you waiting." He walked further into the living room. "Hello Jason," Kyle spoke and extended his hand. He still hadn't seen the face of his private dancer just yet. When she turned and looked in his direction, he found it hard to shield the faint feeling that suddenly washed over him. *Oh my God, no. This can't be*, he thought to himself. Without hesitation he extended his hand out to hers and she released a captivating smile, not recognizing the well disguised Chandler Larson.

"Hello, I'm Kyle."

"It's nice to meet you Kyle. I'm Luscious." He hoped she couldn't see him reeling with disbelief. The undercover cop disguised as the Asian maid walked in with their drinks. The minor distraction gave Chandler time to refocus on his assignment. Aisha and Jason took their drinks.

"Mr. Taylor, unless you need something else, I'm going to leave now. I'll return for Luscious when I receive your call."

"That's fine.. I'll talk to you later." He turned to the maid and asked her to escort Jason to the door.

"Luscious, ahhh. What a lovely name," Kyle managed to say.

As they continued to make idle chatter, he realized she had no idea who he was, which was a good thing for him. He didn't want his cover blown when he was so close to unveiling the inside operations going on at The Lynx. He knew that Jason and Elisa were the two who worked directly for the illusive mastermind behind the whole trafficking operations at The Lynx. But what part did Aisha play in this sordid game? Did she know what she was involved in and who she was involved with? He thought he knew her so well. Though they hadn't been completely intimate with each other, he had already been hypnotized by her beauty and charm. How could she have deceived him like she had? From all indications, she had fooled him into believing she was a good girl who loved God. But looking at her tempting attire and remembering her lies about her second job, he couldn't fathom her being a part of anybody's church or religion. He began to second guess everything she had told him. And to add insult to injury she had pretended like she was so shy and reserved. He thought of Tracye and her betrayal. At that moment he loathed the very sight of Aisha. Instead of striking her like he so wanted to do, he reached for her hand and stood up. "Come with me," he commanded.

Aisha stood up and allowed him to take her hand inside his own. He led her into the master suite. She walked inside the mammoth bedroom. Lights were dimmed and seductive music played softly on the surround sound system. He strolled over to the taupe wraparound chaise and sat down. He stared at her with lust and became aroused at the very sight of her presence.

Aisha began to sway seductively back and forth, becoming one with the music. She knew what her clients liked and she had no problem giving them what they wanted. Thoughts of her father, friends and of course God were replaced with what she was doing at this very moment. She flung her head back and the locks of her hair blanketed over past the back of her shoulders. With each pulsating beat of the music, she moved rhythmically, masterfully luring Kyle in to her web of femininity. As if reading his mind, she moved in closer to him. The scent of her cologne wafted underneath his nostrils, sending him into a world where he was Kyle Taylor, a wealthy executive with an insatiable sexual desire. For the next few minutes, he totally forgot that the woman dancing before him, enticing him, luring him was Aisha.

Aisha danced several more dances for her client. She couldn't help but think about how handsome he was. He reminded her of someone but she couldn't put her finger on whom. Lost in her thoughts, she barely realized when he reached out and grabbed her around her waist and pulled her down on the chaise next to him. His breathing was heavy. She could actually smell the faint scent of liquor on his breath. She had never allowed a client to get this close and personal with her but something about him ignited a flame within her. She allowed him to kiss her without any resistance. He sucked in her breath as if it was part of his own. His kisses engulfed her and he became rough and more demanding. His hands briskly explored her thin body. When she heard his heavy breathing and felt his hands go places she'd never let any man visit, she yanked away from his tight grasp.

Her heart pounding and flesh tingling, Aisha pushed herself away from him. "Hold on, Kyle. This is not what I'm about. You're, you're out of line," she said, finally mustering up enough control over her body and emotions.

The sound of her voice awoke him from his lust filled state of mind. He sat upright on the chaise, pressing the wrinkles out of his shirt with his sweaty hands. Though he was physically attracted to her, at the same time he was sickened at the thought of her profession. Whatever he once hoped and thought they could have together was gone. It took every fiber of his being not to do to her what he'd been forced to do to Tracye. The longer he looked at her, the more infuriated he became. He abruptly stood up and looked down on her. Fear rose in the base of Aisha's throat. *What's going on inside his mind?* she thought. *I hope he understands that when a woman says no, she means no. He's fine as all get out, but I'm not going to give up my virginity unless it's my choice, certainly not by force. And there's not enough money he can pay to make me either.* Her eyes revealed her fear. Fear he'd seen in the face of his ex-fiancé that fateful day. And just like with Tracye, seeing Aisha's fear was Chandler's pleasure.

"You really don't know do you?" He asked her in a rough voice.

"Know what. What are you talking about?"

He grabbed hold of her wrist and squeezed it tightly. Aisha winced and tried to break loose from him. He loosened his grip only after he remembered that the undercover maid was in the house. "Call your ride and tell him I'm finished with you," he ordered and stormed out of the bedroom. He turned and took one last look at her and said, "Get out of my house now. Go wait for your ride outside. You're no better than the rest. A two bit…" He stopped in mid-sentence. He huffed and the feeling he had for her was swallowed up in the thought of how he had been deceived yet again. Thoughts of Tracye's betrayal flooded his mind. He was fast approaching the breaking point of self-control. There was no telling what he would do if she didn't leave his house pronto. "Get out," he roared.

Aisha moved away from the chaise and dashed madly out of the house. She felt the wind of the door close behind her. Calling Jason on her cell she told him to come and get her. Out of all the clients she'd entertained, she'd never been so humiliated and treated so disrespectfully as she had just been treated by Kyle Taylor. The limo finally pulled up some twenty five minutes later she jumped in it before it came to a full stop.

"What happened?" Jason asked her, obviously furious at the thought that Aisha had somehow displeased Kyle. "What did you do?"

"What did I do? Aren't you going to ask me why I'm standing outside? Aren't you going to ask me if I'm okay?"

"Don't tell me you acted like some uptight religious prude. Don't even go there. Because if you did, you're going to pay dearly." Jason said furiously. "Now tell me what happened."

"Why don't you go and ask that fool inside. I guess he thought he had himself more than a private dancer tonight. But baby I'm not the one and I've told you that before." Aisha screamed and climbed inside the limo. She slammed the door before Jason had a chance to say another word. Jason went inside and talked to Kyle. After waiting in the limo impatiently for him to return, Aisha was fuming. She watched as Kyle stood in the doorway while Jason exited the house.

Instead of Jason taking her side, he chose to totally ignore her. On the way back to The Lynx he refused to say anything to her. She suddenly became sick of the whole thing with The Lynx. For the first time she understood that Kyle, Jason and any of the rest of them, didn't care the least bit about her or her wellbeing. They were all about self-gratification.

God, I'm tired of this, she prayed within. I'm sick of living a lie. I've gotten myself in way too deep and I don't know how to get out of it. When the limo pulled up in front of The Lynx, Jason hopped out of it so fast it was like a whirlwind had come and swooped him up. Aisha grabbed her purse and yelled at him.

"You wait just a minute," she yelled. "I don't know what just happened back there and why you have a major attitude with me But I did what you wanted me to do so give me my money and I'll be out of here," she said in a raised voice.

"Every penny you deserve is in the limo," Jason grumbled and walked inside The Lynx.

Aisha whirled around and opened the door to the limo. A brown envelope was lying on the seat next to where Jason had been sitting moments before. The driver sat motionless as if nothing had occurred. Aisha opened the envelope and counted thirty, one dollar bills instead of the thirty, one hundred dollar bills she was supposed to have been paid. Slamming the door with all of her force, she mouthed a string of expletives while each step led her closer to the main entrance of The Lynx. Just as she was about to open the door, she stopped and then turned around. She was no match against Jason or anyone else inside The Lynx. And if she had gone inside, she would be stepping into God knows what. She went straight to her car, jumped in and sped off.

As she neared her apartment, her cell phone rang. She looked down and saw an unfamiliar number. "Hello. Helloooo," she said again but no one answered. She glanced at the caller ID but it all it showed was an unfamiliar number. "Look I don't have time for games. If this is you Kyle, you know where you can go." she yelled and hung up the phone. It was almost three o'clock in the morning and she needed to change and get back to the hospital. She thought about calling Elisa to tell her what had happened but decided to wait until later in the morning. Her cell rang again. "Hello," she screamed. The whimpering sound over the phone reminded her of a crying baby. "Who is this?" "Aisha."

Aisha pulled over on the shoulder of the road and screamed. She didn't need to hear anything else her mother had to say. The sound of her mother's grief stricken voice on the other end told her everything she dreaded to hear. Her father was dead.

When she arrived at the hospital and saw her father's lifeless body lying in the bed, she wanted to be the one lying there instead of him. Her mother watched her with rage as she entered the hospital room.

Without warning, Sandra Carlisle bolted out with a tirade of seething anger. "Get out of here, get out of here now. You're too late!" Nurses in the room tried to calm her down but she was out of control. The words spewing from her mouth dripped vile and vicious accusations against her only daughter. Aisha's tears erupted like a volcano. She placed her hands over her ears to drown out the condemning words coming from her mother. She hated the words her mother spewed against her. But within Aisha believed every word her mother said.

"You are so selfish. You always have been selfish," her mother said pointing at her and reaching towards her like she wanted to tear Aisha apart. "He was asking for you, Aisha. He took his last breath with your name on his lips. You were always his favorite. I had to compete with you. Selena had to compete with you. But you always won. Didn't you?. And in the end, you were the one who let him down!"

"Momma, please, please," Aisha begged mercifully. "Please don't say that. I don't know what I'm going to do without my daddy. Mother," she kept repeating. A male nurse entered the room and led Sandra Carlisle away. The doctor ordered a sedative for her and then returned to check on Aisha. Aisha stood in the room frozen, watching as they prepared to take her father to the morgue. She held on to the side of the bedrails screaming.

One of the nurses told Tameria what was going on. She and Chase rushed to CCU. The sight of Aisha ripped at Tameria's heart and she couldn't control her own tears of pain. She ran up to Aisha to try to settle her down but there was no consoling her.

"Aisha, come on honey. Come on now," Tameria repeated while she and Chase led her out the room.

"Noooo, Tameria. I can't leave my daddy. I can't."

"Shhh, it's going to be okay." Tameria cried. "It's going to be okay." Tameria leaned over to tell Chase that she was going to take Aisha home as soon as her shift ended in about half an hour. "Aisha, come on, I want you to lie down for a while. I'm going to take you home in just a few minutes, okay?" One of the resident doctors approached Tameria and told her that he would work the remainder of her shift so she was free to leave. Chase gave Aisha a sedative before he took her downstairs to Tameria's car.

"Where's Mrs. Carlisle?" Tameria asked one of the nurses. "The wife of the deceased patient?"

"She's down the hall. We had to administer a tranquilizer. She was inconsolable. Some people are here from the CCU waiting room area. I think they're friends or church members. They said they would make sure she gets home or she'll spend the night with some of them."

"Okay, that's good. I'm going to go and check on her. Then I'm leaving to take Aisha home." Tameria was relieved to walk in the room and see the faces of several of Mr. and Mrs. Carlisle's friends and church members She walked over and hugged the distraught woman and kissed her on the cheek. "Momma Carlisle, I'm so sorry." Tameria hugged her again. "I'll call and check on you a little later. I'm going to take Aisha home, okay? If you need anything, you just call me or my mom and dad. You know we'll be here for you."

"I don't have a daughter anymore, Tameria. I don't." A man dressed in a dark suit with a white Nehru collared shirt approached Sandra and Tameria. Tameria assumed it was the minister from Mr. and Mrs. Carlisle's church. Kneeling beside the grieving widow, he took her shaking hands inside of his, then looked over and nodded at Tameria.

"Sister Carlisle, everything is going to be all right. Brother Carlisle is resting in the bosom of Abraham. He's with God now. One day you're going to see him again." Sandra fell against his chest. This time quiet tears of pain trickled from her eyes.

27

One deceit needs many others, and so the whole house is built in the air and must soon come to the ground.
Baltasar Gracian

For the fifth day in a row, Chandler's cell phone had gone straight to voice mail. Aisha hadn't heard from him since the night her father died. She scrolled through her caller ID on both of her phones but Chandler hadn't called. The last time they'd seen each other, things were great. She reminisced about the kindness and compassionate he'd shown when he came to the hospital to sit with her. What could have happened? She hoped he was all right. She became agitated and worried. It wasn't like Chandler not to call. Was he sick? Maybe he had gone out of town and forgot to mention it to her. Picking up her purse and her cranberry parka, she stepped outside and met a zesty breeze. Pulling her parka in closer, she jogged the short distance to her car. She tried Chandler's number for the umpteenth time while she waited on the car to warm up. She'd left a message on his phone telling him that her father had died but he hadn't shown up at the funeral nor had he sent any flowers. Not even a card. That further indicated to Aisha that something was terribly wrong. She'd driven over to his apartment a couple of times but his car wasn't there either time. The only thing left for her to do was to go back over to his apartment and knock this time. She hated it when people

came to her apartment unannounced. But she felt she had
no other choice.

Turning down Ross Avenue, she drove the next few
blocks with the radio playing a rap song by Kanye West.
There was a time not long ago when you couldn't pay her
a million dollars to listen to rap, but here she was now,
moving in rhythm to the beats.

She pulled up in front of his apartment and searched
around to see if his car was in view before she stepped
out of the car. There was a car parked a few spaces away
from his apartment that looked similar to his but she
couldn't be sure that it was. She went upstairs and
knocked on the door of apartment 104. After knocking on
the door several times she finally gave up and left.

Chandler peeked through the side blind and watched
Aisha as she returned to her car. He just couldn't stomach
her right now. Everything about her had been based on a
bold faced lie and at that moment he felt nothing but
disgust towards her. How could she be involved with
drugs and the trafficking of young girls? How could she
live her life knowing that men were raping and abusing
these girls? Girls whose parents were probably at home
crying their hearts out because they didn't know what
happened to their daughters. How could she? He became
even more determined to shut The Lynx Association
down. And women like Aisha could burn in hell for all he
cared. Soon everything was about to come to an end
anyway. He had managed to gain young Hallie's trust.
She had told him everything she knew about The Lynx
including the name of the owner, Ronald Shipley. When
Chandler first heard the name it hadn't meant anything to
him. It was just another name. But after further
investigation and background checks he quickly surmised
that busting The Lynx was going to make national news
when it was revealed that Ronald Shipley was the

fraternal twin brother of none other than the renowned Donald Shipley, Senior Pastor of Greater Faith Community Church.

Hallie told Chandler that at least once every couple of months that Daddy-O, the name they were forced to call Ronald Shipley, sent Elisa and Jason to different cities to bring in new girls. The members of The Lynx provided funding for these excursions, as Hallie had heard them call the mysterious trips. She didn't see Daddy-O very often and she was lucky for that, she told Chandler. Daddy-O could be quite brutal and sadistic. Not to be called to his private suite was a blessing to Hallie.

Over the course of his undercover investigation Chandler arranged with Jason for Hallie to come to his room on a regular basis. He informed Jason that he wanted exclusive rights to the girl. Of course Jason was glad to oblige. Chandler made sure whenever she came to his suite that she relaxed, watched TV and ate. He allowed her to be the young girl that she was. For a short time she didn't have to think about the hell hole she was being held in against her will. Chandler promised Hallie that he would get her out of The Lynx and back to her mother and sisters. He was going to make sure her father was prosecuted to the fullest extent for selling his own daughter.

Hallie had managed to find out more than Chandler could have hoped. His investigation had netted him enough evidence on Shipley, Jason and Elisa to put them away for years. But Hallie pleaded with him to let Elisa go. She told him that Elisa was the one who looked out for the young girls and tried to make sure they were taken care of. But Kyle made her understand that Elisa was in this for her own selfish reasons and keeping the girls safe wasn't one of those reasons. He further explained to the girl that if Elisa really was on their side, then she would never have been part of manipulating and kidnapping innocent girls and bringing them to The Lynx in the first place. Hallie's green eyes grew large like Rockwell figurines. Tears formed in each corner when she realized that Elisa was going down with the rest of them. As for Aisha, it appeared that she just so happened to be naïve and stupid. Chandler didn't think she realized what kind of mess she was in by being linked to The Lynx, but she was about to find out. He was definitely going to see to that. But first he had to cut all ties with her as Chandler Larson. He couldn't and wouldn't take any chances of his cover being blown.

It was a total surprise to him when she came to his apartment unannounced. He never would have known had he not decided to stop by just to check up on things. A prick of sympathy had tugged at his heart when one of her voice messages told him about her father's death. But Chandler's sympathy didn't last for long. He remembered saying to himself before erasing the call, *what goes around comes around, Aisha Carlisle*

Peeking out of the window one last time to make sure Aisha had left, he shuffled back to his bedroom to relax for a couple of more hours until it was time to become Kyle Taylor yet again.

28

Everyone can master a grief but he that has it.
William Shakespeare

Ever since her father's death three and a half weeks ago, Aisha had retreated into an impenetrable shell. She hadn't been to her dance studio or The Lynx. She refused to answer her phone calls or listen to messages. Not even the sound of Elisa and Jason pressing down on her doorbell day after day could bring her from her self-induced reclusiveness. Only Tameria was able to get in the apartment and that's because the two of them kept a key to each other's apartments for emergencies.

When Tameria arrived she moved slowly around Aisha's apartment. Garbage overflowed from the trash can. The bathroom had a stench that had begun to permeate out in the hallway. The bedroom made Tameria think of a militarized war zone.

Aisha was sprawled across the bed with her head face down and her arms dangling over the side.

"Aisha, come on girl, get up. You need to take a shower or a bath. It'll make you feel better. Please don't make me call Chase to help get you in the tub," Tameria threatened her. To Aisha, the words coming from Tameria sounded like the glob, glob, glob of the character Charlie Brown's parents.

Aisha's mother hadn't talked to her since the funeral. She was swallowed up in her own grief and still blamed Aisha for not being at her father's side when he died. She believed Aisha had put her mysterious part time job before everything, including her dying father and she refused to have anything to say or do with her daughter. One week after her husband died, Sandra packed her bags, closed up the house and moved back to her home town of Little Rock, Arkansas. She wanted to be as far away as she could from the painful memories, not to mention the daughter she believed had betrayed Benjamin.

After much poking and prodding, Tameria managed to convince Aisha to take a hot shower. While Aisha was in the bathroom, Tameria started to clean up her room. She started by pulling the dingy covers from Aisha's bed. Her eyes became glued to the brown glass vial lying underneath Aisha's pillow. She looked over her shoulder to see if there was any sign of Aisha before she opened the vial and poured out a tiny portion of the white powder. After placing some of it on her tongue, within seconds the tip of her tongue started to become numb. *Oh my God, no, not Aisha*, she whispered to herself when her suspicions were confirmed. *No wonder she's lost so much weight and barely eats. She's using drugs*. Tameria fell back on the bed and silent tears fell from her eyes. She hurt at the thought of what Aisha had gotten herself involved in. Losing her father had been tough on Aisha. The two of them had been thick as thieves. But why had she turned to drugs? Tameria couldn't understand any part of this whole nightmare she'd stumbled on to. Aisha had always been the strong minded one. Her Christian convictions were rigid and she used to put nothing before God. But Tameria began to look back over the past few months. There had been a serious change in Aisha. They used to talk all the time but when Aisha had to get another job their conversations became sparse and with Tameria's medical rotations, the two of them just couldn't spend time together like they used to. The first time Tameria had noticed a physical change in Aisha was when she came to the emergency room to see her father. Aisha looked like a ebony version of Olive Oil. But she didn't want to believe that Aisha could be on drugs. Now she was faced with the truth. Things were worse than she had imagined. Tameria went to the door of the bathroom and knocked lightly.

"Aisha, are you okay in there?" she asked in a soft like whisper.

"Yes, I'm fine. I'll be out in a minute."

Tameria finished cleaning Aisha's bedroom. When Aisha came out of the bathroom, Tameria was seated in the wingback chair next to Aisha's bedroom window.

"You want some soup or something?"

"No, I'm not hungry. Tameria?"

"Yes?"

"Thanks for coming over here and being the friend that you are. I feel like my whole life has spun out of control. The funny thing is, I don't remember how it happened."

"Why didn't you tell me you were in trouble?"

In a sarcastic voice, Aisha responded, "I'm not in trouble. Unless being in trouble means missing my father and feeling guilty for not being there when he died. Or maybe you're talking about the fact that my mother hates me now and I feel so alone. I can't even pray right now, Tameria." Aisha started to cry, something she hadn't done since the day they buried her father. She felt like she didn't deserve to shed tears of grief because she had let her father down.

"I'm talking about this." Tameria held up the vial. "Why didn't you tell me you were on drugs? Why?" Tameria pleaded.

A stunned look spread over Aisha's face.

"Who are you supposed to be? Some private eye. You had no right to search through my things. No right at all," Aisha screamed.

"No, see that's where you're wrong. I have every right. I'm your best friend. You can try to avoid the issue if you want to. You can try to blame me for being a snoop. Whatever you want to say is fine, but when you get finished I still want to know how you, of all people, Aisha, could do something like this.

Aisha felt like nothing. Tameria had always admired her, looked up to her and respected her for her Christian values. Now here she was standing before Tameria feeling like the lowest of the low. *Is this what hitting rock bottom means?* She questioned herself.

The anger in Aisha's voice turned to a shallow whisper. "I, I didn't know how to tell you. It happened so fast. I went from abhorring the very thought of drugs to needing a hit every day all day. I can't explain it. It, it just happened. That's all I know to say."

"Well, that's not good enough. I'm sorry if I sound harsh. But I won't let you give me some half-ass excuse. I can't. When was the last time you really looked in the mirror? You look like a walking skeleton. I thought it was because you were stressed about the studio. Since you eat like a rabbit anyway, I didn't think too much of it when I saw you at the hospital. But drugs? Oh my God. Talk to me. Tell me if any of this has to do with this part time job you have. Because it seems like that's when you began to change."

Aisha paused, thinking about whether she should confide in Tameria. There was nothing the two of them hadn't been able to share. But this time things were different. They were both adults now and some things, no matter how close you were to someone, just couldn't be shared. She looked at Tameria again. Tameria's gaze remained fixed on her.

"I'm waiting," Tameria spoke up and said in a hurtful voice.

"All I can tell you is that I'm in way over my head. You know I needed money desperately to keep my studio going."

"Go on," Tameria encouraged her.

"I couldn't let the studio go under. If I lost that building, you and I both know it wouldn't have been long before everything would have started to fall apart. I couldn't allow that to happen."

"What happened to having faith and trusting God, Aisha? All the things you used to tell me about? When that man first told you about buying the building you really didn't seek God's will about it. You know that and I know that. Instead, you panicked and started making things work the way you thought they should work."

Aisha didn't open her mouth.

"Remember, when my parents wanted me to become a teacher because the both of them were teachers? What did you tell me Aisha?"

Aisha didn't budge from her spot on the bed. Her wet body was still wrapped in her bath towel. The natural air in the room slowly dried her. "That was different," Aisha said under her breath.

"No, that's where you're wrong. Because it wasn't different. You told me to pray and seek God's will and purpose for my life. You reminded me that all of my young life I had believed that it was God's will for me to be a doctor. You told me that I had to do what God wanted me to do and become what God ordained me to become. You prayed for me and with me Aisha. You prayed for my parents and for my future. And God showed me and them what He wanted for me when I got a full four year scholarship to attend college. Then remember when I got a stipend for room, board, books, meals and transportation when I entered medical school? All because I sought God and waited for Him to do what He willed in my life." Crocodile tears streamed from Tameria's eyes with each word she spoke. "Aisha, I don't know what you've gotten yourself involved in and honestly I don't care. But what I do care about is you finding your way back to God, back to the only one who can deliver you from this evil." Tameria held up the vial again in front of Aisha. "He's the only way and you know it."

"But I feel so foolish. I feel dirty and disgusting. You don't know the half of what's been going on in my life these last few months."

"Then tell me. I'm listening."

"When I found out about the building going up for sale, I told the parents of my students that I was going to increase my fees." Aisha wiped tears away from her eyes.

"Keep talking," Tameria insisted.

"At the Mayor's charity ball, one of my student's mother told me about a job that would pay me a lot of money in a short amount of time. I know. You don't have to say it. I should have known then that it wasn't something that was in my best interest. But I listened to her proposition anyway. I was in a state of panic because I didn't want to have to tell my students that the dance studio would have to close. So when she..."

"Wait, wait right there. Who is this she that you're talking about?"

"Elisa Santana."

"Gabby's mother?"

"Yes. Gabby's mother."

"But isn't she a stripper?"

"She's an exotic dancer. There's a difference."

"I don't know who you think you're talking to. But you know and I know that's just a fancy name for stripping. But anyway, keep talking. I'm listening."

"I know you're probably going to think badly of me. But at the time, I thought I could do it for just a few weeks, get the rest of the money I needed to buy the building and that would be the end of it."

"Are you telling me that you're a stripper?" Tameria tried to hide the deep disappointment she felt. She didn't want to pass judgment on Aisha, but at the same time she couldn't believe that Aisha could stoop so low as to defile her body by displaying it to God knows who.

"Not a stripper, Tameria. I'm a private dancer. I dance for wealthy clients at a private men's association."

"Please tell me I'm not hearing this. Please, Aisha. Tell me this isn't true."

"Believe me. I wish I could. But I can't. That's where I was the night Daddy died. Elisa called and told me a huge bonus was in it for me if I could dance for one of the new members of the association. So I told her I would do it. I left the hospital, went to the association and got dressed. I had only planned to be away from the hospital for a couple of hours. My employer took me to the client's house. I started dancing for him but he wanted more and I wasn't about to give him what he wanted.

"You mean he wanted to have sex with you?"

"Yes. But believe me, Tameria, I have never given my virginity to anyone. I made that vow to God and to you. I would never give my body to anyone but my husband. You know that."

"Do you know how ridiculous you sound?" Tameria rose from the chair and walked toward Aisha. Her voice escalated and she pointed her fingers in anger at Aisha. "Well, let me tell you how you sound. You sound like a fool, a hypocrite Aisha." Tameria shouted. "On one hand you're telling me that you haven't given your body to any of these tricks. And yes I said tricks because that's what these men are. And you may as well have given it to them because you had them lusting over you Aisha. Maybe you didn't go all the way, but you still gave your body to who knows how many men, just in a different kind of way. Now you want to sit here and sound all sorry and pitiful and try to make me believe that you're still little miss church lady? Well, I don't think so."

Aisha's face had turned beet red. She'd never seen Tameria so angry. Not in all the years of their friendship had Tameria lashed out at her like she was doing now. But Tameria was right. How could she even try to justify her actions?

"I'm so sorry. I really am. But think of how I feel about myself now. I not only gave in to something that was totally against my Christian morals but I succumbed to using drugs. The first night I was supposed to dance I was so uptight, so afraid Tameria. Elisa offered me a valium to relax my nerves and that was the beginning of my addiction. I went from using valium to cocaine. Little by little I began to want *baby girl* more and more." Aisha cried and looked at the vial of cocaine.

Tameria held the vial up in front of Aisha's nose. "*Baby girl*?" Is that what you call this stuff?

"Yes." Aisha hung her head down and turned away. "I can't do this anymore,. I've said too much already. Please, just go. I have to be alone right now."

Tameria hated to admit it, but she was glad Aisha wanted her to leave. She couldn't digest all of what Aisha had just confessed to her. She needed time away from her to think and pray about the things Aisha had confessed. Tameria drew in a deep breath before she spoke again. Maybe she had been too harsh. Aisha was human. She was subject to the same mistakes as anybody else. Tameria thought about the sin she'd committed with Chase that she hadn't told Aisha about. Only God, Chase and she knew that she was no longer a virgin. So how could she condemn Aisha? Aisha got up from the side of the bed and began walking toward the hallway. She wanted Tameria to leave right away. The shame she felt was too great.

"Sure, I'll leave. But before I go, let me say this. I know I sound like I'm condemning you for the choices you've made. And I'm sorry for that. Regardless of what you've done, you're still my best friend and when you hurt, I hurt. I love you. I just wish I could have been there for you and that you would have come to me before things escalated out of control the way they did. But just like you've always told me, God forgives. When He died, He died for our past sins, the sins we commit now and the sins we will commit in the future. We will sin every day of our lives for the rest of our lives, so please, please don't sit in this apartment and beat up on yourself, Aisha. God doesn't condemn us, so don't condemn yourself. Maybe you should get some counseling." Tameria hugged her before she turned to leave.

♦

Bright and early the next morning, the piercing sun poked through Aisha's window shades. She rose up and sat upright in the bed and began to pray.

"Lord, please forgive me. I need your help. I can't fight this battle by myself any longer." When she finished a calm peace had filled her body. For the first time in months she felt a heaviness leaving her. She climbed out of bed, took a bubble bath and prepared herself for the eleven o'clock church service. It had been weeks since she'd graced the doors of Greater Faith but she was determined to go, no matter what kind of thoughts were going through her mind. She leafed through her walk-in closet. After several minutes, she settled on wearing a dusty rose cascading dress and a pair of black Astor pumps. After finishing up with light touches of makeup, she grabbed her cell phone and purse then set out to church.

Her cell phone rang minutes before she turned down Elvis Presley Boulevard. This time she decided to answer when she heard Elisa's ring tone. "Hello, Elisa" she said in a voice that lacked enthusiasm.

"I can't believe you finally decided to answer the phone. I've been worried sick about you. How are you? I've called the studio and Angie wouldn't give me any information. She just said you were taking some time off because of your father's death."

"No need to worry Elisa. I'm fine. I just need some time alone, that's all."

"I understand. And I feel really bad about your father, Aisha." Elisa sounded genuine and Aisha accepted her sentiments.

"Thanks. And look, I know you and Jason have been calling and leaving messages, but I just haven't been able to talk to anyone."

"I understand. Believe me I do. I just wanted to hear your voice and believe it or not, Jason is concerned about you too. He really is. We've been by your apartment several times as well."

"Like I said, I'm sorry. Look, I'm about to turn into the church parking lot so I have to go right now. I'll call you in a day or two. You take care Elisa."

"Sure, I will. Bye now.

"Oh, wait, Elisa."

"What is it?"

"How is Gabby?" She's fine. She asks about you all the time. I don't know if you know it or not, but the studio isn't holding many classes since you took time off."

"Yes, I know. Anyway, I'm thinking about closing it for a while. I need time to get my own life in order. You know what I mean?"

"I think I do. But you go on in church. Say a prayer for me, okay?"

"Yeah, I'll do that. I just hope God still wants to hear from me," Aisha said with a grim look and squeezed in a parking space.

29

It's so much darker when a light goes out than it would have been if it had never shone. John Steinbeck

Aisha shuffled inside Greater Faith Community Church with the rest of the crowd. The church was filled to overflowing and this was the third service of the morning. She scanned over the crowd for familiar faces. Several members spoke to her as she made her way down to the middle section of the church.

"Girl, where have you been lately?" asked a woman named Paulette who Aisha used to sit next to at the nine o'clock service. Aisha turned, looked at her and smiled. "I've been working a second job. How have you been?"

"Oh fine. I can't complain. Like they say, it won't do any good anyway."

"I know that's right," Aisha agreed.

"Do you still have your dance studio?"

"Well, yes and no. I mean right now I've closed it for a while. Since my father passed, I just haven't been in the frame of mind to do too much of anything."

"Oh, that's right. I heard that Mr. Carlisle passed. I'm sorry about that," Paulette said and laid her hand over Aisha's in a sympathetic gesture before leaving. "It's good to see you Aisha. You take care of yourself and remember that nothing is too hard for God."

"Sure will, see you, Paulette." Aisha hoped that no one else would say anything to her. She wanted the service to start to avoid any more such uncomfortable encounters. When she was active in church, she had done the same thing Paulette did when she ran into someone she hadn't seen at church for a while. Now she knew how those people felt and decided that if that ever happened again, she would just say hello and keep on stepping. She skimmed through the church bulletin at the order of service and the weekly announcements.

The sound of a man's voice interrupted her reading by calling her name, "Aisha, Aisha Carlisle is that you?" Aisha jerked her head up to meet the sound of the gentleman's voice. She barely recognized him. It had been several years since she'd seen Leland Parker. After graduating from high school he had joined the Peace Corps and that was the last she'd seen or heard from him. It wasn't like they were ever close friends but like Paulette they had been members of Greater Faith since they were youngsters. They used to be active in youth functions around the church and participated in almost everything that had to do with the youth. But when they became adults, they went their separate ways.

"Leland, right?"

"Yeah, in the flesh," he grinned and his glistening uneven teeth seemed to sparkle. He sat down next to her and immediately began talking. "How've you been?"

"Pretty good. Are you still in the Peace Corps?"

"No. I've finished with that. I just made it home a few months ago. , What are you up to these days?"

"I own a dance studio in South Memphis," she remarked without much excitement.

"Wow that sounds great. How's your friend, Tameria? You two still thick as thieves?"

"Yeah, we are. She's doing fine. She's in her second year of medical residency."

"Gosh, I sure would like to see her. You know I always had a crush on her," he added. "I haven't seen her at church since I returned but of course I guess with the growth of this church, it's easy to do. Like you for instance, I've been here every Sunday and Wednesday evening since I made it back to town but this is the first time I've run into you."

Aisha was getting bored with Leland's conversation. She looked at her watch to see how much longer it would be before the service started. Leland must have taken a hint because he stood up and said, "Look I'm going to move up closer. I usually don't sit this far back."

"Sure, Leland. It was really good to see you again." To erase some of the guilt she felt for brushing him off she said, "Like you said, since the church is so big we don't get a chance to see each other as often as we used to and then we have three services on top of that. But I'm really glad you're home."

"Thanks, and remember to tell Tameria I asked about her." He turned and walked down the aisle until he made it to the second row.

Aisha's eyes focused on the handsome man walking up the steps leading to the pulpit. She hadn't seen him before but ministers joined Greater Faith regularly so she wasn't surprised. She listened intently at him when he stood at the pulpit and began to speak.

"Good morning," his voice boomed throughout the sanctuary. "I said good morning. It's good to be in the house of the Lord." The congregation responded with rounds of praise and waving of hands. Aisha studied the gentleman who spoke so articulately. He was attractive, spoke like he was highly educated and he moved with an aura of self-confidence. He moved slowly back and forth across the podium as he led the congregation in praise and worship. Not only was his voice magnetizing, his swagger added a slice of charm that sucked her in like a vacuum. When he started singing, *Lord we lift your name on high*, Aisha couldn't resist the urge to stand up along with the rest of the congregation and sing. When the people standing on both sides of her raised their hands in praise, Aisha felt unworthy. On one hand she wanted to clap and wave her hands too. But the other voice in her head told her she was nothing more than a hypocrite, one of those folks Jesus talked about in the Bible who shout Lord, Lord, but they're none of His true children. She used to believe that she couldn't lose her salvation. That's what she'd been taught since she was a small child in Sunday School. But now she wasn't so sure anymore. She'd betrayed God and she couldn't see how he could ever forgive her for turning her back on Him. She continued to stand and sing, *You came from heaven to earth, to show the way…* When he raised his hands for the musicians and congregation to stop singing, he said a short prayer and motioned for everyone to be seated.

"Who is he?" Aisha couldn't resist asking the lady sitting to the right of her.

"Are you talking about the minister?"

"Oh. Yes, I'm sorry."

"He's one of the associate ministers. He's been here for about a month. We love him," she whispered.

"What's his name?" Aisha asked leaning in closer to the woman so as not to disturb anyone.

The lady responded in a friendly voice, "Minister Jackson Williams. He's over Pastoral Care. He does counseling too."

"Thanks." Aisha sat upright and listened to the choir sing. By the time Pastor Shipley made it to the podium to deliver his sermon, Aisha was ready to receive his message.

◆

"That was a powerful message wasn't it?" the woman who she talked to earlier remarked.

Aisha's response was, "Yes it was. But Pastor's messages are always prolific. And I needed to hear it too."

"I did too. Well I guess I'll get out of here. It was nice talking to you. You have a blessed day."

"You too," Aisha said and walked down the corridor in the opposite direction of the woman. She weaved through the crowd that had formed a line for tapes of today's sermon. She paused and contemplated whether or not she wanted to purchase a copy. Turning around, she walked until she reached the end of the line.

When she made it outside with her tape in tow, the departing crowd had thinned out.

"Oh, excuse me," the mild mannered voice said when she accidentally brushed against Aisha causing her to drop her purse. "I'm so sorry," she apologized again.

"No problem," Aisha stooped down and picked up her purse. She didn't know what to do when she stood upright and saw the man standing next to the woman.

"Hi," Aisha said trying to shield her surprise at seeing Chandler. The attractive woman looked confused.

"You two know each other?" she asked Chandler and glanced at each of them.

"Why, uh yes." he stumbled over his words. "We used to…"

"Work together," Aisha quickly added before Chandler could say anything else.

"Oh, are you a policeman too?"

"Policeman?" Aisha was totally baffled. She eyed Chandler curiously.

The woman waited anxiously for a response. She had a feeling that these two had done more than work together. She'd been dating Chandler for several weeks but he told her it had been quite some time since he was seriously involved with anyone. If that was the case then why were they acting so suspicious? She folded her arms and looked at Chandler.

Aisha spoke up. "No, I'm not a policeman. We worked together a long time ago when we were younger," she lied.

"Are you a member here?"

Aisha replied, "Yes, I am. What about you?"

"No, we're just visiting but I really enjoyed the sermon."

"Well look it was nice seeing you again Chandler but I'd better go. I have to be somewhere shortly. It was nice meeting you. Uh what did you say your name was?"

"I didn't say. But it's Candyce."

"Okay, Candyce. Bye, Chandler."

"Goodbye, Aisha," he said coldly.

A policeman? Aisha's thoughts were scrambling together as she repeated the word policeman over and over in her mind. *Someone is definitely lying,* she told herself as she made her way to the car. *Chandler said he was a land developer. And if he isn't a land developer what could have been his reason for lying to me about his profession?* When she got in the car, she dialed his cell phone. *Let's see if he's going to pick up this time. He can't hide any longer.* She pushed the number four and the phone dialed Chandler's number. After three rings, the mechanical voice answered and said, "The subscriber you're trying to reach is no longer available." She looked down at her phone and saw his name on her screen so she knew she hadn't dialed someone else's number. She dialed the number a second time instead of pushing speed dial. The same recording came on. *He must've changed his number.* She started her car and pulled off. She watched as Candyce and Chandler got inside a champagne colored Nissan Altima. *Unless he has a new car, that must be her car, Aisha surmised.*

On first thought, she wanted to follow them but if he really was a policeman, she didn't want to get caught up in any mess. She dialed Tameria's number.

"Hey, how are you?"

"I'm okay. I'm just leaving church."

"That's good to hear. How was service today?"

"Actually it was good. Remember Leland Parker?"

"Yeah, is he back in town?"

"Yeah, and still boring as ever. But he looks good. He still has that crush on you. He wanted me to tell you he said hello." Aisha managed to smile.

"Puhleeze. You should have told him I was already taken. What did Pastor preach about?"

"Something I guess I needed to hear. Accepting yourself as you are instead of trying to live your life for others. He said we should stop being something other than what God has purposed us to be."

"I think we all need to be reminded of that from time to time." Tameria responded. "Look, I'm at the hospital so I'm going to have to hang up in a second."

"No problem. I was just calling to let you know that I took your advice and went to church. I didn't know we had a new minister over Pastoral Care."

"I didn't know that either. That's one reason I really miss church. I'm losing out on what's going on by having to do these long rotations. But listen, I'll call you later tonight when I get a break. That is if it's not too late. Hang in there."

"Yeah, I will. Bye Tameria."

Tameria was elated when Aisha told her she'd gone to church. Maybe Aisha would get herself together. And the first step she needed to take was turning back to God. She'd been praying for her and Mrs. Carlisle. The next thing was to convince Aisha to take her suggestion and get some counseling. Tameria believed things would begin to turn around for Aisha if she did that.

Chase appeared from out of nowhere and grabbed Tameria around her waist and twirled her in the air. She loved him deeply. It was a blessing to have someone in her life who shared her same dreams, goals and aspirations. Chase was someone who accepted her just the way she was. She wasn't the prettiest girl neither did she have a model's figure but she possessed compassion, concern and a gentle spirit for others. That's why she fit perfectly in the medical field. She loved people and wanted to spend her life helping them. Chase asked her if she could take a break but as soon as she was about to tell him yes his name blared over the intercom.

"Sorry, baby, duty calls," he said apologetically.

"I'm going to the nurses' station and grab me a donut and some coffee. I'll see you later on I hope." She smiled and kissed him on the cheek.

◆

Aisha dialed Elisa's cell. She had promised Elisa that she would call her and tell her about the maniac client, Kyle Taylor since she'd never gotten the chance after the devastating news about her father. Elisa picked up right away.

Elisa began to question Aisha as soon as her number appeared on her cell. "How was church? Did you remember to say a prayer for me?"

"Dang girl, can't you at least say hello first?" Aisha laughed over the phone.

"No, I can't. We already said hello before you went to church," Elisa responded in a carefree voice.

"Whatever. Anyway, to answer your questions, church was quite enjoyable and second, I did remember to say a prayer for you and Gabby. So there. Anything else?"

"Yea, what are your plans for the rest of the day? I don't have to work and we haven't hung out in a while. You game?"

"Why not. If you're hungry why don't we meet at Ruby Tuesday downtown? I haven't had a thing to eat and I'm starving." Aisha suggested.

"Okay, let me get ready and I'll meet you there around two-thirty."

"Okay, see you then because I have to tell you everything that happened the night I met Kyle Taylor. Remember?"

"Do I remember? I've been itching to hear the details. I'll see you in a little while."

Since Aisha was already dressed, she had time to go by her dance studio, something she hadn't done in a couple of weeks. There was a time that no one or nothing could pull her away from A-Carlisle Studio of Dance and Choreography. She drove to the location, unlocked the door and stood in the vast space. She inhaled while outstretching her arms and closing her eyes. Imagining the room was full of students, she pictured her them dancing gracefully around the studio. When she opened her eyes, she felt a tear traveling along the contours of her cheek. Being at the studio reminded her of how much she missed doing the one thing she used to live and breathe for. Not dancing at The Lynx because that wasn't the same. But teaching the girls the art of dancing and how to feel the music in your spirit and show your passion in every movement. She went into her cold office and eased down in the chair. Her desk was piled high with messages and other paper work that Angie had left for her to go over. Angie, she thought. *Lord, thank you for her. Angie has kept things going virtually on her own, like this is her studio.* She wrote a note to remind herself to do something extra special for Angie, like giving her a nice bonus. Dialing into her voice mail, she heard the robotic woman's voice tell her that her mailbox was full. She listened to the messages, deleting unimportant ones and saving the ones that required her attention. When she heard Kyle Taylor's message, she shivered at the sound of his voice. He sounded exceptionally charming. For a moment she forgot about the way he had treated her. Then she became somewhat uneasy. He had called her studio and he knew her real name. How could he have discovered who she really was? She trembled at the thought of how he'd talked to her the last time she'd seen him. Now here he was, sounding so charming and sensitive. She'd have to ask Elisa what was going on. *Maybe Jason's sorry behind told him.* Her nostrils flared at the thought of how low down Jason could really be. She replayed Kyle's message. "Aisha, Kyle Taylor here. First let me say how sorry I am about your father. I also want to apologize for my totally senseless and cruel behavior when you came to my home. Will you forgive me and allow me to make it up to you by taking you to dinner? Please call me at The Lynx. I'll be waiting."

You sure will be waiting, and you'll be waiting a long time too if you think I'm going to call you, she exhaled a heavy sigh of disgust at his unmitigated gall and proceeded to delete his message. She listened to the last two messages, erased them and stood up to leave.

Before locking up, she turned and surveyed her turf one more time.

Elisa waltzed into Ruby Tuesday like she was a runway model. Dressed in a gold colored parchment silk tube skirt and a black tailored blazer, she turned the heads of several gentlemen with each long stride she took. Her soft patent and linen sling backs added height to her already gazelle like frame. She asked the hostess to seat her in the back of the restaurant near the window so she and Aisha could enjoy the breathtaking view of the mighty Mississippi while they dined.

Aisha skimmed over the restaurant until she saw Elisa's hand waving back and forth in the air motioning for her.

"It's about time. It's after three. I was beginning to think you weren't going to show," was Elisa's response as she stood up and hugged Aisha.

"Now you know I would have called if I had a change of plans. I stopped by the dance studio and just lost track of time, that's all. Have you ordered yet?"

"No, just this Cosmopolitan. I wanted to wait on you before I ordered."

"Well, let's check out the menu because I'm starving." After placing their orders the two friends laughed and talked endlessly about Gabby. Aisha laughed when Elisa told her that she had taken Gabby to the school parking lot and let her practice driving. Elisa said she thought she was going to pee in her pants when it looked like her daughter was about to run into the side of the school. The waiter brought Aisha's gold margarita and a glass of water with lemon. Another server came up behind the waiter with their orders. Pausing their conversation, they allowed the server to place their orders on the table.

Between bites, Elisa started talking again. "Enough said about Gabby's driving techniques. Let's get to the juicy stuff. Tell me about this Kyle Taylor and what happened with him." Elisa urged.

"Every time I think about that night, I almost lose it, Elisa. If it wasn't for him, maybe I would have been there when my father died. But let me tell you what happened."

"Look, if it's too painful for you to talk about, then don't tell me. We haven't been out in a relaxing atmosphere for a while now and I sure don't want to ruin it by asking you to relive something that's obviously still hurting you quite a bit." The look on Elisa's face expressed her genuine empathy for Aisha. By choice, she didn't have many women friends but Aisha was the exception to the rule. Aisha possessed the kind of personality that drew people to her and Elisa was one of those people. Forming friendships with any of the girls she and Jason brought in to The Lynx was definitely taboo plus most of them were far too young anyway. The only girl who had tugged at her heart was Hallie. Hallie reminded her so much of herself when she was a teenager. Shy, frightened, and afraid to trust anyone. Elisa managed to gain her trust after a few months and slowly Hallie opened up to her about how scared she was. Elisa promised her that she would never let any of the men at The Lynx hurt her and so far, she had kept her word. Whenever Ronald Shipley asked for one of the girls, Elisa made sure it was one of the older girls and never Hallie. When the new member Kyle Taylor joined The Lynx, Jason assigned Hallie to him before she could intercept. So far, Hallie told her that Kyle Taylor was a nice man. That's why she couldn't believe it when Aisha told him how mean he was to her. She was even more surprised to hear about how he had put her out of his house and made her wait outside until the company limo came to pick her up. There was another side to him and Elisa wanted to know what made him tick.

"So when he put me out of his house," Aisha continued with her story. "I called Jason and told him to high tail it to that fool's place and get me."

"What did Jason say, girl?" Elisa bent in closer so she wouldn't miss a word.

"I don't know what he and Kyle talked about. All I know is that Jason went inside the house and stayed in there about five or ten minutes. When he came back to the limo, he didn't say one word to me. The dog didn't even ask me if I was okay or anything. He acted like I was some hooker on the street or something. All the way back to The Lynx he refused to say one word, Elisa. I hate him for that."

"Jason can be low down when he wants to be, Aisha. But that was a bit much, even for him, especially when it wasn't your fault."

"I guess he expected me to sleep with Kyle but I'm not about to lose my virginity to some oversexed executive. I don't care how much paper he has," Aisha insisted.

"I can't believe that he acted like that. But I'm proud of you for standing up for your beliefs. So I say hats off to you." Elisa raised her glass up in the air toward Aisha and took a sip of her second Cosmopolitan. "Did you get paid or did the lowlife hold back the three grand he promised you for meeting that chump."

"I wasn't about to let him mess me out of my money. No way. So since he was playing the silent treatment with me in the limo, when we made it back to The Lynx I asked him where my money was. He turned around like he was the exorcist or somebody and said it was in the car. I looked back inside the limo and saw the envelope lying next to where he had been sitting.

"Shoots, as long as you got your money, then I say to hell with him."

"Oh, let me tell you about that! Instead of the three thousand I was supposed to get, Jason gave me thirty, one dollar bills. I was so pissed I could have killed him. Forgive me, Lord, but that's the way I felt. Then I grabbed hold to my senses and I let it go. I told myself he wasn't worth it. I didn't even go inside The Lynx. I was too angry. He'll get his. You can bank on that. Anyway, it was my intent to go home and change clothes but before I could do that, I got the call from my mother." The two ladies became deftly quiet. Aisha drank some of her water and Elisa stirred her plate of Carolina Chicken Salad around with her fork.

Aisha broke their momentary silence. "You know I told you I stopped by the studio before coming here." Elisa nodded her head in response. Aisha continued. "Can you believe I had a message from one Kyle Taylor?"

"Are you kidding me?"

"I wish. But I'm not. Jason had to tell him how to contact me, Elisa. He even called me by my real name. He offered his condolences over my father's death. If Jason did that, he's stooped to an all-time low! He doesn't know what Kyle Taylor is up to."

"You're right. I think you should confront Jason about it. I know I would."

"I'm thinking about it. But one thing I don't have to think about is calling Kyle back. He said he wanted to have dinner with me."

"Girl, he must be on something more potent that either of us," Elisa laughed and took another sip of her drink.

"Seriously though. Elisa, it's over for me. I'm not going back to The Lynx. I have to get my life together in more ways than one. I'm a wreck. I'm no better than the crack heads that walk up and down the streets doing any and everything for a hit of that pipe."

"No you're not, Aisha. That's not true at all. Sure you snort a little coke every once in a while. So what. I've been doing coke and valium for years and I'm fine. If I wanted to stop, I could. But I don't want to. It relaxes me like a person who smokes cigarettes or drinks a glass of wine every night before bed. So we do our thing – we snort coke. What's so terrible about that?"

"For one, it's illegal. Two, it's addictive. And three, it fries your brain, which is obviously true if you think that what we're doing is okay. I am a drug addict. That's what's so terrible about this. I even have a name for the coke – *baby girl*. I have to have it. I don't care if I'm in church, at my parents' house, at The Lynx or the dance studio. I take it with me wherever I go. It's like that commercial that says American Express – never leave home without it. Except I say *baby girl*, never leave home without it. Before I got out of the car and came in here I took a hit. And you tell me there's nothing wrong with that?"

"There isn't. But have it your way because somehow you always manage to make insignificant things into huge mountains. Everybody has a vice of some kind, Aisha. None of us are perfect. At least that's what you've told me time and time again. And now you're being hard on yourself because you like to snort a little coke. And the money you're making at The Lynx, you're ready to kiss it goodbye because you're feeling guilty because of what happened to your dad?"

"Don't you dare bring my father into this! Don't you dare." Aisha raised her voice in hurt and anger. "If I had been where I was supposed to be I could have told my father goodbye."

"I don't mean to sound insensitive, but when it's your time to go, there's nothing anyone can do about it. Who's to say that you would have been there to tell him goodbye if you hadn't been with Kyle? You could have easily been doing something else. It could have been something as simple as having been in the hospital bathroom and before you made it back to his side your father could have died."

For the second time, they both remained silent. Aisha was lost in her thoughts and Elisa in hers. Both of their lives had connected along the pathway of life but they had started on two entirely different roads. Aisha's faith and convictions were what used to hold her up and keep her keeping on during trials and tribulations.

Elisa grew up living a hard knock life where her parents constantly fought each other verbally and physically. When she was about the same age as Hallie, Elisa was the victim of being 'recruited' after having run away from home. The day she ran away, she was supposed to be at school. But she had made other plans. Plans that included a life of living on her own and becoming a famous model. All of the cussing, fighting and threats at home had escalated to a point where she had begun to fear for not only her mother's life but her life and the lives of her two younger brothers. The day she ran away, she vowed to make a life for herself and then go back to Kansas City to rescue her brothers. She had saved up enough money from babysitting and her after school job at McDonald's to purchase an airline ticket. She had been saving her money for almost a year and a half. She arrived in Houston, Texas with high hopes and fast dreams so when the well-dressed man and woman approached her while she was eating alone at Wendy's she was thrilled. They both told her how beautiful she was and how they were searching for models for some of the top magazines like Seventeen, Vibe and Essence.

They told her that they operated an exclusive modeling agency located in Memphis, Tennessee. They offered her what they called, 'the opportunity of a life time." They told her they would be willing to take her to Memphis and introduce her to the owner of the agency. Something within told her not to go, but what if what they told her was true. She couldn't pass up this chance. If things turned out differently than what they said, she still had enough money to last a couple of weeks for her to get a room and food. She climbed in the car with them and within two hours she was on a flight from Houston to Memphis. She couldn't believe the stroke of luck that had come her way and she'd only been gone from home for a little over two days. It wasn't until a few days after her recruitment she realized something was wrong.

Soon after arriving at The Lynx, she met the owner and for her it was love at first sight. His charm was magnetic and he treated her like a queen. He lavished her with gifts, clothes, jewelry, trips all over the world and lots of money. But six months later when she told him she was pregnant, he flipped. He accused her of screwing the other members without protection. Soon after that, his demeanor toward her did a 360 degree turn. He became physically and verbally abusive just like she remembered her father being toward her mother. She wasn't allowed to leave her room until after she gave birth. When a doctor who was a member of The Lynx delivered her precious *baby girl*, she was overcome with love at the sight of her tiny daughter. She named her Gabby. The baby's daddy, notorious Ronald Shipley, wanted nothing to do with her. Life for Elisa became a living nightmare. What she had seen and endured at home was nothing compared to the way she was used as a sex slave by

Ronald and the men at The Lynx. During her first few months as one of the girls she wanted to run away but she was kept secluded on a locked floor along with several other girls. The only time she was allowed off the floor was when she was forced to perform sexual acts and illicit dancing for the men. Eventually, money started flowing way of tips from the men. Finally after a year, Elisa was raking in over $750 a week. That was a heck of a lot of cash for a sixteen-year old teenager. When Gabby turned two years Ronald allowed Elisa to move into a place of her own with the understanding that he owned her. He couldn't have a child, especially his, running around The Lynx. Elisa was relieved to have her own space. She was willing to do whatever it took to keep Gabby from the clutches of her pedophile father and his sick buddies. Elisa understood that she was forever bound to do whatever she was told.

Gabby was fifteen years old herself now. To protect her from the horrid life she'd led, Elisa made it her business to keep her end of the bargain with Ronald over the years. That meant going out with Jason to recruit new girls. Whatever Ronald wanted from her, she gave it to him. She couldn't understand how totally opposite Ronald Shipley was from his twin brother. Ronald had no problem with carrying out his threats. Elisa had witnessed his anger unleashed on many of the girls. Through the years, she had been the recipient of it as well. Though she couldn't prove it, she knew that he had committed murder as well. It was like Ronald was Jekyll and Pastor Shipley was Mr. Hyde. They were as different as night and day.

◆

Aisha and Elisa finished their meals and Aisha was ready to leave. She couldn't listen to Elisa's denials about their drug addictions and sinful lifestyles. Elisa was certainly in denial but Aisha sure wasn't. She needed help and maybe it was time to take Tameria's advice. She would seek spiritual counseling.

"What are you going to do about Kyle?" Elisa asked her as they exited Ruby Tuesday. "Are you going to return his call and accept his apology?"

"You really think I'm that stupid. I told you Elisa. It's over. I'm never going to The Lynx again. And I'm certainly not going to call that scumbag Kyle Taylor."

"All I can say then is good luck. You're a better woman than I am."

"Why don't you quit too? You can come and help me at the studio. I can use a good director. You're talented, smart and good with the students. You're a great dancer too. What do you say?"

Elisa's face beamed at the thought of being able to get away from The Lynx. She could have a new start and a real job. For once things could be normal for her and Gabby. *Gabby*, she thought to herself. *If I leave, he'll take Gabby.* "Aisha, I wish I could but I've been at The Lynx for a long time and you can't begin to pay me the kind of money I make there. I'm sorry." Elisa explained reluctantly without telling her the real truth about why she couldn't leave The Lynx.

"Suit yourself. But still at least think about it?" Aisha pleaded with her.

"Okay, I'll give it some thought. Now come on. I've got to get home. I promised Gabby that I'd take her to get a new outfit at the mall. She's going to a spring fling at school so you know that she insists on having a new outfit." Elisa hugged Aisha tightly. She hoped that Jason or no one else from The Lynx would give Aisha any trouble for quitting. Poor Aisha had no idea what Ronald Shipley was capable of.

30

There is nothing more deceptive than an obvious fact.
Arthur Doyle

Chandler sat in his suite at The Lynx thinking about his last two encounters with Aisha. As Kyle Taylor, he almost gave his cover away when he saw her walk into his bedroom that evening. He wanted to ask her why she doing what she was doing. He had her pegged all wrong and he began to doubt his intuitive side. Being intuitive was what had helped to make him an outstanding veteran cop. All the years he'd worked undercover, his cover had never been blown. That said a lot about him. But he almost blew it when he saw Aisha. He thought back on that night and remembered the sexiness she exuded as she danced to the music. Before he knew it, he was in Kyle Taylor mode. As Kyle he was a member of The Lynx Association. As a member he could have any and everything he wanted from any of the girls there. Watching Aisha or Luscious as she called herself, moving back and forth with her hair swaying against the flow of her body, aroused him and he wanted her. When she brushed off his advances, his ego was severely wounded. He went into Chandler Larson mode and lashed out at her before forcing her out of his house. After he'd done it, he felt horrible but the thought of how she had been deceiving him soon made the sympathy he had for her subside. When he ran into her at church the following Sunday he felt awkward at first because she still had the power to captivate his thoughts and his body. When he saw it was her, he moved in closer to Candyce. He could tell Aisha was hurt to see him with another woman. The look plastered across her face was one of shock and dismay. Yet, he continued to act cold towards her. She was no longer worth his time. He had left her a message at her studio several days before using his Kyle voice and asking her for forgiveness. It was all part of trying to get into her head to find out the part she played with The Lynx. He could have called her on her cell but decided against it, hoping that somehow a positive outcome would from calling her at the studio. The knock on the door jarred him from his thoughts of Aisha and the indictments that were about to go down in the next few days. He had located the files of the members of The Lynx, found out how they shipped their drugs into the city and the method they used to traffic girls. He had taped conversations, videos and a reliable inside informant, not to mention Hallie. All Chandler had to do was give the final word to his Chief and his back up team was ready to spring into action. Every facet of Operation Lynx was in place. The backup team was prepared just in case there was any trouble when they delivered the indictments to Shipley, Jason and Elisa. But first Chandler had a few loose ends to tie up. One of those loose ends was Hallie.

"Who is it?" Kyle asked.

"It's Hallie, Mr. Taylor," the familiar sound of the child's voice responded. He opened the door and ushered her inside.

"Hi, sweetie. Everything all right?" he asked her. He was glad he had everything set up to get her out of The Lynx first thing tomorrow morning. The plan was for his inside informant to pretend that he was going to take Hallie to the mall to get her new clothes. Periodically the girls were allowed to venture outside the confines of The Lynx but only with escorts. Either they went with some of the older girls who had gained trustee status or they were carried by Elisa herself.

"Hallie, I want you to do everything I've told you to do tomorrow morning. Do you understand me?" He asked the anxious girl.

"Yes, Mr. Taylor I understand."

"You're going to be picked up around nine thirty. I want you up and ready. Don't take anything along with you. Absolutely nothing. Do you hear me?"

"Yes, I know. I promise I won't take a thing."

"Hallie, things are about to change for you. You'll never have to worry about being hurt again. You hear me?"

Without any advance warning she reached around his waist and hugged him as tightly as she could. Tears flowed freely from her child eyes. He stroked her hair gently like a loving father would his child. He fought back his own tears at the thought of all Hallie had experienced in her young life. Anger mounted in the base of his throat when he thought of Aisha again. He moved Hallie back and looked down at her. He wiped her tears away with the back of his hand.

"Hey, I have your favorite. Chocolate chip cookies and vanilla ice cream." he smiled at her.

"Wow, thanks Mr. Taylor." A big smile exchanged places with her tears and she ran off into the kitchen.

While Hallie was in the kitchen he went to the study and looked over the final plans for the down fall of The Lynx and Ronald Shipley. He looked at the pictures he'd taken when he was at Greater Faith and searched for any evidence that the Revered Donald Shipley knew about The Lynx operation. For the past few weeks the Feds had kept a close eye on the reverend too. So far neither

Chandler nor his police partners had evidence or proof that the illustrious Pastor Shipley was part of his twin brother's scandalous, illegal lifestyle. From all indications, Donald Shipley was everything he portrayed himself to be. A man of integrity with upstanding Christian morals, who displayed a love for God that appeared to be sincere. But Ronald on the other hand was a bad seed. That much Chandler was sure Donald Shipley knew about his twin. But Reverend Donald could not be responsible for his brother's sick minded actions.

31

*The risk of love is loss, and the price of loss is grief – But
the pain of grief is only a shadow when compared with
the pain of never risking love.* Hilary Zunin

Sandra Carlisle sat in the living room staring blankly
out the picture window on to the sidewalk. She missed
Benjamin's hearty laughter, the way he ambled around
the house. She missed the way he took care of everything
from grocery shopping to paying the bills. The house
echoed a silence that she was not accustomed to. Maybe
she would go to Springfield and visit her brother and his
wife for a few weeks. Her small church family was
supportive and there was always someone calling her to
check up on her or stopping by to see her, but things
weren't the same and never would be without her
husband. Selena called almost every day to see how she
was doing. Sandra was really appreciative for that. When
he was alive, Selena and Benjamin had an on again off
again father-daughter relationship. She had grown up
being poisoned by her mother's constant belittling of
Benjamin. It wasn't until Selena was a young adult that
she began to see that most of what her mother had told
her about her father had been untrue. However, the
distance between them made it difficult for them to ever
establish a close bond like he had with Aisha.

The day Sandra discovered she was pregnant with
Aisha, Benjamin ran through the house yelling and

215

screaming for joy. He pampered and petted Sandra's stomach and did everything he could to make sure she had an easy pregnancy. When seven pound eight ounces Aisha Carlisle entered the world, Benjamin cried so hard the nurses and doctor thought they were going to have to give him a sedative. He was allowed to cut her umbilical cord and since then the cord of love he had for Aisha was never broken.

Sandra soon took second place to her husband's love and attention. It was like he was trying to make up for all the years he'd missed out on with Selena. Over time, jealousy slowly creeped up on Sandra. Benjamin still handled everything and he tried to be a good husband but it was no secret that Aisha was his treasure. Sandra began to pour herself into her work as a social worker at the Department of Human Services. If she didn't make it home from work until late, she wasn't missed. If she stayed out all day on Saturday, Benjamin didn't mind. As long as Aisha was around he was happy and content. There was nothing too good for his little princess.

Since his death, and her move to Little Rock Sandra hadn't seen or heard from Aisha for weeks. Initially that was the way she wanted it. Benjamin loved Aisha and for her to be out in the streets somewhere while he was dying was unforgivable. How could she have even thought about going to some job when her father had been on his death bed? Sandra thought her daughter was insensitive and selfish and because of her, Benjamin's last request to see her went unfulfilled. Sandra Carlisle cried until the doorbell rang and invaded her loneliness. She hurriedly wiped away her tears. As she pressed the wrinkles out of her cotton dress with both of her hands, she moved closer to the side entrance. Unlatching the door, her mouth dropped open wide when she saw Aisha standing on the other side. At first thought she felt anger and rage at her child. She was unable to say anything to her and so she stood in the doorway staring at her.

"Momma, may I come in?" Aisha asked in a sorrowful voice. Without waiting on her mother to reply she eased past her and stepped inside the kitchen. "How are you Momma?"

Her mother followed Aisha with her eyes. "I'm, I'm okay. What are you doing here?"

"I came to check on you. To see if you were okay. You won't accept or return my calls."

"And you wonder why I won't? Aisha, please. Why don't you think of somebody else other than yourself for a change?" Her mother retorted.

"That's why I'm here Momma. I care about you. My God, I love you Momma Don't you know that for the rest of my life I'm going to remember that I wasn't there when Daddy needed me the most? I wasn't there to hold him and tell him I loved him for the last time. Momma, knowing he died asking for me is tearing me apart. But if I lose you too, I don't know what I'll do."

Sandra's heart began to soften somewhat as she listened to her daughter. The hurt Aisha felt was evident as she expressed her sorrow for what she had done. "Aisha, I know you're sorry but sometimes sorry just doesn't cut it. Some things can't be fixed no matter what you do."

"And I know not being there for Daddy is one of those things. Believe me, if I could turn back the hands of time and do things differently I would. But I can't. What I can do is let you know that I love you and ask you to forgive me. I want us to have a real mother - daughter relationship. I know things between us have always been strained but it's just you and me now. Can't we be there for each other?"

"I don't know. I need time to think. I miss your father so much. It is lonely here without him. But right now I can't allow anyone in my life."

"What you mean is that you can't allow me into your life." Aisha lashed out. "I'm your daughter, Mother. Your only child."

Sandra Carlisle turned and walked toward the family room. When she got to the hallway she looked back over her shoulder and said, "Lock the door when you leave."

Aisha was blinded by tears as she made her way out to her car. The clouds grew dark in the sky and she knew it was about to rain. But she didn't care because it was already raining inside her heart.

◆

"Angie, thank you for all of your help. I know I haven't been around much lately. I've all but let the studio run itself. If it wasn't for you, everything would have fallen apart." Aisha passed the white envelope to Angie along with a bouquet of colorful mixed flowers.

Her eyes grew big as marbles when she opened the envelope and saw the bonus check inside. "Oh, Aisha, you shouldn't have." She jumped up and ran from behind the receptionist area and hugged Aisha. "Thank you, thank you, thank you."

"I owe all the thanks to you, Angie." Looking at the envelope, Aisha added, "and that's just something to show how much I appreciate your loyalty and dedication. I haven't been the best person to get along with lately or to get in touch with for that matter," Aisha grinned.

"Maybe we can get things back to normal, huh, Aisha?"

"I hope so. I'm going to take things one day at a time. I have a lot of healing to do mentally, emotionally and physically before I can give my all to anything else."

"Well, listen. You do what you need to do to take care of you. The studio will be here. The instructors you hired are really good with the girls and as long as you want me here, I'll be here."

"I don't just want you at the studio Angie. I want to offer you a job as Assistant Director. Of course there'll be a hefty raise for you and really, if you think about it, you're already doing the job anyway. Whaddaya say?"

"Oh, my God," she yelled and started jumping up and down like a bunny rabbit. "Are you serious?" she squealed.

"As a heart attack."

"Then yes. I'll be glad to accept the position. Aisha I have to call my husband. He's going to be ecstatic. Thank you. I don't know what else to say."

"There's nothing for you to say. Just continue to do the outstanding job that you're doing. That's thanks enough for me. I'm going to go in my office now. I need to try to dwindle down some of the mountain of paperwork on my desk. We'll talk later about your salary increase if that's okay with you. But I'm sure you'll be pleased."

Angie squealed again. "Of course. Let me know if you need me. I'm going to call Kevin and tell him the good news now."

Aisha clicked on Yahoo Yellow Pages and entered the name Greater Faith Community Church. When the number came up she dialed it nervously.

"Good afternoon, GreSater Faith Community Church. How may I help you?"

"I, I need to make an appointment for counseling please."

"Let me transfer you to Pastoral Care. They can help you with that. Please hold." Aisha tried to keep her voice from trembling. The thought of a hit of *baby girl* weighed heavily on her mind. If she could have just one hit, she'd feel better. It had been a week since her last hit of coke. Her body craved the drug and the sense of hopelessness and depression was almost unbearable. . Her nights were filled with paranoia and insomnia. She was irritable and anxious. Her thoughts about her life and where she would go from here were inconceivable to think about.

Just as she was about to change her mind and hang up the phone, she heard another pleasant, calming voice over the phone.

"Hello, Pastoral Care, Natalie speaking."

"Uh, Natalie, I need to make an appointment for counseling please." Aisha stammered.

"Sure, I just need you to answer a couple of questions, if that's okay with you."

"Yes, I guess so."

"Are you a member of Greater Faith, ma'am?"

"Yes, is that a requirement?" Aisha asked.

"No, ma'am. We ask that because we want to see if our members are utilizing the ministry, that's all."

"I see. What else do you need to know?"

"I need your name please and your membership number."

"Aisha, Aisha Carlisle. My membership number is 72054."

"Miss Carlisle, I need to ask you just a couple of more questions then we can schedule your appointment." Aisha gave the administrative assistant the information she requested and her appointment was scheduled for Thursday morning. Two days, I hope I can hold out until then, she said to herself. "Natalie, which minister will I be meeting with?"

"Minister Jackson Williams. You'll love him. He's really good and he'll make you feel comfortable. Everyone who talks to him leaves the office praising him," she continued to babble.

"Okay, thank you, Natalie. I'll be there Thursday at ten." Aisha answered cutting off Natalie's spill. She reflected on the handsome minister and how she was drawn in by his presence when she initially saw him in the pulpit. She admitted she needed someone to confide in who would keep things confidential. If Jackson Williams was everything Natalie made him out to be then maybe, just maybe he was the one who could help her. She'll know for sure after Thursday's meeting.

32

At the empty dance studio Aisha kicked her legs up on the futon in the break room. She sipped on a cup of green tea while flipping the remote at the same time. Earlier she thought about going home to her apartment but there were times such as this when she found more solitude at the studio. Reflecting on the past few months she quickly zoomed pass the red background on the TV with the words Breaking News Alert flashing across the screen. She turned back just in time to see the Memphis Police Chief and Chandler talking to Tony Williams, anchorman for Channel 24 News.

'Tell me, Chief, what led to the indictments of some of this city's most notable and well known constituents, especially Ronald Shipley the brother of Reverend Donald Shipley." Tony placed the mic directly in front of the Police Chief.

"Let me say this, Tony. Our department has worked diligently with the Feds in Operation Lynx for over a year. Ronald Shipley may be the twin brother Donald Shipley one of the most well-known and respected preachers in the South, but he is certainly not at all like him. Ronald Shipley is suspected of being the mastermind behind the kidnapping of underage girls brought against their will to serve as sex slaves for members of The Lynx Association. He's also been indicted for drug trafficking and is thought to be responsible for three fourths of the cocaine and crack distributed on the streets of Memphis."

"Chief, I see you have Detective Chandler Larson standing here with you. What part did you play in Operation Lynx Detective Larson?"

"Like the Police Chief said, we've been working on this case for a long time. I'm proud to be part of getting scumbags and lowlifes like Shipley off the street. There are mothers and fathers out there who've been searching for their children, not knowing that some of these very children have been abused and misused as sex slaves for wealthy perverts that call themselves members of this so called private gentleman's association known as The Lynx."

Aisha sat frozen on the cold hardwood dance floor directly in front of the TV. She continued to listen. Aisha quickly thought about what Candyce said that Sunday she saw her with Chandler. Candyce had asked her if she worked with Chandler at the police station or something like that. After not hearing from Chandler, she soon dispelled the thought of what Candyce had asked her. *What Candyce said is true. Chandler really is a policeman,* she said out loud. Anger formed in her chest and rose through her throat, extending out to her arms and fingers. A lump formed in her throat when she heard him telling about the indictments. Suddenly she thought about Elisa. *Where is Elisa? And what about me? Suppose they suspect me of being involved with what was going on at The Lynx. God please say it isn't so.* She jumped up off the floor and ran over to the cordless phone lying on the sofa. She dialed Elisa. The phone rang until Elisa's voice mail picked up. The same response was received when she called her cell phone. Gabby, where is Gabby? Aisha became increasingly frantic at the thought of Elisa and her whereabouts. Aisha's purse was in her office and her cell phone was in her purse. She hurried to her office to get her purse. When she retrieved her phone, she scrolled through her contacts until she landed on the name *Gabby Cell*. She pushed the green button to dial Gabby's number. Gabby didn't answer either. Beads of sweat formed on Aisha's brow. She started to pray. *Lord, hear me. Please don't let Elisa be involved in this. Please Lord. Let her just be out of reach right now. Let Gabby be safe. And please don't let me be pulled into this either.* Aisha went back into the break room to see what else was being said. She caught the tail end of Tony Williams' last comments.

"And there you have it folks. Five people have been indicted for human trafficking and drug trafficking. One of them being the twin brother of Pastor Donald Shipley of Greater Faith Community Church, the largest Baptist congregation in Memphis. Greater Faith is evolving into one of the largest Baptist churches in the South with over 8,000 members. Join us tonight at ten for more about Operation Lynx. I'm Tony Williams, News Channel 24, good evening." Aisha flicked off the television and prepared to leave the studio.

She hoped she wouldn't get caught speeding. A ticket was the last thing she needed but she wanted to go by Elisa's to see what was going on. She dialed Chandler's number, hoping and praying for once that maybe he hadn't changed it after all. *Come on Chandler, please answer*, she mumbled as the phone began to ring.

For the first time in weeks, he'd finally decided to unblock Aisha's number and answer her call. The detective in him knew that once she heard about The Lynx she would be running scared. Now was the time to get the truth out of her. "Hello, I take it you saw the five o'clock news," Chandler's voice loomed over the phone.

"Chandler, what's going? What is all of this about?" Aisha's anger mounted and Chandler could hear it in her voice.

"If you really want to know, you'll meet me in fifteen minutes at Java, Juice and Jazz." He hung up the phone without any regard to Aisha or her feelings. Part of him was relieved when there was no evidence that tied her to the illegal operations at The Lynx. But her friend, Elisa was a horse of a different color. He turned his unmarked police car in the direction of Bellevue Boulevard and Java, Juice and Jazz Cafe.

Aisha arrived at the restaurant, known for hosting spoken word and literary events, just as Chandler was walking inside. She sat in her car for a few seconds and watched his Denzel swagger and his Brad Pitt butt before she climbed out. *Stop lusting after someone who doesn't give two cents about you,* she told herself. She strode inside the dimly lit restaurant and felt the tug on her arm.

"This way," Chandler ordered.

"Well, hello to you too," she said in a gruff voice. She was just about sick of his disrespectful treatment of her lately. He had no reason to treat her like this and before she left she was going to tell him exactly how she felt.

"Would you like something to eat or drink?" he asked.

"I'm not hungry and no alcohol for me tonight. But I'll take an iced tea." He went to the bar and came back with a beer for himself and her requested tea.

"Okay, let's have it. Exactly who are you, Chandler? Or is Chandler even your real name?"

"Chandler is my real name. But I'm the detective. So I think I should be the one asking you questions?"

Aisha's eyebrows raised and she flung her twists back off of her face which was a sure way to determine that she was nervous. "What are you talking about? I'm not the one who lied about my profession. As I recall, you told me you were some big shot land developer. Now I find out from your little girlfriend that you're a cop. Plus your true identity was confirmed on the five o'clock news. What, you think I couldn't handle dating a policeman or something? Or maybe you have even more to hide Mr. Larson."

Chandler took a swig of his beer and listened to Aisha. He still found her attractive. There was a time he thought she could be the one for him, but again he had misjudged her like he had Tracye. Maybe he should give up the pursuit of finding that special girl and concentrate on his career. Or he could become the playa he used to be and start lovin' 'em and leavin' 'em.

"Let's see, Mizz Carlisle of Carlisle Dance Studio. Or no, no. On second thought, perhaps you're not that Mizz Carlisle. Maybe you're Mizz Carlisle behind door number two." His words were cutting and confusing.

"What are you talking about?" Aisha looked at him like he was crazy. It was times like these when she missed *baby girl* the most. She could have shrugged his weird antics off if she had a snort of coke, but she didn't so she couldn't. She sat across the table twitching and searched the faces of people coming into the Jazz Cafe.

"I guess you don't hear me now, huh?"

"Chandler, I don't have time for your games. I want to know what happened to Elisa. I really don't care who you are. Just tell me where she is."

"Elisa's exactly where she needs to be. Like all the rest of them. She's like that song that goes something like this, *'locked up they won't let me out...'*

Ignoring his mockery through song, she continued her line of questioning. "How long have you been involved in this Chandler? Will you at least tell me that much?"

"Only if you'll tell me how long you've been stripping and having sex with men at The Lynx." He cursed and looked at her like she was nothing.

"I, I don't know what you're talking about," she stuttered. *Surely he doesn't know that I was one of the dancers at The Lynx. Did Elisa tell him or Jason? Oh my God, no wonder he all of a sudden didn't want to have anything else to do with me."*

"What? Cat got your tongue? You see, I know all about you. How long you've been working at your so called part-time dance instructor job. I know about the men you danced for as a private dancer. I even know about Kyle Taylor and you. So, who's the liar Aisha? You want to sit up here so self-righteous and all and go off on me for not telling you something I obviously wasn't at liberty to tell you. But tell me something. What's your excuse for being a ho!"

Aisha rose up from the chair like a lion about to pounce on its prey. Her petite hand curled up in a fist in striking mode.

"Don't you dare or I'll lock you up so fast, it'll be tomorrow already when you walk outside to my police car. Now sit down." He ordered.

Aisha did as she was told. How could she not have recognized that Chandler was no good? She should have seen through his façade. "What do you want from me?"

"I don't want anything from you anymore. I thought you were a classy lady but you're nothing. You're no more than a high priced hooker. Just like your friend Elisa. You're so concerned about her. Well you better be glad that you got out in the nick of time. I know you'll never tell me the part you played in all of this. But believe me, I swear if I ever find out you were mixed up in this, you'll be teaching dykes how to dance instead of young girls. For all I know maybe you planned on pawning off some of the girls at your studio to Shipley and his group. After all, didn't you say you'd do anything to save your studio?"

Aisha felt her blood pressure rising. The words spewing from Chandler's mouth stung her repeatedly. How could he even form his lips to say the things he was saying to her? It became impossible for her to hold back her tears. She sat at the table and cried. Pellets of tears landed in her glass of tea.

"You really don't know me at all do you? If you think for one minute," she spoke between crying, "that I would allow harm to come to any young lady at my studio or anywhere else, then you're the psycho. Yes, I was a dancer at The Lynx. But I didn't know anything about the illegal side of that place. I was there to make some money to save my dance studio and that's it."

"Don't put on the sad little girl act now. You were there to support your coke habit. That's why you were there, *baby girl*." His tone was evil and his words were wounding and full of sarcasm.

Stunned again, Aisha hated Chandler at that very moment. How could he have known her secret name for coke or that she even had a coke habit? She never thought it was possible to feel like this toward another human being. She had always been taught to love others and have compassion for other people. But Chandler made her life's teachings null and void. The sound of his cruel words wafted in and out of her mind. The more she listened and watched him, the more he looked and sounded like someone other than the Chandler she thought she knew. He continued his verbal onslaught. Like a photographer focuses and zooms in with his camera, her mind zoomed in on Chandler. Then it clicked. She pointed an accusatory finger at him. "It's you. sure am. So you see. I know all about your little habit. I know what you've been doing at The Lynx. You can't lie to me anymore."

"How could you? I hate you," she screamed and jumped up and ran out of the cafe. Just as she made it to her car, Chandler was beside her.

"Sorry to bust your bubble, Luscious. But like the good book teaches, my sista," he mocked, 'what's done in the dark surely will come to the light."

"Where is Elisa?" Aisha shouted at Chandler. "Is she in jail? At least tell me that much."

"Elisa and Gabby are fine. That's all you need to know. And if I were you, I wouldn't waste my time trying to go to her place. You won't find her there," he smirked. "Now you go and have yourself a good night." And with that being said, he turned and walked off leaving Aisha standing next to her car shocked and hurt.

33

No sin is hidden to the soul. Bengali

It was Thursday. Aisha called in to the studio and told the receptionist she wouldn't be in until after her appointment. Usually she went to the studio first to check her messages or return calls up until it was time to leave for her counseling session with Minister Williams. But this morning she just wasn't feeling it. She lounged around the apartment, sipped on a cup of hot decaf tea with lemon and listened to the morning news.

The reporter talked about a murder that happened on the East side last night that was thought to be the result of a botched up robbery. Then the reporter followed up with something more pleasant. "Urban Knowledge Memphis bookstore is hosting a book signing event for New York Times Bestselling author Carl Weber Tuesday at six p.m." the red haired reporter stated. Next, Aisha listened to the meteorologist tell about the weather. "Weather today is going to be breezy and mild with a temperature of 64 degrees. Temperatures will remain between a low of fifty-three to a high of sixty-three the remainder of the week with a forty percent chance of thundershowers on Saturday and Sunday." The same red-haired reporter came on again after a commercial break.

Aisha got up from her favorite tomato red chair. She halted when she heard the reporter mention The Lynx. "Ronald Shipley, former owner of The Lynx Association indicted last November for capital kidnapping, drug trafficking and human trafficking. was sentenced to thirty five years to life. The remaining three people indicted in the sting will stand trial in the next few weeks. It has been reported that a fifth accomplice, Elisa Santana, the prosecution's star witness has not been seen since the reading of the verdict. Speculation has it that she's been placed in the witness protection plan. Stay tuned to the five o'clock edition of News Channel 24, giving you up to the minute news."

So that explains Elisa's sudden disappearance, Aisha said out loud. It all makes sense now. *Maybe she'll be able to make a decent life for her and Gabby now without fear of Ronald's revenge. Take care of her God. Take care of her.* Aisha clicked off the television and turned the radio on in time to hear Yolanda Adams singing In The Midst Of It All. She listened like she was hearing the song for the first time. *"I've come through many hard trials…not because I've been so faithful…"* God you have kept me in the midst of it all, she said. She listened to the rest of the song before getting up to dress for her meeting with Jackson.

Aisha waved dryly when she passed the receptionist and continued her way to her morning session. She felt exceptionally down today and dreaded her meeting with Jackson Williams. If only she could have a hit of *baby girl*, she'd be fine. Most of her nights were spent tossing and turning and dreaming about the drug. When The Lynx was raided, her supply line was cut off. There were times when she considered going to some of the same drug infested neighborhoods where she once used to knock on doors and witness to people. Only she wouldn't be witnessing about the Lord. She'd be searching high and low for her drug of choice. So far she'd resisted the strong urge to do it. If Elisa was here, she'd know where to get some without having to result to a street dealer.

Dang, I miss her. What am I thinking? I've got to get a grip. She hurried along the familiar corridor leading to Jackson's office. With each step the tug of desire for *baby girl* intensified. She stopped, turned around and went back outside to her car in desperate search for even a crumb of coke. She rambled through her glove compartment, under the seat cushions and floor mats. There had to be some coke somewhere. She was growing more and more frantic by the minute. When she caught a reflection of herself in her rear view mirror, she sat upright in the seat and then leaned back. She pounded her fists against the dashboard, jumped out of the car and strode back inside the church.

Chandler watched her from across the street until she disappeared inside Greater Faith Community Church. For the past several weeks he'd been following her. Now that the trial had ended and Ronald Shipley would never walk the streets of Memphis or anywhere again, he could concentrate on finding out if Aisha had any secrets he should know about. He didn't really want to see her go to prison, but if he discovered that she knew anything about The Lynx operation, he had no choice. He wouldn't rest until she was prosecuted to the fullest extent of the law. He looked at his cell phone to check the time, wondering what she could possibly be doing at the church every week. Like clockwork, he watched her arrive at Greater Faith between 9:30 and 9:45 a.m. every Thursday. Maybe she was going before the altar to confess her sins.

◆

Today's session with Jackson left Aisha feeling somewhat invigorated. Almost as soon as she heard his voice, she dispelled any thoughts of her drug craving.

"Aisha, we're going to delve deeper into some personal issues going on in your life. Are you willing to open up a little more today?"

"I think so. But I don't know if you're going to like what I have to say," she answered nervously and rotated her fingers over and over again in a circular motion.

"Like I told you, Aisha, I'm not here to judge you. I'm here to listen and give you Godly counsel. Now why don't you start from the beginning," he urged. He clasped his hands together and placed them underneath his chin. He didn't want to stare at her and make her feel uncomfortable, but she was ravishing. He could tell that whatever her problem was it must be really working her nerves because while she was indeed beautiful, he saw dark circles underneath her round dark eyes. She was jittery too, like she had a whole lot on her mind. Out of all of his past relationships, none of them had been as lovely as Aisha Carlisle. During college and seminary he could have had his choice of women but staying true to his faith, he refused to be a player. He dated for the sole purpose of finding a lifelong mate instead of physical gratification. Being celibate was indeed hard, especially since he wasn't a virgin. He'd had his share of sexual encounters but since he entered ministry full time, he vowed to God that He would present His body as a living sacrifice. He believed that a major part of having a body that was acceptable to Christ was not subjecting it to activities that were outside of the will of God. Namely fornication, drinking, smoking and drugs. Though some of his friends of which some were ministers that smoked, indulged in sex and drinking, Jackson didn't have the desire to do any of it. But he didn't knock them for their habits because he believed that every person had a shortcoming. Just because some of his buddies smoked or had a drink from time to time didn't automatically mean they were hell bound. It was all about if they believed and accepted Jesus Christ as their Lord and Savior. That was what mattered. He fidgeted in his plush wide back chair and leaned back to listen to Aisha.

Aisha was afraid at first but after several minutes of talking about her love of dance and telling Jackson about her studio, she began to feel relaxed and eager to tell him more. He watched the way she moved her lips in a pouting manner and resisted the urge to tell her how pretty she was to him. The more she talked, the more he wanted to hear.

"The studio was my dream, my answered prayer," she had told him.

"So tell me, when did things take a turn for you Aisha?"

"When the studio turned from a dream into a nightmare. You see, the owner of my building decided to sell it. But I didn't have enough cash or assets to buy it. I couldn't borrow enough money, which I wasn't supposed to do anyway. And I didn't have anyone who could loan me thirty-five thousand dollars."

"Wow, I understand your dilemma. But why didn't you just find another location for the studio?" he asked in a sincere voice.

"Because. My students are mostly inner city students. They already have enough trouble getting to practice. Moving the studio would have meant that I would lose a considerable number of talented students. For some it was all they had to look forward to. The other thing was my credit. It stunk. I had overextended myself and my debt ratio was really out of proportion. I had student loans, rent, car note, bank notes, credit cards, and anything else you can think of. When the realtor contacted me and told me the owner was going to sale the building I went into action.

"What did you do?"

"I petitioned for investors, went to my bank but I still came up short. So I did what I thought was best for me at the time."

"And what exactly was best for you at the time, Aisha?"

Aisha thought of how genuine he sounded. His voice echoed compassion and understanding. She hoped her intuition was right because she was about to confess to him the double life she had been living. Taking a deep breath, she looked down at her shaking hands.

♦

"I'd like to go into the sanctuary to pray. I won't be long." Chandler spoke in a low, reserved type voice.

"Sure, go right ahead. You do know where to go don't you?"

"Yes ma'am. I think I know every square inch of this church," he quickly lied.

"Go on then," she prompted.

"Thank you," he answered and tipped his hat toward her. In the massive sanctuary there were only a handful of people. An elderly man sat on the front pew with his head bowed and eyes closed. There was a young couple kneeling at the altar holding hands. Perusing the rest of the sanctuary and balcony he saw several other people but none were even close to fitting Aisha's description. Just to be certain none of them were her, he quietly walked along the sanctuary and glanced at each person he passed. He did the same thing when he went upstairs to the balcony. Next he went to the other side of the church where the sign read Staff Offices with an arrow pointing straight ahead.

◆

"Aisha, there's nothing you can tell me that will make me think differently of you. So come on, relax and talk. Jackson coaxed."

"One of the parents of my students made me an offer I couldn't possibly refuse. But, I should have. The money was not only good, but it was quick money and I didn't have to do a lot for it." She couldn't bring herself to look at Jackson's handsome face. She kept her head bowed and continued to talk.

"I'm a private dancer at an exclusive men's club. No, wait. Let me rephrase that. I was a private dancer until the club was shut down by the Feds. I had special clients who were extremely wealthy, I must say. They paid me a lot of money to dance for them."

Jackson stared at her. His thoughts were scrambled but his attraction to her was still in place. "Would you like to take a break before going on?" Jackson offered. "I can get you a soda or coffee."

"No, I want to continue while I can. Anyway, I accepted the job and my friend was right. The money was good. I made enough to buy the building, pay off my credit cards and then some. But that's not all. I don't know if I can tell you the rest," she said in shame.

"Don't stop now. The only way to confront what's attacking you is by talking about it and praying about it. I've been praying every day about you and your situation. But you've got to have faith for yourself and hope for your problems."

"Well, I'd never done anything like private dancing in front of men. I believed that a woman's body should be reserved for her husband. As for being physically intimate with them, I didn't engage in that. I've preserved my virginity but what I have done is to showcase my body in an undesirable manner that I know God is not pleased with. I was no more than a stripper. The only difference in what I did and what a stripper does is that I happened to work for extremely wealthy clientele. And while I'm confessing, I guess I'll tell you the other part."

"What is it?" Jackson sat upright in his chair trying to prepare himself for what she was about to reveal.

"I'm a cocaine addict." As many confessions and stories he'd heard, Jackson Williams couldn't believe that the woman sitting before him was an addict. He noticed that her eyes were dark and her body was frail but to be on drugs, no way. He definitely would have to pray for God to deliver her from such a powerful stronghold.

"Do you snort it, use a pipe, a needle? What?" Jackson had to know. He had to find a way to help her.

"I snorted it. I haven't done it in a while now. Not because I haven't wanted to, but because they shut down The Lynx. That was where I worked. But anyway, I lost my connection when they were busted. I called it *baby girl*. I know that sounds crazy, but that's one of the names some of the other girls called it. So I used it too. I didn't mean for it to get out of control. I only meant to use it to help me relax before I danced for my clients. I started out with crushed Valium and that made me feel relaxed. Then I graduated to snorting coke. It kept me energized and less shy and reserved. Before I realized it, I was using it all day every day. I had an endless supply available to me at no charge at my place of work. The more I became addicted to *baby girl*, I mean cocaine, the less I turned to God and the church. I gave more and more time to my night job and my next hit of coke that I lost all perspective. I couldn't even pray Jackson," she started to cry. Before I came in here, I wanted a hit so bad that I searched around in my car like a car thief trying to hot wire it and get away before being caught.

Jackson opened his side desk drawer and pulled out a box of tissue and passed it over to Aisha. He wanted to sit beside her and hold her. He wanted to tell her everything would be all right but she was in a fragile state of mind and he was too attracted to her to do such a thing. "Aisha, please don't cry," he begged. "I tell you what. Let's stop right here. You've shared a lot with me today and by confiding in me, you've shown that you trust me. What I want you to do when you finish your day is to read some scriptures starting with Romans chapter seven, verses fourteen through twenty-five." Jackson used his note pad to write down the passages of scripture for Aisha. She looked so hopeless and helpless sitting across from him. "I also want you to read Romans eight verses one through four. Don't just read the scriptures. Meditate on them. Pray for spiritual understanding. It's well and fine for others to pray for you Aisha, but you have to learn to pray for yourself too. You're just as much a child of God as I am. And yes, you've made some mistakes and you've walked outside of God's will, but it doesn't change who and whose you are."

Aisha cried even harder. "I'm sorry, Jackson, I can't help it. I hear what you're saying but it doesn't make me feel better about the decisions that I've made. It doesn't change what I've done."

"Aisha, please stop crying." This time he walked over to where she was sitting and kneeled down beside her. She could smell the scent of his cologne and the minty freshness of his breath as he spoke. Reaching for her hands, he looked her straight in the eye. "I promise you right here and right now that everything will be all right. Just don't give up Aisha. Don't throw in the towel. Allow God to do a new thing in you. It may not happen overnight, but you have my word. No, I take that back. You have God's promise that He is forever by your side, loving you just as much as He did before all of this." Without thinking he reached up and pushed aside one of her fallen twists from her face. He grabbed a tissue and patted her cheeks until they were dry. Aisha stopped crying and began to watch the caring man kneeling before her. Her heart fluttered.

"Will you read the scriptures Aisha?"

Aisha didn't respond immediately. But after several seconds of silence, she told him that she would do as he asked.

"There's one last thing I'd like you to do before you leave this morning. And that is to pray with me. Do you mind?"

How could she turn him down? Between sniffles she answered, "Okay."

Jackson prayed and asked God to guide Aisha's thoughts, her actions and her body. He prayed for deliverance from her addiction and for the guilt and condemnation she felt to be moved out of her life. When he finished his prayer, he got off his knees and sat down next to her. "Feel better?"

"Yes, I do. Thank you, Jackson. Thank you so much."

"I'm just doing God's will Aisha. Just doing God's will." He took hold of her smooth hands and gently helped her up to her feet. "Are you going to be all right?"

"Yes, sure. I'll see you next Thursday," she told him as she walked out of his office.

"Next Thursday? What about Sunday? You've come the last few Sundays and I expect to see you again this Sunday."

A slight smile filled her face. "Sunday it is."

As Chandler made his way along the winding hallway, several office doors were open. He saw several staff members busily working. He had never thought about the inside operations of a church but today he was getting a lesson in the behind the scene functions of a mega church. Approaching the other end of the hallway, and still saw no sign of Aisha, he was about to give up his search. Where could she have gone?" he pondered.

The sound of the woman's voice made him pause. "You have a good day too, Natalie," the woman said. "Yes, I will be in church on Sunday," and began walking in Chandler's direction. As she made her way closer to him, he recognized her clothing and her walk and knew that it was indeed Aisha. Then as she approached him, he saw her. Without looking in his direction, she turned down the opposite hallway.

Chandler walked to the office where Aisha had just come out of. Though the door was still open he could see the sign on it – Pastoral Care Offices. Chandler peeked inside at the woman sitting at her desk working on something at the computer. "Excuse me, miss."

Startled at the unannounced intruder, she jerked her head around quickly. "Yes, do you have an appointment?"

"No, no, ma'am. But my, my uh fiancé was here and I was supposed to meet her after her session ended."

"Oh, well what's your fiancé's name?" Natalie asked, knowing that it had to be Aisha he was talking about since she was the first appointment of the morning.

"Her name is Aisha. Aisha Carlisle, soon to be Aisha Green," he smiled charmingly.

"Oh yes. I didn't know she was engaged. But anyway, you just missed her. Her session with Minister Williams just ended a few minutes ago. I don't see how you missed her."

"Is that right? Oh well, let me see if I can catch her. She's probably out on the parking lot waiting for me. Thanks for your help." So *she must be running scared and now she's trying to make things right with God,* Chandler thought. *Poor baby, guilt must be eating her up,* he snickered and proceeded down the corridor leading to outside. By the time he made it to the front of the church entrance, Aisha had disappeared.

After saying goodbye to Natalie, Aisha had proceeded to walk down the winding hallway. She didn't notice the gentleman at the opposite end of the hallway. She looked at her watch. She was glad that she had made plans to be with Tameria today. After today's session, she needed some girlfriend time.

34

Friends are God's way of taking care of us. Unknown

Aisha maneuvered her car in and out of the morning expressway traffic. Arriving at the Kirby Parkway exit, she pressed speed dial button 7 on her cell phone to call Angie.

Kaye, the geeky receptionist picked up and answered in an overly happy voice. "Good morning Miss Carlisle. Are you on your way to the studio?"

"No, as a matter of fact I'm not. I forgot to let you know that I won't be in until around three. The girls should be coming in around that time. Is Angie close by where I can talk to her?"

"Yes, hold on just a minute. I'll get her."

"Hi, Aisha, how did your appointment go this morning?" Angie didn't know the details of Aisha's weekly sessions but she assumed they had to do something with her father's death. Angie waited on Aisha's slow response.

"Everything went okay, I guess. But what I wanted to tell you was that I won't be in until later this afternoon. Tameria called last night and told me that her schedule is free today so we're going to hang out," Aisha explained.

"Oh, good. I know you two don't get the chance to see each other often. I tell you, when you get involved in the medical field, it's a big sacrifice isn't it?"

"Yes it is. But you know Tameria loves it. That's why I know she's doing exactly what she's supposed to be doing. I'm about to turn down her street now, so I'm going to hang up. I just wanted to let you know that you can reach me on my cell if anything comes up."

"Sure. See you later," Angie was about to hang up the receiver but stopped when she saw the receptionist waving her hands and telling her that she needed to speak back to Aisha. "Aisha, hold up," Angie squealed. "Kaye wants to talk back to you."

"What is it, Kaye?" Aisha asked as soon as she heard the girl breathing over the phone.

"I almost forgot. Someone called for you earlier. A guy, but he didn't want to leave his name."

"Is that right? What did he want?" Aisha asked with a puzzled look on her face. Turning into Tameria's drive, she placed the car in park and opened the door while listening for Kaye's response.

"He wanted to know if you were back in the office."

"Back in the office? And he didn't say who he was?"

"Nope. When I asked him his name, he hung up. I looked on the office caller ID and it said unknown name – unknown number."

"It was probably some salesman wanting to sell me some more equipment or something. If anyone else calls, just send them to my voicemail. I'll check it later." *Who was it that called and knew that I was out? Who could it have been?* She thought about Chase, but why would Chase call her? *Maybe it was Minister Williams. No, I just left him. Plus he would have left a message.* Tameria opened the door and halted the guessing game playing in Aisha's mind.

"Good morning."

"Hey, Tameria," she replied and stepped inside Tameria's cluttered apartment. Walking over to her favorite chair Tameria had owned since high school, Aisha rested her butt on the arm of it. Tameria used to be the kind of person who kept everything in order, but since med school she was hardly ever home and the other free time was spent at Chase's place. Aisha looked around at the medical books spread out over the sofa and floor.

"I know. Don't even say it. The place is a disaster but I'm off tomorrow too and I've already made plans to clean up this place from top to bottom. I can't stand all of this clutter."

"I know that's right." Changing the subject Aisha asked, "What's on the agenda for us today? If you want, we can stay here and I'll help you tidy things up."

"No way! Off days from the hospital are far and few. I do not want to spend it cooped up in this apartment cleaning. I thought we'd go shopping and then have lunch. Whaddaya say?"

"That'll work. Let's get out of here then." Aisha pounced off the arm of the chair.

◆

The two friends shopped until they dropped. Aisha bought a tangerine jogging suit, a diamond print DKNY mermaid skirt and two pairs of sling backs. Tameria couldn't resist going into Victoria's Secret. Aisha couldn't believe it. Tameria was never shy or inhibited but she'd never guess that she'd want to get something out of Victoria's Secret.

"Tameria, I know you aren't going to get anything in here," Aisha leaned over and whispered. Tameria continued to browse through the undergarment section until she chose two pair of no-show panties and a fire red thong and bra set. Aisha was speechless but she refused to voice her say about Tameria's choices.

"Don't start your criticizing, Aisha. I know you don't want me to go there with you again."

"I wasn't criticizing you. I was just going to say that you're really flaunting your stuff aren't you," she managed to release a fake laugh.

"How is buying panties flaunting my stuff, Aisha? You can never have enough bras and panties. That's what my mother always said and working in a hospital emergency room, you better believe I've seen the worse of the worse when it comes to undergarments." Tameria turned her upper lip until it covered her nostrils. Without missing a beat she pulled out a couple more bras for her size DD breasts and happily went to the counter with her garments tucked safely in her hands. Aisha chose not to respond. While Tameria paid for her items, Aisha browsed through some of the lotions and oils.

"Okay, on to the next store."

"Hey, let's go inside that new store over there." Aisha suggested. Quickly putting aside their near confrontation just a few seconds earlier, the two of them giggled when they saw a guy and girl pass in front of them holding hands, both with pink and blue hair.

"Can you believe that?" Tameria turned her head and followed the odd looking couple with her eyes. "Love truly is blind."

"I just can't believe they're black. If they were white, I wouldn't think anything of it 'cause white people will die their hair green, orange and any other color without thinking a thing about it. But us? No way.

"Yea, but wait a minute," Tameria added and kept on laughing. "You know we can be ghetto fabulous ourselves. We'll dye ours Kool-Aid burgundy and bleach blonde in a minute." They were still laughing and chattering as they made their way over to the store. They searched through the sale items until they each found a pair of jeans they liked and shirts to match.

With their bags in tow, their next stop was the food court. While munching on chicken nuggets and waffle fries, they people watched between bites. "So you're telling me that you still haven't heard from Chandler?"

"That's right. And I don't want to either. Chandler said some cruel, disrespectful things to me the last time we talked. I refuse to go through that with him or any other man. Not to mention he lied about his profession. All the time I thought Mr. Right had come along and he turns out to be a liar and a skeezer. I guess he was using me all along so he could make himself look good. I think he thought he was going to catch me mixed up with those terrible men at The Lynx. But thank God, I didn't know anything about it."

"You got that right. Instead of sitting here eating in the mall, you could have been serving time. You see why you need to get your life back on track? God has been far too good to you for you to keep on doing what you were doing. You need some help."

"Puhleeze, Tameria, don't ruin the day. I don't need to be preached to." Aisha shrugged her shoulders and held her head down.

"Preaching is exactly what you need. Have you still been using drugs? And tell me the truth too." Tameria insisted. "I'm your friend but I'm a doctor too, and doing drugs can be not only addictive but deadly."

"I've started going to Cocaine Anonymous meetings at the church. Minister Williams convinced me to try it. I've been a couple of times. To be honest, once I got over the initial shame of walking into my first meeting, I've been doing okay. I haven't had a hit of coke for four weeks and a day."

Tameria stood up and went over to hug Aisha. "I knew you could do it. You just have to take it one day at a time. I'm proud of you," she said as she went back to her seat. "Sounds like Minister Williams has some influence, huh."

"You can say that. I think it's the way he listens without making me feel worse than what I already feel for what I've done. He doesn't look at me like I'm a terrible person. I feel comfortable talking to him. To be honest, I look forward to our sessions on Thursdays. I really do." Aisha looked as if she were in a daze as she talked about Jackson Williams. Tameria noticed the sparkle in her eyes and the manner in which Aisha spoke about him. Maybe Aisha wasn't aware of it, but Tameria could tell that Aisha liked Jackson Williams a lot.

Tameria changed the subject. "Have you heard from your mother?"

"I've tried talking to her but she's so cold towards me. I don't know what else to say or do. I love my mother and I'm sorry for so many things, Tameria." Aisha's voice dropped and Tameria detected her sadness.

"Just give her time. She has her own burdens to bear too."

"That's what Jackson, I mean Minister Williams said."

Tameria raised her eyebrows when Aisha called Minister Williams by his first name. *So things are on a more personal level*, Tameria thought to herself but acted like she hadn't notice Aisha's slip of the tongue.

"He told me to give her time to come around because she's still grieving. I just don't know how much more time she needs though. I wish I could help her in some way. If we pulled together instead of apart, maybe Daddy's death wouldn't be so hard to deal with."

"Everything will work out. You'll see." Tameria reached over and grabbed Aisha's hand and squeezed it. "Come on, let's get out of here." Looking at her watch, Tameria remarked, "Didn't you say you wanted to be at the studio by three?"

"Yeah," looking at her watch Aisha added, "It's one forty now. By the time you take me to your place to get my car and I drop off my clothes at the apartment, it'll be close to three. So you're right. Let's go.

The drive to Tameria's afforded the two friends more time to talk and enjoy each other's company. Tameria told Aisha that she'd met Chase's parents and they loved her. Tameria said she couldn't see herself spending her life with anyone else but him. Her cell phone rang and she looked down to pick it up and almost rear ended the car in front of her. Aisha tightly gripped the door handle. Tameria giggled and made smooching sounds in the phone. She was still talking to Chase when she turned off the I-240 exit on to Bill Morris Parkway Aisha used her time to check her voicemail and retrieve her messages. She didn't want to keep listening to Tameria's side of her and Chase's conversation.

35

He who wants to do good, knocks at the gate; he who loves finds the gates open. R. Tagore Thakur

Jackson Williams positioned himself on his extra-long blumarine sofa. He fluffed its pillows, stretched out then crossed his legs one over the other. He turned his big screen to channel 633 to watch the Memphis Grizzlies' basketball game. Tonight they were playing against the Cleveland Cavaliers. He wanted to see if the Grizzlies could do a repeat of their last win against the Rockets. Normally he would be putting his season tickets to use by rooting for the Grizzlies in person at the FedEx Forum but the day had been a long, tiring one so he had made a hard decision to stay at home. He had counseled over ten church members today and attended the weekly youth meeting. He awarded two young men with his tickets for tonight's game. They deserved it and Jackson wanted to show them how much he thought of them. Living in one of the worse areas of the city, the two young men had been involved heavily in drugs and gang activity. Both of them were high school dropouts who lacked parental influence and supervision. The Youth Program turned out to be their saving grace. During the past year, they had managed to make a 360 degree turn by giving up drug dealing and gang involvement. It hadn't been an easy road for either one of them. There often were deadly circumstances when a gang member wanted out but it was God's grace that had kept them safe. The gang was a small time neighborhood gang perpetrating to be as bad and as dangerous as some of the more notorious ones. Their bark however was far worse than their bite.

The two youths had recently accepted Jesus Christ into their hearts. The difference in their personalities was remarkable. They attended the GED classes offered at Greater Faith and the Human Resources manager hired them at the church to work along with the sound engineer. When Jackson gave them the tickets, they were ecstatic and humble at their blessing. Jackson felt just as good, knowing he had brightened the life, if only for a moment, of the two young men.

"Oooohhhh! he screamed when Gasol made a three pointer. At half time, he went into his modern kitchen and fixed himself a turkey burger on his George Foreman grill and added ice to his all-time favorite drink, root beer. Returning to his spot on the sofa, the past week's events flashed through his mind. When he landed on thoughts of Aisha, he put his mind on pause and gave himself permission to reflect on the woman who pricked his heart each time he was in her presence. She had no idea that he understood her hurt and pain. The relationship with his mother had been a strained one as well. He never wanted to become an attorney like her. His mind was always focused on Jesus. Every time his father made a step toward their front door, Jackson was at his heels determined to go along. Unlike most children, any time the church doors opened he wanted to walk through them. Any and everything that had to do with God and church, Jackson yearned to be part of it. His father was thankful that his youngest son, Jackson loved the Lord as much as he did. Jackson's father and mother often argued about all the time Jackson's father spent away from home preaching, counseling, visiting the sick and doing anything he could to help save someone else's soul from going to hell. She disliked it even more when he started taking Jackson along with him. The friction intensified in the couple's relationship and after fifteen years of marriage, Jackson's mother left his father. Jackson refused to move with her and his two brothers. Once it was made apparent how much he wanted to stay with his father, she relented and allowed him to remain with his dad. She had very little to do with Jackson and his father after that. It took years for Jackson to let go of the anger he felt toward his mother for walking out on him and his daddy. But once he did, he began to slowly allow her back into his life. She told him she felt like he chose his father over her. But Jackson wanted her to know that it wasn't his father he chose over her, it was God and that choice was something he would never be sorry for doing. How could anyone be jealous of a man who was called to do God's work? Jackson decided he would stop trying to answer that question and instead he did like God wanted him to do, which was to love his mother unconditionally and to forgive her.

Sitting on the sofa taking small bites from his sandwich, he decided that at the next session he would share his story with Aisha. He wanted her to know that he truly understood some of her pain. She seemed to be doing better physically and mentally since she started attending Cocaine Anonymous. For that e was grateful. He noticed that the last time she came to his office, she looked much healthier. In the beginning he knew she was fighting hard not to let him know she was snorting cocaine. But he'd seen enough people on drugs to recognize that she was one of them. One of his close friends from high school was on crack back in Ohio. From what Jackson had heard from some of his other buddies back home, the guy was basically living on the streets and walked around begging for money to buy his next rock. Jackson had him on his long prayer list. Every day he called out the man's name. He did the same when it came to Aisha. He believed with all of his heart that God had great things in store for her. Now he had to get her to believe it as well.

Of all the people he had counseled, Aisha was rather special. She possessed some of the qualities that he wanted in a wife. She was kind and humble with a spirit that radiated love and sincerity. Sure she had a lot of healing to do, but he saw past her imperfections and focused on the Godly woman he knew was inside of her. He thought about her smile, the way she threw her head back when she laughed and how it broke his heart each time he witnessed her tears and pain. Out loud he made his requests for her healing to God then assumed his previous position and started watching the ballgame again.

◆

Aisha climbed out of the bath tub, dried off and curled up in her favorite chair. She was exhausted after coming home yet again from another Cocaine Anonymous meeting. When she initially joined the group she made a pledge to attend ninety meetings in ninety days. It was tough but she was determined to beat her drug addiction and make things right in her life.

This time when she opened the nightstand drawer, she wasn't searching for a hit, she was looking for the white sheet of typing paper with the twelve steps of Cocaine Anonymous printed on it. She picked up the paper, went over to her chair and began to read the twelve steps.

She made it a daily ritual to recite the steps after she prayed every morning and before she prayed at night. Her sponsor, a recovering addict named Beverly, had been clean and sober going on three years. Whenever Aisha felt the pressure of the drug tugging at her, she picked up the phone and called Beverly for support. The program was her lifeline to a drug free life. She prayed that she would not go down the destructive path of using drugs again.

The ringing of the phone startled her. Her first thought was to let it ring. Whoever was on the other end could leave a message if it was important. Her decision was quickly changed when an unfamiliar Little Rock number appeared on the Caller ID.

"Hello."

"Aisha?"

"Yes, who is this?"

"It's Mrs. Simmons. Your mother's next door neighbor." Aisha didn't know if she could take what she believed Mrs. Simmons was about to tell her. Her heart started pounding against her chest and her hands shook.

"Is my mother all right?" Aisha asked in a panic.

"She didn't want me to call you but I did anyway. My husband and I had to take her to the emergency room. She kept complaining about being short of breath. She was sweating and could barely talk."

"Mrs. Simmons, is my mother okay?" Aisha asked again in a loud voice.

"Darling, calm down. She's going to be fine. They kept her in the hospital though because they suspect she has a bout of pneumonia. We just left there, me and my husband and some of the other church members."

"What hospital did you take her to, Mrs. Simmons?"

"She's at St. Vincent Hospital, baby. Now you be careful driving over here. You need to get somebody to come with you because you're too upset."

"Thank you for calling me, Mrs. Simmons," Aisha didn't respond to Mrs. Simmons advice. She hung up the phone, hurriedly threw on some clothes and dashed out the door.

◆

"Mother, how do you feel?" Aisha's voice was tender as she spoke to her mother and stroked her forehead. "I came as soon as I heard you were here."

Sandra Carlisle removed the oxygen mask from over her nose and mouth. "You didn't have to do that. I'm fine. I bet Mattie Simmons called you didn't she?"

"Mother, it doesn't matter who called because it was the right thing to do."

"I told her not to call anybody but my church members and the pastor. There was no need for you to come all the way over here."

"Well, I'm here and I'm not going anywhere until you're better. Now you just close your eyes and get some sleep." Aisha kissed her mother's sweaty forehead and pushed back the loose strands of gray hair away from her mother's face. Within a few minutes, Mrs. Carlisle was asleep. Aisha sat down in the chair next to her mother's bed and watched her while she slept. Her own eyes became heavy and she succumbed to the call of her body to rest.

"Mrs. Carlisle, how are you feeling, hon?" a short white chubby nurse asked her. Aisha's eyes flew open and she sat upright in the chair, rubbing her eyes.

"I'm feeling better. My breathing is better too."

"Good. Who is this young lady here with you?" Aisha's mother looked over to her right at Aisha.

"My daughter," Mrs. Carlisle responded.

"Hi, daughter," the nurse teased.

Aisha stood up and said, "My name is Aisha. Nurse, is my mother going to be okay?"

"Yes, but she does have pneumonia and it can be rough on our older patients. The doctor will be able to tell you more when he makes his rounds first thing in the morning. Will you still be here?"

"Yes, I'll be here. And thank you."

"No problem. Mrs. Carlisle, I want you to take this pill for me, hon. It'll help you rest easier tonight." She gave her a glass of water with the pill and without any protest, Aisha's mother swallowed it. "Good girl," she said like Mrs. Carlisle was a child instead of a seventy two year old woman. The nurse patted Mrs. Carlisle on the legs and said, "Press the button on the side of the bed if you need anything hon."

The following morning the doctor came in. He assured Aisha that her mother would be fine. He explained that he was going to keep Mrs. Carlisle in the hospital for at least another few days just to make sure the fluid on her lungs was clearing up.

"Aisha," her mother called out soon after the doctor left. Aisha leaped up from the chair and rushed to her mother's bedside.

"What is it, Mother?"

"Shouldn't you be at work? I told you I'm fine and you heard what the doctor said."

"Mother, I'm not going anywhere. I already called Angie and told her where I was. She knows how to reach me if she needs me. Anyway, I'm not worried about the studio right now. I'm going to be here for you as long as I have to." Aisha became upset when she witnessed the tears falling from her mother's eyes.

"Momma, what's wrong? Are you in pain? Do you want me to get the nurse?"

"No, no. I was just thinking."

"Thinking about what Mother?"

"Never mind, I'd just like to rest now." Sandra Carlisle turned over away from the glares of her daughter.

"I wish you wouldn't do that, Mother."

"Do what? What have I done now?"

Aisha felt her anger rising against her mother but managed to keep it in check. Now was not the time to explode. But this was her mother's typical way of getting Aisha on edge and she was sick of it. But there was nothing she felt she could do about it because disrespecting her mother was the last thing she wanted to do.

"Mother, look you go on and rest. I'm going downstairs to the cafeteria and grab a bite to eat. I'll be back shortly."

Without turning to look at Aisha, her mother responded curtly, "No need to hurry. I told you anyway that I would be fine. You should go back to Memphis and see about your dance studio."

Without responding, Aisha proceeded to walk out of the room. *Not tonight. I am not going there with tonight*, she repeated to herself. She went outside and sat on the veranda. Inhaling the fresh air and feeling the night air against her body sent a shiver up and down her spine. Why did she let her mother get under her skin? It was time she learned to do like her father told her – "let it roll off you like water rolls off of oil," is what he would often tell her. But through all these years, she'd not yet learned how not to let her mother's harsh reprimands and stinging comments affect her. Reaching on the side of her jeans, she removed her cell phone from its clip and turned it on. Aisha phoned Beverly and told her where she was. Beverly got on the internet with Aisha on the other end of the phone and searched for meeting places in or surrounding St Vincent Hospital. The two of them were elated to discover that a nearby community center held a nightly meeting seven days a week. It was remarkable how God had opened another door for her to walk through.

36

Love will find a way. Unknown

"Natalie, have you heard from Miss Carlisle this morning?" Jackson was concerned that Aisha hadn't shown up for her session. During the time they'd been meeting she had never missed a meeting nor had she ever been late. Now he hadn't heard from her for two weeks. The fact that she hadn't bothered to call had him on edge.

Father God, please let Aisha be safe. I pray that she hasn't relapsed. Take care of her wherever she is. He paced back and forth in his office. Scrolling through his palm pilot, he stopped when he reached her office number. For reasons he didn't know, this was the only contact number Aisha had listed on her membership and counseling forms. Dialing the number, his hand slightly shook from nervousness. He told himself he was calling from a professional standpoint, but his heart kept insisting it was something more. Something more personal.

"Good afternoon, is Miss Carlisle in please?" He was extremely polite and without him knowing, he had already won over Kaye because of his courteous attitude.

"No. Miss Carlisle isn't in the office today. May I take a message?" Kaye was equally polite.

"Is there another number where I can reach her? It's sort of important." Jackson insisted.

"I'm afraid not. Would you like me to put you into her voice mail? She checks it regularly." Kaye offered.

Where is she? Jackson paced across the deep purple carpet in his office. "Yes, you can transfer me to her voice mail. And thanks so much. God bless you," Jackson told her before she transferred him. *I have to get it together. This happens all the time. Once they feel that the counseling sessions have helped them over the hump, most of the people stop coming. Seldom do they call and notify Pastoral Care – until the next time that is, when they need more help.* That was fine with Jackson because he wanted the members to benefit from his spiritual counseling and then move on to stand on their own faith. But Aisha had tugged at his heart in a way no other member had done. The woman was intriguing regardless of the things she'd confided in him about. Just because she'd ventured down the wrong path didn't make her a terrible person. To Jackson, it only confirmed that she was just like the rest of God's children – imperfect. He sat back in his chair, pulled out his Bible and meditated over several scriptures. An hour later he informed Natalie that he was leaving the building. He offered to bring her back a sandwich.

"No thanks, Minister Williams. I'm going to the cafeteria to get a salad and a sandwich a little later. Thanks anyway."

"No problem."

"Are you going to be away long? Because if you are, I want to remind you that tonight is the Ministers' Meeting."

"I know. I have it in my palm pilot. I shouldn't be gone more than a couple of hours. Call me on my cell if something comes up."

"Yes sir." Natalie made a thumbs-up sign and smiled. She loved being Minister Williams' admin. He was easy to work for, considerate and thoughtful too. *If I wasn't close to being a senior citizen, I'd give these young women at the church a run for their money. And that Aisha Carlisle doesn't seem to be aware that he has a special attraction for her. I can see it and I'm blind as a bat. Too bad she's already engaged.* She laughed out loud then turned around in her swivel chair to resume working on the quarterly membership Pastoral Care report.

◆

Jackson floored the accelerator of his pearl blue Chrysler Crossfire. There was barely any traffic on the interstate, which was unusual. But it was to his benefit because he felt like he had the road to himself. For some reason, driving was a means of relaxation for him. He drove until he read the green sign that said Bailey Station exit. He took the exit and continued his drive through Collierville. The town was growing rapidly and the hustle and bustle of traffic was more than what he expected. Nevertheless, it worked in his favor because it forced him to slow down and take in the beauty of God's world. He could no longer ignore the rumbling sounds of his stomach so he drove into the parking lot of O'Charleys for a quick lunch. After placing his order for Cajun chicken pasta, he reached for his cell and dialed Aisha's office again. The receptionist transferred him to her voicemail once again. His initial thought was to hang up. But before he could follow through on that thought, he heard her sweet, tender voice instructing him to "please leave a message and your call will be returned."

◆

Aisha met the doctor at the entrance to her mother's hospital room. Opening the door for her, she anxiously stepped ahead of him to hear his latest report concerning her mother.

"Mrs. Carlisle, how are you feeling today?"

"I'm feeling fine doctor. I want to go home. I've been lying in this bed for God knows how many days," she complained.

"Well, the last series of tests we performed late yesterday show significant fluid decrease. I'm pleased with your rate of recovery."

"Thank you, God. Doctor you have made my day. Now tell me, when can I get out of here and go home?" Mrs. Carlisle eased upright in the hospital bed and waited on his response.

"You can be discharged this afternoon if you promise to follow my instructions."

Mrs. Carlisle raised her left eyebrow and slowly folded her arms.

"You are not completely over this and until you've regained some of your strength, I want someone with you around the clock. If that's not possible, I'll have to insist that you remain in the hospital for a few more days." He shifted his piercing green eyes in Aisha's direction.

Observing him carefully, Mrs. Carlisle spoke up. "Doctor, there's no need to look at her. She has her own life to lead in Memphis. I have good neighbors and church members who won't mind watching out for me."

Aisha managed to hold back her embarrassment over her mother's thoughtless comments. *Just who does she think she is. Acting as if I don't have time for my own mother?* For now, she held her tongue so the wrong words wouldn't spill out. *Lord have mercy.*

"I understand that your daughter has her own life. And I'm certainly not one to tell you who should or who shouldn't take care of you over these next couple of weeks. My main concern is that you have someone with you. You're still weak and you still have some healing to do. Is that clear?" The doctor was stern and refused to leave until Mrs. Carlisle promised to follow his directions.

"I understand, Doctor. Like I told you. I have plenty of people, thank God, to help me."

"That's fine, Mrs. Carlisle. Oh by the way, I want to see you in my office first thing Monday morning." He studied her chart like he was searching for anything he may have forgotten to cover. "Any questions before I leave?" he finally asked Mrs. Carlisle and Aisha.

Both of them shook their heads. "No I don't have any," was Aisha's response.

"I think you've answered all of my questions," was Mrs. Carlisle's response. "But I know how to call your office if I think of anything. No need to worry about that because you know I will."

"Yes, how well do I know," the doctor laughed. Sandra Carlisle was not one to mince words. Whenever she came to his office for any reason she commanded the full attention of his staff.

Aisha reached out and shook his hand and thanked him for taking such good care of her mother.

"Aisha, I meant what I said to the doctor. There's no need for you to keep staying over here. You haven't been home in God knows when. Mattie will help look out for me. She told me that yesterday when she came up here to see me. And my church has some of the sweetest members. Pastor already made it clear that it's the church's responsibility to take care of the elderly and the widows. I don't want to stop you from living your life. I'll be just fine."

"Why do you do that?"

"What on earth are you talking about now?" her mother sighed, eased down in her bed and pulled the dingy white hospital covers up to her shoulders.

"Mother, please. You know fully well what I'm talking about. Telling the doctor that I needed to get back home to Memphis. I've been here for you ever since Mrs. Simmons called and told me you were sick." Aisha fussed.

"Exactly. And that's what I'm talking about. You need to get back to a sense of normalcy. If you keep on, you're going to let that studio of yours go down the drain. You can't keep putting all of your responsibility on poor Angie."

"Will you let me handle my own business? Angie is totally capable of running things while I'm away. Plus, I talk to her every day. Sometimes three or four times a day."

"Look, I don't want to argue with you. I'm trying to get well. You're just like your father – stubborn and strong willed. He never wanted to listen to what anybody else had to say. And you're a carbon copy of 'em."

"I do listen to you. But I also listened to the person who knows what you need better than you right now – your doctor. So I don't want to hear about what I can do or should be doing. Or talking about daddy like it's so terrible for me to be like him. The only thing I'm going to be doing is taking care of you. And that's that." Aisha walked over to the huge picture window and looked out over the city. Looking over her shoulder in the direction of the sound of heavy breathing, she realized her mother had fallen asleep just that quickly. Aisha stole the opportunity to begin gathering the small wardrobe and the mini florist her mother had managed to collect during her hospital stay. One thing was for sure, her mother had many friends at the church she'd joined when she moved to Little Rock. The small congregation of Holiness Tabernacle of Praises was the perfect size. It offered Sandra the attention she always craved from others. The people adored her. In spite of this, Aisha was her mother's only daughter, her only child for that matter. She felt it was her responsibility and no one else's to take care of her mother. Sure she wouldn't deny any one from helping out but ultimately she wanted to be her mother's caretaker. It took almost an hour for her to finish packing everything together. Next she went to the Nurse's Station to check on the discharge papers and the medications the doctor wanted her mother to take home with her. Once she finished doing that she called and talked to Angie. She filled her in on what was going on with her mother.

"Angie, I haven't received any more strange calls have I?"

"No. Not that I know of. Kaye hasn't said anything to me. The calls she passes my way have all been regarding something legit pertaining to the studio. Is everything okay?"

"Yeah, sure. I was just checking that's all. I guess I'll hang up now. You know where to find me if you need me. And again, thanks for handling everything at the studio."

"Girl, please you're not only my boss, you're my friend Aisha. And friends help each other out during times like this."

"Well, I definitely couldn't do this without your support. But anyway, I'm going to let you go before I start boohooing. Just put me in my voicemail so I can check my messages. I'll call you later. Bye bye."

"You have seven messages. To listen to your messages, press…." Aisha quickly bypassed the mechanical instructions and hit the pound key which took her straight into her voice mail. A couple of calls were from people checking to see if she had any available slots for new students. She forwarded the message to Angie's voicemail. Another message was from Tameria. She quickly erased it because whenever Tameria couldn't reach her at the office, she knew how to call her at home or on her cell and she had done just that. Tameria once offered to drive over to Little Rock when her rotation shift ended but Aisha refused. Tameria's plate was already full and she wasn't about to add undue pressure on her by allowing her to come and sit with her, *I'll say whatever's on my mind and I don't care who likes it mother*. Tameria had become used to Mrs. Carlisle's overly expressive ways over the years. She'd witnessed her during some of the best of times as well as the drama queen tantrums that Mrs. Carlisle was good at throwing. The next call totally took Aisha by surprise. It was from Minister Williams. She had totally forgotten about their Thursday meetings. When was the last time she had attended a counseling session? *Oh my God, I can't believe this and I haven't even bothered to call him. He must think I'm an idiot, she shouted at herself.*

"Aisha, Minister Williams here. I hope you're all right. I haven't heard from you. Natalie said you haven't called to cancel any of your appointments. Give me a call when you can to let me know how you're doing." The next two messages were also from Jackson. "Aisha, it's me again. Jackson Williams. Are you okay?" I'm really worried now. Please call me. And remember, God is everywhere you are. Call on Him Aisha."

Aisha could tell by his somewhat pleading voice that he was genuinely worried about her. He probably thought she was back on drugs which she thanked God was far from the truth. His last call sounded even more desperate than the others. "Aisha, I contacted the young lady who works with you at the studio. Don't worry, I didn't tell her any of your business. I told her I needed to talk to you and asked when you would be in. Guess what? She put me in your voicemail, so here I am again, leaving you a message. Please call me. If you don't want to attend any more counseling sessions, then call me or Natalie and let one of us know. I promise I won't be mad at you." Aisha could tell by the way he said that, he must have had a smile on his face. "And Aisha even if you decide that you don't want to attend anymore counseling sessions, please don't stop going to your CA meetings. Call me if you need me. I'm praying for you. Goodbye."

He sounds so sweet, Aisha said to herself. I do owe him an explanation as to why I haven't been coming to my sessions. The man must think I'm really crazy now. She picked up her cell phone and scrolled through her contacts until she reached the church office number. The receptionist forwarded her to Pastoral Care. Natalie answered the phone.

"Natalie, is Minister Williams available please?" Aisha asked politely.

"May I tell him whose calling?"

"Yes. This is Aisha Carlisle."

"Aisha. I mean, Miss Carlisle."

"No, you were right the first time. Please call me Aisha."

"Well, Aisha, Pastor Williams and I have been really concerned about you. It's like you just dropped off the face of the earth. And Minister Williams said he hasn't seen you at any of the services. But you and I both know that's no easy feat anyway with all the people coming through these church doors," she babbled. "I didn't tell him, but I thought to myself, maybe you were on your honeymoon."

"Honeymoon? What are you talking about Natalie? Why would you think something like that?" Aisha was flabbergasted to say the least. Sometimes Natalie didn't know when to shut up.

"Well, I thought that since you're engaged that maybe you had gotten married and you and that handsome man who came looking for you that time had gone on your honeymoon."

"What on earth are you talking about? What man?"

Natalie went on to explain to Aisha about the gentleman who had come looking for her several weeks ago, minutes after one of her sessions. She described the man to her. Aisha became frightened. Was it one of Ronald Shipley's goons or somebody Jason had looking for her to bring harm to her? A lump rose in the back of her throat at the thought. She vaguely heard Natalie going on and on about how shocked she was to learn there was no fiancé'. Aisha then focused in on Chandler. It had to be Chandler. He would do something like that. She finally convinced Natalie that what the stranger told her was indeed a lie and asked her not to repeat it to anyone. Natalie assured her that she hadn't told a soul, not even Minister Williams.

"Thank you, Natalie. Did you say Minister Williams was in his office?"

"Oh, no I didn't say. I'm sorry. I get carried away sometimes you know. Anyway, he's out of the building right now. I can take your number and have him call you when he returns if you'd like."

"Yes, yes that would be fine." Aisha left her cell phone number. "Please let him know I called."

"I sure will. You take care and have a blessed day." Natalie hung up the phone. She wondered what was going on with Aisha Carlisle and who that strange man could have been since she wasn't engaged. She shrugged her shoulders. After a few seconds of contemplating the situation, she returned to shuffling papers around on her desk.

37

The mother-daughter relationship is the most complex.
Wynonna Judd

"I'm ready to get out of here." Sandra woke up from her two hour nap. "Have they finished writing up my discharge papers?" she asked groggily.

"Mother, everything is fine. By the time you get dressed, we should be able to call for a wheelchair. Then I'll take you home. Come on. Let me help you out of the bed so you can get dressed. And please, take your time Mother. You may think you're okay, but you still have a long way to go before you get your energy level back up to where it was before you came down with pneumonia.

"I hear you. And I know what the doctor said. I was here, remember?" Mrs. Carlisle retorted.

◆

In between taking care of her mother, Aisha took the time to clean out her mother's cupboards and closets. When Sandra moved to Little Rock, she moved many of Bennie's belongings right along with her. There were still plenty of clothes of her father's that needed to be given to someone who could use them. Before she washed them, she breathed in for the last time, his scent. Folding and packing the freshly washed clothes, she placed them in several large bags before carrying them to her car. After her CA meeting, she planned to stop by her mother's

269

church and donate the remaining clothes to the Clothes Closet.

Her mother listened to Aisha shuffling about the house doing things that she'd wanted done but hadn't been able to do. "Thank you God for my daughter," she prayed. Her face was crimson and tears poured down landing on her satin nightgown. It was time she made things right with Aisha. Tomorrow was promised to no one and she didn't want to leave this earth without asking for her daughter's forgiveness.

"Mom, I'll be back," Aisha yelled from the front room. I'm going to drop the last of Daddy's things off at your church for their Clothes Closet." She turned around and headed to her mother's room to make sure Sandra heard her. "I'll bring us some Chinese food back for dinner. That is unless you want something else." When her mother didn't acknowledge her, Aisha walked over to her bedside. "Mom, are you all right? You look like you've been crying. Are you in pain?" Aisha sat on the side of her mother's bed and felt her forehead to see if she was warm.

"I'm fine. You go ahead and take care of your daddy's things. I've wanted to do it for so long but I just couldn't bring myself to. I'm glad you're doing it for me."

"Well, I tried to do it several times before but you wouldn't let me."

"I know, but I just couldn't at the time."

"I know, Momma. I understand. It was difficult for me too. Somehow even though I know he isn't coming back, when I was packing his things, it hit me again and I began to miss him terribly." She felt herself tearing up. The last thing she wanted to do was get her mother upset. That's probably why her mother had been crying. She had been thinking of Bennie, as Sandra often called him.

"You go on before it gets dark out there. Chinese is fine with me. You know what I like."

"Okay, I'll be back as soon as I can. I've already talked to Mrs. Simmons and she's going to come over and sit with you until I make it back."

"I wish you wouldn't worry Mattie. I'll be fine."

"Well, I won't be fine if I know you're here alone." Aisha kissed her mother's forehead and turned to leave. Just as she made it to the back door, Mrs. Simmons ambled up the concrete path.

"Hi, Mrs. Simmons. Thanks again for coming over."

"Honey, please, I don't mind at all. Me and Sandra are close like that. There's nothing I wouldn't do for that woman and I know she'd do the same for me. So you go on. Take your time too."

"Yes, ma'am. I'm going to stop and get some Chinese. Do you want me to bring you something back?"

"No, young lady. Me and Chinese don't see eye to eye. Plus I just ate not too long ago." She reared back and laughed.

◆

"Did you get everything taken care of?"

"Yes, ma'am. Pastor told me to tell you that he's been praying for you. He said that he and the First Lady would be over tomorrow to sit and pray with you."

"Oh, that man is such a blessing to me. And his wife, that woman knows she stands by her man," Sandra remarked.

Aisha helped her mother into the kitchen and they sat and ate their Chinese food.

"Aisha, I want to talk to you about something."

"Mom, please. I already told you. I have everything under control with the studio and my apartment. I have enough clothes here already and Tameria checks on the apartment. So there. Now let's talk about something else," Aisha demanded.

"Actually, that's not what I wanted to talk about anyway."

"It's not?" Aisha wrinkled her brow and appeared puzzled. "What is it then?"

"I want to talk about all the time I've wasted being angry and jealous. I want to tell you that I'm sorry. For all the things I said when Bennie died. It wasn't your fault. None of it was. Before Bennie died, I felt neglected by him. Don't get me wrong. I know that he loved me. He loved me dearly, but sometimes I believed he loved me because I gave him you. You were the center of his universe outside of God."

"Mother, please don't say such things. I'm the one that's been wrong all the years before Daddy died. I didn't want to cause problems between the two of you Momma. Honest, I didn't. I'm the one who's sorry."

"You didn't cause problems honey. I wanted you to believe you did because I was jealous of my own daughter's relationship with her father. You see, you had the kind of relationship I always wanted to have with my daddy when I was a little girl. I wanted to have all of his love and attention but he was too busy working all the time, trying to make a decent living for us. He worked hard too Aisha. And instead of being thankful for him, I despised him for being away from home so much. When I met your father, he was attentive and romantic. He showered me with his time. There was nothing that man wouldn't do for me."

"Momma, don't say anything else. Why don't you rest? We'll talk when you're better."

"No, I want to say this now. The day you were born, I don't remember ever seeing him as happy as he was at that moment. You were always a Daddy's girl. In the beginning it was fine. But when you became older, it seemed like everything centered around you. Whenever he was at home, it was you not me that he showered with attention and gifts. It was you he wanted to spend his time with. Not me. But I didn't make it easy for him either. I was always so critical of him. Nothing he ever did was good enough for me. But you, you were so easy to please. He loved and adored you. Baby, won't you forgive me? Mrs. Carlisle pleaded. "I love you sweetheart."

Aisha laid her head on the side of her mother's shoulder. Wrapping her arm around her mother, Aisha wept. Between sobs, she said, "I love you too. For so many years I thought you didn't love me. And I didn't know what to do about it. I would pray to God over and over again asking him to make you love me. You have no idea how much you mean to me Momma."

Sandra stroked the top of her daughter's head and brushed Aisha's hair with the back of her hands. At that moment, Aisha felt the weight of the heavy burden she had carried during her life being lifted from her. A sense of release washed over her soul. She felt a spiritual cleansing taking place. *Jackson was right,* she thought. "When the time is right, things will work out. Each day is an opportunity for a new beginning," was what he told her. Aisha silently thanked God for yet another miracle.

After a long tiring day, Aisha retired to her bedroom. She collapsed on the full size bed and curled up in a knot. Staring at the phone next to the bed, she pondered over whether or not she should call Jackson. The clock radio displayed 9:00 p.m. *Jackson left his cell number in my voicemail. And he did say call him whenever I got his message.* She placed her hand on the receiver, picked it up, then abruptly placed it back on the hook. *Naw. It's too late. The man didn't mean for me to call him this time of night. I'll call him tomorrow.* To keep her mind off of him, she took a long bath, then climbed up in the bed and started reading an old J. California Cooper novel, *Some Love Some Pain* until sleep overtook her.

For the next several days Aisha remained at her mother's side almost constantly. They talked, went on short walks along the sidewalk to help build her mother's strength. They laughed and had a good time watching Sandra's favorite daytime show, *Judge Mathis*. They spent time getting to know each other all over again.

38

*Friendship is born at that moment when one person says
to another: 'What! You too? I thought I was the only one.*
C.S. Lewis

"It's good to have you back, girl. Things haven't
been the same since you've been gone."

"Angie, thank you. I missed this place." Aisha
looked around the studio, noticing every detail around
her. It felt good to be back at home. Her mother was
doing fine. Things between them had drastically
improved. Every now and then, Sandra Carlisle had
snapped at Aisha or said something out of line, but Aisha
had come to understand that there were some things that
would never change. Finally, she had been able to let her
mother's sometimes insensitive, thoughtless remarks,
'roll off of her like water rolled off of oil.

◆

"Come on, girls. Let's get with it. Just because I've
been away doesn't mean you should be unprepared.
You've had some great instructors and I want you to
show me what you've been doing in my absence. Now,
come on. Get with it." She clapped her hands and yelled
out her instructions.

"Rock forward on the right. Recover weight back on
to the left, three and four. Step right foot. Half turn to the
right. Step slightly forward onto the left. Now facing the

six o'clock wall, shuffle forward. Right, left and right. Step left. Forward and pivot half turn. Right foot. Weight onto the right and step to the left. Bend slightly forward. Now facing the twelve o'clock wall I want you to…"

Dancing and choreography was her calling. Watching the girls perform energized her. She was back where she belonged. Her body seldom harassed her about doing drugs. The seven and a half pounds she'd gained had given her a healthier glow. For now, things for her couldn't be better.

◆

Aisha, Tameria and Angie danced around Aisha's spacious living room while Beyoncé's *Check On It* blared on the stereo. *"Ohh, boy you looking like you like what you see,"* the three women sang in unison and laughed wildly. It had been such a long time since the three of them had gotten together for a girl's night out. It felt good to Aisha to have her friends around her. Having been off of drugs and alcohol for close to six months, her outlook on life was upbeat again.

"Tameria, I thought you were going to fix us some more daiquiris and margaritas," Tameria asked while sipping the last bit of her peach margarita.

"Hold up, girl. Don't you see I've got my dance on," Aisha yelled over the music.

"She doesn't need any more anyway. You know she can't hold water, let alone a third virgin margarita. No telling what she'd be doing if alcohol was really in our drinks," Angie teased before breaking out in a twerk.

After the song ended the exhausted girls fell on the sofa and chair.

"Tameria, what's up with you and Chase?" Angie asked while Aisha got up to go and mix some more drinks.

"We're going strong. I tell you, I love me some Chase." She tilted her head back and laughed loudly again.

From the kitchen Aisha added, "Tell us something we don't know already. We know he's got your nose wide open."

"Angie, I don't recall you asking Miss Know It All anything," Tameria shot back.

"Okay girls, settle down." Angie remarked and jokingly raised her hands like she was trying to part them. Aisha put a two more pitchers of the non-alcoholic peach daiquiris and margaritas on the living room table and then stood in front of Tameria with her hands positioned on her hips.

"And? What are you supposed to be doing?"

"I'm about to get my groove on again. That's what I'm about to do." Aisha pranced over to the stereo and turned on another song. This time it was Unpredictable by Jamie Foxx. After putting the CD on, she looked at the girls and said, "you know I'm unpredictable myself," and started laughing.

"Yeah right, I think it's Minister Jackson Williams that's unpredictable." Tameria answered and swayed to the beat of the music.

"I know you didn't go there. Jackson and I, I mean Minister Williams and I are just friends. He's been a great counselor."

"What? Naw she didn't just play us for crazy," Angie looked over at Tameria with a huge smile plastered across her face.

"I don't know what y'all mean. There's nothing going on between me and Minister Williams."

"Go on, call the man Jackson. No sense in pretending to be all professional now. It's too late for that." Again, Tameria and Angie laughed while Aisha looked at them like she had no idea what they meant. She was still somewhat uncertain about her feelings for Jackson Williams. He was a minister and she couldn't see herself becoming caught up with a man of the cloth. Her life had been far too complicated for her to start living the life of a preacher's lady.

"Okay, okay, I admit it. I do like him, but that's about it. The man is a preacher for God's sake. What kind of relationship can we have?"

"A real one, just like anybody else," Angie interjected. "He's a man who happens to preach for a living. He's no different from any other fine brother out there."

"Except if you cross him, he's got the power to report you directly to God," Tameria teased again. Aisha picked up the fluffy sofa pillow and threw it at Tameria. In return, Tameria grabbed one and threw it at Aisha. .

"Angie, don't think you're getting away," Aisha yelled between laughing and dodging pillows. "We know you and your man are going at it like forty going north."

"I'm not like you," Angie said as she ducked the flying pillow. Almost out of breath she responded, "I'm not ashamed about anything. I do what I do," she breathed heavily, "and I do it good. My husband and I aren't trying to hide a thing."

"Oh, that we know. Don't we Aisha. When you have a husband things are different," Tameria answered.

"That's for sure. Especially when you have a good man like you do Angie." Aisha giggled and plopped down on the sofa, tired from the pillow fight. "I like it when we get together like this."

"Yeah, me too," Tameria replied.

"We just don't do it often enough," Angie added. "Maybe when you finish your residency we'll have more time to hang out."

"I don't know about that. By that time she'll be doing her full time doctor thing, you know. And she and Chase will be tying the knot."

"Tying the knot," Angie sat up right and glanced over at Tameria in surprise. "You and Chase are getting married? When?"

"Girl, puhleeze. Don't listen to Aisha. Chase and I haven't talked about marriage, well not lately anyway. We have to get our careers going first. I'm not saying that I don't want to marry him, but first things first. Shoots, Aisha will probably be married before Chase and I get hitched. Isn't that right Aisha?"

"Yeah, right," Aisha mocked.

"I'm hungry." Angie got up and went into the kitchen. "If you're going to invite your friends over you're at least supposed to have something for us to munch on."

"You know I am not a cook. The best I can offer is Pizza Hut."

"Sounds good to me. Tameria, are you going to order? You always know how to talk them into giving us something free."

"All right, as if I have a choice. Aisha passed the phone to her. "What would you two do without me?" Tameria asked.

The three of them burst out laughing again.

Tameria and Angie didn't leave until two o'clock in the morning. After they left, Aisha reflected on the evening's events. It was times like these when she was reminded of how valuable it was to have true friends in her life. It was hard to have women friends because other women could become jealous easily at another woman's relationships, success or whatever. But Angie and Tameria had never displayed a jealous or envious bone in their bodies. She and Tameria were childhood friends and Angie joined their small circle a few years ago. Tameria and Aisha liked her immediately. The only thing different about Aisha's relationship with Angie was that Aisha didn't confide everything to her like she did with Tameria. There were just some things you didn't share with everyone. Aisha believed in degrees of friendship. Some friendships were meant to be deep, totally giving and last forever. Others were the kind friendship that filled another void in a person's life but yet not meant to be as deep as the best friend kind of relationship. Angie fell into the latter category. Nevertheless, Aisha felt truly blessed by both of the ladies. Before she settled down for the night, she thanked God for her friends.

During her sleep, she dreamed about her and Jackson. The two of them were standing in front of Pastor Shipley. She couldn't tell what they were saying in the dream, but Pastor Shipley was smiling. She and Jackson were holding something in their hands. Jackson pulled her underneath his arm and held her close to him while they continued to stand before of Pastor Shipley. A glowing bluish light suddenly appeared and she and Jackson smiled as they looked toward the light. Jackson turned to face her. His lips met hers. He thrusted his tongue into her mouth. The alarm clock jarred her from her sleep. She stretched in the bed. She smiled when she remembered that she'd dreamed about the exceptionally charming, handsome Minister Jackson Williams. Looking around the room, she envisioned him standing at the foot of the bed smiling at her with arms outstretched, waiting to hold her. *Don't go there, Aisha. Don't even go there.*

She stopped off at the coffee house before she went to the studio. As usual, this time of morning the place was crowded. Finally she was able to place her order. She moved through the crowd of people and headed out of the shop with her steaming brew.

"Well, hello Miss Carlisle." The voice startled her and she almost spilled her hot cup of caramel apple cider. The man grabbed her by her arms and steadied her. "It's good to see you too." He mocked.

Aisha's face reddened. Her mouth hung open but no words came out.

"Don't you have something to say to me? Or is it that you don't speak to your clients outside of your former place of employment, The Lynx?"

"What do you want Chandler?" she asked nastily. She hadn't seen or heard from him since her unpleasant meeting with him at Marlowe's. And she did not miss him one bit after she found out what kind of guy he really was. A lying snake.

"Now that's no way to treat me is it? If it wasn't for me, you would be locked up along with Shipley, Jason and the rest of them."

Aisha turned from him and briskly walked away but he wasn't about to let this opportunity pass him by. He'd been waiting for such a time as this. He'd called her office several times but never left a message. His anger with her was still raw since he found out how she had deceived him in to believing she was a saint. There was a time he thought about a long term serious relationship with Aisha. No one knew how it crushed his heart when he found out she had been dancing at The Lynx and doing drugs. But seeing her today somehow rekindled some old feelings that he forced back into the safe place within his cold lonely heart.

"Hey, what's your hurry?"

Aisha didn't bother to turn around. She wanted to get to her car as quickly as she could. The strong hand latched onto her arm and pulled her back with such force that this time she did drop the cup of cider. She was furious and frightened at the same time.

"Let go of me, Chandler." He ignored her pleas and proceeded to pull her into the alley on the right of them.

"Where are you taking me? I swear, if you don't let me go I'm going to scream."

"Go on. Scream. I'm a cop remember. Who's going to help you?" He flashed an evil grin at her that made her stomach turn.

In the alley he pushed her backwards hard against the brick wall. The pain in her back was excruciating and she couldn't stop the tears that formed in her eyes. *Chandler must be crazy*, she thought. *Lord help me*, she prayed to herself.

"What do you want?" she cried.

"Oh, let's put it this way. You're nothing but a slut and a whore. You're just like your friend Elisa."

At the mention of Elisa, Aisha jerked her head up and looked at him. "Where is Elisa? Is she all right? Tell me Chandler, please."

"I guess whores stick together huh. Well, Elisa is long gone. You'll never see her again. I guess you'll just have to find yourself another whore to fool around with. Maybe I can do you a favor and turn you on to some of the girls at the Platinum Plus."

"How dare you talk to me like this. Let me go or I'll report you to Internal Affairs."

"Don't you threaten me! He tightened his already vice grip on her. "If you do, I'll make sure you're locked up for a long time. You see this?" He pulled out a package of white powder. "How'd you like to go down for this? This little package can get you oh say about twenty years at the least." He laughed wickedly. "Better yet. Wouldn't you like a little hit of this Aisha. Huh?"

He opened the package of cocaine. He moved it back and forth underneath her nose. Aisha jerked her head away before any of the powder went up her nostrils. Seeing the drug for the first time months was tempting but Chandler would never know it. She fought against him but his grip on her was way too tight.

"Why are you doing this?" Her tears were flowing heavily and she didn't know what to do.

"Because you're walking around thinking you got away with something. You should have gone down with the rest of them. Do you know they were using little girls as young as thirteen and fourteen years old to satisfy their sick sexual desires. You know that, Miss Luscious? Do you?" He stood so close to her she could smell the breath mint on his breath. His chest was against hers. He still had her pinned between him and the wall.

"I didn't know anything about that. I told you that, Chandler. If I had known anything or suspected anything illegal was going on at The Lynx, I would have gone straight to the police."

"You're lying and you know it. You fooled me once, but you won't fool me again. You're not going to tell me that you didn't notice that some of those girls looked like little teenyboppers. And you sure as hell can't convince me that you thought the coke they were giving you was legal. Whore puhleeze."

"Stop calling me a whore. I'm not a whore," she finally yelled back.

"Oh, we're getting a little feisty aren't we? Well let me tell you this. Then I'll bid you farewell. If I ever, and I mean ever catch you doing so much as pausing at a stop sign instead of coming to a complete stop or jay walking, whatever it is, I'll lock you up so fast you won't know what day it is. You better watch your back every step of the way Aisha because you never know just when I might pop up." Without warning, he shouted "Boo!"

Aisha jumped. Loosening his grip on her, Chandler laughed loudly and walked off.

"Now you go and have yourself a good day."

Aisha was shaken. When she arrived at the studio, she barely spoke to Kaye. She went straight to her office and called Jackson's office.

"Good morning, Natalie." Her voice was shaking as she spoke. "This is Aisha."

"Good morning, Aisha. Are you all right? You sound a little strange."

"No, I'm fine. I wanted to know if I could schedule an appointment with Minister Williams. I really need to see him. I know it's short notice but if you'll ask him and get back with me, I'd really appreciate it."

"Hold on. He just walked in. I'll let him talk to you."

"Good morning, Sista Carlisle. How are you?" He was surprised to find out she was on the other line. Their sessions had ended several weeks ago. Since then he'd seen her at church a few times but he never had a chance to talk to her.

"Jackson. I, I need to talk to you." Her voice trembled. Right away he could sense that something was wrong.

"Sure. How soon can you get here? Or would you prefer that I meet you somewhere?"

"Would you do that?"

"Of course. I don't usually make house calls, but since you're high on my list, I'll make an exception," he laughed.

Aisha didn't respond to his humor. She was still trembling from her traumatizing encounter with Chandler. When she didn't laugh, Jackson became worried.

"Look, tell me where and when."

"My, my studio. Say in about one hour."

"I'll be there."

"Jackson?"

"Yes. Thank you. You don't know how much this means to me."

"I think I do. I'll see you in an hour."

True to his word, within an hour, Jackson was walking through the studio doors.

Kaye admired the handsome stranger as he walked up to her desk. Mercy, mercy, she said to herself. "How may I help you sir?" she asked in her usual polite manner.

"I'm here to see Aisha Carlisle. She's expecting me," he answered pleasantly.

"Your name?"

"Jackson. Jackson Williams."

Kaye immediately recognized his name from calling the studio. Dialing Aisha's intercom, she informed her of his arrival. "Mr. Williams, you can go on back. Just go down that hallway," Kaye pointed to the hallway on the right of her. "Her office is the first door on the left."

"Thank you. Uh" he paused and looked at her name plate, "Kaye," he said and proceeded to walk away.

Knock, knock.

"Come in." As soon as he entered her office he noticed her face was puffy and her eyes were red. She'd obviously been crying. What could have her so upset?" He walked over to her and knelt down beside her.

"Hey, what's wrong? Tell me what happened," he urged.

"It's awful. I'm scared, Jackson. I'm really scared." She was shaking. She grabbed the center of his arm in a tight grip.

"I'm getting you out of here. You're no good to anyone in this shape. Come on," he ordered and gently grabbed her by her arms and pulled her up from the chair. Tugging at her hand, he led her out of the office.

Without looking directly at Kaye, Aisha said, "Kaye, I'm going out. Please send all my calls to voicemail. Tell Angie when she gets in that I'm with Minister Williams."

Kaye's eyes grew large when she heard the word Minister." She had no idea he was a minister. "Okay sure. I'll tell her."

Jackson opened the passenger door of his Crossfire and waited for Aisha to get in. He ran to the driver's side and jumped in. Speeding off, he asked, "My place or yours?"

"Mine, I guess." Aisha suddenly thought about Chandler and quickly changed her mind. She didn't know what else Chandler was capable of and she didn't want to find out. "No on second thought I'd rather go to your place. If that's okay with you."

"Sure." They rode the twenty minute drive to his place in total silence. He didn't say anything to her on purpose. There would be time for talking. Pulling up in front of Riverfront Condominiums, he keyed in his security code and the massive iron gates slowly opened. Aisha slightly lifted her head to survey her surroundings.

He parked his car and led her into his domain. Upon entrance into his split level condo, Aisha immediately noticed it was immaculate beyond belief.

"Come on. Have a seat in here." He led her to the den and motioned for her to sit and relax on the plush melon couch. "Can I get you something to drink or eat?" he offered.

"A cup of decaf if you have it."

"Yes I have some. How do you take it?"

"One sugar and two creams."

"Give me a minute. I'll be right back."

"Okay." Her eyes zeroed in on the mantel over the fireplace that was to the right of her. She stood up and walked over to the fireplace and looked at the pictures.

"That's my family," he said, startling her. Walking up beside her, he placed the coffee mug in her hands. "That portrait there is of my father." He pointed to the oil painting on the wall above all of the smaller pictures. He's a minister in Ohio."

"Oh. I didn't know that."

"There's a lot you don't know about me," he responded. "These are my cousins," he picked up a couple of more pictures and explained who each person in the photo was. And here's my best friend, Jeremy with his wife and kids. But look, enough of that. Let's sit down so we can talk. I want to know what has you so upset this morning. When I got your call, you said you were frightened."

"I was and I am," she answered in almost a whisper.

"What is it, Aisha? You know you can talk to me."

"I know. That's why I'm here. You remember the policeman I told you about?"

"The undercover guy who you ran into at church?" he asked. He eased in closer to her and held her hand. "What about him?" The look on her face was one of utter fear. *What could have happened?* His mind traveled round and round with thoughts.

"I, I stopped at the coffee shop this morning. On my way out, I ran into him."

"Okay," he wanted to be as patient as he could but he also wanted her to go on and tell him what he'd done to make her this upset.

"Remember, I told you that he was the man who portrayed himself as a member of The Lynx. I had no idea who he was. When I met him at The Lynx he was in disguise and he said his name was Kyle Taylor."

"Yes, I remember. But what did he want this morning?"

"He always thought I knew about the illegal operations going on at The Lynx, but I didn't and you know I told you that Jackson. But this guy, Chandler, he seems to think I was involved in the whole thing. I know I was accepting coke from Jason and yes I knew it was wrong to do that. But I swear I had no idea that they were involved in sex and drug trafficking." Aisha's face turned red again. He saw the tears swell up in her eyes once more. He reached behind him and took the box of tissue off the sofa table and passed it to her.

"Are you okay?" he asked her.

"Yea, I think so. Well, this morning Chandler forced me into an alley beside the coffee shop. I tried to get to my car and get away from him but I couldn't."

Jackson's jaw tightened. The fury he felt was hard to keep under control.

"He called me nasty names. He pushed me hard against the wall and pinned me there. He, he pulled out a bag of coke and told me he could easily plant it on me if he wanted to. He said if he caught me doing anything that even looked illegal, whether it was jay walking or anything, he would lock me up so fast..." she stopped and started to cry in the tissue.

"That good for nothing, crooked..." Jackson stopped himself before he said something he would later regret. He wanted to go out and find this chump and beat him to a pulp but he knew that he had to exercise restraint. He was a minister, for God's sake. But at this moment, his thoughts were far from being Godly. But he didn't dare let Aisha know how angry he was. "Aisha, there's nothing to be scared of. This guy is trying to control you, to put you in a state of panic and fear." A soft spot formed in his heart for her

She looked up at him. . "He's succeeded Jackson. I'm terrified. I can't live like this. Looking over my shoulder. Wondering if he's watching me. Or if he's going to plant drugs in my car or at my studio. Or anything.

"Shhh, he's not going to hurt you. I promise I won't let him." he assured her and pulled her trembling body next to his. He held her. Her mild fragrance wafted tantalizingly underneath his nose. He leaned back against the sofa, still holding her. She lay against his chest and allowed her tears to flow freely. Cautiously, he lifted her chin up until her face was almost even with his. His heart raced as he resisted his emotions. "Aisha, I want you to listen to me. God is greater than anything you're facing. Chandler has no control over you. You haven't done anything wrong so believe me, he's just trying to do just what he's doing to scare you. But God has not given us a spirit of fear. Put your total trust in Him. Believe me. He won't let you down."

Aisha looked in his eyes and listening to him, she began to feel calm and peaceful. He was such a gentle, compassionate man. His words penetrated her heart and she believed him. Pushing back and sitting upright, she listened as he continued to reassure her that everything would turn out just fine.

"As for the name calling, you know who you are in Christ. No man can take that away from you. You're God's child, fearfully and wonderfully made. You hear me?"

"Yes, I hear you. I, I was just so scared when he came at me like that. I had no idea that he was such an evil man. And to think that I really did like him at one time."

Jackson hoped she didn't detect the look of surprise on his face. During their sessions she had never divulged that she had been involved with Chandler at one time. "Let it go, Aisha. You can't let him do you like this. He's manipulating you. God wants you to live your life free. Chandler wants to make you miserable. But what he's trying to do is a lie from the pit of hell and we are coming against that right now." Jackson squeezed her hand tighter and whispered a prayer. When he finished he stood up and looked down at her.

"What?" she said, looking confused.

"I'm going to fix you some brunch. I did tell you that I'm an excellent cook didn't I?" he laughed

The heaviness was lifted from her heart and she smiled. "I'm not sure you did," she stood up and followed him into the kitchen. "But I'm going to hang around. Then I'll be the judge of that."

The rest of the morning, the two of them laughed, talked and enjoyed the delicious French toast, sausages and grits that Jackson prepared. Their time together ended when Jackson's phone rang.

"Excuse me, please." He picked up the cordless phone. "Hello. Yes. Uh huh."

Aisha moved away from the breakfast table and walked back into the living room so Jackson could finish his conversation in private. She sat in the bay window and looked out over the Muddy Mississippi River. Being here had a peaceful effect on her. Looking out on the water, she felt safe and secure. She watched as the waves brushed up against the shore. People were walking along the river walk, some hand in hand. Others walked alone or with their pets. Some were jogging.

"Earth to Aisha," Jackson's voice boomed. She jerked her head around swiftly. "It's beautiful isn't it?" he asked as he moved in closer to her.

"Yes it is. I could sit here forever. I didn't tell you, but your condo is beautiful.

"Why, thank you. That was Natalie on the phone. I'm needed back at the church. But come on," he reached for her thin hand. "Let me give you the full tour before I take you back to the studio. That is unless you want to stay here until I return."

"Are you kidding me?" she responded with a look of awe on her face.

"No, I'm not. You can get you some rest and there's plenty of food in the fridge. Plus we have excellent security here. So at least for a while your mind can be at ease. He led her through each room while he continued his spill.

Aisha followed him around and was continually impressed with his style of decorating. "I don't know if I should stay here while you're gone Jackson."

He stopped at the top of the curving stairway and turned to face her. "Look, if I didn't want you here, I would tell you. I'm going to a staff meeting which usually lasts a couple of hours. I have two counseling sessions after that. In the meantime, you can take a nap, eat, watch satellite, read or whatever. I should be back around four. Then I'll take you to get your car. How does that sound?"

"Well..."

"Okay. It's done," he said before she could finish her sentence. "You can finish looking around while I grab my briefcase and a couple of other items I'm going to need for the staff meeting."

When he finished gathering his things he turned and without thinking, kissed her on the cheek. Immediately after doing so, he stepped back. "I'm sorry. Really I am. I didn't mean anything by that."

She was reeling from the touch of his soft, thick lips pressed against her cheek. Electric sparks tingled throughout her body. "Jackson, please. There's no need to apologize. Now go before you're late for your meeting."

"I'll see you later," he said with a sheepish look on his face.

When he closed the tall oak door behind him, Aisha leaned against it and breathed in slowly. Her heart still fluttered from the kiss. She smiled then proceeded over to the bay window again and became lost in the thought of where she was. *Minister Jackson Williams, you are truly one of a kind,"* she said out loud. She sat on the window bench and folded her legs up to her chest.

Lord, I can't believe I did that. Jackson prayed out loud in the car. I like her. I like her a lot. But I don't want to scare her off. So please guide me every step of the way. Help me to do things in the way you see fit and not succumb to my own fleshly desires. He displayed all thirty-two teeth as he drove to the weekly staff meeting.

39

When a man loves a woman, periodically he needs to pull away before he can get closer. John Gray

Turning the key to the door, Jackson was eager to see Aisha again. The alarm beeped as he closed the door behind him

"Aisha," he called out while he keyed in the alarm code. The apartment met his call with silence. He laid his briefcase and keys on the granite kitchen countertop. He slowly maneuvered his lean, physically fit body throughout the lower level. There was no sign of Aisha. Maybe she had decided to leave and called one of her friends to pick her up. He climbed the stairs and peeped in the guest bedroom. No Aisha. He checked in his office. No Aisha. Looking back over his shoulder he spied the petite frame in his master bedroom. The pace of his heart settled down when he spotted her laying on his bed sound asleep. He stood in the entrance of the bedroom and watched her. She reminded him of a fragile child in need of love and affection. *Sleep, my beautiful angel.*

Jackson retreated back downstairs. He opened the door to one of the hall closets and pulled out a pair of casual slacks and a shirt before going into the bathroom to take a shower. The piping hot streams of water pounding against his creamy colored skin released some of the tension of the day. Afterwards, he dressed and went to the kitchen to prepare something to eat.

Searching through the freezer, he settled on preparing a vegetable casserole with grilled chicken slices.

Aisha turned lazily in the supple king sized bed and opened her eyes. It took her a few seconds to remember that she was still Jackson's condo. She hadn't meant to fall asleep in his bed. Aisha jumped up and sat on the edge of the bed and listened to the noise coming from downstairs. Her instincts told her to sit quietly and gather her thoughts. *Could Chandler have broken into Jackson's apartment? Oh God, please no, don't let it be him.* Beginning to feel frightened, she tightened her grip on the edge of the bed. Her fear was replaced with a smile when she smelled the tantalizing aroma of food that filtered through her nostrils. Jumping up, she ran barefoot down the stairs to greet Jackson.

"Hello, there. Did you sleep comfortably?" he asked her.

Aisha blushed and lowered her head. "I'm sorry for falling asleep in your bed. Believe me when I tell you that I don't go around sleeping in strangers' beds," she said with an embarrassed look.

"Stranger? And here I thought we were friends. When did I lose my status?" he smiled and closed the door to the convection oven.

"No, we are friends. I, I didn't mean strangers as in strangers, I meant…"

"I think I know what you meant. I was just teasing anyway. I'm actually glad that you felt comfortable enough to get you some sleep. Why don't you sit down and after I feed you, I'll take you to get your car. Unless you want to crash here for the rest of the night."

Aisha was surprised at Jackson's offer. It must have shown on her face because Jackson immediately clarified his statement. He didn't want her to get the wrong idea about him. "Hold up. I didn't mean anything by that. I just thought you might like to lay low for the night, no funny business. Before I go to the office in the morning, I can take you to get your car."

"Jackson," Aisha paused. "I really appreciate the offer. I'm tempted to accept it."

"Then do it."

"Not this time. I think I'd better go and get my car this evening. I don't want to invade on your privacy. You've already done more than enough for me today by rushing to my rescue and allowing me to stay here. Gosh, I can't thank you enough. And on to of all of that, you're feeding me too."

The smile on her face when she spoke resurfaced emotions he'd suppressed for the past several years. The more he was around her, the more his desire grew. His vow of celibacy was being tested but he was determined not to allow his flesh to make him forget that he was a man of God. His father often reminded him that if there was ever a time that he started to feel weak to his fleshly desires that he should find a wife. "Son, it's better to find a wife than to burn. The Word of God says, the man that finds a wife, finds a good thing. Just make sure she's a Godly woman and that her beliefs and convictions are just as strong as yours. You know not every woman can handle being a preacher's wife."

"Jackson, what's that you're cooking?" Aisha asked in the middle of his thoughts. "It smells heavenly."

"Vegetable casserole with grilled chicken, madam. I'm almost done. I hope you enjoy it."

"I'm sure I will. Tell me. Where did you learn to cook and clean too for that matter? This place is immaculate."

"I wish I could say that I'm responsible for the cleanliness of my apartment. But I have a confession to make."

"Okay, I'm listening." Aisha placed her head in her hands and leaned on the table.

"Some of the senior women at church do a great job of taking care of me. Two times a week they come over and clean my apartment. As for the cooking, they taught me how to do that as well but I did have some experience already from living with my father growing up. We had to learn how to fend for ourselves unless some of the church ladies brought food over to our house. I also have plenty of prepared foods that the mothers of the church have cooked and frozen for me. All I have to do is come home, pop a meal in the microwave or the oven and *waallaa!*

"Well aren't you special."

"I guess you can say that. Not having my mother around when I was growing up makes me enjoy the attention showered on me. The church has been good to me. God has shown me favor. I can't thank Him enough."

Aisha gazed at him. Listening to him, watching him move around the kitchen, his kindness and gentle spirit touched her deeply. The more she talked to this man and spent time around him, the more she felt safe and secure. They ate the meal he prepared and just like he promised, when they finished eating, he drove her back to the studio to get her car. He waited patiently for her to go to her office and grab some paperwork she wanted to take home with her, then he followed her home to make sure she arrived safely.

"Let me check everything out inside before I go," he said as he took her keys gently from her hand and opened the door to her apartment. He walked in ahead of her, clicking on lights and checking every closet and room. She followed closely behind him. When he had made a full search of the apartment he walked to the door and turned to tell her goodnight.

"Jackson, thank you. Thank you so much."

"If you need me I want you to promise me that you'll call. Or better yet, if you get frightened, just jump in your car and come back to my place. You hear me?"

"Yes, I hear you. And..."

He placed two fingers against her lips. "Please, don't say thank you again. Just accept the fact that I'm here for you. Now lock up. I'll talk to you tomorrow."

Chandler watched from his car across the street as Jackson walked to his car. With a smirk on his face, Chandler drove off just as Jackson opened the door to his Crossfire.

40

If a relationship is founded on love it doesn't end.
Rosanne Cash

The past four and a half months had been heavenly for Aisha and Jackson. She'd taken him to meet her mother. Aisha felt like a miracle occurred when her mother doted over Jackson like he was the best thing since ice cream. He had a way about himself that brought out the best in Sandra Carlisle. The fact that he was a minister made Sandra like him even more. She bragged to her friends, her church family and anyone who would listen, telling them that her daughter was seriously dating a minister at Greater Faith Community Church in Memphis. Aisha hadn't seen her mother this excited in a long time. Whenever she brought Jackson around, Sandra's whole demeanor changed. Every time Aisha called her, Sandra was sure to ask about Jackson.

Jackson reciprocated by taking her to Ohio for a weekend. She met the man who mirrored Jackson in mannerisms, looks and spiritual strength. His father reminded her of her own daddy. Just like Benjamin, he was easy to talk too and he made her feel comfortable during her stay. Aisha often visualized herself as Jackson's wife. Could she fulfill the role that was expected of a minister's wife? Would she be jealous of the late night phone calls from distressed women? Could she handle the times when he'd have to spend away from her and their family? Would she be able to attend

298

numerous church services? Being Jackson's wife surely wouldn't be an easy task.

As if someone suddenly poked her with a pin, she jumped up from his sofa and focused on what she'd been doing instead of daydreaming. It wasn't like Jackson had proposed. He hadn't come close to talking about marriage. Things were going too good and she wasn't about to blow it with her thoughts of anything as serious as marriage.

Thank God Chandler had miraculously stopped stalking her. The last time she'd seen or heard from him was that night in the parking garage at her dance studio. She hadn't received any more hang up calls nor had anyone called at the dance studio. For once, everything seemed to be going her way. God had smiled on her. For the first time in a long while, she allowed herself to accept what He had already done in her life. She had made peace within and had forgiven herself.

She strolled over to the bay window and sat down, folding her legs up on the window seat. Jackson had gone to visit some of the sick and elderly members who were unable to attend church. There were times she'd go along with him, but today she chose to hang around at his condo until it was time to go to a dance competition she had scheduled for later that afternoon.

Jackson's apartment was like a sanctuary to her. It provoked an inexplicable sense of peace, calmness and security. Whether he was there or whether she was alone, her spirit felt at home. She loved this feeling and though she hadn't told Jackson, within her heart she knew that she loved him too.

◆

Jackson had a long day. He had visited several church members at Baptist East Hospital, Methodist University and Methodist South Hospitals. In addition to the hospital visits, he made a couple of stops at nursing homes as well as homebound members. After he finished, he stopped off at the church then rushed home to the love of his life. He had promised Aisha he would go to the dance competition with her. His emotions were hard to contain whenever he saw her dancing. Dancing was her calling, a God-given talent that continued to flourish and blossom in her life and the lives of the kids she taught. He'd suggested that she start a dance class at church. She told him that she would give it some serious thought. Driving along the BMP expressway, he realized that Aisha was the woman for him. He loved her with all of his heart and it was time to let her know. He already knew that he wanted to spend the rest of his life with her. But the timing had to be right. He wasn't going to ask her to be his wife until he was sure about her feelings for him. Their level of intimacy was another obstacle in his way. If he didn't make a serious move soon, his desire for her would be even harder to suppress. He flipped the radio from 95.7 to 103.5 solid gold just in time to hear Stevie Wonder singing one of his favorites, *"everyone has got a certain weakness in life, your love just happens to be mine..."* He smiled and sang along with the song.

Jackson pulled the car up in his parking space and rushed to his condo. Knowing Aisha was inside waiting on him made his heart flutter. It felt perfect for her to be at his place. The more time he spent with her, the more time he wanted to spend with her.

He turned the lock and went inside. The apartment was relatively quiet except for the sound of some reggae music playing on the stereo. He walked further into the apartment. "Boo," Aisha yelled and pounced from behind the hallway door onto Jackson's back. He grabbed her by the waist and brought her around to face him. Without saying a word, he kissed her with fervor and passion. She responded by caressing his face and shoulders with her delicate hands. His lips traveled to her ear lobes and he gingerly kissed them before moving to her cheeks, her forehead and her eyelids. The sounds of pleasure emanated from each of them as their desire rose to a feverish pitch. He became consumed by the taste of her lips and the feel of her soft mounds that pressed against his taut chest. Moans escaped and pushed their way up and out of her mouth. "Jackson," she whispered before he pulled away from her. Each time he held her in his arms, pulling away from her became more difficult.

"Come on, Aisha. We can't do this. Not until. Not until it's right."

She slowly shook her head in agreement and stepped aside. She exhaled before changing the subject, "How did visitation go?" she asked with her face still flushed.

He forced himself to answer, though his body was still begging for something else.

"Everything went well. I managed to visit fifteen of our members. I know that may not seem like a lot, especially when we have a church roll of what? Six to eight thousand? That means every week we have a growing list of sick and shut in members reported to the church office. Think of the ones we don't know about. But hey, thank God for the different ministries we have that address the needs of our sick and elderly. They do an excellent job too, which makes the jobs of the pastor and the ministers somewhat easier. There's no way our ministry staff, even though we have a huge group, can cover all of the members who are sick or unable to get to church." Talking about church relaxed him and soon his flesh quieted down. Jackson could count on his love of

God and the church to help him regain his focus whenever his flesh tried to dictate to him.

Like Jackson, Aisha as much as she wanted him, accepted that there could be nothing sexual between them unless they said those three words I love you, followed by those two words –I Do.

♦

The dance competition was the third one this month for Aisha and her A Carlisle Studio. The girls looked forward to it and so did Aisha. They were competing against several other top dance groups from the tristate areas.

Aisha waved both hands in the air when she spotted her mother, Tameria and Chase, Angie and her husband sitting in the bleachers. It was simply unbelievable that Jackson had convinced her mother to come to the dance competition. Attending any of her competitions, even when she was a teenager was almost unheard of when it came to her mother. It was always her father who supported her dream and love of dance. But Jackson's effect on Sandra was remarkable. For Aisha it was another prayer God had answered in her life.

Tameria and Chase sat up in the bleachers talking to Jackson and the rest of the group. Tameria was glad that she and Chase's schedules had made it possible for them to attend the competition. It was a huge event for Aisha and Tameria wanted to be there to show her support. If A-Carlisle won, they would move on to the national competition. It would be a dream come true for Aisha.

Angie and her husband laughed and talked until the band marched out across the gymnasium floor. Sandra Carlisle stuck under Jackson like glue. She linked her arm inside of his and continued her praise of him to the others. Her dramatic performance whenever he was in her company was something that Jackson had become accustomed to. And welcomed.

The competition went on for almost three hours. At the end, *A-Carlisle Studio of Dance and Choreography* went home with the first place trophy in lyrical dance and second place in the hip-hop category. Aisha screamed and jumped up and down when they announced their first and second place wins. Afterwards, she pushed through the crowd to find Jackson. When she reached him, his embrace sealed the exhilarating triumph of the night.

Chandler stood undetected on the other side of the gym, He watched the couple who obviously were in love. *Why couldn't that be him?* He had to do something that would make her understand how much he loved her. He'd been silent far too long. It was time to make his move. Threatening her and acting like a stalker had been the wrong thing to do. He didn't know why he had acted like such a dimwit. Maybe it was because he had been hurt to find out about her job at The Lynx. But that was over and he was convinced that she had been telling the truth about not knowing what was going on there. She wasn't anything like the other females he'd dated. He had confessed to his partner, Jay what he'd done to her. Jay called him a lunatic and a stalker. As bad as Chandler hated to admit it, Jay was right. If he was going to have any chance with her, he had his work cut out for him. Jackson Williams had stepped up his game and Chandler had become Aisha's least concern. He turned and walked out of the gym.

♦

Aisha was still on a natural high from the dance studio's win. She entered her empty apartment. The lights flicked on as she walked through it. She twirled around with joy. After a warm bubble bath, she curled up in her bed and pulled out her Bible. Turning to one of her favorite passages, Psalm 30 she read the words that brought her to tears. *I give you all the credit, GOD; you got me out of that mess, you didn't let my foes gloat. GOD, my God, I yelled for help and you put me together. GOD, you pulled me out of the grave, gave me another chance at life when I was down and out.*

Her home telephone rang and disrupted her quiet time. She looked at her caller ID. Private name, private number flashed across the caller ID screen. Must be some telemarketer or something. She hesitated before answering.

"Hello."

"Aisha. Please don't hang up." Chandler's voice sounded almost childlike and innocent.

She recognized the voice instantly. "Chandler, I thought you were out of my life and moved on to torment some other woman." She mocked in anger. Everything had been going well. Today had been totally one of the best days of her life. Now Chandler had to pop up and ruin what was left of a perfect day.

"Okay, I deserved that. But if you'd just wait and listen to me. I don't want to start any trouble with you. I promise if you'll see me tonight, I won't bother you again. But I need to talk to you Aisha."

"Sounds like a personal problem to me." she rebuffed. "Whatever it is you have to say, you'd better say it in the next thirty seconds or I'm hanging up this phone."

"I need to see you face to face," he insisted.

"Why? So you can set me up for the kill. I don't think so." She slammed down the phone. *The nerve of that man. Why won't he leave me alone?* She paced back and forth for several seconds before she glanced down at the phone. Dialing Jackson's number, she listened as the phone rang. When he answered, she immediately relaxed. They talked for almost two hours. By the time she hung up, she had forgotten all about Chandler's pathetic pleas.

♦

The next morning she met Jackson for breakfast. She didn't tell him about her call from Chandler. She'd decided to leave well enough along. The two of them enjoyed what was becoming a weekly ritual. At least twice a week they'd meet up for breakfast at The Kettle before he went to the church office and before she went to the studio. The relationship she had with him was what she'd envisioned in her dreams The time they spent together was always fun. He was easy going and his Christian convictions were real. There was no pressure to engage in sexual intimacy. That alone made Aisha comfortable around him. They could sit at each other's apartments for hours, listening to music, watching movies or television or doing nothing and the both of them would be content.

Aisha walked into the studio and just as she turned the knob to walk inside, she was met by a man with the most beautiful bouquet of mixed flowers she'd ever seen. There were roses, carnations and lilies in the oversized arrangement.

"Are you coming here?" she asked him.

"Yes, ma'am."

"Follow me then." Aisha proceeded to walk inside the studio. "Good morning, Kaye."

"Good morning, Aisha. Wow, who are those for?" she asked when she saw the flowers.

"Angie." Aisha answered. She turned and looked at the delivery man. "Oh, I'm sorry. I know that vase of flowers must be heavy. You can sit them right over there on that round table." *Angie's husband is something else,"* Aisha said to Kaye. He's always so thoughtful when it comes to his wife. "Has she made it in yet Kaye?"

"Not yet."

"Ma'am, I need one of you to sign here please?" The delivery man passed the paper to her. Aisha noticed her name on the yellow slip.

"Wait. I thought you said these were for Angie Walker."

"No, ma'am. I didn't say who they were for. But uh, let's see. Okay, they're for," He turned the slip of paper around so he could read it. "Miss Aisha Carlisle. Is she here?"

Kaye jumped from behind the receptionist' counter so she wouldn't miss a word of the conversation between Aisha and the delivery guy.

"I'm Aisha Carlisle."

"Good, then have a great day. Enjoy your flowers too," he said before turning to leave.

"Who are they from?" Kaye inquired.

"I don't know." Aisha hurried over to the bouquet and pulled out the card tucked on the side. *"Won't you giv'a brother another chance. Everyone deserves to be forgiven, including me. Chandler."*

"Who is it?" Kaye continued to urge her for an answer.

"No one. I mean the card doesn't say." Aisha lied. She refused to air her dirty laundry with Kaye. She placed the card in the pocket of her sweat pants and turned and walked to her office. She noticed that the light on her voicemail. She dialed into it to listen to her morning messages.

"Aisha, I hope you'll accept my peace offering. I know flowers can't begin to convey how sorry I am for being so foolish. But people can change. I should know because I'm one of them. I know I've frightened you. I've said some horrible things about you. But please, let me talk to you. I want to ask for your forgiveness in person. Call me and tell me that you'll see me."

Aisha listened to his pleading. He sounded like the Chandler she'd first met. The one who had been sensitive, kind and attentive. Maybe I should consider his request. She paused before pushing the button to move on to the next message. The last message was from her mother telling her that she might go to Dallas to visit one of her friends who'd recently retired and relocated there. "Call me back Aisha. I'm thinking about flying out of here Wednesday." Aisha returned her mother's call. She assured her that she thought it was a good idea for her to visit Charlene. "Mom, you and Charlene have been friends for years. So I say, go. Have a good time." Sandra agreed and told Aisha she would call her back to let her know when she would be leaving.

Aisha sat behind her desk and leaned back in the chair. Reminiscing about her and Jackson made her giddy inside. She soon came from behind the desk and went into one of the practice rooms. For the next two hours she worked on a series of new dance moves that she'd planned to teach her students. The national competition was four weeks away and their routines had to be the best ever. It was almost noon by the time she walked out of the room.

"Hey, those new routines looked great," Angie remarked when she saw Aisha coming down the hall in a sweat.

"Thanks, girl. I've got to keep working on 'em until they're perfect. I'm not planning to come home from the nationals without a trophy.."

"With what I saw when I peeped in on you, the girls will be hard to beat if you can teach them to do what you were doing in there."

"*If* I can teach them? Now you know me better than that. If is not in my vocabulary when it comes to dancing. They will learn this routine plus two more. Before long, we're going to be the national champions." Aisha used the towel around her neck to wipe the sweat from the side of her face.

"I saw the flowers. Kaye told me they were for you but that you didn't know who they were from." Aisha motioned for Angie to join her in the break area. She opened the fridge and pulled out a cold blue PowerAde before sitting on the bench in the room. When she finished telling Angie about Chandler and his sudden change of heart, Angie appeared just as dumbfounded as Aisha. She didn't trust Chandler Larson as far as she could throw him. But listening to what Aisha said about him, she almost felt a tinge of pity for the guy. Still she told Aisha to keep a clear head when it came to Chandler and not to let him force her to do anything she didn't want to do. Angie reminded her friend that the relationship between her and Jackson was going too well to allow someone like Chandler to come in and mess it up. Aisha agreed to some point. But on the other hand, if Chandler was serious, then it was her Christian duty to accept his apology by forgiving him. *Even the Bible says that we should forgive seventy times seventy* she reminded herself. She hadn't forgiven Chandler one time yet. She so wanted to believe that he had recognized the vast error of his ways. If he was willing to ask for her forgiveness, she had to at least afford him that chance.

Kaye's voice blasted over the income. "Aisha. Line two. Aisha. Line two please."

Aisha pushed the button on the phone in the break room. Angie gestured that she was leaving the break room and then disappeared.

"Hello, this is Aisha."

"Hi, beautiful."

"Hi, Jackson. How's your day going?"

"It's been busy. I can say that much. But hearing your voice makes me feel better already. How's that new routine you've come up with coming along?" he asked. She'd told him over breakfast about the new choreography she'd planned to teach the girls for the nationals.

"I've been practicing my butt off all morning. I feel pretty certain that once I perfect all the moves, we'll have a winning routine." Her confidence was obvious with every word she spoke. "I'll probably be here late this evening. Once the girls come in and leave, I'm going to stick around for a while. So it's unlikely that I'll see you tonight."

"I understand. But I don't like it."

Aisha could hear the smile in his voice. Having someone who understood her was such a wonderful gift.

"You're too good to me. You know that," she said.

"Yeah, I do." He laughed. "I'll call you later."

"Okay."

"Line three, Aisha. Aisha. Line three." Kaye said the minute she'd hung up from talking to Jackson.

It must be Jackson calling back. He must've forgotten to tell me something. "Hello, Aisha speaking."

"Aisha, hi. It's Chandler."

"I know, Chandler. You have one of those distinguishable voices. I've told you that before, haven't I?"

"Yeah, you have. Did you get my message?"

"Yes, I did. The flowers are beautiful. Thank you very much."

"You're welcome. I just want the chance to make things right with you. I don't want to come off as pushy or like the stalker I once was. So this time if you tell me not to call you again and that you won't see me, then I'll accept that. But seriously, all I want is a chance to talk to you face to face."

"I, I don't know, Chandler. You've done some crazy things that gave me a totally different view of you. You've scared the mess out of me. You've had me constantly looking over my shoulder wondering if you were lurking around somewhere to hurt me. It hasn't been a good feeling either. Now you're calling me and telling me that you need to see me. How do I know if you're telling the truth or not? I just can't do it."

"Look, Aisha, I'll meet you in a public place. That way you won't have to be afraid. We can talk or rather I can talk. All you have to do is listen to what I have to say." He waited on the other end of the phone. Her silence let him know that she was considering his offer. If he could get her to meet up with him, he felt certain he could convince her of his feelings. She finally responded.

"Okay, I'll do it. But I'll pick the place."

"Wherever you say, I'll be there," he answered. A big smile covered his face. He'd made it over the first hurdle.

"Meet me at Interstate Barbeque on Third Street this evening at seven thirty." Aisha didn't allow him time to reply. She hung up the phone and quickly returned to working on her choreography.

◆

The waitress seated her at a booth near the middle of the restaurant. Chandler walked in just as the waitress was bringing Aisha's order of tea.

"Thank you for seeing me," Chandler said and leaned over so he could kiss her on the cheek. Aisha quickly moved her head before his lips met its intended target. He chose not to comment. He gave the waitress his drink order and proceeded to sit down.

Seeing him for the first time in months, she studied his profile. He was a handsome man, always had been. He looked more chiseled, like he'd been hitting the gym around the clock. His crystal white teeth and mustached lips enhanced his already good looks.

"What do you want to talk to me about? If you're going to start stalking me again and trying to set me up, I'm telling you that I'm not going to put up with it anymore. I'll go to Internal Affairs, the newspaper, whatever I have to do. But I won't live in fear of you anymore."

Chandler watched her as she demanded him to leave her alone. He had to make things right with her. He wanted to convince her that he wasn't out to harm her. He reached across the table to grab hold of her hand. She quickly removed it before he could grasp it. Anger formed inside of him but he couldn't let her know that she was pissing him off. *Who the hell does she think she is? Don't blow this, man Keep your cool.* He told himself. "Aisha, I know I've done some questionable things. I understand why you feel the way you do about me. But the fact is, I didn't know how to deal with my feelings when I found out you were working at The Lynx.

Imagine how I felt when I saw you walk into that house as my private dancer. I almost blew my cover right then and there. I was devastated. I loved you Aisha. I know I never told you but I was planning to tell you as soon as my assignment ended. But seeing you dancing that night reminded me of my ex-girlfriend Tracye. I felt like I was being betrayed all over again."

Aisha's eyes grew as big as golf balls when she heard Chandler's confession. Her heart began to soften as she witnessed the hurt look on his face. She remembered the night she stood before the man who she thought was Kyle Taylor at the time. Putting herself in his shoes, she imagined how she would have reacted had the situation been reversed. She admitted that their relationship was ruined because of her actions. For that she was sorry.

"I'm sorry but I can't do anything to change that. All I can tell you is that I didn't mean to hurt you. I didn't mean to destroy what we had together. Things in my life plummeted out of control so fast. I got caught up in the game of making fast money. Along with the fast money, came drugs to help me keep making the fast money. With the drugs came a downward spiral of my life. But I never meant to hurt you."

"Aisha, you don't know what it means to hear you say that. I know I said some atrocious things to you. That's why I wanted to see you face to face. I'm asking if you can find it in your heart to forgive me. I didn't know how to react, or how to express to you what I was feeling, so I retaliated by calling you names and stalking you." Tears crested in the corner of Chandler's eyes. "Aisha, I'm here to confess that my feelings still haven't changed. I love you. I want the chance to make things work for us. But if they can't, then at least please tell me that we can be friends."

The waitress brought their orders and placed them on the table in front of each of them. Aisha glanced at her barbeque salad. Chandler didn't bother looking at his jumbo shoulder sandwich and onion rings. He concentrated on her, afraid if he looked away that she would be gone from his life forever.

Aisha picked up her fork and picked over her salad. She was taken aback by Chandler's outpour of love for her. She didn't know what to say or how to counter what he'd said. There was a time she had believed that Chandler was the man of her dreams. The one who might possibly be her knight in shining armor but it hadn't worked out that way. Yes, she blamed herself for hurting him, but she also believed there was a reason for everything. She believed that Chandler was basically a good man with a lot of love to give. But time brings about a change and now her heart belonged to Jackson.

"What are you thinking?" Chandler asked sullenly.

"I'm thinking of how much I hurt you, Chandler. I don't want to hurt you ever again. That's why I have to be honest with you. First, let me say that I do forgive you. I really do. I hope you can find it in your heart to forgive me as well. I once cared deeply for you. I think I can even say that I was starting to fall in love with you. But that was then and this is now. I can't change the series of events that took place. Neither can you. And now I'm in love with someone else."

"Is it that minister? Jackson Williams?"

"Yes," she answered, confessing to Chandler something she hadn't yet admitted to Jackson. She loved Jackson. Sitting across from Chandler confirmed her feelings.

The look of disappointment was evident on Chandler's face. He'd treated her harshly and now he had to pay the ultimate price of losing her and the chance to work things out between them. This time it was her turn to reach out and console Chandler. She held his hand and tenderly squeezed it. Reaching across the table she used the back of her hand to wipe away his falling tears.

◆

Jackson dialed Aisha's cell for the fifth time and for the fifth time it went straight into her voice mail. He hung up and dialed her apartment number again, still no answer. He scanned his memory to see if he could remember whether or not Aisha had told him she was going somewhere after leaving the studio. It was almost ten thirty and she wasn't at the studio. He knew because after he couldn't reach her, he had driven by there to see if her car was still there. The lot was empty and all the lights were off at the studio. He sat at his kitchen table and ran both hands through his hair, a sure indication that he was worried about her. He picked up his keys and stormed out of the door. He needed to make sure she was all right.

Aisha and Chandler left the restaurant. "I'll follow you home to make sure you get there safely." Chandler offered. "If that's okay with you."

"That's not necessary."

"Please. Let me do something. I can at least make sure you get home safely."

Aisha relented. "Okay. But I'm tired Chandler. I just want to get home. I've had a long day and an even longer day tomorrow."

"Sure, no problem. I'll just follow you and then go on about my way."

Arriving at her place, they spent a few minutes sitting in his car in front of her apartment. For the first time in months, they were able to enjoy one another's company. Aisha felt convinced that Chandler had been sincere with his apology. "Everyone deserves a second chance," he'd told her and she agreed. That was all Chandler had hoped for. Thoughts of Tracye's betrayal resurfaced in his mind. The more he watched Aisha, the more she began to look like Tracye. Tracye was a slut. She stooped to an all-time low when she slept with his friend. Aisha was no better.

"I'll walk you to your door." The two of them stood in front of her door. Without warning, Chandler grabbed her shoulders. He pulled her towards him. His breathing became heavy within seconds.

"What are you doing? Turn me a loose." Aisha tried to yank away from his grip. But his lips crushed hers violently. She twisted her body but his massive hands were unyielding. The force of his teeth against her lips bruised hers.

"Chandler. Stop it. No. Let…me…go." she tried to yell as her head went back. But he held her so tightly she could barely speak.

"You know you like it like this. You don't really want that jacked up preacher. You want some roughness in your life. Don't you!"

Aisha was petrified. How could she have allowed Chandler to deceive her again. She should have known better. He kissed her forcefully again while his hands invaded the most private areas of her body. Her salty tears flowed but her tears only excited him more as he lapped them up with his tongue. He viciously pulled her hair back and sucked on her neck while he squeezed her breasts hard. His legs forcefully parted her thighs and he used his knee and hands to do vile things to her.

Jackson pulled up in front of the complex. Getting ready to step out, he witnessed Aisha and Chandler kissing. Furious, he was about to jump out of the car and attack Chandler. *How could she do this? How?* Jackson's heart skipped a beat when he saw her head tilt backwards. From what he could tell, she appeared to be laughing. His head rested on the steering wheel. He pounded his fists against the dashboard and put the car in reverse. Unable to watch the two any longer he sped away.

Chandler slammed Aisha against the door. He jerked the keys to her apartment from out of her hand. He pushed open so hard it sounded like it was about to pop off the hinges.

"Chandler, please. Please don't do this," she begged him.

Chandler's laugh was wicked. His eyes narrowed menacingly. He grabbed her between her thighs again then violently pushed her inside her apartment before he turned to leave. Aisha fell on the cold hardwood floor. Looking back at her, he saw Tracye's face plastered on hers. He walked back over to her just as Aisha tried to use her feet to push the door close. She didn't have the strength. He bolted inside, stood over her and spat on her. "Did you really think I would want somebody like you? Well, I never have. And I never will! Now let's see you forgive that!"

41

Do not sabotage your new relationship with your last relationship's poison. Steve Marabol

She lay still on the floor for almost forty-five minutes. She was too scared to move, afraid that Chandler was still lurking outside. When she mustered up the nerve, she started crawling over to the door. She pulled herself up enough to lock the deadbolt. She slid back down to the floor, bent over and sobbed into her hands. For the next several minutes Aisha lay next to the door trembling in fear. She was traumatized. Should she call 911? What would she tell them? He hadn't raped her in the sense of what they called rape. It would be her word against the well-respected undercover detective Chandler Larson. Once he finished telling his chief about her past, no one would believe her. She screamed like a wounded animal. A wave of nausea sent her rushing to the bathroom where she threw up her day's food consumption. *Oh God*, she continued to sob as she ran a hot tub of water. She climbed inside and began to scrub her violated body until her skin started to tingle from her roughness. It was over an hour before she stepped out of the tub. Dripping wet, like a zombie she walked into the bedroom and fell across her bed.

Aisha climbed between the covers and wept until she succumbed to the voice of sleep. Even in her sleep, Chandler's assault tormented her. She bolted upright in the bed. Glancing over at the clock on her nightstand, she saw that it was 3:45 in the morning. *Jackson. Oh my God. I told him I was going to be working late but I didn't tell him about my plans to meet Chandler. I know he's worried sick.* She reached for the phone to call him so she could explain to him what had happened. Just as she was about to dial his number, she looked on the caller ID. He'd already called her several times. *I can't tell him. He won't understand. He'll ask me why I met him in the first place. Why did I?*

She glanced over at her answering machine and saw the message light flashing. *Why didn't he call on my cell?* she asked herself. She got up from the bed and stumbled into the hallway where her purse and keys were still lying on the floor. She shivered again in fear. She quickly grabbed up her purse and raced back into her bedroom, slamming and locking her bedroom door behind her. Frantic, she searched inside her purse until she found the razor thin phone. *Oh, dang, I didn't even turn it on when I left the restaurant last night.* Throwing the phone down on the floor, she pushed the buttons to listen to the messages on her home phone. With each message, Jackson's concern escalated. She heard the sound of worry in his voice as he spoke into the machine. *"Aisha, pick up the phone. Beep. Aisha, where are you? Beep. Aisha, are you okay? Call me."* Beep. "Aisha, you won't answer your cell." Beep. "Aisha, sweetheart, call me and let me know you're all right." After listening to the messages, she picked up the phone to call him. She thought about what she would tell him. *I'll remind him that I worked late. Then I'll tell him that I was worn out so I came home, took a shower and fell asleep. I can't tell him the truth. I just can't.* There was no answer at his apartment. *He must be asleep himself. Good, maybe he'll believe me when I talk to him later today..* Rubbing her hands through her hair, Aisha rocked back and forth on the bed. Her eyes had begun to swell from crying and her body ached from Chandler's abuse.

♦

Early the next morning, before the sun came up, Jackson was awakened by the familiar ring tone *My Girl* by the Temptations on his cell phone. It was Aisha's ring tone. But Jackson ignored her phone calls, the same way she'd obviously ignored his calls last night so she could be with Chandler. He couldn't believe that she had been lying to him all of this time. She had managed to convince him that Chandler was some kind of crazed maniac cop who was stalking and harassing her to no end. But what he witnessed surely hadn't looked like someone who was afraid of Chandler nor did Chandler look or act like a stalker. Had she been fabricating these tall tales all along? And if so, how many more lies had she been feeding him? For the first time he had serious doubts about Aisha's honesty. If he couldn't trust her, there was certainly no way he could hope to continue a relationship with her, let alone contemplate asking her to become his wife. His phone began ringing again. He turned it off and jumped up and got dressed in a pair of sweats. The more he thought about it, the more he dreaded being at home. He didn't want to chance her popping up, something he wouldn't have minded her doing before the events of last night. Without thinking, he grabbed a few clothes and left the condo.

He exited off the Ridgeway exit and drove until he arrived at AmeriSuites on Park Avenue. He checked into the hotel, went to his room, turned his cell on vibrate and lay back on the double bed. Thoughts tackled his mind about the good times he'd spent with Aisha and the love that had evolved in his heart for her. He had prayed for God's hand of guidance and direction to be upon him throughout this relationship. Time and time again he had asked God to reveal to him if Aisha was the one. Dropping down on his knees and clasping his hands together, Jackson cried out to God. At this point, he believed that God had allowed him to witness Aisha and Chandler's secret rendezvous to show him that she wasn't the girl for him. As bad as it hurt, he trusted God. He determined within his spirit that he would get through this painful situation with God's help. After his prayer, he undressed, pulled back the covers on the bed and lay between the cool white cotton sheets. Staring at the ceiling as if watching a movie, a flash of pain enveloped him. He allowed his tears to flow freely until he succumbed to exhaustion and fell asleep.

♦

Aisha yawned and sat up in bed. She looked at her cell phone to see if she had any missed calls or voice mails but there were none. Neither were there any messages on her home phone from Jackson. Her concern mounted even more after she had called him and didn't get an answer. Checking the time, she decided to get up and drive out to his apartment before going to the studio. She left a message for Angie telling her she would be running a little late, then headed toward the Bill Morris Parkway e-way. Arriving at Jackson's apartment, she saw an empty space where his Crossfire would normally be parked. She dialed his apartment number again. Again his voice mail picked up after four rings. Sitting in the parking space, she tried his cell again, no answer. Her cell phone rung and before it went to the second ring, she'd answered.

"Hello, Jackson?"

"No. This isn't Jackson. It's your mother, Aisha." Aisha's chest sunk.

"Good morning, Mother. How are you?"

"I'm fine. Are you okay? You sound like you're anxious to hear from Jackson. I hope you two haven't had a lover's quarrel. You know you can be excessive and overly dramatic Aisha."

"Mother, please, not this morning. Jackson and I are doing fine. And I don't know what you're talking about. I am not excessive or dramatic. I just haven't talked to him since early yesterday. I guess he had some emergency calls from the church or something." Aisha tried to mask her emotions. "Are you back from Dallas?"

"Yes. I called last night to tell you that I made it home. But of course, as usual, I didn't get an answer."

"Sorry, Mother," Aisha said in a somber voice. *But I was busy being brutally assaulted last night,* she wanted to say but held her tongue. Knowing her mother, Aisha knew Sandra would manage to blame Aisha for what Chandler had done to her. For once, Aisha would have agreed with her mother's conclusion. She ignored her inner voice and continued talking. "I had a lot of things going on yesterday. But I'm glad you made it back home safely."

Sandra didn't like the sound of her daughter's voice. There was something she wasn't telling her. Sandra stood in the kitchen with one hand positioned on her hip. "Have you tried calling him on his cell phone?"

"Of course I have. He doesn't answer. But if he's with a church member at the hospital or sitting with someone who's dying, then you know he isn't going to answer." Aisha explained while trying not to get annoyed with her mother's drill.

"Seems to me like there's something more going on. Certainly Jackson would call and let you know he's okay even if he can only talk a second or two. Let me see, it's almost eight o'clock. The church office opens around eighty thirty doesn't it?"

"Yes. Why?" Aisha responded with her own question.

"Because you need to get on that phone and call his secretary as soon as that clock strikes eight thirty. Do you hear me?" Sandra's voice raised up an octave.

"Look Mother. How many times do I have to remind you that I am not a child? I can handle my own affairs and I can certainly handle my relationship with Jackson, which is none of your business anyway," Aisha retorted.

As if she hadn't heard a word her daughter had said, Sandra ordered, "Find out where he is. Do not mess this up. Jackson is a good catch and I'd hate to see you lose out because of your lackadaisical attitude about things. Now do what I say and be sure to call me as soon as you hear something. Goodbye." Sandra hung up the phone, shook her head and positioned her eyes toward heaven. "Lord, help that child of mine. She's just like her daddy. Stubborn, naïve and narrow minded. And wherever Jackson is let him be safe." Sandra grabbed her house keys and headed out the door for her daily three mile walk.

Aisha called the church office twice. Both times Natalie told her that Jackson wasn't available. She could barely concentrate on the choreography moves. Her worry was beginning to transform into anger. She needed him. Whenever she reached him, she planned on giving him an earful!

Another day had come to an end. It was well after midnight. There had still been no word from Jackson.. Aisha laid in her bed trying to concentrate on writing out the final dance steps for the nationals. Each sound she heard in her apartment caused her heart to skip a beat. She said a prayer of protection for herself as well as Jackson. Before retiring for the night, she got up and checked the locks on the doors and windows. Peeping outside, she exhaled when she didn't see any signs of her attacker. Returning to her bed, she laid her notebook on the nightstand and gave in to the tiredness that consumed her body.

42

Don't let your past relationships ruin your future relationships because everyone is not the same and true love might not always be what you want, so accept who God blesses you with. Dionta Long

Tameria prepared for her impending graduation. This was another milestone that moved her closer to reaching her goal to become an internist. The next step would be to complete her medical residency like Chase was doing now. By the time she completed residency Chase would have three years under his graduation belt and would be either working with a group of doctors or entering into private practice for himself. Tameria looked forward to their careers as doctors. She couldn't have chosen a better field. The hours were long, the work was extremely difficult but the thought of being blessed to help save lives was awe stupendous to her.

She and Chase were practically living together and she no longer felt a need to hide the fact that they were. At this point Aisha had definitely shown her that just because a person behaves one way in front of one set group of people, that it surely doesn't mean they're who they say they are. Aisha was still Tameria's best friend and there was nothing she wouldn't try to do for her, but let's face it, when Aisha told her about her double life, Tameria had been absolutely floored by the revelation. Aisha? Nice, innocent, church lady Aisha? Every time Tameria thought about Aisha's past, she was yet still amazed and shocked by the things Aisha had gotten herself into. But now it looked like her friend's life had truly taken a turn for the best. Jackson was not only good to her but he was good to Aisha. And as far as Tameria knew, Aisha had told Jackson everything about her past.

Chase entered the bedroom and sat down beside her. "Hi there, Dr. Matthews."

"Hello yourself, Dr. Gray." she answered, smiled in return and kissed him on the lips. "Tired?" she asked him as she noticed his wrinkled brow and the circles forming underneath his deep brown eyes.

"Yeah. The past thirty six hours were hell. We had eight serious head trauma injuries. This city is becoming more violent as we speak and the increase in the number of African American teenagers coming into the emergency room is alarming." Chase had grown up with parents who were teen activists. The same sense of concern, compassion and the need to help make a positive difference in the lives of teens had been passed down to Chase and his three other brothers, one of whom was an attorney, the second a physician's assistant and the third brother was a high school English teacher.

Tameria climbed on the bed and rested on her knees behind Chase. Gently pulling his head back to rest just above her breasts, she massaged his temples in a slow relaxing motion. Chase groaned from pleasure and his body became almost limp as she moved her hands along his neck and on to his shoulders.

"How does this feel?" she whispered in his ear.

"Hmmmm," was his response. His eyes closed and within minutes she heard his labored breathing and light snore. Carefully moving from underneath the weight of his body, she eased him down on the bed, removed his shoes and pulled the covers up to his chest.

◆

"Aisha, 'sup girlfriend?"

"Hi, Tameria, nothing's going on. Unless you're talking about the fact that my whole life is in a shambles." Aisha said in a monotone voice which immediately signaled to Tameria that something was bothering her friend.

"What is it? You and Jackson okay?"

"Not really. But then I don't know

"What do you mean by you don't know? Either you're doing good or you're not. Which is it?"

"He's acting really strange. I mean, we went from talking two, three four times a day to him barely returning my calls. It's been like this for the past week and a half."

"Have you come out and asked him what's bothering him? Maybe he has a lot on his plate, which I'm sure he does by him being a minister and a counselor."

"Yeah, I know that. But I'm telling you it's not that. Jackson's whole conversation has changed. The few times I have gotten through to him, he's been distant and he won't talk but a few minutes."

"That does sound weird. You need to sit him down and find out what the deal is Aisha." Tameria suggested.

"I know but that's the problem too. He keeps telling me that he's busy and that he's going to get back with me. I'm beginning to think that there's someone else involved. Maybe he's met another woman Tameria. I wouldn't blame him if he has."

"Don't get all crazy on me. It might be possible that he's met someone else. But Jackson doesn't impress me as the kind of man to string a woman along. I would think that before he did that, he would at least tell you."

"Girl, whatever. A man is a man. Whether he's a preacher, minister, blue collar worker, a scrub, a man of the law. It doesn't matter."

"Here you go. Get your butt off your shoulders, Aisha. Don't tell me that Chandler has been bugging you again."

"I don't have my butt on my shoulders. I'm just tired. My life is so screwed up."

"It's no worse than anybody else's, Aisha. Now. Like I just asked you. Has Chandler been stalking you again? He's the only 'man of the law' that I know who fits the description of lu..na…tic!"

Aisha thought that she should confide in Tameria but again she dismissed the thought. "No I haven't heard from Chandler. Not lately anyway."

"Well I don't agree with your analogy of our men. That's what's wrong with us women. We're always going around bashing them. No wonder they turn to women outside their race. Our brothers are good, decent and they know how to treat a lady. But just like us and anything in life, there's always a bad apple somewhere in the bunch. You just have to find the bad apple and remove it from the rest of the bunch."

"Well, I never would have thought Jackson would have turned out to be a bad apple," Aisha rebuffed.

"Who said that he is? The man probably is overextended, that's all. Give him a break. You watch what I tell you. He's going to sit down and talk to you."

"We'll see. Anyway, talking about good men, how are you and Chase? I take it you're at his crib."

"Things couldn't be better. And yes, I'm at his place. You already knew that before you asked. I've told you before. Chase and I spend as much time together as we can and with the hours we spend at the hospital then every minute is precious to us. If that means I have to camp out at his place or vice versa then that's what I'm going to do."

"Suit yourself, but it's still shacking up anyway you look at it." Aisha insisted.

"Whatever, but let's not get all self-righteous and judgmental Aisha. I know you aren't even going to try to go there." Tameria shot back.

"I'm not trying to be self-righteous or anything else Tameria. All I'm saying is if he gets it all without marrying you, why would he feel he has to ever marry you?"

"That's something Chase and I have already discussed. You know I'm graduating from med school next month and he'll be finishing his residency shortly thereafter. When he finishes he's more than likely going to go into practice with some other neurosurgeons. Once he starts making enough money to support us both, then we're going to tie the knot and I'm going to continue with school. You may have a hard time believing it, but it's true. I love Chase and he loves me. We are going to get married and we are going to spend the rest of our lives together," Tameria said with force behind her words.

"Okay, okay, no need to get your panties in a wad. I only want the best for you. You know I have your back." Aisha replied.

"I know. And you'll see. Well, look I've gotta go. I have some studying to do. Why don't you try calling that man of yours again and see if you can get him to open up."

"I think I will. But I need to tell you something else."

"Yeah, what?"

"Chandler did call me a couple of weeks ago."

"Chandler? You need to report that fool for real. The man is a bonafide stalker. I knew that he had to have something to do with the way you're feeling.

"No, no, wait a minute. Let me tell you what happened. He begged me to listen to him so I met him and we sat down and talked. He told me he was sorry for the way he had been following me and harassing me."

"Really?"

"Yes, really. And there's more. He told me that he only said and did the things he did because he had a hard time accepting the fact that I was involved with The Lynx."

"That's understandable but he sure had a scary way of showing it. I thought the guy was an undercover serial murder instead of an undercover cop," Tameria laughed.

"I know that's right. But really, I listened to him and I believe he was sincere. He told me that he loved me and he wanted to start over again."

"What did you say?"

"I told him I loved Jackson. He didn't like what I said, but he accepted it. He asked if we could be friends and he wished me the best."

"Oh my, there is a God," Tameria teased again. "Anyway, that's good but I'd still be careful if I were you. Make sure this isn't another one of his games, you know."

Too late for that. I already fell feet first into the stupid bucket. "Yea, I know and I'm going to be cautious."

"If you begin to have any negative vibes about him, promise me that you'll report him without so much as a blink."

Oops. Already made dumb move number two. My life is a living nightmare and Chandler is the monster in my closet. "I will." Aisha responded without conviction.

"Listen. I'm sorry but I have to get ready to leave in a few. Take care of yourself. Stay prayerful. Oh, why don't you call Jackson again too. Everything will turn out fine. You'll see. Bye. We'll talk again soon."

◆

Aisha thought about Tameria's suggestion to call Jackson. Before she could pick up the phone to call him, her phone rang.

After hanging up from the call, Aisha left to go and talk to Jackson. Whether he wanted to or not she made up in her mind to find out what was going on with him and why he was taking it out on her.

Aisha listened to one of her favorite gospel artists. His songs could lift her up from the deepest bouts of depression. She needed to hear the words of his song in order to drown out thoughts of Chandler. At the end of the track, she turned off the CD player and flicked on the radio. She turned abruptly into Wal-Mart's parking lot when she heard the reporter. She sat and listened, stunned at what he was saying. "Memphis Undercover Detective, Chandler Larson, pleaded guilty last Friday to stealing money from drug dealers. Larson admitted to stealing over two hundred seventy-five thousand dollars from drug dealers over the past year and a half. Larson is a ten year veteran police officer with several commendations. He has also admitted to conspiring with Sabatio Foxx, known gang leader and suspected mastermind behind the Memphis Drug Cartel to distribute over three and a half million dollars' worth of cocaine on the streets of Memphis. Larson and three other officers have been charged with official corruption in an ongoing investigation labeled Operation Cruise Control. Wearing a blue detention jumpsuit, Larson tried to shield his face from the news media. He is being held on a five hundred thousand dollars bond. It is also reported that Larson is being held at the Criminal Justice Center under suicide watch. Larson faces thirty-five years to life in prison plus a four hundred seventy-five thousand dollar fine.

Lord, have mercy. I don't know whether to be happy or sad. Aisha sat in the parking lot for fifteen minutes. Her head ached. She decided to take advantage of where she was. She headed inside Wal-Mart to purchase something for her headache. With each step she took, the frown of pain on her face slowly evolved into a smile of gratitude. *God is so good.*

43

It is difficult to know at what moment love begins; it is
less difficult to know that it has begun.
Henry Wadsworth Longfellow

"Northwest flight fifty-seven eighty departing for Chicago is now boarding at gate eight." The ticket agent spoke into the mic, repeating the call for passengers to board. Jackson looked around the area where he had been seated to make sure he wasn't leaving anything. He reached for his carryon bag and laptop then proceeded to get in line to board his flight. Pastor Shipley's schedule was already overloaded. So he had asked Jackson if he would run revival on his behalf at Faith Missionary Baptist Church in Chicago, whose shepherd was none other than the infamous Pastor Curtis J. Black. Jackson jumped at the opportunity to preach his first revival and rejoiced that Pastor Shipley had faith that he could carry it out. It was the perfect occasion for him to get away and clear his head. It was getting harder and harder to escape Aisha's calls and her unscheduled visits. And staying away from home or parking his car somewhere other than in his apartment parking space, was working his already frazzled nerves. He would be in Chicago for two weeks and he had made up his mind to be over and done with Aisha Carlisle by the time he returned to Memphis.

◆

Aisha stood at Jackson's door with her thumb pressing full force against his doorbell. When he didn't answer for the umpteenth time, she curled her hand in a rigid fist and pounded on the heavy steel and oak door. Disgusted and defeated Aisha turned around in anger and stomped back to her car. "Jackson Williams, to hell with you," she mumbled underneath her breath before speeding out of the complex.

I'll call his office one more time. If he doesn't answer, then I'm through. "Natalie, I need to speak to Minister Williams please. And will you please tell him that it's important," Aisha emphasized. Natalie had no idea what had happened between Minister Williams and Aisha Carlisle, but something was going on, that much she was sure about. Over the past couple of weeks Minister Williams had been quiet and elusive, almost with a sad countenance in his usually cheerful persona. He rarely accepted Aisha's calls. Now Aisha was calling for him again and Natalie wasn't sure what kind of response she'd get from Aisha after she told him that he would be out of town for the next two weeks.

Slamming the door to her apartment, Aisha slung her purse on the sofa and stomped into the kitchen for bottled water. Maybe the ice cold water would somehow soothe her mounting furor towards Jackson. "The nerve of him. He's gone to Chicago for two weeks," she yelled. I've got to get it together. I don't know what his problem is and I'm beginning not to care." The ringing phone snatched her from her self-talk.

"Aisha, will you tell me what's going on?" her mother's piercing voice told Aisha that she was less than pleased.

"Mother, I don't have time for this tonight." Aisha scolded.

"I don't know what your problem is young lady. But you have managed to screw up the best thing that's ever happened in your life. Jackson Williams is a man any woman would kill for. But oh noooo, *Miss Aisha* has to go and find a way to lose him. I tell you, sometimes I just don't understand you."

"You know, I thought you had really changed Mother. But you're still the same selfish, thoughtless human being you always were. As for Jackson, maybe the two of you belong together. He seems to have some of your senseless, heartless ways." Aisha didn't let up with her assault on Sandra. "It's always me who's at fault, let you tell it. Well, I'm tired of always getting the blame for everything. Jackson is the one who dropped out of sight. Jackson is the one who decided he didn't want to have anything to do with me but didn't bother telling me. If he's such the perfect man, looks like Mr. Perfect would have the decency to tell me when he doesn't want to be bothered. Now look, I'm tired, I'm fed up and I really don't want to continue this conversation Mommie Dearest," Aisha said sarcastically. "Good bye."

Sandra Carlisle's jaw fell open as she listened to the tone of her daughter's voice. The more Aisha talked, the angrier Sandra Carlisle became. "Whether she wants to accept responsibility for blowing this relationship or not, the truth is that child is a duplicate version of Ben– irrational, bull headed and impossible to please. Aisha," Sandra walked through the empty house talking as if Aisha was standing next to her. You're making a hard bed for yourself. If you want to spend your life alone, so be it. Stupid, stupid girl. Lord, she's in your hands 'cause she surely doesn't want to listen to her dear mother."

◆

Jackson loomed over the pulpit of Faith Missionary Baptist Church and preached his heart out. "I tell you my people, now is the time. Oh yes, now is the time to lay aside every weight that's holding you down. Now IS the time to turn your lives over to the one who can give you life. I say, Now IS the time for you to come to God. Don't wait until things have gotten better. Don't wait until you stop doing the stuff you know you shouldn't be doing. Don't wait until you don't cuss anymore or you don't go to this place or that place anymore. Don't wait until you don't sell this or smoke this anymore. Come now. Jesus wants you to come. Just the way you are. If you'll only come, He'll do the fixing up and cleaning up, I tell you. Paul says in Romans chapter one verse sixteen, I am not ashamed of the gospel, because it is the power of God for the salvation of everyone who believes. Not just some of us but for everyone who believes."

After eating dinner with Pastor Black and his deacons, they drove Jackson to his hotel room. This was his last night in Chicago and the experience had served its purpose. Not only had he been blessed to minister to lost souls, but he himself felt like he had been released from a vice grip that had been wrapped around his heart. Night after night, he'd prayed to God to help him decide about his relationship with Aisha. His sermon the night before had been on forgiveness. In his heart, he knew God had given him that message for himself as well as the congregation. He was the one who had to exercise forgiveness. He lay on the hotel bed and relived the night he saw Aisha and Chandler. Why hadn't he allowed her the chance to explain rather than ignore her? There could be a logical explanation for what he'd seen, though he didn't see how it could be anything different from what he'd witnessed with his own eyes. *They were kissing for God's sake.* How much more did he need to see? But no matter how it had hurt him, within his heart he knew that he had to bring some closure to their relationship. Closure meant that he would have to talk to her and then he could move on with the rest of his life. Picking up his cell, he dialed her at home. He was about to hang up when he heard her sweet voice.

"Aisha? Hi, it's Jackson." He barely spoke loud enough for her to hear.

"I know. So you finally decided to call."

"Okay, maybe I deserve that, but…"

"But nothing, Jackson. Just tell me something. Why are you calling me?" Aisha's obvious anger was apparent with every word she spoke.

"Listen," Jackson answered.

"No, you listen. I have tried calling you God only knows how many times. I've been to your house. I've called the church office. I've called and called. And now, you happen to be ready to talk to me and you think I'm supposed to just listen to what you have to say just because you're Minister Jackson Williams. Well, I don't think so. Find yourself another toy 'cuz I'm not the one." She slammed the phone down so hard that the phone and the receiver fell to the floor. She folded her arms in anger and paced back and forth through her apartment. "The nerve of that man. He really has me messed up. Here I am, running, chasing, wondering, thinking about what I could have done wrong. Blaming myself for everything. But no more. Aisha's smarter than Minister Jackson Davis Williams."

Jackson listened to the sound of the dial tone buzzing in his ear. It took several seconds for him to hang up. The initial shock left him dazed and speechless. Should he try to call her back? He thought for several more minutes about his next move. *For now, I'll let her have it her way. But when I get back to Memphis, one way or the other, we're going to resolve this, Miss Carlisle.* He went into the bathroom, turned on the shower and stepped under the rain of hot steaming water. Maybe, just maybe the water would wash away the sense of loss he just felt, but was afraid to own up to.

44

*You have to walk carefully in the beginning of love; the
running across fields into your lover's arms can only
come later when you're sure they won't laugh if you trip.*
Jonathan Carroll

It had been three days since Jackson's return to
Memphis. He hadn't seen Aisha at any of the Sunday
church services or mid-week Bible study. But, even if
she was there, it wouldn't be hard for her to blend in with
the thousands of members who poured inside the
sanctuary week after week. The tables had indeed turned
because no matter how many times he called her, went by
the studio or her apartment, she managed to make herself
unavailable and out of sight. His mind was filled with
thoughts of her and Chandler. *Could she be with him?
Why couldn't she just tell me she was still hooked on that
cop?*

Jackson wheeled his car into the lower level parking
garage. Parking next to Aisha's car he planned on waiting
for her for however long it took. The clock in the car
assured him that she should be finishing up her last dance
class. To pass the time, he pulled out a Bible
commentary from his briefcase and began studying
passages of Old Testament scriptures. After waiting for
almost forty five minutes, he looked up and saw the
familiar silhouette of her figure walking towards him.
When she was within a few feet he opened his car door
and got out.

338

Aisha looked at him, and without saying a word proceeded to open the door to her car.

"Aisha, please wait. We need to talk." Walking over to where she stood, he blocked her from getting inside her car.

"Move out of my way Jackson. I have nothing to say to you."

"You have nothing to say to me. Isn't that some bull," he said in a voice that resonated his dislike for her attitude.

Her glare let him know that in no uncertain terms, she was angry.

"You can act like you're the victim all you want Aisha, but let's face it. You're the one who betrayed me."

"What are you talking about? Betrayed you! Let me refresh your memory. You're the one who dropped out of sight without any explanation whatsoever. You're the one who wouldn't return MY phone calls or answer your door. It was you Jackson. Not me." She huffed and tried to push him out of the way.

"And you're the one who's been seeing Chandler behind my back," he yelled back. The look on her face let him know that she was totally caught off guard. Her shoulders slumped and her eyes were like round gleaming balls.

"Are you accusing me of cheating?"

"Like they say, if the shoe fits…" The two of them exchanged silent words between each other. The tension was thick as sorghum syrup.

"I don't know where you came up with these accusations, but to set the record straight, I have not cheated on you with Chandler or anyone else for that matter."

"I guess kissing him in front of your apartment just happened to be your idea of Chandler stalking you, huh?" he mocked, his jaw tightening in anger.

"Is that what this is about? You saw me and Chandler together?" Aisha cocked her head to the side and let out a sarcastic type laugh.

"You know something. You men are all alike. Insecure, fault finding and plain old jerks. Obviously you're no different from Chandler. You had to have been watching me. How else would you have seen what you thought you saw?"

"I was on my way to see you. I had something I wanted to get off my chest, Aisha. But what did I find instead? You and Chandler all lovey-dovey. From what you led me to believe, you were supposed to be so terrified of this guy. Then I drive up and see just the opposite. What am I supposed to think Aisha?"

"You're not supposed to think anything, Jackson. You're supposed to trust me. You could have gotten out of your car and approached both of us, especially if you were uncertain about what was going on. But no, you'd much rather assume that I'm a cheater and a betrayer, I guess."

"Aisha, look I didn't know what to think. I got crazy when I saw you and Chandler together." He grabbed both of her shoulders and gingerly turned her to face him.

"Why didn't you just talk to me, Jackson? I thought we had something special. I trusted you with the sordid details of my past. I trusted you with my hurts and my deepest emotions. And you, you couldn't trust me with what you were thinking and feeling?"

"It wasn't that." Jackson's face took on a somber expression. His heart beat wildly. Part of him was relieved to find out that Aisha hadn't betrayed him. And the other part didn't know if there was anything she wasn't telling him.

"What is it then? I guess you want to know everything. Well, let me tell you this and then I'm done. Chandler, for your information, contacted me and begged my forgiveness. And since you're a man of the cloth, you should know better than anyone, that when a person asks for forgiveness, there is no question that we should accept their forgiveness. He admitted that what he had been doing to me was wrong and that he was truly sorry. He told me that he loved me."

Jackson's face became flushed. Had he lost her to Chandler? "What did you tell him?" Jackson paused and waited on her answer.

"I told him that I didn't love him. That my heart belonged to someone else. I told him that all he could ever expect from me was friendship. At first I found it hard to believe when he said he understood. I thought maybe he was trying to trick me so he could set me up and do something terrible to me. Turns out that I should have listened to my spirit."

"What do you mean? What happened?"

Aisha drew in a deep breath. She told Jackson everything that happened that dreadful night. Tears formed in her eyes and droplets slid along her face.

Jackson stepped closer to Aisha. Aisha stepped farther away from Jackson. Jackson's anger mounted with each thought of Chandler's cruelty. When Aisha told him the part about Chandler being arrested, he was relieved. He wanted him to rot in jail for the rest of his life. Although he was a minister, his flesh overruled his spirit when it came to Chandler Larson. He would have to pray and ask God for the strength to see Chandler the same way God saw Chandler. "Aisha, baby," Jackson cried with her. "I'm so sorry this happened to you. I'm so sorry I wasn't there for you." He reached out to pull her to his chest but again Aisha stepped back in haste.

"That terrible night I tried to call you. I needed you so bad. I needed to tell you what had happened but you didn't answer me. But that's neither here nor there now. Because the man I loved didn't trust me or believe in what I once thought we shared." She pushed Jackson to the side and climbed inside her car.

"See you around Minister Williams." And with that she put her car in reverse and drove off, leaving Jackson standing alone in the garage with his own supply of fresh tears pouring from his eyes. She loved him. It was the first time he'd ever heard her admit she loved him. Someway he had to convince her that he loved her too. He had reacted out of jealousy and distrust. Aisha had been right and he had been wrong. As a man of God, he knew she had done the right thing by accepting Chandler's plea to forgive him. She had been the bigger person while he had operated out of his own fleshly thoughts and desires. Standing in the moldy damp parking garage, Jackson purposed in his heart and his mind that if necessary, he would spend the rest of his earthly life showing Aisha how much she was loved by him. With that being settled, he climbed in his car and sped off to catch up with the woman he'd pray for all of his life.

Aisha stopped off at the grocery store to purchase some fruit and the makings for a Caesar salad. It had been hard to see Jackson without the urge to fall into his arms. The thought of seeing him again stirred up emotions she thought she had pushed aside.

Grabbing the plastic grocery bag and heading for her apartment, she was startled by the sound of footsteps rushing towards her. Abruptly turning around to face whoever was behind her, she stopped in her tracks when she saw it was Jackson.

"Jackson, what are you…"

He didn't give her a chance to finish her sentence. He walked up to her and placed his finger over her lips. "Aisha, I was wrong. I've been crazy with jealousy over the thought of you loving someone else. I tried to bury my feelings, tried to pretend that what we had wasn't real. But the more I ran, the more my heart pulled me closer to you. I hope you can forgive me. Forgive me for being so stupid. Forgive me for not telling you how much I really do love you."

The callous expression on Aisha's face softened. The look in her eyes exposed what was in her heart. Hearing Jackson confessing his love for her made her weak in the knees. As if he could read her mind, he removed the grocery bag from her hand, sat it on the porch and pulled her close inside his arms. She allowed herself to relax and breathe in his familiar scent. At last she felt at home. She felt safe and protected. Jackson caressed her and kissed her hair. Running his hands tenderly up and down the length of her shoulders, she could hear his heavy breathing and feel his excitement. Her head raised up to look at him and his lips passionately overpowered hers. The hunger they felt for each other was enhanced as the cool night breeze kissed their bodies. Aisha eased back, and without saying a word, turned the key to unlock the door. Jackson picked up the grocery bag, and his other hand gathered around her waist. The two of them walked inside the apartment and closed the door behind them. On the other side they opened the door to a new beginning.

45

Press forward. Do not stop, do not linger in your journey, but strive for the mark set before you. George Whitefield

Walking across the stage, Tameria felt like a kid in a candy store. It was hard for her to contain her excitement. When she exited on the other side, she spotted Chase standing in the corner near the stage exit. He walked over to her and grabbed her around her full figured waist and nibbled on her neck. "I'm proud of you girl," he said between nibbles.

"Chase, I made it. And baby," she said, turning around to face him. "I couldn't have done it without you. You've been my rock, the one who believed in me and I love you so much," she said and kissed him on his lips.

Tameria along with her friends and family gathered at the dance studio after the commencement exercise. Aisha and Angie had everything decorated. The menu included fresh salads, fruits, baked chicken, salmon and fresh turkey cutlets. There were green beans, turnip greens, fresh corn, broccoli and several deliciously tantalizing desserts.

"Tell me. How does it feel Dr. Tameria Matthews?" Jackson remarked teasingly.

"Yeah, how does it feel?" Angie interjected as she joined the group. "You're a doctor! Wow!"

"Speech, speech, speech! Some of the guests chanted.

Tameria stood up and looked around at the long table of family and friends. At that moment she felt such a tremendous thrill at how much God had blessed her life. Chase eased his hand on top of hers. She looked down at him and smiled then she began to speak. "I can't begin to put my feelings into words. I'm absolutely in shock. I've made it over the first hurdle and I'm looking forward to the next one. And with the support of my loving parents, Chase's and all of you, and of course the help of God, I know I'm going to be just fine. I am happy than I ever have been. It's good to know that I have your love and your blessings. Your prayers have sustained me these past years and they will continue to sustain me as I move forward into my residency. I love you all." Tameria walked over to her parents and gave each of them a hug of thanks.

"I say we should drink to that," Angie suggested. "Wait right here. Come on sweetie," she ordered her husband. Seconds later the two of them returned with a tray of wine glasses filled with sparkling grape juice. Passing around a glass to each of them in the circle, Angie lifted her glass in the air. "Aisha, on second thought, why don't you do the toast?

"Of course, I'd be happy to. Today marks a new beginning in the life of my dearest and best friend, Dr. Tameria Shante' Matthews. We've seen some good times and some not so good times. There have been some ups and there have been some downs. But through it all we've persevered. God has watched over you and he has placed his angels charge over you. I'm thankful for your friendship and for your love. So, Tameria, may God's blessings continue to abound in your life. May you forever be happy and may your career be all that you have hoped and dreamed. Cheers," she said and smiled, then turned up her sparkling beverage and drank.

46

Change your life today. Don't gamble on the future, act now, without delay. Simone de Beauvoir

Aisha strolled across the stage and took her place front and center behind the glass podium. She couldn't believe that she wasn't nervous at all. When Jackson first asked her to share her life's testimony with the hundreds of youth who were there for the annual youth conference, Aisha quickly accepted. If it meant that through sharing her testimony she could possibly help to change one child's life for the better then she was gung-ho for it. She had prayed leading up to the youth conference for God to tell her what He wanted her to share with the young people who would attend. She had scribbled notes after notes and searched scripture after scripture. Days before the conference, she tore up the notes. When Jackson asked her if she'd finish preparing her speech she told him that she didn't have a speech prepared. She was going to speak from her heart.

The day had arrived. It was time to stand up and allow God to use her in the way He saw fit. Facing the diverse group of youth she cleared her throat before she began.

"All of my life, I've had a passion for dancing. My father often told me stories about when I was but a toddler; how I would go through the house pretending like I was a ballerina. As soon as I was old enough my parents fed my passion and enrolled me in dance and ballet. I blossomed like a flower. Each waking moment I thought about dancing. There was nothing I wouldn't do if it would afford me the opportunity to fulfill my lifelong dream." Aisha shifted her weight to one side and continued to speak. "Shortly before my grandparents died in a house fire, I had graduated from college. They left me an inheritance that enabled me to start my own dance studio called A-Carlisle Studio of Dance and Choreography. It was the greatest blessing of my life. I couldn't thank God enough for what he was doing in my life. I was actually doing what I loved to do. That's a feat in and of itself because so many people leave this earth without ever fulfilling their dreams, goals and aspirations. The room full of youth sat in the auditorium as if they were each hypnotized. Her words were powerful. The impact of her words was powerful. Scanning the crowd, she continued to speak. "Even though I was able to share my love of dance and choreography with young ladies and young men, I still had a business to run. That meant that I had to have financial resources that would keep the studio open.

Well, unfortunately things changed. I found myself sinking. I didn't know it at the time, but what had happened was I began to put dance before God. I got in financial difficulty and instead of turning to God for answers and guidance, I looked within myself. I'm standing before you today to tell you that whatever you do in life, always and I mean always put God first and keep God first. You see, I thought I could handle my problems on my own. But boy was I wrong. I became involved with drugs, began dancing for money at this exclusive gentleman's organization. I justified what I was doing by telling myself that I wasn't like some of the other women who danced there. After all, I was a Christian and a virgin too. So what I was doing couldn't be all that bad and I was only going to do it for a while, just to save up some money to keep my studio going. All along, I was fooling me," she said and pointed at herself. "I started using valium and cocaine because I listened to someone who convinced me that it was just to help ease my nervousness of working at the association. It's so important for you to be your own person. Don't let anyone pressure you into doing what you know is not right. Listen to God and those people who will tell you the truth. I learned that the hard way. Anyway, it didn't take long for me to become addicted to the drugs and the money I was making." The eyes of the teenagers were focused in on every word Aisha spoke.

"I loved my daddy. He was my rock of Gibraltar. But you know what? I let him down. To this very day, I wish somehow that I could turn back the hands of time just for a moment. But I can't. I wish I could have been there with my father when he took his last breath, but instead I was at the club snorting coke and shaking my butt to 50 Cent and Mike Jones. I know God has forgiven me because His word says that all we have to do is confess our sins and he is faithful and just to forgive us and cleanse us from all unrighteousness. But the fact remains that I had trouble forgiving myself. So what I'd like to leave with you today is that we all make mistakes. There are some roads you'll travel on this journey through life that will lead you to some undesirable places. There are some people who are around you that don't mean you any good but they will pretend to be your friend. There may even be family members who won't and don't support your dreams and aspirations. But even if all of this is true, there is hope for each of you. Don't cling to the mistakes of your past.

"Don't allow negativity and trouble to hinder and destroy what your divine purpose is in life. The best advice I can give you is to make Jesus the Lord of your life. Keep Him first because no matter what you do or where you go in life, He will forever be by your side if you'll only receive Him into your heart. Then like me, when things get hard as they sometimes do, when you don't know where to turn and it feels like the weight of the whole world rests upon your shoulders, He'll be there to uphold you and keep you safe. When others won't forget or forgive you, or when you won't forgive yourself, God will and does forgive. What's so amazing about Him is that He accepts you and me just the way we are. So if you're sitting out there feeling like all hope is lost and that you've messed up and you're at the point of no return, then I'm telling you that what you're thinking and feeling is a trick of the devil. Because we are more than conquerors. We've overcomers. We're beneficiaries of the kingdom of God and His throne.

"Since I came to that realization, my life is much different now. There's no more guilt over the things I've done in my past. Whatever I did is done and I can't make anything change. And there are going to be other times in the future when I'm sure that I'll mess up. That's because I'm human which means that I'm not perfect. None of us are. But what I am is Forgiven and that makes all of the difference in the world. And what I can do is live this day to the best of the ability God has given me.

"God's blessings have continued to run me down and overtake me. I now have two locations for A-Carlisle Studio of Dance and Choreography. One which is located at this very church. I've also been blessed to love and be loved by a wonderful man, Minister Jackson Williams." The gym full of young people began to snicker at the thought of Minister Jack, as they called him, with a girlfriend.

Aisha smiled too. "So today, I'm encouraging you to forget what lies behind and strain forward to what lies ahead. When I graduated from college my late grandparents gave me this locket." Aisha pulled the locket out from underneath her melon colored blouse. "The inscription on this locket says Jeremiah twenty-nine eleven. Do any of you know what that passage of scripture says?"

The young people remained fixated on Aisha and no one acknowledged that they knew the scripture by heart, so Aisha started up again. "Well, it says something that I truly believe with all of my heart. 'For I know the plans I have for you,' declares the LORD, 'plans to prosper you and not to harm you, plans to give you hope and a future.' What more could I or any of you ever ask from such a loving, all powerful heavenly father." Before turning to leave the stage, she paused. Scanning the church auditorium full of young people, her eyes rested on the man she loved with all of her heart. Jackson stood up with the group of young people as the crowd gave her a standing ovation.

Her heart flooded with pride and thanksgiving. God had used the bad, sinful things in her life to bring about the good and perfect gift He had designed for her. Her life was a changed life and her relationship with God was strengthened by the adversities, trials and troubles she'd experienced. But the ultimate lesson gained was that of unconditional love, acceptance and forgiveness. And because of that she knew that she wouldn't trade her journey for anything.

THE END

Words from the Author

Our lives are but for a fleeting moment. Many of us live on the verge of desperation, hoping and clinging to things, people and stuff. We often become lost and caught up in what we can gain from the world. The pleasures of sin often catch hold to many of us because of its ability to entice us. Don't be mistaken my readers, Sin IS captivating. It feels good. It looks good. It dresses well. Sin is articulate and can take on any form it so chooses – for a while. And it's only for a while because even though its mask is temporary. It lingers just long enough to pull you into its grasp. However, it eventually has to rear its ugly, vile, deceitful head and reveal what it really is. Don't think that for one moment you can fight against it under your own strength, because if you think that, you have already been deceived by it. The only sure way to fight it, to get through it, to overcome it, is to go to the one who has the power to destroy it – that one true sovereign one is God. Without Him, we are nothing. With Him, we are more than conquerors. With Him all things are eternal.

Readers, thank you for your continued support of my literary career. Because of you, I am able to Live My Dreams Now. Be Blessed!

To arrange speaking events, book signings, and or workshops please contact the author at sheliawritesbooks@yahoo.com You may also reach this author through http://www.twitter.com/sheliaebell; http://www.facebook.com/sheliawritesbooks; www.sheliawritesbooks.com

If you enjoyed this book by Shelia E. Bell, PLEASE LEAVE A REVIEW ON YOUR FAVORITE ONLINE REVIEW SITE

Additional titles by Shelia E. Bell
(Some titles can be found under former name Shelia Lipsey)

Young Adult Titles
House of Cars
The Life of Payne
The Lollipop Girl
The Righteous Brothers (Coming 2019)

Standalone Novels
Show A Little Love (*out of print*)
Always Now and Forever Love Hurts
Into Each Life
Sinsatiable
What's Blood Got To Do With It?
Only In My Dreams
The House Husband
Cross Road
Forever Ain't Enough

Series Books

Beautiful Ugly
True Beauty (*sequel to Beautiful Ugly*)

My Son's Wife Series
My Son's Wife: The Beginning (Book 1)
My Son's Ex-Wife: Aftershock (Book 2)
My Son's Next Wife (Book 3)
My Sister My Momma My Wife (Book 4)
My Wife My Baby…And Him (Book 5)
The McCoy's of Holy Rock (Book 6)
Dem McCoy Boys (Book 7)
My Brother, Father…And Me (Book 8)
My Truth, My Time, My Turn (Book 9)

Adverse City Series
The Real Housewives of Adverse City
The Real Housewives of Adverse City 2

The Real Housewives of Adverse City 3
The Real Housewives of Adverse City 4

<u>Anthologies</u>
Bended Knees
Weary to Will
Learning to Love Me

<u>Nonfiction</u>
A Christian's Perspective: Journey Through Grief

www.ingramcontent.com/pod-product-compliance
Lightning Source LLC
Chambersburg PA
CBHW032054180726
48284CB00004B/1344